# *Luke's Dream*

## Cassie's Legacy—Book 4

by Yvette Blake

**Skinny Brown Dog Media**

Copyright Page

*Luke's Dream* © 2025 Yvette Blake
All rights reserved. No part of this book may be reproduced, scanned, stored, distributed, or transmitted in any form or by any means—electronic, mechanical, photocopying, recording, AI-generated processing, or otherwise—without prior written permission from the publisher or author, except for brief quotations in reviews or critical analysis.

AI & Machine Learning Restrictions and TDM Opt-Out

All rights reserved. Without prior written consent, no part of this work may be used to train, fine-tune, or improve any AI/ML system; to conduct text-and-data mining (TDM); or to create datasets, embeddings, or corpora, including by scraping or ingestion. Unauthorized use may constitute infringement under U.S. and international law (including the DMCA). The rights-holder expressly opts out of any TDM exceptions.

Copyright & Intellectual Property Protection

All characters, concepts, and original content in this book are protected under U.S. Copyright Law, the Digital Millennium Copyright Act (DMCA), and international copyright treaties. Unauthorized adaptations or reproductions based on this work constitute infringement and will be subject to legal action.

Identifiers Library of Congress Control Number (LCCN): [Pending]
Hardcover (Case Laminate) ISBN: 978-1-965235-94-2
Hardcover (Cloth™ with Dust Jacket) ISBN: 978-1-965235-95-9
Paperback (Perfect Bound) ISBN: 978-1-965235-96-6
eBook (EPUB/Kindle) ISBN: 978-1-965235-97-3

Contact the Author @ YBlake.com

Additional Books available @ YBlake.com

Permissions & Licensing

For bulk purchases, translation rights, subsidiary rights, or AI/licensing inquiries, contact:
Skinny Brown Dog Media
Website: https://www.skinnybrowndogmedia.com
Email: info@SkinnyBrownDogMedia.com

Printed in the United States of America
10 9 8 7 6 5 4 3 2 1

# Dedication

I dedicate *Luke's Dream* to those who remain true to their culture, spiritual beliefs, and family values while navigating the world and finding their place in it. You are an inspiration to us all.

Like Luke, may you continue to find joy, purpose, and the courage to live your dreams to the fullest.

# *Chapters*

# *Luke's Dream*

# Chapter 1

# Homecoming, June 1889

Without thinking, Luke bent and pressed his lips to hers, overcome by the joy of being near her again. The kiss felt as natural as breathing.

Megan didn't pull away. Her lips were soft, welcoming, and for one blissful moment, the world vanished. When he drew back, her brilliant green eyes shimmered with love and longing. Something deep stirred within him—a love that had never faded.

Then reality crashed in. Panic surged.

"I—I'm sorry. I shouldn't have done that," he stammered. But even as he apologized, he didn't regret it. He'd dreamed of kissing her more times than he could count. His heart said it was right; his mind warned otherwise. They were family—adopted, yes—but still, some would find it wrong.

But Megan didn't look away. Her whisper was calm, steady. "It's alright."

Her hands, trembling slightly, cupped his face and drew him back down. This time, she kissed him—with yearning. His lips were warm, firm, sending a shiver through her.

When he eased away again, she stared at him, dazed and breathless.

"Megan," he murmured, his heart racing. Her touch

felt so right. Their bond had never broken. But how could he explain it? She'd think he was crazy.

She gave a breathless laugh, cheeks flushed. "I don't know what came over me. I'm sorry," she said, turning away, blushing. *What must he think—kissing him like that?*

"Don't." His knuckles brushed her cheek, voice gentle. "Don't be sorry. I didn't mind."

His hand found the small of her back, thumb gently stroking. When she looked up again, he smiled that familiar boyish grin—full of mischief.

She laughed softly. The tension eased. "We should probably get home." She still couldn't believe it—he was here, teasing her like old times.

"You're right." He grinned. "I can't wait to see everyone."

He let out a sharp whistle that cut through the trees, and a copper-coated stallion trotted into view.

"Wildfire!" Megan gasped, eyes wide. "You still have him!"

She stepped closer, hand trembling as she stroked his black mane. Somehow, the day had transformed—from heartbreak to wonder. Luke was finally here, standing beside her—the one person she thought she'd lost forever.

Luke ran his hand along the horse's neck. "He's been with me through it all."

Megan's excitement returned. "Let's go!" She mounted her white Arabian mare, her ebony braid catching the sun.

Luke swung onto Wildfire bareback. "That's a fine horse."

"She was my birthday gift," Megan said, patting her horse's shoulder. "Her name's Snowfire."

"A beautiful name for a beautiful horse. Wildfire and Snowfire. We've got a matching pair."

Her heart leapt. She remembered her 16th birthday, whispering Snowfire's name into the night, imagining Luke heard it. She'd spoken to him in spirit all those years, as if he'd never truly left, those years of longing tightening her voice. "Yes, we do."

They rode side by side around the pond. The once-young saplings had grown into towering trees, casting dark shadows over the water.

"This place has changed," Luke said, glancing around. "The trees are bigger."

He smiled, slowing. "Where's that tree you fell out of?"

Megan laughed, pointing. "Right there. I'm surprised you don't remember. We were trying to touch the sky."

"I remember now. That was terrifying. But nothing compared to today," he added, thinking of Theo—how he'd nearly put an arrow in the man for attempting to defile Megan. One moment too late, and Theo would've succeeded. Fury simmered beneath his calm exterior. "You've got to stop scaring me like that."

"I'll try," she said softly, her cheeks flaming at the thought of the lustful man's attack. His forced kiss and groping hands—felt much worse than a broken bone. She remembered her painful arm, Luke racing for help. He was still her protector.

"Do you remember that mean teacher?" he asked, breaking through her thoughts. "The one who made you cry on the first day of school?"

She groaned. "How could I forget? It was awful. He thought I put the tack on his chair."

Luke's jaw clenched. He still saw the fury on the teacher's face, threatening to thrash her. But Luke had taken her place, enduring every blow.

"And watching you take my punishment…" Her voice cracked. "That was excruciating."

He met her gaze. "And I'd do it again—a hundred times."

His eyes lingered on her. She wasn't the round-cheeked girl anymore. She was a woman now—radiant and spirited, with a strength he hadn't known before—but still the same soulful green eyes.

Her voice was a whisper. "I really missed you." She reached for him, and he took her hand.

"I missed you too," he said. "Every day." One day he would tell her how hard it had been without her, how he'd held on just for her.

They rode in silence, fingers entwined, hearts finally whole.

As the forest thickened, they moved into single file, light filtering through the tangled canopy. Eventually, they emerged to the sound of a distant train and followed the road north, side by side once more.

Luke reined in slightly, eyes drifting east. His brow furrowed as Cheyenne came into view.

"Cheyenne sure has grown," he muttered, barely recognizing the place he once called home.

Megan followed his gaze. "Yes, it has. Our little school's gone. They built a two-story schoolhouse in its place." She turned to him, eyes shining. "I graduated there."

Luke glanced at her, impressed. "All twelve grades, huh?"

She nodded with quiet pride. "All twelve."

He smiled, remembering the wide-eyed girl she'd been—marveling at the woman she'd become. "You've always been smart," he said softly.

"Did you ever go back to school?" she asked, glancing at him.

He looked away. "For a while," he said flatly, shutting the door on that subject. "What else is new?"

Megan caught the shift and let it go. "We have electricity and telephones in town now. I work at the telephone company part-time."

Luke raised his brows. "Electricity and telephones?" He shook his head, trying to imagine it. "I'm surprised."

They rode in silence for a moment, the road winding through green hills. On their left, cottonwoods and aspens shimmered beside a lazy stream. On the right, prairie grass rippled in waves, dotted with grazing cattle.

Luke inhaled deeply. The scent of sun-warmed grass and sage filled his lungs. *I'm home.* With each mile, the feeling deepened—a sense of belonging that had never truly left him.

"When did all this happen?" he asked, frowning at the posts and barbed wire now lining the road.

"Farmers are trying to keep animals out. Ranchers are trying to keep them in," Megan explained with a shrug.

"Farmers?" he echoed, surprised. "There weren't any before."

She pointed toward distant fields, where rows of crops stood in perfect lines. "Lots of new homesteaders have come in. It's helped in some ways, but it's shrunk the open grazing land."

Her voice softened. "We had a terrible winter a few years ago. Then a drought. A lot of big ranches went under." She glanced toward the horizon. "We were lucky. Lost some, but not everything. This year's looking better—the grass is thick, and the water's high."

Luke's jaw clenched. He remembered that winter—the brutal cold, the endless wind. He didn't want to dwell on it.

"I'm glad you made it through," he said quietly.

"I'm glad *you* did too." She imagined him braving those winters in a teepee with his tribe.

They rode on. His pulse quickened as they passed the Holden and Hartford ranch—his extended family's land. Though adopted, they'd always felt like blood.

"How are Grandma and Grandpa Hartford?" he asked. "And Aunt Joy, Uncle Clancy, all the cousins?"

"They're well," Megan replied. "Grandma and Grandpa are older but still going strong. Uncle Clancy and his four sons run the ranch now. They added onto the house to fit them all."

Luke's eyes widened. "Four sons? They had more after Jeremy and George Jr.?"

She nodded. "Two more. Jeremy's married now—to a classmate of mine, Penny."

Luke smiled. "Good for Jeremy. I always loved his sense of humor." He glanced over. "And Aunt Beth and Uncle John? Melissa?"

"They're doing fine. Melissa married a young pastor this spring. They live in Idaho Territory."

"She'll make a lovely pastor's wife," Luke said.

He looked back toward town. "What about Bart and Bea? Still running the clothing stores?"

Megan watched him reach into his satchel and pull out a fringed tunic, slipping it over his bare torso. Her gaze caught—broad shoulders, lean muscles, copper skin—she quickly looked away, cheeks flushing.

She cleared her dry throat. "They're doing well. Both stores expanded. Still making the best suits and dresses around." She hesitated, hoping he wouldn't ask. But he did.

"And Andrew? Is he working with them, or did he go off to college?"

Her throat tightened, tears pricked her eyes. "He... was killed. Two years ago."

Luke's head snapped toward her. "Killed? How?"

She stared ahead, voice trembling. "Andrew and I were courting…"

Luke's stomach twisted. *Courting?*

"One night, after a play, we were with friends when Shane cornered us in an alley. He was getting revenge—Andrew had broken his nose at the New Year's Eve Ball. He tried to protect me but was shot while trying to disarm Shane."

Luke struggled to picture gentle Andrew in a fight to the death.

"Why would Andrew break his nose?" he asked. "That doesn't sound like him."

Megan's voice cracked. "It was my fault." Tears spilled over.

Luke pulled his horse to a sudden halt. "Wait. Stop."

He swung down from Wildfire, reaching for her, easing her from the saddle. She slid down, her chin quivering.

"It started at the New Year's Eve Ball...about two and a half years ago. Melissa went with a man named Shane. He was a bad sort—like Theo." She shuddered. "He kept making advances toward me, even though he knew I was with Andrew. I rejected him. He was furious...so, to spite me, he called me a—" Her voice caught.

"A what?" Luke's hands tightened around her arms.

She hesitated, then forced the word out. "A...'half-breed.'"

Luke's jaw clenched.

Megan saw the flash of pain in his eyes—the flinch he tried to hide.

"Those were his words, not mine," she whispered. "He thought we were half-siblings. I told him we weren't, but he wouldn't believe me."

He shook his head, heart twisting.

Megan continued, voice trembling. "He said he knew you were my Indian brother. He taunted me—insisted I was like you—had Indian features. My skin, my hair, my cheekbones…" Her eyes met his. "I told him you were adopted. But he wouldn't let it go."

Luke swallowed hard. *She was branded Indian because of me.*

"I didn't believe him—not at first," she said quietly. "But later, in the ladies' room, I caught my reflection. I really looked at myself. And I...I could see it then."

Her gaze drifted, unfocused. "I fainted. I was so overwhelmed."

"I'm sorry he hurt you...because of me." His head dropped.

"No!" Megan cupped his face, forcing him to meet her

eyes. "It wasn't you. When I turned him down, he lashed out at Melissa. He attacked her—like Theo attacked me today." Her voice quivered. "Andrew stopped him, pulling Shane off and knocking him out cold."

*Good,* he thought grimly.

"We thought it was over," she sighed. "But Shane spotted Andrew later that night. He taunted him...said cruel, filthy things about me and Melissa. Andrew never told me exactly what. He didn't want me to know. But it was bad enough that he broke Shane's nose. Said he was teaching him manners."

"I'm glad he did," he said tightly. "I'd have done the same. I hate that Shane said those things. I hate that he hurt you."

"It's what Shane said that made me ask Ma. And that's when she told me…" She whispered, tears spilling. "I *am* half-Indian."

The words hit him like a blow.

"You're...half-Indian?" Luke was stunned. "This can't be real."

She nodded, her lip trembling. "Remember how Ma's family was killed by Indians in Missouri?" she asked softly. "She was discovered—then left for dead." Her voice cracked. "She came here afterward—to Aunt Mabel and Uncle George. That's when she realized...she was pregnant."

"She was carrying *you*?"

"Yes. She told Pa after they fell in love. They married quickly and he raised me as his own."

Luke shook his head slowly, trying to process it.

"Poor Ma," he whispered, eyes brimming. He squeezed Megan's hands. "I never knew. I can't imagine what she went through. All this time, I thought Pa was your father."

"Me too, but Pa knew the truth. I think Grandma and Grandpa Hartford do too." She hesitated. "I had to tell Andrew."

"You did?"

"I needed him to understand why Shane hated me." Her voice trembled. "And after Andrew was killed, I told Mr. Clark, too—so he'd know why Andrew died."

"That's not why Andrew died," Luke said firmly. "Not because you're half-Indian. That's not your fault. Evil men do evil things. You're not to blame."

Megan's frown deepened. "Mr. Clark said the same. But sometimes, I still think...if Andrew had been with someone else that night, he might still be alive."

Luke pulled her into his arms.

"Megan," he murmured, voice thick with sorrow. "I'm so sorry. That must have been awful."

She clung to him, trembling with silent sobs as he stroked her hair.

"Poor Andrew," he murmured. "And his parents… what a terrible loss." A tear slipped free. "I always loved little Andrew. He was such a sweet boy."

"He was," she wept against his chest. "He was my friend after you left. He loved me—truly. He didn't deserve to die." Her voice faltered. "He was shot, trying to protect me. I'll never forget it."

"I'm sorry I left you. But I'm glad he was there for you...when I couldn't be."

The weight of all they'd lost pressed in. For a long time, they stood in the empty road, their horses grazing nearby. Leaving her had been the hardest thing he'd ever done.

When his father came for him after seven years, Luke had been torn. He'd been eleven, barely remembering the man, yet something deep and ancient stirred—a longing for kin, for roots. His father had asked him to return to the tribe, to live among his people, learn their ways. Although it broke his heart, Luke had felt compelled to go. But part of him had never left Cheyenne. Never left her.

Now, holding Megan, he realized: she'd always been with him. In the quiet by the fire, in the wind through the trees, in every lonely mile—she'd lingered.

"Please don't ever leave me again," Megan whispered, clinging to him, her tearful gaze searching his. "Andrew's gone, and I couldn't bear to lose you again."

Her raw words pierced him. He cupped her face, brushing away her tears with his thumbs.

"I'm here now," he said gently. "And leaving you is the last thing on my mind." He kissed her forehead, lingering for a moment before drawing back, glancing toward the horizon. "Come on. Let's get home. We can talk more later. Ma's probably wondering where you are."

Megan's eyes widened. "Oh goodness—the time! She'll be worried." Then, a wry smile formed. "But the second she sees *you*, she'll forget all about it."

Luke chuckled, but his gaze dropped to her torn shirt. The missing buttons left a gap, partially revealing her soft curves. He quickly looked away. She noticed.

"Oh, that." She held the gap closed. "My vest will hide the worst of it," she said, sheepishly. "You distract Ma while I go change." Up to mischief, just like old times.

"I will." Luke smiled.

Mounting up, they nudged their horses into a brisk trot. As they turned onto the familiar lane, they slowed. Luke's throat tightened at the sight. The old dirt road, flanked by towering trees, formed a canopy of green over the lane.

He inhaled deeply, closing his eyes. "Mmm. It even smells like home."

Megan studied his peaceful profile, his head tipped back. High cheekbones, chiseled jaw, strong nose, smooth copper skin—pure masculinity.

"You look happy."

His eyes opened, meeting hers. "I am—very happy."

As they rode into the yard, Luke took in the cottage—familiar yet subtly changed.

"You've added on," he said, surprised.

Megan nodded. "When I turned thirteen, they decided I needed my own room. Pa expanded the house—a bedroom, a bigger kitchen, and a bathroom off the side."

They dismounted and tied the horses to the porch rail.

"That's odd," she murmured. "No one's come out yet." She glanced toward the quiet house. "Ma's probably busy in the kitchen. Let's check."

Luke paused, his hand gripping the handle.

"What if they're not glad I came back?" he whispered. "What if they don't want me here?"

Megan took his hand, squeezing it gently. "They will. Come on." She pushed open the door and stepped inside.

"Ma, I'm home!" she called, her voice bright. "You'll never guess who's with me!"

Cassie's voice floated from the pantry. "No need to shout, Megan—I'm not deaf," she teased, emerging with a jar of preserves in hand.

Then she saw him. Her fingers went slack, the jar slipping to the floor, preserves and glass scattering at her feet.

For a heartbeat, everything stilled.

"Ma, it's Luke," Megan said, her voice catching. She stepped aside to reveal him fully.

Cassie stared, disbelieving. Her hands flew to her mouth.

"Luke?" she gasped. "Oh—oh my goodness. Luke!"

Tears sprang to her eyes. With a choked sob, she rushed forward and threw her arms around him.

"My boy," she wept. "My sweet boy is home!"

Luke wrapped his arms around her, his breath shuddering as he buried his face in her hair.

"Oh, Mama," he choked. "I've missed you so much."

She squeezed him tighter. "We prayed for this. Every night. And now—here you are."

Megan embraced them both, tears spilling over.

Outside, Ed rode in from the range, his gaze catching on the horses tied at the rail—then locking on the copper stallion.

"Wildfire?" His heart jolted. He swung down and leapt up the porch steps. Throwing open the door, he froze in the threshold.

"What's going on?" he asked, in disbelief.

Megan turned, joy shining through her tears. "Pa—it's Luke. He's home!"

"Ed, our boy's come back."

Luke turned toward him. "Hello, Papa."

Ed crossed the room, pulling him into a fierce embrace.

"Luke!" he rasped. "You're really here."

Luke clung to him. "I'm here."

Cassie and Megan held each other, weeping.

"I still can't believe it," Cassie whispered, then asked, "Where in the world did you find him?"

Megan brushed her damp cheeks, smiling in amusement. "Actually, he found *me*. I was out riding near the pond when he came to water Wildfire. I gave him quite a scare—he wasn't expecting company." Her smile softened, gazing at Luke. "It took a moment to recognize each other. Then we decided to come home and surprise you."

Cassie shook her head. "It's a miracle."

Ed released Luke, the two wiping their faces, chuckling under their breath.

"We're so glad you're back, son," Ed said, voice rough. "We weren't sure we'd ever see you again." He clasped Luke's muscled arm, his gaze sweeping over him. "And look at you now. A full-grown man."

Luke stood shoulder to shoulder with Ed, though a bit taller and broader in the chest. The lanky boy had become a hardened man.

Cassie and Megan let out a breathless laugh, the sound tangled with tears as they clung to each other.

"We love you so much, Luke," Cassie whispered. She reached for him again, and he pulled her into his side. "We tried to be patient." Her voice broke. "We told ourselves you'd come when you were ready. But oh, Luke...we almost stopped believing."

Luke swallowed hard, pressing a kiss to her hair.

"Oh, Mama. Wild horses couldn't keep me away. I'm here now." His chest ached with love. "I missed you more than I can say."

Just then, David came charging in.

"Pa, there's a—" He stopped short, eyes wide, confusion knitting his brow. *Why is there an Indian in our house?* Then realization struck.

"Luke?" he breathed.

"David?" Luke asked. The sixteen-year-old boy looked like Pa—tall, blond, and wiry, with sea green eyes.

David lunged forward, clutching his brother. "Luke!" he cried. "You're back! After all this time."

Kurt dashed up the porch steps, skidding to a stop, eyes landing on the group.

Ed smiled. "Kurt, come here, son. This is your brother, Luke." He squeezed Kurt's shoulder. "You were too little to remember when he left."

Kurt studied the stranger.

Luke offered his hand with a warm smile. "Hi—not-so-little brother."

Kurt gripped Luke's hand with surprising firmness. At fourteen he was nearly as tall as David but broader, dark-haired, and green-eyed like Megan.

"Nice to meet you again... I mean, see you again," he stammered, wringing his hat. "Johnathan's right behind me. You've never met him—he wasn't even born yet."

"I have *another* brother?" Luke asked in wonder.

As if on cue, Johnathan bounded up the steps, bumping into Kurt in the doorway.

"Hey, move! I'm starving," Johnathan muttered, trying to push past.

Kurt stepped aside. Johnathan froze at the sight of the Indian, eyes wide, mouth dropping.

David explained. "Johnathan, this is Luke—our big brother."

Johnathan gasped. "Oh, yeah! The one everyone talks about. My adopted Indian brother." He glanced at David. "He's way bigger than you said."

Luke chuckled. "It's good to finally meet you, Johnathan."

The toe-headed boy threw his arms around him.

Luke startled, embracing his youngest brother in awe. The boy barely reached his chest but held him with surprising strength.

"I'm glad you're back," Johnathan mumbled against Luke's shirt. He looked up, eyes gleaming. "Now I'll get to know you, too." He grinned. "I *love* Indians."

Laughter rippled through the room.

"How old are you?" Luke asked, pulling back to see him more clearly.

"Ten," Johnathan declared proudly. "I've even got my own horse!"

Luke was impressed. "That's great." He ruffled the boy's hair. "You're almost a man then."

Johnathan's smile widened. "One day, I'll grow as big as you and Pa."

Luke patted the boy's shoulder. "I don't doubt it."

Johnathan's eyes filled with admiration. Luke smiled, falling in love with this little brother he'd never known.

Laughter bubbled up again—as if the house itself was exhaling after a long-held breath.

Ed clapped Luke's shoulder, his grin widening.

"Kurt," he said, "ride over to Grandma and Grandpa

Hartford's. Then swing through town—invite everyone for supper at six. We'll roast a pig."

Joy filled Ed's voice. "We're going to have ourselves a family reunion. Luke's finally home—and that calls for a celebration."

# Chapter 2

## Family Reunion

That afternoon, the homestead buzzed with activity as the family prepared for the homecoming celebration. In the yard, chairs and makeshift tables were arranged beneath the shady cottonwoods. Across the way, a pig roasted on the spit, the boys taking turns cranking the handle. In the kitchen, the women were hard at work cooking.

Luke carried in another load of firewood, filling the wood box.

Cassie glanced over her shoulder and smiled warmly. "Thank you, Luke."

"Anything else I can help with?" he asked.

"I think we've got it. But when you go back out, remind Johnathan to keep the spit moving."

"Sure thing, Ma."

Her eyes shone with love at the sound of him calling her "Ma".

"Would it be alright if I cooked a traditional Shoshone dish?"

"That sounds delightful. What's it called?"

"Camas—it grows nearby."

"Sounds great," Cassie replied, giving the bubbling peas and potatoes a good stir.

Megan wiped her hands. "If you want help, I'm done with the salad. Just need to set it in the cellar."

"I'd love help," Luke said. "Let me take that—you grab a basket."

He took the large bowl of potato salad and lifted the trapdoor to the root cellar. He paused, breathing in the cool earthy scent, the shelves lined with preserved bounty. *What a luxury this would've been on the reservation.*

"Just put it on the shelf by the butter," Cassie called, as if he'd never left.

Back upstairs, Megan waited with a basket.

"We'll be back in a little while," Luke said, leaning in to kiss Cassie's cheek.

Her eyes misted, but she quickly turned back to her work, blinking the tears away.

As they emerged, Kurt galloped into the yard, waving a white envelope.

"Megan! You got a letter from your beau—Clint!" he called, reining in beside them.

Her cheeks flushed as she snatched the letter, tucking it hastily into her apron.

Crossing the yard, they spotted Johnathan half-heartedly cranking the spit.

"Ma says to keep that turning," Luke called.

Johnathan straightened. "I will."

Luke and Megan followed the path beyond the garden, tracing the winding edge of Crow Creek, its gurgle blending with the melody of birds and wind in the trees.

Walking quietly ahead, Luke asked, "So... who's Clint?"

Megan's fingers tightened around the basket. "He's a student at the University of Wyoming—just a friend."

Luke stopped abruptly, turning to face her.

"The University of Wyoming?"

Megan's cheeks warmed. "In Laramie. I'm going to teachers' college."

"You're going to be a teacher?"

She nodded. "I want to teach on the reservation when I graduate. I hoped I'd find you there."

Luke smiled, chest tightening. "Well... I found you first."

She returned his smile, the air between them full of longing.

"Do you remember?" he asked quietly. "I asked you to wait for me."

She lowered her gaze, afraid he'd already moved on.

"I remember," she whispered.

Luke studied her face. She wasn't the girl he'd left behind. She was a woman now—still lovely, but deeper, wiser. He reached for her hand, lacing his fingers with hers, resuming their walk.

Luke broke the comfortable silence. "I worried you'd be married by now." He kept his eyes ahead, but his grip steady.

"No," she said softly. "I'm not married."

A satisfied smile crossed his face. He gave her hand a playful squeeze. "I figured that out."

She grinned, and confessed, "I thought *you'd* be married. Maybe with a family." Her heart hoped it wasn't so.

"No one ever felt right." His voice grew quiet. "Some hoped I'd ask... but I couldn't."

She wondered *why* but wasn't sure she wanted the answer.

"I'm sure they were disappointed," she said lightly. "A big, strong, handsome man like you? You must've broken a few hearts."

Luke turned to her, a slow smile forming.

"And I hope to never break another," he said seriously.

Her heart skipped. His eyes held hers—filled with unmistakable longing. Her breath caught. She looked away, cheeks flushing.

Attempting to relieve the tension, he asked, "And what about you—planning to break Clint's heart?" he half-teased.

Megan's blush deepened. She slipped her hand free, adjusting a strand of hair.

"Clint's a friend," she said, avoiding his eyes. "We've been writing during summer break... but I don't know how I feel about him."

Luke's chest eased—her uncertainty gave him hope.

He took her hand again, thankful she didn't pull away.

He led her beneath the shelter of tall trees, where violet-blue flowers blanketed the earth.

Megan's eyes lit up with excitement. "Oh, I love these." She crouched to pick one. "They're my favorite color." She peered up at him, joy spreading across her face.

Suddenly, a glimmer of the little girl who'd once chased him appeared—but this woman's smile now stirred something deeper—sending his heart racing.

"You found a camas lily," he said proudly.

Luke took a sturdy branch and began working the soil, gently tugging the bulbs free.

"This is what we eat," he explained. "We make flatbread or roast them over coals. They're sweet like yams."

"Here—I'll make Ma a bouquet." Megan held out her hand for the flower.

He handed them over, his fingers brushed hers, sending a warmth up her arm that landed in her chest. She'd dreamed of him for years and now he was here working beside her. It seemed unreal.

Once the basket was full, Luke helped her to her feet, keeping her hand in his.

She closed her eyes, inhaling the bouquet of indigo blooms.

"I'm glad we came out here." Megan sighed softly. "I've missed this. I haven't had time to enjoy nature with work and college. You don't realize how much you've missed something until it's back."

Luke squeezed her hand, his voice low. "I completely understand."

She studied him, wondering out loud, "I don't know how you stood being away so long. But I guess you were going home."

His mood shifted. "I was... but they were strangers. It was hard, being away. You all—*you* were my family. *You* were all I knew."

"I'm so glad you're back," she whispered, her heart rejoicing after the years apart.

"Me too," he murmured, brushing the back of her hand with his thumb.

When they approached the yard Luke released her hand, leaving her missing his touch.

Ed sat by the fire pit, slowly turning the spit. He looked up and smiled.

"Those are pretty," he said, eyeing Megan's bouquet.

"They're for Ma," she said proudly. "Camas lilies—

flower of the bulbs Luke wants to cook."

"Pa, I'll need a Dutch oven for these." Luke motioned to the basket.

"If you'll take a turn at the spit, I'll go find it."

"Thank you, Pa."

"I'll wash the bulbs." Megan headed toward the house with the basket and bouquet.

Luke took Ed's place at the spit.

A moment later, Johnathan came bounding outside and dropped to the ground across from Luke.

Eyes full of curiosity, he asked, "Did you scalp anyone while you were gone?"

Luke sputtered, then laughed at the unexpected question.

"Well, did you?" Johnathan pressed.

"No! And I never will."

"Oh." Johnathan said, mildly disappointed.

"What grade are you in?" Luke asked, shifting the subject.

"Third!" the boy beamed.

"I remember third grade," Luke said with a nostalgic chuckle. "In my tribe, boys start learning the bow and arrow by your age. Want to learn?"

Johnathan's eyes lit up. "You bet!"

"Go get my bow and quiver—they're on the porch swing."

The boy dashed off but paused halfway. "What's a quiver?"

"The case that holds the arrows," Luke called, grinning.

Luke had propped up an old stump for a target by the time Johnathan returned—quiver slung over one shoulder, bow in hand.

"Pa! Luke's going to teach me to shoot a bow!" Johnathan shouted as Ed approached.

Ed chuckled, setting the pot down. "Sounds like fun."

Luke demonstrated how to hold the bow and arrow and took a shot. The arrow hissed through the air, striking the stump dead center.

"Wow!" Johnathan clapped. "Pa! Did you see that?"

"I saw it," Ed said, grinning.

Luke handed the bow to Johnathan. "Your turn."

He took the next few minutes instructing Johnathan, then let him shoot on his own.

The arrow skimmed the grass and thudded into the dirt.

"Oh! I missed!" Johnathan dashed after it.

Megan joined them with the basket of washed bulbs.

"Oh! Can I try?" she asked.

Luke grinned. "Sure. You and Johnathan can take turns—after I get these ready for the pot."

She handed him the basket and watched him prepare the bulbs and set the pot on the fire.

"We'll let it cook slow," he said, brushing off his hands. "Your turn."

Megan's eyes sparkled as Johnathan handed her the bow.

Luke stepped behind her, helping her get the right stance and nock the arrow.

Her pulse quickened, but she remained focused as he put his hands over hers. Her arms trembled from the tension.

"Can you hold it if I let go?" he asked softly beside her ear.

"I... I think so," her voice breathy.

He slowly released her hands. She exhaled and loosed the arrow—it soared past the stump, into the grass beyond.

Megan laughed. "At least I didn't hit the garden."

"Not bad for a girl," Johnathan teased.

She shot him a playful glare. "Let's see you do better."

"She did great," Luke said, smiling. "When I got to the reservation, I wasn't good either—they made fun of me."

Ed's brow furrowed. "They teased you?"

"For a lot of things—my short hair, my clothes, not knowing how to ride bareback or hunt like they did. The worst part was the language. When I spoke English, they laughed... or spit at me... kicked dirt in my face."

Megan's heart ached at the thought.

Luke looked at Johnathan. "But the younger boys—ones your age—they helped. They weren't cruel."

Johnathan stood straighter. "Show me again, Luke. I'll practice and get better—just like you did."

"Alright. Let's do it again."

As afternoon waned, Luke tended the coals and Megan and Johnathan practiced. The sun dipped behind the trees as the savory scent of pork and camas bulbs filled the yard.

"So, tell us more," Pa prompted. "What was it like when you first went back?"

Crouching by the fire, Luke stirred the coals thoughtfully.

"It was a long trek through the mountains. We hunted and camped for about a week before reaching the reservation."

The fire hissed with dripping fat, but all eyes were focused on Luke.

"At first, the tribe was welcoming—they pitied me, thinking I'd suffered among 'white men.'" His smile faded, eyes distant, remembering.

"We moved in with my aunt, uncle, and their two boys. The teepee was crowded but felt safe. I was glad to see the ones I'd forgotten. They hugged me, cried, and gave me special gifts. I was eager to learn—hunting, fishing, cooking—the things I'd only read about. But soon, I felt like I didn't belong. I couldn't understand the language. I kept making mistakes—so many misunderstandings."

Megan felt a pang in her chest at the sorrow in his eyes.

His voice dropped. "I was so lonely. I kept comparing life *there*—to life *here*. But over time, I picked up the language, started learning their ways. And I realized— just because it was different didn't mean it was wrong."

He glanced at Megan with a quiet smile. "Eventually, it felt like a long family camping trip—except without Ma's cooking."

Ed chuckled. "I bet you missed that."

Johnathan set the bow aside and joined them. "What else? What did they eat?"

"The food was strange at first—everything smoked, dried, or roasted over a fire. Except the soup—*that* was made in a leather bowl."

Johnathan blinked. "How do you cook soup in leather?"

"They'd stretch a thick hide over a tripod, filling it with water, meat, and wild vegetables—then drop in hot stones until it boiled."

Johnathan's eyes widened. "That's incredible."

Pa leaned forward. "What's pemmican? I hear you eat a lot of that."

"Berries, dried meat, and fat—all ground together," Luke said. "Gives you energy. Good for travel—you can eat while you walk."

His expression dimmed.

"But once we got there... no more reason to trek. My people used to move with the seasons, let the land rest. Now, they can't so there's limited game."

"Has it gotten any better?" Megan asked, stepping closer, slipping a comforting arm around Luke.

Luke slowly exhaled. "No. It's worse. The Arapaho— our old enemies—were relocated to Wind River. With more people—less space. And the government hasn't sent what they promised. My people are losing hope. I left—unable to find peace there."

Ed placed a firm hand on his shoulder. "We're glad you came back. You and your family are always welcome here."

Luke's throat tightened, blinking back tears.

"I'm the only one who can leave," he said. "The Indian Agent over the reservation requested proof of my adoption. I have papers now—because of you. They say I'm free to come and go. But not them. I felt guilty leaving my family behind. But my grandfather saw how restless I was…how sad. He told me to go."

"My heart was *here*." He quickly glanced at Megan, tucked under his arm.

She pressed closer into his side, knowing her heart was always with *him*.

Cassie called out from the porch railing, "It's almost time. Let's get the food out."

Kurt and David emerged from the barn and together, the family set the last of the dishes out, placing the roasted pig on a long plank, just as the first wagons rolled in.

Grandma and Grandpa Hartford arrived with Clancy, Joy, and their boys, followed by Beth and her family.

"Howdy!" Ed called, striding over to greet them, helping Joy down from the wagon. Soon, laughter and warm greetings filled the yard.

Luke lingered by the fire, unsure. Megan slipped her hand into his and guided him forward.

Luke was immediately embraced—tearful hugs, hearty backslaps, voices calling his name. The lump in his throat made speech impossible.

Grandma Hartford shuffled forward, her eyes teary. "My, my... how you've grown," her voice trembled, "oh, Luke... we love you so much."

Her embrace was as warm as he remembered. Tears spilled down his cheeks.

Grandpa Hartford followed, slower now, but his grip still firm. "Luke, we were sad we never got to say good-bye," he said hoarsely. "But we're so glad you're back."

Grandma and Grandpa O'Malley arrived next, their eyes bright with joy.

"Welcome home, lad!" Grandpa O'Malley's Scottish lilt clear as ever, his weathered face grinning. "And just in time—I could use a good hunt, or maybe some fishing."

Luke smiled, his heart full. "I'll take you up on that."

One by one, he embraced them all. With each tearful hug, the long years apart melted away. The tightness in his chest eased; their love warmed him to the core.

Last to arrive were Bart, Bea, and their three daughters.

Bart pulled Luke into a strong hug. "It's a good thing you're home," he said gruffly. "We've been missing you... and worried sick. But look at you—you've grown strong." He stepped back, giving Luke a once-over. "We sure hope you're here to stay."

"I have no plans to go back. Not yet." Luke's voice was quiet. "I'm just grateful to be here. It's been too long... and I've missed you all."

He hesitated, "I'm so sorry about Andrew. He was one of my favorites." His voice broke. The grief in Bart's eyes mirrored his own.

Bea gently embraced him. "We wish you'd seen him one last time," she whispered. "He was such a fine young man. It was a terrible loss... but we're getting by."

She cupped Luke's face with trembling hands, eyes shining. "We all missed you... but Megan especially." Her voice dropped. "She needs you, Luke. After you left, Andrew became her rock, leaning on him. She's tried to stay strong... but she's not the same. You'll bring her light back."

She kissed his cheek and slipped away, dabbing at her eyes.

Ed clapped his hands. "Alright, everyone—it's time to eat."

The family formed a wide circle beneath the evening sky, with the scent of roasting pork hanging in the cooling air.

Ed offered the blessing, giving thanks for the food, and most importantly, Luke's return.

At "amen," the circle broke, giving way to cheerful chatter.

The feast was abundant—the roast pig fell apart beneath the carving knife. Bowls of creamy salads, garden vegetables, and golden cornbread crowded the tables. Even Luke's camas bulbs drew praise.

Plates were filled and refilled as children clamored for seconds of pie and cookies, cheeks flushed with joy. Adults lingered, their conversations warm with memory and laughter.

When the last crumbs were gone, younger children spilled into the yard, dashing and shrieking in games of tag and hide-and-seek, their delight echoing into the twilight.

Closer to the fire, older children and adults gathered. With Bart's violin, Ed's guitar, and Clancy's harmonica, music drifted through the twilight, voices joining in the harmony. Some danced, stomping boots and clapping hands while others watched with smiles, content in the glow of family.

As night fell, lanterns were lit, casting warm halos across the yard. The fire died down, smoke curling into the star-pierced sky as the families began bidding farewell.

***

Later that night, after the last wagon rolled away, the homestead settled into a peaceful hush. Everyone turned in, except Luke and Megan, lingering on the porch swing, savoring the quiet.

The lantern on the porch flickered in the breeze while the swing creaked softly as it swayed. Megan leaned into Luke, her head resting on his shoulder, releasing a satisfied sigh. Eyes closed, she felt perfectly at ease—content to stay there forever.

"What a day," she murmured. "I never would've guessed it'd turn out like this."

Luke's gaze drifted to the star-scattered sky. The moon had just risen, casting a silvery glow across the clearing.

"It was a great homecoming. I can hardly believe it's real. I wasn't expecting to find you at the pond...and then all of this—it's a day I'll never forget."

"Me either," she whispered.

She slipped her fingers through his. The warmth of her touch sent a gentle shiver through him. He leaned in, resting his head against hers, not wanting the moment to end.

The long, hard years were behind him now. And though the road ahead was still uncertain, one thing was clear—he felt whole.

He was home.

# Chapter 3

## *Revelations*

As Megan finished her breakfast, she sighed. "I wish I didn't have to work today. I wanted to catch up with you."

Luke smiled. "When you get home, we'll go for a ride after supper. I'll save all the good stories till then."

***

The day passed quickly at the telephone company, though Megan's thoughts kept drifting to Luke. She hurried home eager for supper and the promise of their ride.

At the table, she asked, "What did everyone do today?"

Ed wiped his mouth, eyes gleaming. "The boys and I spent the day with Luke—checking fences, crops, and cattle."

"It was great!" Johnathan leaned in. "Luke told us about the buffalo hunts. Thousands of them—riders with bows and arrows chasing buffalo across the prairie. And after the kill, they'd cut out the heart and—"

Cassie cleared her throat, giving him a look.

He winced. "I mean—the heart gave them strength."

Megan smiled, turning to her mother. "And you, Ma?"

Cassie beamed. "Luke helped me in the garden. He showed me herbs and plants they use for healing."

Megan looked at Luke, captivated. She had always admired his quiet strength—but now, she saw his wisdom, too.

After supper, Luke met her at the door. "Are you ready to go?"

He hadn't forgotten. "I'm ready." She hung up her apron and called, "We'll be back before dark."

Cassie stepped onto the porch. "Have a good time."

Ed followed with his guitar. "Have fun, you two," he called, settling beside Cassie on the swing.

Luke led the horses from the corral. Megan secured her hat over her braided hair and swung up onto Snowfire as he held the reins. His gaze lingered— she was a vision in red atop the white mare.

She caught his look and smiled. "Where to?"

He hesitated. "Away from town. I'm not ready for all the looks and comments."

She nodded. "I'm tired of people too. North or south?"

"Let's ride out to Horse Creek."

He mounted Wildfire, and together they turned north onto the open plains. For eight miles they rode, the world slipping away behind them.

It was Megan's favorite time of day—long shadows stretched across the prairie, the land exhaling into evening.

Luke broke the silence. "How was work?"

"Good. Mostly connecting calls in a little room with a few other operators. The girls are nice."

Snowfire snorted softly. Wildfire answered with a low whinny.

Luke glanced over. "What about the restaurant?"

Megan hesitated. "It's fine, usually. Just... busy. Some customers aren't very kind." She forced a smile. "But I manage."

"You work two jobs *and* go to school—hard worker."

She chuckled. "I get it from Ma and Pa."

"I believe that."

"What about your Indian parents?" she asked.

Luke grew quiet. "Most of what I know about my mother comes from my father. I was so young when she died... but I remember her love. My father says I used to fall asleep stroking her braids as she'd sing and tell me stories."

"She sounds lovely. What was her name?"

"Wogweruiyuh," he said quietly. "It means Bluebird."

"That's my favorite bird." She thought of the cheerful mountain bluebirds on her morning rides.

"My aunt Rose cried when she saw the Bluebird of Happiness. I didn't understand until I told my father where I got it—that it was from Ma, on the day my mother died."

His voice thickened. "That's when he told me—my mother's name was Bluebird."

"She must have been special."

"She brought joy wherever she went. Even when she was sick, she never complained."

"It must have been hard losing her." She thought of losing Luke—all those years of heartache.

"He still misses her. My father and mother fell in love young," Luke added with a playful wink. "They were best friends—like us. My father used to chase her, and she'd slow just enough for him to catch her."

Megan laughed. "That sounds familiar."

Luke's smile became wistful. "When they got older they met by the river, held hands, talking. He gave her a black rock that sparkled like stars—her lucky stone."

The sun dipped as they turned toward the creek.

"She'd sit by the river while he played her a song, called *Bluebird's Song*."

"Played on what?"

"An Indian flute. Some call it a courting flute."

"Do you play?" she asked. Each part of Luke's past painted a deeper picture of him.

"I do. Maybe I'll play for you sometime."

"I'd love that," she said, picturing Luke playing her a song by the river. "What's your father like?"

"Quiet. Wise. A deeply spiritual man—like his father, the Shaman. My grandfather healed, married, and interpreted visions—like a pastor *and* a doctor."

"Your family is remarkable."

"My father left the tribe to protect us. The Spirit told him it was the only way to save our family. Still, my mother and baby sister died. For a while, he felt lost. Now he sees—it was me who was meant to survive. I grew up with Ma and Pa—I had everything I needed to grow strong."

He looked out across the prairie. "Life on the reservation was hard. Some turned to war. I chose a different path. I wanted to help the tribe adjust to change."

Megan's chest tightened. "Oh, Luke, how difficult."

The steady rhythm of their horses' hooves filled the quiet space as their thoughts wandered on different paths.

Luke broke the silence, voice gravelly. "My grandfather passed a few weeks ago. Now my father is the Shaman."

Megan's eyes filled with sympathy. "I wish I could've met him."

"You would've liked him. I miss him."

They rode in silence until they reached the line of cottonwoods and willows where the stream wound lazily through. The gurgle of water met their ears, the air cool with the scent of fresh water.

"We're here," she said.

Luke slowed, eyes fixed on the stream, its waters whispering like memory. "It's just the way I remember it."

They dismounted by the sloping bank, letting the horses drink while their tails swished lazily at flies. Luke tied the reins to a low branch, his gaze drifting to Megan.

She slipped off her hat and loosened her braid, letting the breeze tease her hair. With a sigh, she removed her shoes and stockings, tucking them beside a fallen log. Lifting her skirt just enough, she stepped into the water.

Cool sand met her feet, and she sighed again as the stream lapped over her ankles, soothing the weariness of the long, hot day.

Luke watched her step deeper, water swirling around her calves. Without a word, he shed his tunic and moccasins and followed, bare chest catching the last of the light.

Megan stopped when the water reached her knees. "Oh, this feels heavenly."

Water splashed behind her. She turned and smiled. His dark hair clung damp to his face, his chest and shoulders glistening with water droplets. He looked utterly at home—part of the land itself.

"It does," he agreed, his voice low. The hush of

water, the privacy of the trees—it felt like the edge of another world.

"Remember the stream behind the house?" Megan asked. "How we used to play there?"

Luke grinned. "I remember dunking you."

She laughed, recalling sunlit summers and shrieks of laughter. Then, seeing him edge closer, she narrowed her eyes and lifted her skirt. "Don't you dare. We're not children anymore—this isn't proper—"

Too late.

With a flash of mischief, Luke scooped her into his arms.

"You were saying something about proper?" he teased.

"No!" she squealed, arms tight around his neck, legs kicking.

He laughed, the sound deep and full of remembered joy. "I'm sorry," he said, mock-serious. "I've forgotten how to be proper. I'm a *wild* Indian now."

"You know what I meant," she huffed, blushing. "We're too old for this."

"Too old?" He hoisted her higher, water rising to his waist. "Where I come from, no one's too old to play in the water."

Before she could reply, he let go.

She splashed under, then surfaced with a gasp, hair plastered to her cheeks. "Luke!" she shouted, half-outraged, half-laughing.

She lunged, shoving at his chest—but he didn't move. Her wet dress clung to her curves, and Luke swallowed hard, trying not to stare. She was wild and lovely, just as he remembered.

"You needed to cool off," he said, grinning. "I was helping."

"Oh, I'll help *you*!" she warned, splashing him in the face. He laughed again, the sound echoing off the trees as water streamed down his chest and back in rivulets.

With a wicked gleam she relentlessly splashed him.

"I'm cool enough!" he growled, laughing as he shielded himself.

With a sudden lunge, he hoisted her onto his shoulder like a sack of grain.

"Luke!" she shrieked, pounding his back. "Put me down!"

"Oh... like this?" he teased, tipping forward, dropping her into the stream with a splash.

She surfaced sputtering, water streaming down her face, eyes blazing.

"Now you're soaked too," she said, trying for indignation. "Serves you right."

"Will you forgive me?" he asked, clearly unrepentant.

"Never!"

She waded toward shore, dress clinging to her legs, skin tingling in the evening chill.

She glanced over her shoulder. "What will Ma think, seeing us come home like this?" she huffed. "Honestly, Luke—how could you?"

He caught her wrist and gently tugged her back.

She turned, startled by how close he stood—his warmth rising through her damp blouse. His eyes searched hers, suddenly quiet and serious.

"I couldn't bear it if you were truly angry," he said softly.

Megan's jaw clenched. The sparkle in her eyes had dimmed, replaced by something guarded.

"I'm sorry," he murmured. "I got carried away. I forgot we weren't children anymore."

Megan looked up, her breath shaky. Tears welled before she could stop them.

"Megan…" His voice cracked. "Please don't cry."

He pulled her into his arms, her frame trembling against him. Pressing a kiss to her hair, he whispered, "What's wrong?"

She clung to him, in shaky sobs. "I... I don't know."

He pulled back slightly, brushing her wet hair from her face. "Was it the dunking?"

She shook her head, pressing her cheek against his chest. "No. It's not that. I don't care about getting wet."

"Then what?"

Without thinking, she said it. "I'm mad that you left me."

Luke froze.

"You were my best friend. And you left. I needed you. I was lost." Her voice cracked. "And then Andrew... I lost him too."

Her grief pierced him. He lifted her from the water, holding her close as she buried her face in his neck. On the bank, he sat and cradled her in his lap, as if she might slip away again.

"I'm not leaving you," he whispered. "I came back as soon as I could." He wished she knew how long he'd dreamed of this—of her.

Her trembling slowly stilled. The warmth of his embrace seeped into her bones.

Luke brushed a strand of wet hair from her cheek.

She looked up at him, eyes shimmering.

"I love you, Megan," he said, voice rough. "I always have. I always will. Nothing will ever change that, not time or distance."

A tear slipped down his cheek.

Megan stared, breath held. Then she cupped his face, hands trembling, and kissed him—softly, with years of longing between them.

When she pulled back, her lips curved into a soft smile.

"I love you too, Luke. I've waited twelve years to say it." Her voice dropped to a whisper. "You've always been more than a brother to me. I love you like I've never loved anyone."

Luke's eyes closed, a breath catching. When he opened them, they were full.

"You don't know how much I needed to hear that," he said. "All these years, I've missed you. I've loved you. It's what kept me going."

His lips met hers again—deep and lingering. Tears slid down his face, sealing a long-delayed promise. The dream he'd clung to for so long was finally real.

When they parted, their foreheads rested together, hearts pounding, both smiling through their tears.

Megan's fingers traced through his damp hair, brushing it back. Her gaze searched his, blinking away fresh tears.

"I used to talk to you like you were still there," she whispered. "In my room, I'd tell you everything—how much I missed you. Every year, I said 'Happy Birthday,' 'Merry Christmas.' Sometimes I almost believed you could hear me." Her voice wavered. "I imagined you growing older... wondered if you'd fallen in love with some beautiful maiden."

Luke's eyes darkened with feeling. "I felt you too—saw you in my dreams." He swallowed hard. "There's so much I need to tell you—things I buried deep. I tried to be strong, but I'm not. I'm lost... broken."

He lowered his head in grief. "I don't even know who I am anymore. All I know is that I had to come home—to you."

When he looked up, the vulnerability in his eyes stole her breath.

"You're the only thing I'm sure of," he said softly.

Her heart ached. "Oh, Luke…"

He glanced away. "My father was furious when I refused to marry the chief's daughter. He said it was my duty. But when I told him I was coming back to you... he was ashamed." His eyes locked on hers. "But this—being here with you—is the only thing that feels right."

"I saw you in my dreams," he said again, voice low. "Your green eyes always begging me to come home." He held her hand tighter. "I told my grandfather, before he died. He told me to follow those dreams."

Luke's voice faltered. "My father... maybe he'll understand someday. But right now, he's still angry." He searched her face, his own vulnerable and bare. "Please, Meg... don't be angry too. I couldn't stand to disappoint you."

Her heart squeezed. She touched his cheek, voice soft. "I was never truly angry. Just young—and hurt." Her eyes glistened with sorrow. "Your family needed you too. They missed you as much as I did." Her hand slipped to his jaw, thumb brushing gently.

Her words sank deep, soothing a long-held ache. With a sigh, she leaned against his shoulder, arms wrapping around him. He held her tightly, eyes closed, as though she might vanish.

Her warmth seeped into every broken place. With his chin resting on her head, he whispered, "I don't ever want to make you sad again. I just want to bring you joy. To love you."

She drew back slightly, smiling through tears. "I'm not angry anymore." Rising to her feet, she took his hand.

"We'd better get home," she murmured, glancing toward the dusk-painted sky. "Ma and Pa will send a search party if we're not back by dark."

Luke grinned, mischief lighting his face. "Hmm... we'll need a good excuse for being soaking wet."

Her laughter lifted into the evening. "We'll be dry enough by the time we get home." She gathered her hat, shoes, and stockings, tossing him a teasing look. "No one needs to know we were splashing around like children."

He chuckled as they walked to the horses, the sound of their laughter drifting into the warm evening air.

They rode side by side, speaking in low tones as the sun slipped below the horizon. The sky flared with gold and rose, fading into lavender dusk. Crickets began their nightly chorus, blending with the gentle clop of hooves along the dirt road.

As the homestead came into view, Megan smoothed her wrinkled dress. "Do I look alright?" she asked, tugging at the fabric. Her dress had dried unevenly, hair loose and windblown.

Luke glanced over. Even disheveled, she was breathtaking.

"You look beautiful," he said quietly.

A blush touched her cheeks. She smiled, gaze lingering on his before turning away.

Twilight had deepened as they rode into the yard. On the porch swing, Ed and Cassie rocked gently, fingers loosely intertwined. The swing creaked to a stop as they spotted Megan and Luke.

"Did you have fun?" Ed called as they dismounted.

They exchanged a quick glance, thankful for the shadows that masked their damp clothes and glowing smiles.

"Yes," Megan said with a hint of mischief. "Very refreshing." She shot Luke a sideways look. He turned quickly, hiding a grin.

He led the horses toward the corral. "Goodnight, Ma. Goodnight, Pa. Goodnight, Megan," he called over his shoulder.

"Goodnight, Luke," they answered as Luke disappeared.

Though welcome in the house, Luke still chose the barn. The walls inside felt too close. Out here, beneath tall rafters and the scent of hay, he could breathe.

He spread a blanket over the straw and lay back, moonlight slipping through the cracks above. A long, contented sigh escaped him. He closed his eyes, the memory of her kiss still warm.

Tonight, he would dream of Megan—the girl he'd always loved, and the woman who had finally brought him home

# Chapter 4

## Vision Quest

Megan slipped into her room and closed the door. The soft flicker of lamplight danced across the walls as she lit the wick. She undressed slowly, still warm from the memory of his arms. In her nightdress, she sank onto the stool before her dressing table.

She brushed her hair in long, steady strokes, lost in the sweetness of the evening. Her lips curved into a dreamy smile. Catching her reflection, she paused. Her face glowed. Eyes bright, cheeks flushed—she looked radiant. And she knew why.

Luke was home. This time, for good.

Her chest tightened with joy. Their kisses replayed in her mind—tender, lingering, soft as promises. It had felt right. Natural. And yet... was it? She didn't know how their bond had shifted—from innocent affection to something deeper—but it had. She loved Luke. Not as a brother. Not anymore.

She'd always adored him—the brave boy who made her feel safe. But after Andrew's death, affection turned to longing. Luke became the man she dreamed of—the steadfast protector she yearned for. And now he was here. In flesh and blood. Her heart knew what it wanted.

Still, beneath the joy stirred a quiet ache. No one would understand. How could they? She barely did. This beautiful, bewildering truth would remain tucked away—for now, belonging to her and Luke alone.

She crossed to the wardrobe, lifting her damp dress to hang it. A flash of white peeked from the pocket of her green dress. The letter from Clint. Her stomach sank as she pulled it free.

"Oh no," she whispered. Perching on the bed, she unfolded the page.

*My dearest Megan,*

*I've been thinking about you so much lately. Time is moving too slowly. I can't wait to see you again in the fall. Maybe I'll come out to Cheyenne for a visit, if that's agreeable.*

*I've found no solace in my work or among friends. I feel I need to see you. We've been apart too long. Tell me you'll let me come.*

*Yours always, Clint.*

Her hands trembled as she pressed the letter to her chest. A knot formed in her stomach.

"What am I going to do?" she whispered.

Clint couldn't come. Not now. But how could she tell him? How could she explain something she didn't fully understand herself?

She folded the letter and set it on the nightstand. With a weary breath, she reached for the lamp and snuffed out the flame. Darkness settled, but her thoughts would not.

She slipped beneath the covers and curled onto her side. The letter tugged at her thoughts, but she let it go. Not tonight. Tonight, there was only Luke—the warmth of his embrace, the tremble in his voice, the tears in his eyes when she whispered that she loved him too.

A small smile touched her lips. It had been a perfect

day—one she would carry forever. Tonight, she knew her dreams would be filled with Luke.

***

Megan rose with the sun, her heart already heavy. She dressed quickly. The thought of leaving Luke behind tugged at her.

She rode into town, each mile widening the distance between them. Though the day was bright, work at the hotel restaurant felt dreary. The clatter of dishes and steady hum of voices passed unnoticed.

Her thoughts drifted to Luke at the homestead. She imagined the sun on his skin as he worked. His smile. The way his eyes softened when he looked at her. The look that made her breath catch and knees go weak.

The hours dragged. She fumbled orders, murmured apologies, and hurried on, her mind never quite in the room.

No one seemed to notice, and for that she was grateful. She kept her head down, refilling cups and clearing plates while her heart wandered home.

She didn't see Theo—and silently thanked God. The memory of his cold eyes still sent a chill through her.

By shift's end, she was spent. She rode toward home, her chest easing as the homestead came into view. A smile spread across her face. She nudged her horse into a trot, aching for Luke's arms—for the quiet strength of his presence, and the belonging she felt with him.

***

After supper, Luke and Megan rode south, the cool evening air laced with the scent of sun-warmed grass. Golden light stretched across the open plains as they spoke in hushed tones, laughter threaded into the stillness of the fading day.

Clearwater Pond soon shimmered into view—familiar, yet different tonight. Quieter. Reverent. The glassy surface mirrored the lavender sky, where clouds drifted like smoke. Silver rings rippled where dragonflies kissed the water.

They dismounted and tied their horses to a low branch and wandered toward the shade of a wide-limbed tree.

"Tell me more about your time on the reservation," Megan said, then glanced toward the place where Theo had once stood. A chill slid down her spine.

Luke followed her gaze. His jaw tightened. The memory twisted in his gut—too close. *A few seconds later...* He let the thought go.

They settled beneath the tree. Megan stretched out on the grass, Luke cross-legged beside her. The breeze carried the scent of wildflowers. Cattails swayed at the pond's edge, shadows dancing across the water. Lily pads floated like scattered coins. From across the pond came the croak of frogs, the song of a nightingale.

Luke felt connected to all of it—the trees, the water, the gentle hum of nature.

"How old were you on your first vision quest?" Megan asked gently.

Her voice pulled him back. "Twelve."

"What was it like?" Megan asked, reclining fully, eyes scanning the canopy above. She felt safe here—with him.

He smiled. "A little like this. Just listen."

A bee buzzed past, dusted in pollen. A frog snapped a fly midair. Luke watched it, his expression softening.

Megan studied him. He looked peaceful, as though the earth itself was speaking to him.

She closed her eyes, letting the stillness envelop her—the chirp of crickets, the hush of wind through leaves.

"How long?" she whispered, opening her eyes a slit.

Luke glanced down, smiling. She was still the sweet girl he remembered—her green eyes bright with curiosity, her dark hair spread like silk across the grass. And more beautiful than ever.

"As long as it takes. Sometimes a day. Traditionally, four."

Megan closed her eyes again. A chipmunk chirped in the distance; water gurgled where the pond fed into a narrow stream. She breathed it in—the thrum of nature's song.

After a while, she opened her eyes. "That's a long time. What do you do?"

"You pray. You listen. You wait."

She turned. "Where do you go?"

"Far from anything familiar. No food, no water."

She thought of fasting when Andrew was sick—how it had drawn her closer to God.

Luke's voice quieted. "You find a sacred place—high up. You sit, day and night. As the fast deepens, your mind clears. You start to hear differently, see differently. Sometimes nature speaks—something comes—an animal, a storm. A sign."

His gaze drifted toward the water. "When you return, you tell the shaman what you saw. He interprets it. That's how I got my name—Standing Elk. Then there's a feast to celebrate. It marks the passage into manhood."

"Standing Elk," Megan repeated, smiling. "I like it. Can you tell me how you got it? Or... is that private?"

His eyes softened. "It's sacred." But he trusted her. "I'll tell *you*."

Megan sat up, eyes bright. She propped herself on her arms, green skirt fanned around her legs.

"You begin with a question," he said. "Something your heart needs to understand. I wanted to know my place. I'd lived with the tribe over a year, but I wasn't sure where I belonged—in the tribe... or the world."

He pulled a small leather pouch from beneath his tunic, its cord worn with use.

"My grandfather gave me this. It holds a sacred bundle—gifts for strength and protection."

She leaned in, intrigued. She hadn't noticed it before.

Luke tucked it back beneath his shirt. "He gave me this and told me to climb the highest ridge. From there, I could see the valley and the mountains beyond. I made a circle of stones, laid my buffalo hide inside, and waited. I prayed and burned sage to the four directions."

"Were you scared?" Megan whispered.

He looked out across the pond.

"Not at first," he admitted. "But when night fell, the fear crept in. Every sound—every twig snap, every rustle—felt magnified. I kept imagining a bear, or a mountain lion in the shadows." His voice dropped. "It was eerie... and lonely."

He pulled his knees close, arms wrapped tight.

"I prayed harder—for strength, for protection. Then I saw it. A star, streaking across the sky." He smiled faintly. "In that moment, I felt her—my mother. Like her spirit had come to comfort me. The fear melted away, and I finally slept."

Megan hugged her knees to her chest, mirroring his posture.

"I woke just before dawn and watched the sunrise." His voice reverent. "I'd seen many, but never like that. The sky lit with gold and scarlet. Everything felt connected, the earth and sky. For the first time, I felt one with it all."

He exhaled slowly. "But the heat rose. Hunger gnawed. My throat burned. By nightfall, I was weak, dizzy. Every sound was sharp. I heard an owl... bats swooping overhead. I swear, I could hear their wings beating the air."

He glanced at her, voice low. "Then I knew—I wasn't alone. Something was circling. I heard slow, deliberate steps over dry leaves. I thought I saw its eyes—two pale orbs reflecting moonlight. I stayed inside the circle, wrapped in my hide. Too afraid to sleep. That night felt endless."

Megan reached out and touched his arm, her voice thick. "You poor boy. That must've been terrifying."

At her touch, the tension in his shoulders eased. But he held his knees close, the memory still vivid in his eyes.

"I slept until afternoon. When I woke, an eagle circled high above, riding the wind. He stayed for hours, just gliding. I watched until my eyes blurred. And when he flew away... I felt hollow. Like I'd lost something."

His voice faltered, then steadied. "That night, I cried—not from fear, but sorrow. I thought about my life, all I'd lost." His voice lowered. "And then I felt them— my mother, my father, my grandparents. I couldn't see them, but I knew they were there. Their love wrapped around me like a blanket. I fell asleep in their presence... and dreamed of Ma, Pa...and you."

He turned to Megan with a tender smile.

"Me?" she whispered. "What was I doing?"

"You were crying. Your green eyes were full of tears."

Her breath caught. "I missed you," she murmured. "That first year without you was so hard. I prayed for you every night."

"I know," he said hoarsely. "Your prayers helped me."

He drew a breath. "By the third night, I could barely move. I lay staring at the stars until I drifted off. And that night...I had the dream."

He leaned forward slightly, voice low. "A long road stretched ahead, scattered with elk tracks. I followed them into a dark forest. Eyes watched me from the shadows—wild beasts, silent and gleaming. I was afraid... but I kept going. I had to—or I'd be lost."

His brow knit. "The path turned steep—jagged rocks, cliffs. I stumbled, but I didn't stop."

His voice softened. "Then I came to a valley—tall grass swaying in the wind, wildflowers gold and purple, and a clear spring at its center. I crawled to the water and drank. It filled me—with life, with light."

He smiled faintly. "And then I saw him. The bull elk. Tall, calm, powerful. His antlers like a crown. He looked at me... and bowed."

Luke's voice dropped to a whisper. "I bowed back."

He paused. "Then he turned and walked away, glancing back once—as if asking me to follow."

Megan leaned in. "And did you?"

"I followed," he said. "Then I woke."

She barely breathed. "What do you think it meant?"

"I wasn't sure. I thought about it all the next day. Then at dawn, I heard a sound. I looked up... and there he was. The same elk, watching from the trees."

His voice caught. "He stood so still. His eyes were calm... knowing. I cried—not from sadness, but something deeper. As if God reached into me and filled me with peace. The fear was gone. I knew then—I was on the right path. Hard, yes... but not alone."

Tears shimmered in his eyes. Megan's own eyes mirrored his. The presence of the Spirit settled between them—warm, still.

For a long moment, neither spoke. Only the hush of the wind and ripple of water filled the silence.

Then Luke's breath caught. His expression shifted.

"I just realized something," he whispered, tears spilling down his cheeks.

"What is it?" Megan asked, taking his hand gently.

His voice trembled. "I understand the dream now."

She blinked. "I thought you already did."

"I thought so too," he said softly. "But understanding takes time. Years, even. Visions are like that."

"Tell me," she whispered.

He held her gaze—those same green eyes he'd seen in dreams—and in that moment, he knew.

"I'm here," Luke said, voice raw. "Right where I'm meant to be. I followed the tracks—through pain and darkness. I didn't know if I'd survive. But the elk...he never stopped leading me."

He drew a breath, steadier now. "He's like Jesus. Just

as the elk led me through the wilderness, Christ leads us back to the Father. No matter how steep or broken the road, if we follow Him, we'll find eternal life. Like the spring in my dream—full of light and peace."

Tears slipped down his cheeks, unashamed. "That's my purpose. To follow Him."

Megan squeezed his hand, her own eyes wet. "Yes," she whispered.

Luke looked toward the pond, gold light flickering across its still surface. "The Spirit led me here," he said softly. "And ever since I came back, I've felt that same peace again." His eyes met hers. "He was leading me... to you."

He paused. "I dreamed of you again and again. Always your eyes—watching, pleading with me to come home." His tone deepened. "When my father said I must marry the chief's daughter, I was torn. He said it was my duty. But my heart knew it was wrong."

His fingers tightened around hers. "I told my grandfather everything. Even the dream I had just a month ago—you were older, like now. You wore a white buckskin dress with a beaded belt, your braids wrapped in white fur."

He smiled faintly. "In the dream, I took your hand— as if we were marrying."

Megan's breath caught, tears in her eyes. "Oh, Luke," she whispered. "That's beautiful."

"My grandfather told me, 'You must follow the path—to the girl with the green eyes.' He said if I didn't I'd be going against God's will." Luke's voice dimmed. "He tried to explain it to my father. But he wouldn't listen."

His voice roughened. "And then... my grandfather died. Just weeks later."

A shadow crossed his face, but he pressed on. "After that, my father insisted I marry her. But I couldn't. I knew the vision was true. Even if it meant leaving. Even if it meant disappointing him." His voice dropped. "I had to follow the path."

He looked down. "I pray... one day he'll understand. And forgive me."

Megan reached for his hand, eyes shining. "I'm so glad you listened to your grandfather," she whispered. "I'm speechless."

"No need to speak," he murmured.

He rose, gently pulled her to her feet, and wrapped her in his arms. Then, with quiet certainty, he kissed her.

Her heart fluttered. She slid her arms around his neck. The kiss deepened, then slowly broke, leaving them breathless.

"I love you, Megan," he murmured, brushing her cheek with reverence.

"I love you, Luke," she breathed.

He exhaled, voice hushed. "I'm so happy." His heart pounded like the tribal drum.

"Me too," she whispered, her cheeks warm, her stomach swirling with sweet delight.

He lifted her hand and kissed it, his eyes never leaving hers. "Let's go home."

***

As the cottage came into view, Megan's voice broke the silence.

"Luke?" she asked softly.

He turned. "Hmm?"

Her eyes lingered on the glow of the cottage windows. "Let's not say anything about this... not yet. I'm not sure Ma and Pa will understand. You've only just come back. Let's give it some time," she added with a faint smile.

"I agree."

55

# *Chapter 5*

# *Boarding School*

The days passed quickly—Megan busy in town, the rest with ranch chores. At last, Sunday arrived, a welcome day of rest. Luke was joining them for church, though nerves stirred his stomach.

Dressed in one of Pa's old suits, he stood by the wagon, tugging at the stiff collar. His hair, usually loose, was tied neatly at his nape.

"Do I look alright?" he asked as Megan stepped outside.

Her gaze swept over him. "You look very handsome."

"And *you* look beautiful."

Color rose in her cheeks. Her dark blue dress, trimmed with lace, hugged her bodice and flared with a bustle. A felt hat with curled feathers perched atop her pinned-up hair, loose curls softening her face.

"Thank you," she murmured, glancing away as her brothers spilled out the door.

Luke helped her into the wagon. She sat on a crate with a folded blanket, and he took the seat across from her, as the rest of the family climbed in.

As the wagon rumbled toward town, Luke squirmed in the borrowed clothes. The collar chafed, the boots pinched.

Megan caught his discomfort and gave a small, reassuring smile.

"You'll get used to them," David teased.

"I still haven't," Johnathan grumbled, tugging at his collar.

Luke chuckled, though his nerves lingered.

Town soon rose into view, startlingly changed. What was once a quiet settlement now bustled with life. Grand homes and tall buildings lined the streets. Luke struggled to keep pace as Megan and the boys pointed out landmarks.

"That's the telephone company," Megan said. "I work on the third floor."

David gestured to a stone building. "That's the Opera House. Megan saw a world-famous play there."

Luke's chest tightened. He looked at Megan, remembering Andrew. Her smile dimmed, and he quickly gestured to another building.

"What's that one?"

"The train station," Kurt said. "It's new."

The old depot was gone, replaced by a towering red sandstone structure.

Luke stared at the wires stretched above.

"Telephone and electricity lines," Megan explained. "The electric lights make the streets safer at night."

*Not safe enough,* Luke thought grimly, remembering Andrew's death.

The wagon slowed as the church came into view—a bright white clapboard building with stained-glass windows and a bell tower that chimed across the morning air. Dozens of wagons lined the street.

Pa climbed down first and helped Ma. Luke's hands were damp. His chest tightened.

*What am I doing here?*

Megan stepped beside him, her voice low. "You'll be fine."

He wasn't so sure. Eyes followed him—curious, guarded. Some scowled, others turned away. His smile faded. *No matter what I wear, they still see me as different.*

Megan noticed, her voice wry. "Don't let them get to you. They don't like anyone—not even themselves."

Luke's lips twitched into a faint smile.

She slipped her hand into the crook of his arm as they walked toward the church. The boys ran ahead, Ma and Pa close behind.

At the entrance, they paused to greet the pastor.

"Reverend Gather, you remember our son, Luke?" Ed asked as they stepped onto the wooden landing.

The pastor's face brightened. "Luke! We're glad to have you home. Your family's missed you."

Luke shook his hand, noting the same kind smile beneath the pastor's thinning hair. "Thank you, Reverend. It's good to be back." He added, voice lower, "Though I'm not sure everyone feels that way."

The pastor chuckled. "Some folks have never seen an Indian. The rest? Just busybodies. They'll move on soon enough."

Luke offered a faint smile.

Inside, they settled into a center pew—Ma and Pa on one end, the boys on the other. Megan sat beside Luke, and when no one watched, slipped her hand into his. Her touch calmed the tightness in his chest.

Reverend Gather's soothing voice rose, familiar scripture washing over Luke. The hymns stirred memories—of childhood prayers, of Sundays long faded. He'd prayed with his tribe, but this was different. This was a forgotten thread to his past.

After the final hymn, they stepped into sunlight where friends and neighbors lingered, exchanging greetings.

Mr. and Mrs. Holden's faces lit up at the sight of Luke.

Mr. Holden clapped his shoulder. "Good to see the family all back together."

"It's good to be back," Luke murmured, the sincerity in their welcome settling softly in his chest.

Despite the glances, it was faces like theirs—familiar and kind—that made him feel like he belonged.

They rode several miles to a neighbor's homestead. Wagons ringed the clearing, while tables were set up.

Megan and Cassie joined the women, setting out food. The men gathered near the wagons or arranged benches. The scent of grilled meat and warm bread drifted on the breeze, mixing with children's laughter ringing through the air.

When all was ready, Reverend Gather called for quiet and offered a prayer.

After the "amen", townsfolk lined up eagerly. Luke and his family waited until the line thinned, then quietly filled their plates.

Families spread across the yard, voices bright with chatter. Bart's kin waved from a nearby table. Children hurried through their meals, then raced off into the tall grass, laughter trailing behind like ribbons in the wind.

Luke ate quickly, not from hunger but from unease. Curious glances pricked at him, pulling his thoughts from the table conversation.

When Megan finished eating, he leaned in. "Want to

go for a walk?"

Her eyes brightened. "Sure. Let's tell Ma."

She carried her plate to the washbasin while Luke talked to Ma.

"Ma said to be back in about an hour," he told her with a smile.

Megan slipped her hand through his arm. "Where to?"

"Remember the woodlot out back? Crow Creek still runs through it. Might be quiet there," he suggested.

They followed a narrow path into the woods, the air thick with sun-warmed pine and summer grass. Megan lifted her skirts to avoid snagging the lace trim. The deep blue fabric shimmered as she stepped lightly through the brush.

Luke kept close, steadying her over rough patches. Though he'd shed his jacket, his vest clung, and the tie felt like a noose. Every step his boots pinched.

As the trees deepened, his voice softened. "Tell me about college. What's it like?"

Megan's eyes lit up. "It's in Laramie—you probably passed it coming home. The university is huge, like a castle. Stone walls, tall windows and a tower. My room's on the third floor."

He smiled, watching her come alive. "Sounds exciting."

"It was, at first. But now…" She gave a soft laugh. "Mostly it's just hard work. The newness wore off."

He grinned. "But you're smart—it can't be that tough."

She shook her head. "I'm not. I work hard."

They walked deeper, the air cooling beneath the leafy

canopy.

"You'll do great," he said. "How much longer?"

"Just one more year. Two semesters."

His heart sank. "That long? When's the next one start?"

"First week of September. I'll be gone until mid-December."

"Oh." His smile faded. Her words settled heavy between them.

Sensing his disappointment, Megan gave his arm a squeeze. "But I'll be home for Thanksgiving. A whole week."

"I'll miss you terribly," he said, chest aching.

She met his gaze, heart twisting. "I'll miss you too." Her voice trembled. She looked away, fingers pressing lightly on his sleeve. "I wish I didn't have to go. But I've already paid, and if I want to teach, I have to finish."

"I know." His voice held both ache and admiration. "And you should. You're following your dream."

The trail opened to a clearing where Crow Creek slipped between banks of green, the air cool and fragrant with moss and moving water. The stream gurgled softly over stones and fallen limbs.

Luke found a fallen tree near the edge and brushed off a spot. "Here," he said.

Megan sank onto it, smoothing her skirts, the quiet returning between them.

"And after college...what then?" he asked, settling beside her.

"I want to teach on the reservation. The one where you were—if they'll have me."

"I'm sure they will," Luke said. "Not many want to

teach there." He hesitated. "But are you sure that's what you want? It won't be easy." He knew the ache of not belonging. And he was Shoshone. For her, it would be harder still.

Megan frowned. "Now you sound like Ma. She doesn't think I can do it either."

"I didn't say that." He turned to her. "I know you can. You're strong. I just don't think you realize how hard it'll be. They'll question your motives."

"My motives?" she asked, bristling.

"They won't trust easily. Especially not white men." His eyes skimmed over her Sunday dress—the graceful slope of her shoulders, the curve of her waist beneath the fitted bodice. "And Megan...even though you're half-Indian, you look every bit a white woman."

Her defensiveness eased as she caught the drift of his meaning—and the glint in his eye. Heat rose in her cheeks. She smoothed the silky blue fabric of her skirt with a teasing smile.

"Well, it's Sunday," she said. "I don't plan to dress like this once I'm there."

He leaned back, arms folded, playful now. "No? What *will* you wear?"

She smiled. "My everyday dresses. Why? What would you have me wear?"

Luke smirked, pretending to ponder. "Hmm...a flour sack?"

She laughed. "You're awful."

He grinned. "You'd still be beautiful, even in that."

The teasing melted into something quieter. Megan glanced down, brushing a finger over the lace at her cuff. Her voice softened.

"So tell me," she asked. "What would I struggle with? Besides the language—you could teach me that before I go."

Luke's smile faded. He watched the stream, sunlight flickering across the ripples.

"They don't usually accept outsiders. Unless you're Shoshone—or at least part Indian." His voice was low. "Maybe they'll make an exception. You're half, after all. But it depends...on how you prove yourself."

He looked at her again, his gaze tender. "But I know you. You'll win them over." A wistful smile tugged at his lips. "I would've liked school better if *you* were my teacher."

His gaze drifted back to the water. "But I hated school where I went."

Megan studied him, hearing the shift in his voice. She'd heard whispers—Indian boarding schools, strict rules, and worse.

Her voice dropped. "Where did you go?"

His jaw tensed. For a long moment, he said nothing. Then his fingers moved to his collar, loosening the tie, unfastening the top button like the memory made it hard to breathe.

"They came in the spring of 1881," he said at last. "I had just turned fourteen."

He paused. "They rounded up all the kids—Shoshone and Arapaho—six to sixteen. Said we were going away to school."

He glanced at her, gauging whether she truly wanted to hear it. She held his gaze, her eyes full of compassion.

"The chiefs hesitated," he continued. "But they agreed. Said learning the white man's ways might help us *survive*." The bitterness in that word clung to the air.

"In good faith, Sharp Nose—chief of the Arapaho—sent his own son. Little Chief was my age." Luke's voice grew distant. "There was talk our families might get to visit...eventually."

He exhaled. "Before we left, our parents gave us gifts—for luck, to keep us from feeling homesick." His voice thinned. "We tried to be brave."

He worked the tie free, unfastened another button. Megan listened, heart heavy.

"They took us to the train station," he said, eyes distant. "Loaded us into a freight car. Like cattle."

Luke was seeing it all again.

"I wasn't scared—I'd seen trains. But the little ones…" His voice broke. "They clung to each other, crying for their parents."

He swallowed. "I told them not to be afraid. Us older kids...we did what we could."

He glanced at his hands, as if remembering the tiny fingers that had clung to his.

"We rode for four days. Hot, cramped, barely any food or water. One bucket for a bathroom. The farther we got from home, the more afraid I felt. I'd just begun to belong with my tribe. Then...I felt lost again."

Slowly, he unfastened his cuffs and rolled up his sleeves, as if the memory was heavy to carry.

Megan's chest ached. "Oh, Luke. Where were they taking you?"

"East. We stopped in Pennsylvania at the Carlisle Indian Industrial School."

Her breath caught. "That's across the whole country."

"When we arrived, they took everything—gifts from our parents, even my medicine bag. They burned them." His jaw tightened. "Stripped our clothes. Gave us stiff uniforms and made us choose Christian names off a chalkboard."

He looked away. "I told them I was already Luke. The others couldn't read. Just pointed."

Megan pressed a hand to her mouth, appalled.

"And then...they cut our hair."

"No!" she gasped, horrified. She knew what that meant to his people. Their identity, strength, heritage.

"Many cried," he said. "I'd had short hair before. But it still felt awful...like losing another piece of who we were."

"I'm so sorry." Her eyes blurred with tears.

"They forbade our language. Beat us for speaking Shoshone." His fists clenched. "Worse things happened, worse than anything when we were little. I can't tell you what happened to some of the girls."

She clutched his arm. "Luke...I wish you'd never gone." Tears spilled.

He met her gaze, sorrowful—but resolute.

"I'm glad I did." His voice was quiet. "I could help. I knew English. I translated. I tried to protect them."

He faltered. "I made friends. Little Chief, and two Arapaho boys."

He turned away. "They all died the second year."

Megan's breath caught.

Luke blinked hard, but the tears rose anyway.

"They buried them by the school," he said hoarsely. "I passed their graves every day." He wiped his cheek, but the tears kept coming. "I got sick too. Thought I'd die. All I wanted was to be home. But I was alone."

Megan wept silently. She remembered those years—missing him, never knowing the depth of his pain.

"I dreamed of you," he said softly. "That's what kept me going."

Her sob escaped.

"I got better. Graduated that year. Never had to go back." His voice darkened. "But we had changed. We spoke more English than Shoshone. The little ones forgot their language."

He swallowed hard. "The ones who remembered... whispered it. In fear."

Megan gripped his hand, her tears glistening.

"They made us all convert to Christianity," Luke said quietly. "I'd already accepted Jesus as my Savior, but for others... it was foreign. We were losing our old ways. And when I came home, I didn't know where I fit anymore."

Megan's voice wavered. "Oh, Luke…your people have endured so much." She shook her head. "No wonder there's such deep mistrust." Her eyes burned with resolve. "I want to teach on the reservation. I won't stand by while another child is taken."

Pain flickered in her gaze. This wasn't just history—it was injustice, and it stirred something fierce within her.

Luke's expression softened. He squeezed her hand. "That's good of you, Megan. I think they'll come to trust you. Your heart is pure."

"I want to help—like you did. Give them opportunities without stripping away their heritage."

He lifted her hand, brushing a kiss across her knuckles. A shiver traveled up her arm.

"The world needs more people like you, Megan."

Her smile was full of feeling. "I think it needs more like *you*. I hate what you suffered…but I'm grateful you were there to protect others."

Megan rose, wiping her eyes with the back of her hand. "We should go help clean up."

Luke stood beside her. "Yes. It's time."

She stepped forward—but her boot caught on a rock. With a soft cry, she twisted her ankle and stumbled.

Luke caught her before she hit the ground, his hands strong around her waist.

"You alright?" he asked, eyes searching hers.

She grimaced, testing her foot. Pain shot through her. "My ankle—I can't put weight on it."

When she tried again, she cried out, clinging to his arm.

Without hesitation, he swept her into his arms.

"I'll carry you."

Flushed and flustered, she looped her arms around his neck. "I feel ridiculous."

"Don't," he said gently. "It happens."

He carried her with ease, boots soft against the path. She glanced up at him—jaw firm, eyes warm with concern. Despite her effort to stay composed, he saw the tremble in her lips.

"Thank you, Luke," she whispered.

He smiled down. "Just looking after my girl."

Her breath caught, heart fluttering. So close, she could smell the sun and soap on his skin, the faint trace of pine.

"Thanks for catching me," she murmured. "I would've ruined my Sunday dress."

He chuckled. "One accident at a time."

She laughed through the pain. "I'll try to behave."

As they stepped from the trees into the yard, sunlight poured over them. Heads turned.

Kurt spotted them first and ran over. "What happened?"

"I was clumsy," Megan admitted, cheeks pink. "Twisted my ankle."

More eyes turned her way. She cringed.

Luke stayed steady. "Kurt, let Ma and Pa know I'm taking Megan home. She needs rest and ice. I'll come back for the rest of you."

"Got it!" Kurt darted off.

Cassie arrived at the wagon, face tight with worry.

"Megan! What happened?" she cried, reaching for her.

"Just a twisted ankle," Megan said, wincing. "I stepped on a rock. It'll be fine—it just hurts."

She lifted her skirt; Cassie gently touched the ankle. Megan flinched.

"It's not broken," Cassie said with relief. "But you need to lie down and elevate it. Let's get you home."

"No need. Stay," Luke said gently. "I'll take her. I'll get her settled and come back to help clean up."

Cassie hesitated. "Are you sure? I feel like I should—"

"Ma," Megan said softly, squeezing her hand. "Luke knows what to do."

Cassie relented with a nod. "Drive slow."

"I will," Luke promised, adding with a nod, "And I'll make her some willow bark tea."

Cassie smiled faintly and stepped back as they rolled away.

The drive was rougher than Megan remembered. Each jolt sent a stab through her ankle, the pain climbing her calf. By the time they reached the cottage, she was pale and shaking.

Luke climbed into the back, brow furrowed. "Megan, breathe."

She exhaled slowly. "Good idea," she whispered with a weak smile.

Luke lifted her into his arms and carried her to the bedroom. He laid her gently on the bed, then rolled a quilt beneath her calf.

"There," he said. "I'll get some ice."

"Thank you," she murmured, removing her hat and sinking into the pillows.

He returned moments later with ice in a towel. Kneeling at her bedside, he began to unlace her boot. He glanced up. "Sorry if this hurts."

Her eyes squeezed shut, lips tight. When the boot slid free, a gasp escaped her.

"It's alright," she said through clenched teeth. "It has to come off."

She helped roll down her stocking, cheeks flushed as his fingers brushed her calf—warm and tender.

His jaw tightened at the swelling—angry and bruised. He palpated the ankle gently.

"Not broken," he said, relief in his voice.

She sucked in a breath as he pressed the ice to it.

"This'll help," he said, heart aching.

"Thank you, Luke."

She let her head fall back, sighing as the cold dulled the pain.

"I'll make willow bark tea. Just rest."

From the kitchen came the clink of iron, the creak of the pump. Megan pictured him—sleeves rolled, brushing his hair from his brow—and felt a flutter deep in her chest.

He returned with a china cup painted in rosebuds. Sitting beside her, he slipped an arm behind her and eased her up.

"Here."

She sipped the bitter brew and winced. "Thank you."

As he reached to set aside the cup, a letter caught his eye—its words unguarded:

> *My dearest Megan...I've been thinking about you...I can't wait to see you...Yours always, Clint.*

His fingers tightened. A weight settling in his chest.

Megan followed his gaze and stiffened. She folded the letter quickly. "I haven't written him back," she said, voice unsteady.

Luke set the cup down with care, face unreadable. "It's none of my business," he said softly, turning away.

She reached out, touching his arm. "It's not what you think."

Luke kept his gaze on the far wall. "I know you had a life before me. I don't blame you for having...*friends*." His voice sounded distant.

Her cheeks burned. She lowered her eyes, blinking back tears. The irony stung—he was finally here, sitting where she'd dreamed of him so many nights. Yet now, he felt miles away.

"Luke," she whispered, "look at me."

After a moment, he turned, dark eyes meeting hers. The shimmer of unshed tears stilled him. She blinked, and they slipped into her hair.

"I'm sorry," he said hoarsely. "I didn't mean to—" He stopped, gut clenching against the knot of jealousy.

"I do have a beau," she softly admitted, fingers knotting in the quilt. "But he's not who I want now."

She glanced away, cheeks flushed. "My feelings for him were never like this." Her voice trembled. "He's a good man. A good friend. But that's all."

Luke's chest tightened. His hands curled into fists. *Clint doesn't see it that way,* he thought grimly. Even those few lines had said enough.

"I don't think he believes he's just a friend," he said softly. "He loves you."

Her eyes flashed. "You don't know that!" The words were sharp, but her protest faded, replaced by guilt. She remembered the day Clint confessed—how she hadn't known what to say.

"It was written all over the page," Luke said quietly.

Her stomach dropped. *He read it.* Regret tightened her throat. She reached for him, fingers brushing his sleeve.

"But I don't love *him*," she whispered. "I love *you*, Luke."

The words struck like lightning. His breath caught as he stared at her—at the truth in her trembling voice, the tears in her eyes.

"Isn't that all that matters?" she asked, a fragile smile breaking through her exhaustion.

His heart swelled. "Yes," he breathed. "That's all that matters to me."

He braced his hands on either side of her and lowered his face to hers. His lips brushed hers—soft, reverent—until she responded, deepening the kiss with quiet yearning.

When he pulled back, he lingered, eyes tracing her flushed cheeks, her slightly parted lips.

"I love you, Megan," he murmured, voice thick with devotion.

Her gaze turned dreamy, sleep tugging at her lashes. Still, she smiled.

"You'd better take the wagon back," she whispered drowsily. "I'm not going anywhere. I'll be right here."

Her eyes drifted shut, her breathing slowing as the tea eased her into rest.

Luke watched her a moment longer, her lashes glistened with the last of her tears. He bent to kiss her temple, letting it linger, then gave her hand a final squeeze and slipped away.

Outside, he broke into a run. His boots barely touched the earth. At the wagon, he leapt onto the seat, hands trembling as he gathered the reins. With a flick, he urged the team forward.

The wheels rattled across the ground—but Luke hardly felt it. His heart had stayed behind, soaring with her.

# Chapter 6

## Fourth of July

Megan's ankle took weeks to heal. The injury kept her home and away from work, but she didn't mind the slower pace. In truth, she cherished the stillness—especially the time with Luke.

No one doted on her like he did. He took her on carriage rides and carried her outside each evening to sit by the stream. When he was away with chores, she filled the hours studying and eventually, with some effort, found the courage to write to Clint.

*Dear Clint,*

*I'm sorry it's taken so long to respond. Aside from a sprained ankle, summer has been lovely.*

*I have wonderful news—my Indian brother, Luke, has come home! After twelve years, we never thought we'd see him again. Now that he's back, it feels like a part of me has returned too.*

*Luke and I were always close. Since his return, we've grown even closer. I'll explain more when we're back at school.*

*I'm sorry but now isn't a good time for visitors. I hope you understand. Things have changed.*

*Your friend,*

*Megan*

The words felt careful—too careful. She wasn't ready to tell Clint the truth about her and Luke. What they shared was still unfolding, too tender to speak aloud.

He would understand in time. At least, she hoped he would.

A week later, Clint's reply arrived. Megan slipped the letter into her pocket before anyone could ask. Alone in her room, she opened it with a trembling hand.

> *My dearest Megan,*
>
> *I was astonished to hear your Indian brother has returned. What a miracle it must be—I'm so happy for your family.*
>
> *I'm sorry to hear about your injury. I miss you more than I can say. I know you said this isn't a good time to visit, but when is it ever? I may not be able to stay away much longer.*
>
> *You wrote, "things have changed." For me, they haven't—except my feelings for you have only deepened. I hope I'm not too forward, but I believe I'm in love with you.*
>
> *Yours always,*
>
> *Clint*

Megan's breath caught. Her hands shook. Luke had been right.

She hadn't wanted to see it—but Clint had imagined something more between them. Her throat tightened with regret. In trying to forget Andrew, she'd leaned on Clint too much, blurred the lines of friendship and affection.

She folded the letter and tucked it into her drawer, but guilt clung to her.

A few days later, with the house quiet and the breeze drifting through open windows, she sat at her dressing table and took up her pen again.

> *Dear Clint,*
>
> *Thank you for your kind wishes. I'm healing well and hope to return to work soon.*
>
> *When I read that you believe you're in love with me, I was deeply touched. But I must be honest—I don't share your feelings.*
>
> *You are dear to me, but my heart belongs to someone else. I thought I was ready for a beau when I left school, but I see now I was still grieving.*
>
> *I hope we can remain friends, but I cannot let you court me any longer. Please don't write again. I promise I'll explain everything when we meet.*
>
> *I'm truly sorry.*
>
> *Sincerely,*
>
> *Megan*

She sealed the envelope with a heavy heart. It felt cruel, but kinder than giving him false hope. He deserved someone who loved him completely.

***

One evening, during one of their wagon rides, Luke finally asked, "So...how's Clint?"

Megan stiffened. Of course he knew—he'd seen the letters. She looked away, heat rising to her cheeks.

"I assume he's heartbroken," she said softly. "You were right. He thinks he's in love with me."

She hesitated. "I wrote to him, told him I didn't feel the same." Her gaze flicked to his. "I told him I was in love with someone else."

Their eyes met. She blushed.

Luke's heart lifted. He reached for her hand and held it gently.

"I'm sure he's hurt," she murmured. "But I couldn't keep leading him on."

"You did the right thing," he said. "It's better he knows. Now he can begin to let go."

She nodded, relief mingling with sadness. Luke squeezed her hand again, holding onto the love blooming between them.

***

About a week later, Megan was back on her feet, slowly easing into her chores. Though she still wrapped her ankle for support and rested it when swollen, she no longer felt like an invalid—and that alone was a gift.

Eager to reclaim her independence, she asked her father to ride into town and let her employers know she'd return to work the following week. It wouldn't be easy—long hours on her feet would test her—but she was determined to be ready.

***

The following week brought the long-awaited Fourth of July.

One morning after breakfast, Megan and her mother stood in the warm kitchen, rolling dough and filling pie tins. The scent of cinnamon and sugar drifted through the open windows. A breeze stirred the lace curtains, making them flutter like white sails.

"I can't wait for tomorrow," Megan said, slicing apples into wedges. "The fireworks will be amazing. I don't think Luke's ever seen them. He'll be so surprised."

Cassie smiled, pressing a crust into a tin. "I'm sure he'll love them. Who wouldn't?"

Megan scraped the apples into bubbling syrup, stirring slowly. "Where are we watching from this year?"

Cassie glanced out the window. "We could sit along the road by our lane, like the year we skipped town. No crowds. Same view."

Megan's face lit up. "Perfect." She paused. "Can we have our picnic here instead of going to the church one? Just the family—the grandparents and cousins? It'd feel cozier."

Cassie's eyes twinkled. "Like another family reunion." She brushed flour from her hands. "The church will survive without our pies. We should ask your father what he thinks."

Just then, the back door creaked open. Ed stepped inside, followed by the boys—hot, dusty, and streaked with sweat. They crowded around the sink, splashing cool water on their hands and faces.

Cassie caught Megan's eye and gave a quick wink. *Now's our chance.*

She handed Ed a towel as he wiped his face, inhaling the spiced air.

"The pies smell amazing," he said.

"Peach, apple, and raspberry," Cassie replied lightly, exchanging a glance with Megan.

She turned to him, tone hopeful. "Ed, what if we celebrate *here*? Just us. We could picnic, visit, then watch the fireworks from the road."

Ed raised an eyebrow, amused. "Sounds like someone's already decided." He turned to the boys. "What do you think?"

"Yes!" Luke said quickly, a quiet rush of relief in his voice. The thought of crowds still made his stomach twist. A celebration at home sounded perfect.

"Yay! Another family reunion!" the younger boys shouted, already picturing the food and games.

Ed laughed. "Alright then. I'll ride over to the grandparents' and check with Beth and Bart after supper."

Cassie wrapped her arms around him, head resting on his chest. "Thank you, darling."

Even as she held him close, her mind had already moved to the details—tables to set, dishes to make, decorations to hang.

It was going to be a perfect day.

*** 

The next afternoon, the family and the Clarks arrived early to help set up. Cassie, Ed, and the children had begun chores at dawn, then arranged makeshift tables and chairs beneath the wide shade trees. A brilliant blue sky stretched above, clouds drifting lazily by.

As the hour neared, they washed up and dressed. Luke pulled on trousers and a crisp linen shirt he'd bought for trips to town. The collar felt stiff after months in buckskin, and he tugged at it, already missing the comfort of his old clothes.

In her room, Megan slipped into a soft green dress that deepened the color of her eyes. She tied back her hair with a matching ribbon and gave herself quiet approval before heading out.

By the time guests began arriving, Ed and David had a fire going for roasting chicken. Tables were covered in clean cloths, dishes stacked neatly, and soon filled with roasted meat, fresh bread, pickled vegetables, and fruit pies.

Laughter rang through the yard. Adults chatted as they worked, the clatter of dishes and bursts of conversation blending with the shrieks of barefoot children racing through the grass.

Luke leaned against the porch railing, soaking it all in—the warmth of family, the hum of belonging.

"Luke, how are you settling in?"

He turned to find Grandma Hartford slipping her arm through his, eyes crinkling with warmth.

"More every day," he said with a cheery smile.

She patted his hand. "I knew you would. We all love you and hope you feel at home."

Her words settled in his heart. "Thank you, Grandma. I do."

She glanced at his shirt. "I see you're in 'white man's clothes,'" she said, teasing gently. "You'll always be Luke to us—buckskin *or* cotton."

Her insight startled him. She reminded him of his Indian grandfather—wise, intuitive, seeing straight through him.

"I guess I *am* trying to fit in a little," he admitted. "I still love my buckskin, but... now and then, I want to wear my 'white man's clothes.'" He echoed her words with a wink.

She patted his hand. "Just so long as it's your choice."

He placed his hand over hers. "It *is* my choice. And I'm grateful you see me for who I am."

Grandpa O'Malley appeared with a grin and clapped Luke on the shoulder.

"Luke, lad, how about fishing tomorrow?" he asked in his Scottish brogue.

Luke grinned. "I'd love to, Grandpa."

"I'll come by at seven." Grandpa's voice lowered in mock secrecy. "Just you and me—my secret spot."

"Sounds perfect."

With a wink at Grandma Hartford, he headed toward the tables. "Better see if Kathy needs anything."

Grandma O'Malley looked up as he approached. Their eyes met, and a smile passed between them. He slid an arm around her waist, murmured something only she could hear, and kissed her cheek—quick and tender.

Luke caught the gesture. A quiet warmth spread through him.

He admired their ease with each other—the kind of love that didn't have to be spoken to be felt. In their bond, he saw the life he hoped for. Among his people, a husband was a protector and provider, honoring his wife as the heart of the home. He'd always known he would be that man. And in his heart, he hoped someday, that woman would be Megan.

His gaze drifted to the fire pit, where Grandpa Hartford stood shoulder to shoulder with his father and uncles. Luke had always respected his elders—but tonight, their quiet strength ran deeper, anchoring him to both the past and the life he was anxious to embrace.

"A penny for your thoughts?" Grandma Hartford's voice pulled Luke back.

He turned with a smile. "Just thinking how lucky I am to have you and Grandpa. You've both been such a good example—especially in how you treat each other."

Her eyes softened. "When you've lived as long as I have, you learn what matters. The most important thing in this world is your marriage."

"I can see that," he said, watching Grandpa Hartford laugh with the men by the fire, then sent her a wave. "You're happy—it shows."

She smiled and waved back. "Put the Lord first, then your spouse—that's the key. Marriage isn't always easy, but if you stick together it gets better and better." Her smile faded slightly. "We couldn't have children. For years, that sorrow weighed heavy between us. But we leaned on each other. Then Cassie came—a blessing we never expected. And now, we have you."

She squeezed his hand, voice firm. "When you face life as a team, you can endure anything."

"Thank you, Grandma. I'll remember that." He smiled warmly. "I always thought I'd marry someone like you," he added with a wink.

Her face lit. "Oh—you make an old woman feel young." She patted his hand. "Whoever you marry will be a lucky girl."

His eyes drifted toward Megan as she stepped onto the porch, a basket of steaming biscuits in her arms.

"Nah," he said with a quiet smile. "*I'll* be the lucky one."

Grandma followed his gaze, her smile blooming with quiet understanding. "You'll *both* be lucky."

***

After supper, the family lingered in relaxed clusters—some by the fire, others on the porch. As dusk settled, firelight danced against the trees, casting playful shadows.

Luke and Megan rocked slowly on the porch swing, a sleepy child nestled between them. When she darted off to join a game of tag, their hands found each other again.

Around the fire, the grandparents swapped stories, their grandchildren at their feet—wide-eyed, giggling at tales both funny and wild. The swing creaked in time with crickets, birds calling goodnight, and the soft crackle of flames.

A warm glow spilled from the house window, softening the porch in amber light. Beyond, laughter and quiet conversation drifted through the dark.

"I can't wait for you to see the fireworks," Megan said, her eyes alight. "There's nothing like it."

Luke smiled, her joy contagious. He gave her hand a light squeeze. "As long as I'm with you, I know I'll love them."

For a moment, the world felt suspended—Megan's hand in his, a cool breeze, the hush of night. It was as if time paused just for them.

Ed's voice cut through the hum. "Time to go! Everyone in the rigs!"

Cheers erupted. Children were called and gathered, excitement rising as they loaded up. Luke helped Ma into her seat, then turned to offer Megan his hand as she climbed into the back with the boys.

Uncle Clancy's wagon led the way, a lantern swaying from its hook, casting golden light along the dark lane.

The trees gave way to open prairie, a sea of grass shimmering beneath the stars. On the horizon, a faint glow of city lights flickered.

In a wide clearing, the wagons stopped. Men set the brakes, secured the horses. Families waited, hushed, as the sky arched wide and moonless above them—an endless canvas pricked with stars.

Megan shivered slightly as a cool breeze skimmed her bare forearms.

"Cold?" Luke asked, noting the tremor.

She shook her head. "Just cooling off. It feels good."

Across from her, he gestured to the blanket on his crate. "Let me know if you need it."

Her heart warmed. "Thank you. I will."

Nearby, Ed and Cassie joined Bart and Bea, soaking up every last moment of the festivities. Children darted through the grass, laughter rising into the starlit sky.

Luke and Megan smiled at the chaos.

Suddenly, a thunderous boom shook the earth. Overhead, red sparkles bloomed into an enormous sphere, trailing streams of light before vanishing into darkness.

Horses jolted in their harnesses, but the men calmed them with low murmurs and firm reins.

Megan laughed, startled as she nearly slipped from her crate. Luke motioned for her to join him, and she happily complied. Protectively, he braced an arm behind her, hand gripping the sidewall, just in case.

Another burst—white, then blue, then gold. Each explosion rolled like thunder, the sky pulsing with brilliant color. Each flash reflected in Luke's wide, awestruck eyes.

It reminded him of summer storms, though the sky stayed clear. A trace of sulfur drifted on the breeze.

Megan's hand found his. He turned his palm up, threading their fingers together. Her touch deepened the rush surging through him, sending his heart into rapid staccato.

She leaned in, watching his wonder with quiet joy.

"It's beautiful," he whispered, eyes fixed on the sky.

When the final spark faded, stillness blanketed the field. For a moment, no one moved, unwilling to break the magic spell. Then murmurs stirred, children's laughter resumed, and families began to gather, bidding farewell.

One by one, the wagons rolled away, lanterns bobbing into the night like fireflies.

Luke sat quietly as they rolled down the dark road. Megan's hand in his, the echo of children's laughter and fireworks floated over the prairie, fading into the night. It was a memory he would carry with him always.

# Chapter 7

## *Surprise Visitor*

"All ready to go?" Grandpa O'Malley called as Luke stepped off the porch.

"You bet. Just need a pole."

"No need—I brought two," Grandpa said, holding up a pair of bamboo rods. "Just saddle up."

At Luke's whistle, Wildfire trotted to the gate, ears perked. Grinning, Luke opened it, and the spirited horse bounded out, eager for the trail.

"Amazing how you trained him like that," Grandpa chuckled.

"Didn't take long. My father showed me how," Luke said, swinging onto Wildfire's back with ease.

From the kitchen window, Megan watched them disappear down the lane. She could have asked to join—they would've welcomed her—but sensed Luke needed this time alone with Grandpa. Instead, she joined Cassie in the garden. They spent the morning weeding and picking vegetables.

Needing another basket, Megan slipped off her gloves and stepped inside the house. As she reached for it, movement through the screen door caught her eye.

A black horse pulled a small buggy down the lane, bouncing over the uneven path. As it drew closer her breath caught.

"Clint!"

Without thinking, she rushed out.

"Clint! What are you doing here?"

"Megan!" He stepped down and hugged her. "So good to see you." He pulled back, taking her in. "You look wonderful. Being home suits you."

Flushing, Megan brushed a stray hair from her brow, suddenly aware of her rumpled dress and dirt-streaked hands.

"Thank you," she said.

"I know you said not to come," Clint said, gently touching her arm, "but I had to talk to you."

Her heart skipped. "Come meet my ma," she said softly. "She's in the garden."

Clint offered his arm, and Megan slipped her hand into the crook of his elbow.

Cassie straightened at their approach, her gaze fixed on the stranger beside Megan.

"And who do we have here?"

"Ma, this is Clint," Megan said, glancing up at him. "He's my friend from college."

Clint removed his hat, revealing blond hair and bright blue eyes. He extended his hand with a dashing smile.

"Ma'am, it's a pleasure to finally meet you. Megan speaks highly of you."

Cassie wiped her hand on her apron before shaking his. "The pleasure's mine. I've heard some lovely things about you, too."

She gave Megan a quick look.

"Let's go in and have some lemonade," Cassie offered. "We can get acquainted properly."

"That sounds wonderful, Mrs. Havoc," Clint said, picking up the basket of peas and following her inside.

Megan's pulse quickened. It felt surreal—her two worlds colliding, college and home, leaving her feeling off balance.

In the kitchen, Cassie poured lemonade while Megan set out glasses, her hands trembling. She stole a glance at Clint, who smiled as if this were the most natural thing in the world.

They sipped the lemonade and nibbled on leftover cookies from the Fourth of July. Conversation flowed easily—Clint spoke of his family and work; Cassie shared stories from ranch life.

"This is delicious, Mrs. Havoc," Clint said, setting down his glass. "If it's alright, I'd love to take Megan for a buggy ride before I head back. My train leaves in a few hours, and I'd like a little time to talk."

Cassie met his gaze, then turned to Megan and smiled. "I don't see why not. You two enjoy yourselves."

"Thanks, Ma." Megan's heart pounded as she braced for the conversation ahead.

Outside, he helped her into the buggy and climbed in beside her. She glanced down at her plain everyday dress, suddenly self-conscious next to his crisp dark suit.

With a gentle flick of the reins, Clint steered them down the lane.

"This place is beautiful," he said, taking in the trees and the cottage nestled among them.

"Thank you," Megan murmured, keeping a subtle distance between them. Clint's kindness only deepened the ache—knowing soon she'd disappoint him.

"So, where to?"

She hesitated. The last thing she wanted was to be seen in town in work clothes—or worse, be seen with

Clint when her heart already belonged to another.

"Clearwater Pond," she offered. "To the right, just a few miles ahead."

"Sounds perfect."

The buggy clattered along the road, past the railroad tracks and into the woods. When the trail narrowed, Megan touched his arm.

"We'll walk from here."

Clint stopped the rig. When he helped her down, his grip lingered too long, and her breath hitched. Thankfully, the path forced them into single file.

The meadow opened before them, the pond shimmered, still and glassy beneath the late-morning sun. Wildflowers nodded in the breeze, and reeds rustled at the edge.

"Wow," Clint breathed. "It's stunning."

She smiled faintly as he led her beneath an old tree.

"I just wanted a place where we wouldn't be disturbed," she said, settling into the grass.

Clint sat beside her.

"Megan," he began, "I came because of what I wrote. I shouldn't have said it in a letter. When you tell someone you love them... it should be face to face." He paused, eyes searching hers. "But I meant it. I love you."

She turned to him, heart aching.

He reached for her hand, hope flickering in his eyes—until he saw the sorrow in hers.

"Clint, I'm so sorry," she whispered. "I don't love you the way you love me."

His hand dropped, the light in his eyes fading.

"You've been such a good friend," she continued. "You deserve someone who feels the same." She looked down, plucking at the grass. "I've fallen for someone else."

Her voice cracked. "I didn't mean to mislead you. I'm sorry you came all this way."

When she glanced at him, his expression darkened.

"I see," he said, blinking hard. "What did I do wrong?"

"You didn't do anything wrong," she said quickly. "You were perfect. But…my brother came home, and everything changed."

Clint frowned, eyes searching. "What does your brother have to do with *us*?"

"It has everything to do with *me*," she said, a bit sharp. She softened. "I don't know if you'll understand."

"Then help me. Please."

She met his eyes.

"It's my Indian brother," she said gently. "I've fallen in love with him." Her eyes shimmered. "I've always loved him. But now…it's different."

"Your *brother*?" Clint asked in disbelief.

"My *adopted* brother, Luke," she clarified gently. "I've told you about him—he was my best friend growing up. Then he left with his father twelve years ago. I missed him every single day."

Her voice dropped. "I felt lost without him. Andrew helped me heal, and I truly cared for him. But when Andrew died… I fell apart again. I planned to finish school and go find Luke—only he found me first. Here."

She clenched her hands.

"He saved me, Clint," she said quietly. "I trusted someone I shouldn't have. I let my guard down, and Luke stopped him…from violating me."

Clint's eyes widened with horror. "Megan..."

She dropped her gaze.

"I know. I was foolish. But thank God Luke was there. I believe... he was meant to be." She hugged her arms. "He came back when I needed him most."

Her voice trembled, a smile tugging at her lips.

"We've been together ever since. It was like we were whole again. I know it's not conventional, but it feels right. He's loved me for years—even from a distance. And now that he's back, there's no denying it."

Tears of relief welled in Megan's eyes. She brushed them away, her heart lightened by truth.

Clint stared at her, emotions warring inside. She'd tried to tell him, but he hadn't wanted to hear. He'd come anyway—hopeful. Now that hope was gone.

"Megan, I'm sorry. You don't owe me anything. I shouldn't have come. I just didn't want to believe it...but I do now. If you never want to see me again, I'd understand."

She blinked, touched by his grace.

"Of course I want to see you. You're my friend, Clint."

He nodded. "I don't like it, but I get it."

He helped her up.

"We should go. I've got a train to catch."

As the buggy rolled into the yard, Luke stepped from the corral, latching the gate. At the sound of wheels, he turned—and froze.

*Megan!*

She sat beside a man—a blond man in a suit. Luke's stomach twisted.

The man jumped down, then turned to help her.

"Luke!" Megan called brightly, tugging the man forward—smile too quick, too deliberate.

Luke didn't move. Arms crossed, face unreadable, he stared at the stranger—polished, clean-shaven, refined.

"This is Clint," Megan said cheerfully. "The friend from college I told you about."

The fringe of his tunic fluttered in the breeze, but his expression remained hard.

Clint cleared his throat. "Megan said you were home. Nice to meet you." His eyes took in the formidable, leather-clad man.

Luke didn't respond.

Clint glanced at Megan, unsure if Luke understood. She nodded.

Clint smiled, extending a hand. "Good to meet you."

Luke unfolded his arms. Slowly. Deliberately. "Likewise." His grip was iron.

Clint flinched. "Uh...may I have my hand back?"

Luke let go.

Clint flexed his fingers with a forced chuckle, stepping back.

Luke's gaze locked on Clint's face, unmoving.

"Well. I should go. It was nice meeting you."

Megan smiled. "Thanks for the visit, Clint."

He tipped his hat and climbed into the buggy. A flick of the reins, and he was gone—dust trailing behind him.

Megan watched Clint go, her emotions churning. When she turned, Luke stood rigid, eyes fixed on her.

"So," he said, hands clenched, "what was that all about?"

She exhaled, the ache still pressing on her chest. "He came this morning. Said he had to tell me how he felt. He told me he loved me. I told him the truth—about us—so he'd understand why I didn't feel the same."

"Good. Better to be clear." He crossed his arms. "So he knows you're not courting?"

"He knows," she said gently. "But we're still friends. He understands that I love you." She touched his arm, trying to soothe him.

He didn't soften. "You think he can just be friends?" His voice held an edge. "Might not be wise to keep him close, Megan."

Her eyes flashed, heat lacing her words. "That's not your decision. I choose my friends."

She turned sharply and strode toward the house.

Luke groaned, raking a hand through his hair. "Nice going, genius," he muttered.

Inside, Cassie looked up as Megan brushed past, heading to her room. A door slammed. Cassie followed, knocking gently.

"Megan, honey? Can I come in?"

A sniffle. "Yeah."

Megan sat on the edge of the bed, tear-streaked and red-eyed.

"What happened?" Cassie asked, sitting beside her, resting a hand on her back.

Megan leaned into her. "I feel terrible."

"Tell me."

"Clint wrote—said he was in love with me. I wrote back, told him I didn't feel the same, that I'd explain in person. He couldn't wait—had to tell me. I care about him, but not like that."

Cassie sighed. "I thought he was your beau."

"I did too. But I don't love him. I told him we could

still be friends. I hurt him."

Cassie handed her a handkerchief. "He'll be alright—in time."

Megan nodded. "I hope. He came all this way—but I couldn't lie."

Cassie studied her. "This wouldn't have anything to do with Luke, *would it*?"

Megan froze, heart hammering.

Cassie's gaze narrowed. "So it *is* about Luke"

Fresh tears welled. "It just happened. When he came back, everything made sense. I've never felt so whole. He loves me, Ma. And I love him." She sobbed. "Please, don't be mad."

Cassie sat still, her thoughts racing. She remembered Megan's grief when Luke left. How Andrew, and then Clint, had helped her smile again. But when Luke returned, Cassie had seen the spark in Megan's eyes—laughter, joy, lightness. She'd wondered.

"Mama?" Megan whispered. "Say something."

Cassie pressed her fingers to her lips. "I'm surprised," she said at last. "But maybe I shouldn't be. You two were always close. And I know you missed him terribly. Still... Megan, it's not exactly proper. People will talk. You were raised like siblings—"

"But we're not—not by blood," she said softly. "We've thought about all that. It doesn't change how we feel."

Megan hesitated. "Luke's had dreams about me. Before he came back, he dreamed of marrying me. Around then, the chief arranged for him to marry his daughter. But Luke refused. He told his grandfather—their shaman—about the dream, and he said to find the girl with green eyes—that I was his mate."

Cassie blinked. "His mate?"

Megan blushed. "That's what he said."

Cassie leaned back. Luke could've had status and security—but he walked away. For Megan. For a dream.

She spoke slowly. "It's a powerful story. But are you sure it's love? Not just the joy of being reunited with your best friend?"

Megan's frustration flared. "Isn't that what love *is*? Didn't you and Pa start as best friends?"

Cassie smiled. "We did. But our love came out of shared pain and healing."

"That's what happened with Luke and me," Megan said, voice rich with emotion. "He's always been my protector—my anchor. When he left, it felt like I lost part of myself. I didn't feel whole again until he came back." Her voice trembled. "And finding out I'm part Indian... it brought me closer to him. We understand each other in a way no one else can. He needs me—and I need him."

Cassie pulled her close, pressing a kiss to her temple. "I understand, sweetheart. It won't be easy. But if it's what you both want...I'm happy for you. I love you both."

Relief swept through Megan. "Thank you, Ma."

She wiped her cheeks. "I need to find Luke. I told him it was over with Clint, but he still seemed...uncertain."

Cassie nodded. "If he loves you, I can see why Clint might feel like a threat. You're going back to school soon. Maybe Luke's afraid he came back too late."

Megan stood. "You're right. He must be worried." She dabbed her eyes. "I need to talk to him. Thank you,

Ma. I love you."

"I love you too." Cassie hugged her tightly, then let her go.

Outside, Megan scanned the corral—Wildfire was gone.

She opened the front door. "Luke's gone. I'm going after him—I'll be back soon."

Megan quickly saddled Snowfire. As she rode past the house, Cassie stepped onto the porch, worry etched across her face.

"I'll be back by dinner, I promise!" Megan called.

"Be careful. I love you."

* * *

Luke knelt beside the pond, sage-scented smoke curling from a small smudge fire. Eyes closed, hands on his thighs, he prayed silently:

*Father, thank You for bringing me home. For Megan. But I fear my love for her clouds my judgment. Jealousy burns in me. Please, help me be better...*

Megan knew he'd be here. The pond had always been her refuge. Perhaps, now, it was his too.

She entered the quiet meadow and spotted Wildfire tied to a tree. Then she saw Luke—still and straight, hair draping over bronzed shoulders, smoke curling around his bare chest.

Dismounting quietly, she tied her horse beside his and sat beneath a nearby tree. Her gaze lingered on him—calm, grounded, strong.

Luke had sensed her coming—the rhythm of hooves, the whisper of her skirts. He finished his prayer, exhaled, and stood. When he saw her reclining in the grass, he crossed to her and lowered himself beside her, mirroring her posture.

"Hi," he said softly.

She smiled up at him. "Hi."

Her eyes drifted to his broad chest, where his medicine pouch rested over his heart.

He took her hand in the grass, fingers brushing hers. "I'm sorry. I was rude to Clint. I've never felt anger like that—seeing him with you…"

"I didn't expect to see him either," she said gently. "I didn't know he still felt that strongly. But you were right—he came to say he loved me." Her voice steadied. "I already told you everything. He knows the truth. He knows I love *you*."

Luke's thumb traced her knuckles. A warm shiver rose through her as her heart quickened beneath his touch.

"And I love *you*," he said. "I was wrong to tell you who you could be friends with. I just…" He shook his head. "When you're away, and Clint's there…I'm just afraid of losing you."

He studied her—high cheekbones, elegant nose, dark lashes shadowing downcast eyes, lips parted to speak.

"You won't lose me." Megan lifted her eyes to meet his. "I hate the thought of leaving you—even for work. Being apart for months?" She shook her head. "It already hurts."

"I don't want you to go either," he said. "But you have to finish school."

His hand slid up her arm, brushing her shoulder before weaving into her hair. The silk of it flowed through his fingers like water.

Megan inhaled sharply, lashes fluttering. "I'm sorry

I snapped," she whispered. "If it were you with someone else, while I was gone... I'd feel the same. We just have to trust each other."

"I do trust you," he said. "It's Clint I don't trust. You see the good in him—and maybe there is. But he's still a man. And I know what he's thinking."

His eyes were smoldering as he leaned in close.

She arched a brow, lips curving. "Oh? What's he thinking?"

Luke smirked, voice low. "That you're beautiful. That once you're away from me, he might win you back—that a gentleman could offer more than a wild Indian."

Megan's laugh was soft and sure. "He's wrong. I *like* that you're a wild Indian."

He leaned closer. "He's also thinking he wants to kiss you. And make you his wife." He paused, eyes dark with intent. "Because that's what *I'm* thinking."

Her cheeks flushed, emerald eyes sparkling. "Oh, you would, *would you*?"

His voice dropped to a husky whisper. "You have no idea."

He kissed her—soft and sure. Her lips yielded, his heartbeat thundered as she responded with a sigh. She melted into him, the kiss deepening. His hand cradled her head, reverently.

He drew back at last, breath ragged, gaze lingering on her face. Megan's eyes fluttered open, her voice a deep whisper:

"I think I do now."

# Chapter 8

## Summer Love

As they rode back to the ranch, Megan recounted her talk with Ma.

"So, she knows?" Luke asked, eyes downcast.

"Yes. Everything." She watched his face tighten. "It'll be alright. She understands. She wants us to be happy."

"I hope you're right." He sighed. "I wasn't ready to talk to Ma and Pa yet…"

He glanced at her, his smile softening. Megan seemed to glow, wind-tossed hair streaming behind her like Snowfire's mane. Horse and rider moved as one— wild, free, and breathtaking.

As they neared the cottage, Ma and Pa stepped out onto the porch.

"Good, you're back," Ma called. "Dinner's ready. Wash up."

They exchanged a glance and dismounted.

Inside, the boys were already at the table. Megan and Luke washed quickly as Ma set down the last dish.

"Sorry to keep you waiting," Luke said, drying his hands and passing Megan the towel with a knowing look.

"Thanks for dinner, Ma," Megan added. "I'll cook tonight so you can rest."

"It's no trouble, dear," Ma said, giving her hand a squeeze. "Let's eat."

They bowed their heads. After the prayer, the room filled with the quiet clatter of dishes and the scent of fried fish and potatoes. A tension hummed beneath it all.

"Hey, Luke, thanks for catching these. They're amazing," David said, trying to lift the mood.

"You're welcome." Luke kept his eyes on his plate.

"I wish I'd gone," Kurt muttered. "I love fishing."

Luke glanced up. "Ask Grandpa. I bet he'd take you."

"So, you had a good time?" Ed asked, handing over the potatoes.

"Yeah. I missed using a pole all those years. Nothing like that first tug on the line."

"What do you mean? How else do you fish?" Johnathan asked.

"In my tribe, we used traps—or spears. But I've always loved sitting by the water with a pole, it's peaceful." He smiled. "And Grandpa O'Malley told me stories—how he met Grandma, and his sheriff days."

Ed's posture eased. Luke was a good man. The truth about Luke and Megan had hit hard—but reflecting back, it made sense. Cassie had been right to ask him to wait before confronting them.

"I'm glad you had a good time," Ed said. His gaze flicked to Megan, who quickly looked down. He turned to Luke. "I'd like to go with you next time. It's been too long since we had time together."

Luke nodded. "I'd like that, Pa."

Across the table, Megan met Luke's eyes and gave a small, reassuring nod.

"How about tomorrow morning?" Ed asked, glancing at Cassie, winking.

Luke hesitated, then smiled. "Sure. That'd be great."

***

The sun had barely risen when Luke hurried through his chores, hoping to finish before breakfast. Though he sat at the table, his plate was barely touched. His stomach churned with nerves.

He and Ed rode in silence through the underbrush, shadows stretching long across the prairie. Birds called overhead, the stillness of the grove wrapping around them as they entered the dense foliage. Ahead, the wide stream shimmered in the morning light.

"This looks like a good spot," Ed said, dismounting. He tied Major to a low branch and grabbed his pole.

Luke followed, slipping from Wildfire's back. "We fished here yesterday," he said, kneeling to lift two worms from beneath a rock. "There's a deep pocket under that log."

The water flowed clear and slow, cool beneath the shade. Luke settled on a flat rock and cast his line. The bobber drifted toward the log, tugged by the current. Beside him, Ed sent his line to the undercut bank, giving it a practiced twitch.

"That's a good spot," Luke said. "Caught a few there."

They sat in easy quiet. Dragonflies skimmed the surface, the stream whispering between them. But Luke's thoughts swirled beneath the calm.

"Luke," Ed exclaimed, nodding at the bobber, "you've got a bite."

Luke snapped to attention, pulling back sharply. The line went taut. The fish darted, fighting hard. After a tense minute, he landed a large brook trout, silver scales flashing.

He struck it cleanly and laid it in the shade.

"Nice one," Ed said.

"Thanks, Pa. I would've missed it if you hadn't said something."

Luke cast again, then exhaled. "So...Ma told you about Megan and me."

"She did. But I'd rather hear it from you."

He told Ed everything—how Megan had stayed in his heart, how thoughts of her had called him home, how he'd risked disapproval from his father and chief just to be near her.

"She's not my blood sister," he said quietly. "I was adopted. So...it's not a sin, right?"

Ed sighed. "No, son. It's not."

Relief flickered across Luke's face, but he pressed on. "She's always been my strength, my everything, Pa. I want to marry her."

Ed watched the water a long moment. "I know you love her, and she loves you. We just didn't realize how deep it ran." He looked over. "As your father, I want your happiness. But others may not understand. They might see it as... wrong."

"I've thought about that. Prayed about it. But, we belong together, no matter what people say. I want her to be my wife."

Ed studied his son, then nodded. "I understand."

Luke stared into the current, the water tugging at his line. He felt like one of the fish—swept along, caught in a current he couldn't escape. Yet unlike them, his path was leading to a beginning, not an end.

Ed's voice broke the quiet. "When I met Cassie, I didn't think I could love again. After losing my wife and daughter...I was empty. But Cassie changed that. She healed my heart. Megan might've told you—before we married, she told me she was pregnant. With the man who—"

"She did," Luke said softly. "It hurt, knowing what Ma went through."

"I didn't care. I loved her—and I loved that child. Megan became mine from the start. I've never once regretted it."

Luke's voice shook. "Then you understand. Megan and I...we were always meant to be family—and so much more."

Ed nodded. "You're right. What you two share—it's rare. Strong."

Luke exhaled, the words loosening something deep inside. "Saying it out loud...it feels heavier than I expected. But it's the truth."

Ed placed a hand on his knee. "It took me time, son. But I see it now. And I'm happy for you."

"Thank you, Pa. That means everything."

"But give it time. Not everyone will understand at first."

Before Luke could answer, Ed's cork dipped. With practiced ease, he hooked the fish and reeled it in.

Luke watched him land it, heart still thudding. He'd hoped this talk would clear the way completely. But maybe Pa was right. Maybe the world still wasn't ready—for an Indian man and a white woman to love openly.

He stared at the stream, remembering the stares, the whispers that followed him into church. Over time, folks had quieted—but not forgotten. And if they'd balked at his presence, what would they say now?

*Maybe Pa's right. Maybe it takes time.*

***

That Sunday, after supper with the grandparents, Luke knew the moment had come. Still dressed in his Sunday best, he rose from the table, walked to Megan, and rested a hand on her shoulder.

"I just wanted to say...Megan and I are courting. I love her—and she loves me."

Megan looked up, cheeks flushed, eyes shining. She reached for his hand, and he took it, heart full.

"Well, if that don't beat all!" Grandpa O'Malley beamed. "I couldn't be happier." He turned to Kathy, grinning. "Look at 'em—practically glowing."

"They are," Kathy said, warmth rising in her chest.

"You two have always belonged together," Grandma Hartford said with a smile, giving Megan's hand a squeeze, then winked at Luke.

"Guess things have a way of working out," Grandpa Hartford said, blinking back tears. "The good Lord brought Luke home and look what a blessing—especially for Megan."

Luke's chest warmed. "Thank you, Grandma. Thank you, Grandpa."

"What about *us*?" Johnathan piped up. "We knew first! They'll probably get married right after Megan graduates—right, Megan?"

Megan flushed, speechless. She glanced at Luke, and for a heartbeat the room fell silent.

Laughter broke the tension.

Cassie stepped in. "Johnathan, let them be. They've got time." She moved to the china cabinet to get dishes.

"Megan, will you go to the icehouse and fetch the ice cream for the cobbler?"

"Sure, Ma," Megan said quickly, grateful for the excuse.

"I'll help," Luke added, grabbing a bucket. "We need more ice for the tea."

Out of sight from the house, Luke slipped his arm around her. "Whew. Glad that's over."

"I thought I might faint," Megan laughed. "Did you see their faces?"

He grinned. "A little stunned, but happy. We're lucky."

She gave him a playful squeeze. "Then Johnathan had to go and make it awkward."

"He just said what I've been thinking. I want to marry you right after you graduate."

Megan hesitated, drying damp palms on her skirt as Luke pried open the door to the icehouse. Cool air hit them as they ducked inside the dim dugout.

"Luke…" she said softly. "Let's take it one step at a time. Let me finish school before we plan the rest of our lives."

He smiled as he chipped at the ice. "Whatever you say." But in his heart, the vow lingered: *I'll wait. I'll wait as long as it takes to call you mine forever.*

***

As summer waned and harvest neared, the ranch pulsed with life. Megan worked in town, helped can the garden's bounty, and stitched a new dress for college. But beneath it all, her love for Luke deepened like roots pressing into the earth.

About a month into their courtship, Luke began riding into town to escort her home. She never knew when he'd come—but each day, she hoped. And when he did, her heart soared.

Today was one of those good days.

"Luke!" Megan waved goodbye to her coworkers and hurried toward him. He stood waiting, polished in a crisp shirt and coat.

He smiled. "How was your shift?"

"Busy, but it flew." She slipped her hand through his arm as they strolled past the shops. "You?"

Luke grinned. "Did chores. Thought about you. More chores. Then this—best part of my day." He patted her hand.

She laughed softly, his hand resting over hers.

Behind them, two men stumbled from a cigar store, trailing too close. Luke noticed. He didn't flinch—just kept walking.

"We should stop by Jeremy and Penny's," he said. "Invite them to picnic on Sunday."

"That sounds lovely! I'm sure—"

A gruff voice behind them cut her short.

"Hey, look at that Injun," his words slurred. "How come he gets a pretty girl, and you don't, Pete?"

Luke's jaw tightened. He caught their reflection in a shop window—scruffy drifters, whiskey-stained and loud, but no real threat.

The second barked a laugh. "Maybe she's blind. Don't even know she's holding on to a filthy Injun. Hey, missy—you best get your eyes checked."

Megan's stomach clenched. Fury surged, hot and fast. She wanted to spin around, to shout, to strike—but Luke's hand gently tightened over hers.

*Not like this*, his touch said.

Luke's quiet restraint only deepened her fury. She'd spent her childhood watching bullies wound and humiliate. She'd sworn never to stay silent again—never to let someone she loved be shamed without a fight.

Luke saw the fire in her eyes and gave a small shake of his head. "Shhh."

Then, louder, his voice turned sharp and cold.

"Megan, remember when I beat up that teacher back in school?"

She blinked. "What?"

He went on, smooth and deliberate. "Kept calling me a 'filthy Injun.' One day, I had enough. Poor guy was bawling when I finished. Never came back."

Megan caught on. "Oh right—his arm was in a sling for weeks. That nose never did heal straight."

Luke exhaled slowly. "Got what he deserved. Still makes my blood boil."

Megan sighed dramatically. "Now, now. Don't lose your temper again."

From the corner of her eye, she saw the men hesitate.

One grunted, "Let's hit the saloon. I'm parched."

The other nodded. "Too hot to be out here anyway."

They shuffled off, glancing back once before disappearing through the saloon's swinging doors.

As soon as they were gone, Megan and Luke exchanged glances—then burst into laughter.

"Think we scared 'em off?" she teased, giving his arm a squeeze.

"Either that," he said with a smirk, "or they really were thirsty."

Still smiling, they walked on, the weight of the

moment slipping behind them.

***

As Megan and Luke spent more time together in town, curious glances often followed. At first, whispers and sidelong looks were common, but over time, gossip faded. Those who knew them chose quiet acceptance. Cruelty, when it came, was from strangers—outsiders who couldn't understand the love they shared.

They never spoke of it, but both felt the sting. It wasn't fair. It wasn't right. Still, as long as they had each other, they refused to let judgment steal their joy.

Jeremy and Penny, newly married and glowing, were eager companions. The four picnicked in shady meadows, rode buggies beneath golden skies, and dressed in their best for plays and dances. Laughter came easily. In those hours, the world fell away.

That summer felt like a dream—one they would carry forever. But time, quiet and relentless, slipped through their fingers. Two months vanished in a blink. The season of endless sun was fading.

***

Summer had begun to surrender, giving way to crisp mornings and shorter days. Cheyenne shimmered in mid-September gold. Fields bowed under the weight of ripe grain, ready for harvest—if the weather held.

"I can't believe I leave in a few days," Megan murmured, fingers laced tightly with Luke's as they walked the path behind the house. The stream's quiet burble echoed the ache in her chest. "I'm not ready. I don't want to leave you."

Luke brushed his thumb across her hand. "I don't

want you to go. I can't imagine not seeing your beautiful face each day."

Megan's grip tightened. "I can't imagine not talking to you...not kissing you." Her voice broke. "I'm not sure I can do it."

Luke stopped, pulling her into his arms. She wrapped her arms around his neck. Cheek to cheek, he breathed her in. Tenderly, he kissed a trail along her jaw until he felt the warmth of her tears against his lips.

She trembled, then broke. Soft sobs shook her shoulders.

"Shh...it's going to be okay," he whispered, holding her closer. "I'll be here. We'll write. We'll see each other on your breaks. It'll go fast—you'll see."

He tried to sound sure, even as his own throat tightened.

"Oh, Luke," she choked. "I've never been so happy. I can't leave you...it's going to break my heart."

"You can dream of me," he murmured, kissing her cheek.

She turned into his lips, and the kiss deepened—tender, then urgent. They were running out of time.

When they pulled apart, breathless, she whispered, "I'll try." Her knees were unsteady, heart pounding.

"I will too," he said, a soft smile rising.

She looked up, eyes glinting with mischief. "Should we go for one more swim before I leave?"

The heat clung to her, dress damp against her back.

Luke grinned. "Let's go."

He'd have said yes to anything. She could've suggested mucking stalls, and he'd have agreed.

They ran to the corral, saddling her horse in a flurry.

"Ma! We'll be back for supper!" Megan called as they mounted.

Cassie stood on the porch, watching them ride off with a knowing smile. She remembered that kind of love. Even now, after all these years, she and Ed still stole quiet moments. He was her everything—and she, his.

Out on the open road, Megan and Luke gave the horses their heads, laughing as they raced beneath the endless Wyoming sky. The grass waved golden, dotted with wildflowers and sage. Hawks circled above, butterflies danced across sunflowers, and cattle grazed in the distance.

Their horses kicked up dust as they galloped. Megan leaned low over Snowfire, her skirt and dark hair streaming. Luke rode bareback, moving fluidly, his long hair flying with the wind.

After a few miles, they slowed, flushed and breathless. Megan's hat flew back, caught only by its string. They laughed, letting the wind cool their skin.

As the horses settled, they followed the familiar trail to Horse Creek—their secret place.

The rushing water beckoned. One last summer adventure waited.

"Whew. Just when I thought it couldn't get any hotter," Megan said, swinging off Snowfire. Dust rose around her boots as she landed. She pulled off her hat and swiped her brow.

"I know. I can't wait to get in."

Luke dismounted, stripping off his tunic and moccasins, then untied his leggings, leaving only his breechcloth. The sun gilded his smooth skin, sculpted muscles carved in bronze.

Megan turned quickly, cheeks burning, pretending she hadn't noticed. She slipped off her shoes and stockings, then her dress. Arms crossed, she stepped carefully toward the stream in her slip, the damp earth cooling her bare feet.

"Come in—it feels amazing," Luke called, waist-deep in the water, sunlight dancing around him. The trees swayed gently overhead, shadows rippling across the surface.

"Don't look." She hesitated, waiting for him to turn before dipping a toe in. A gasp escaped. "Oh! It's freezing!"

"You'll get used to it." He reached out without looking. "Here—take my hand."

His grasp was steady and warm. She stepped in, the chill climbing her legs, sending a thrill through her flushed skin.

"Just a little further," he murmured as the current tugged at them.

"That's deep enough," she said, shivering. "I don't want to get my hair wet."

Luke grinned. "You should've put it up."

"I didn't think of it," she said, lifting the strands.

"Turn around—I'll fix it." He removed the leather thong around his arm.

She obeyed. Gently, he gathered her hair, fingers brushing her scalp, gliding over her neck. A shiver ran through her—but not from the water. He twisted the thick strands and tied them up, his touch lingering as he slid his hands down her arms.

She closed her eyes. His callused hands clasped her

upper arms tenderly, his warmth making her relax.

"There," he whispered, his voice husky. "That should hold."

He nearly brushed his lips against her neck—but stopped himself. She tilted her head back, leaning into him, breath shaky.

"You're shivering," he murmured. "Want to get out?"

"No…just a few more minutes."

The world narrowed to the space between them, Megan unwilling to break the moment. But Luke knew they had to stop. Now.

"Time to get out." He swept her into his arms.

She gasped, wrapping around him instinctively. He held her close, her damp slip clinging to her form. On shore, he set her gently on a log and turned away to dress, his heartbeat thundering. He needed space—to calm the fire she'd lit inside him.

Megan sat still, flushed and trembling. Even with her body chilled, she felt the heat of his touch.

Luke raked a hand through his hair. He loved her—too much. He wanted her, but not like this. Not before it was right. He had to protect her…even from himself.

She wrung out her slip and pulled her dress over her wet frame, fingers fumbling as she let her hair fall loose to dry.

On the other side of the horses, Luke dressed quickly, his back turned.

"Ready?" he asked at last, voice steady, but distant.

She heard the shift. Something had changed.

He held the reins as she mounted up but wouldn't meet her eyes.

Softly, she asked, "Did I do something wrong?"

He shook his head, his eyes on the ground. "No. It's me."

"What do you mean?"

"I'm a fool. I never should've come here with you."

Her brow furrowed. "Why?"

He looked up at her. "Megan...do you know how much I love you? *Really* love you?"

Her heart skipped. "I think I do."

"I want to be *with* you. *Completely*." His voice roughened. "To love you in *every* way a man can love a woman."

She flushed. "Oh...I didn't realize…"

"It's not your fault," he said gently. "It's just...human nature. But I want to do this right. When I marry you, I want you to be...virtuous."

She lowered her gaze, cheeks burning. "Oh."

Luke studied her, glowing in the late sun, hair cascading over her shoulders. She took his breath away. He loved her more than he ever had.

He stepped closer and took her hand, his thumb brushing her knuckles. "I love you, Megan Marie Havoc. And I'll wait as long as it takes. But one day, I'll make you my wife. And then...you'll be mine. In *every* way."

Megan met his eyes, her voice trembling. "One day—body *and* soul."

Luke pressed a kiss to her hand, reverent and slow, knowing whatever came, their love would endure the wait.

# Chapter 9

## College

The day Megan left for college was one of the hardest goodbyes she'd ever faced. Her trunk was already packed, loaded into the wagon.

"Let's go. We don't want to miss the train," Pa called, stepping outside.

Megan turned to the mirror, placing the last pin in her hat. As her throat tightened, she touched the heart-shaped locket, drawing comfort from Luke's photo inside.

Cassie stood behind her. "You look beautiful, sweetheart," she whispered, squeezing her shoulder. "I'm so proud of you."

Megan turned and hugged her. "Thanks, Ma."

Cassie smiled through her tears. "We'd better go."

Megan nodded. "I just need a minute."

Cassie understood and stepped out.

In the front room, Luke turned as Megan emerged. She looked lovely in her dark blue traveling dress, but it was more than that. She was his—Megan.

She closed the bedroom door. "I want you to stay in my room while I'm gone," she said softly. "No more sleeping in the barn—especially with winter coming."

Luke nodded. "I'll take good care of it." He stepped closer, hands settling at her waist, velvet beneath his fingers.

Her gaze dropped, throat clenching.

"I'm going to miss you like crazy," he murmured, voice rough.

"I'll miss you more." She wrapped her arms around his neck. "I don't know if I can do this. I love you so much." Tears spilled freely.

"I love you too." He held her tight, his cheek brushing hers. "I'll pray for you every day."

She closed her eyes, breathing him in. "I'm not sure my legs will take me out that door."

He smiled gently. "Then I'll carry you." His voice wavered. "You can do this, Megan."

She managed a shaky smile. "If you don't write—I'll come home…"

"I promise. Every week." He kissed her, then wrapped her in one last, aching embrace.

"Megan! We have to go!" Pa's voice called.

They shared a watery laugh, cheeks damp with tears.

"Let's go," she whispered, taking Luke's hand and leading him to the door.

On the porch, he stopped. "You go," he said quietly. "I can't say goodbye twice." His voice broke. "I love you, Megan."

Before she could answer, he turned and strode toward the backyard, shoulders stiff, tears streaming.

Megan stood frozen. "Goodbye, Luke. I love you," she whispered.

At the wagon, Pa jumped down to help her climb in beside her brothers.

"Doesn't Luke want to see you off?" Johnathan asked.

"Shh," David nudged him.

"He already did," Cassie said gently, squeezing

Megan's hand. "He just needs a moment."

Megan only nodded, heart aching.

"Ed, let's go," Cassie said.

The wagon lurched forward. Megan looked back—and there he was, stepping from around the house. Their eyes locked.

Suddenly, Luke ran for Wildfire. In one fluid motion, he was on the stallion's back, hooves thundering as he galloped alongside the wagon.

"Stop, Pa!" Megan cried.

The wagon halted. Luke pulled up beside her. Megan stood and reached for him.

He leaned in, hands cradling her face. His kiss was fierce, tender—full of everything he couldn't say.

Then he pulled back, jaw clenched, and spurred Wildfire forward, disappearing in a cloud of dust.

Megan sank down, sobbing.

Kurt slid beside her, wrapping an arm around her shoulders.

Pa clucked to the horses, and the wagon rolled on. When they reached the main road, Luke was gone.

***

Megan pressed her hand to the cool train window, waving as the engine lurched forward. Tears blurred the familiar faces on the platform. She dabbed her eyes, willing herself to stay composed.

Two months until she returned. By then, the golden hills would lie buried beneath snow.

As the train picked up speed, Megan turned back to the window. Autumn's fading brilliance glowed beneath the mid-morning sun. Then, three miles out, her breath caught.

*Luke!*

He sat astride Wildfire at the edge of the grove, waiting.

Her heart surged as their eyes met. She lifted her hand. He raised his in return, a quiet smile on his lips. He didn't look away, tracking the train as it rumbled past.

She twisted in her seat, straining to keep him in view. He nudged Wildfire forward, crossing behind the train. Through the opposite window, she caught one last glimpse of him disappearing into the trees, toward Clearwater Pond.

And then he was gone.

Megan exhaled, fingers twisting the lace edge of her handkerchief. A soft smile touched her lips.

*Luke loves me.*

With that thought, she leaned back and inhaled deeply, ready for the journey ahead—her next great adventure waiting just beyond the horizon.

* * *

Luke emerged into the quiet meadow that cradled Clearwater Pond, his vision blurred with tears. His chest ached—every heartbeat echoing the emptiness Megan had left behind.

He guided Wildfire to the water's edge and dismounted slowly. Shedding his layers, he let the cool autumn air wash over him. Against his bare chest rested his sacred bundle.

Beneath the tall cottonwood, he knelt and lit a smudge fire with dried sage from his medicine bag. As fragrant smoke spiraled upward, he bowed his head, pleading silently for comfort from his Father in Heaven.

Grief surged, raw and unrelenting. His breath hitched,

then broke—sobs overtaking him as sorrow poured out like water from a broken dam.

Time blurred as his hoarse voice rose with the smoke. Gradually, the weight in his chest began to lift. He ended his prayer and stood, lifting his face to the autumn sky, jaw set with quiet resolve.

*Megan, I let you go, but my spirit walks beside you. I will love and honor you always.*

***

Megan arrived at the University of Wyoming by midday, her heart heavy with parting. A porter carried her trunk to the bare room she'd share with Tabitha.

Alone, she sank onto the unmade bed, grief pressing down until the tears came. When the storm passed, she wiped her eyes, blew her nose, and began unpacking.

Tabitha arrived, her radiant energy lifting the room's heaviness. Grateful for the distraction, Megan welcomed her in. As they settled, she quietly confided that things with Clint had ended. Her heart now belonged to someone else—a childhood friend who had returned to Cheyenne last spring.

Tabitha's smile faltered. "I always thought you and Clint made a sweet pair." But seeing the certainty in Megan's eyes, she quickly added, "I'm happy for you. Truly."

"Clint and I were never meant to be," Megan said simply. "It wasn't true love."

The afternoon blurred with orientation—Megan had heard it all before, letting her thoughts wander to Luke.

All day she managed to avoid Clint—until supper.

He spotted her the moment she entered the dining hall. "Megan!" he called, striding forward. Unexpectedly, he took her hands and kissed her cheek.

Her heart pounded. She'd wondered how he'd act—but there he was, confident charm intact.

"It's good to see you! How are you?" he asked with ease.

"I'm well. You?" she managed.

"Wonderful. Glad to be back." He glanced past her. "Tabitha! Welcome back."

He kissed Tabitha's cheek.

Tabitha, ever the opportunist, tucked a loose curl behind her ear and gave her bustle a teasing swish. "Good to see you too, Clint."

"We're all here now—Gwen, Richard, Eileen, Tyler... and you two," he said, gesturing toward their old group. Megan hesitated, but his grip was firm, gently leading her forward.

Tabitha leaned in. "Well, *he's* in a good mood," she whispered. Then, with a wicked grin, "If you don't want him...maybe I do."

Megan arched a brow. Tabitha just smirked.

Clint acted as though nothing had passed between them, but Megan wasn't fooled. Though he smiled and joked, she noticed the moments in between—fleeting glances, the hint of sadness in his eyes.

Tabitha jumped in. "Megan, tell us about your new beau," she said lightly, her intent clear—she wanted it known Megan had moved on.

"You have a new beau?" Gwen asked, twirling a golden curl, eyes darting between Megan and Clint.

The others listened politely, though Megan knew the real questions would be whispered behind closed doors.

She hesitated. "Yes. An old friend. He moved back

last spring." She left it at that. Some things were too sacred to explain.

Clint offered a small smile.

Megan shifted. "So, what have you been up to this summer, Clint?"

Clint straightened slightly. "Working at my father's newspaper." He paused, then added, "Got some time off—visited a *friend* and some relatives."

Megan looked away, cheeks warming. "Sounds nice," she murmured, then redirected. "Anyone else travel this summer?"

Eileen perked up. "We went to California—saw the ocean for the first time. It was *incredible*. I think I want to teach there after graduation."

"I'd love to see the ocean someday," Tyler said, cheeks flushed, secretly adoring her.

Around the table, the old friends laughed and talked, but Megan sat quiet, her thoughts drifting to Luke.

By day's end, she welcomed the solitude of their room.

After washing up, Tabitha and Megan promptly turned out the lights at nine. Megan lay still, listening to Tabitha's breath slow into sleep—only then did she turn to the wall, bury her face in the pillow, and weep.

***

Luke's first night in the cottage felt strange. He was grateful for the warmth and privacy, but an emptiness settled over him.

After bidding his parents goodnight, he slipped into Megan's room and changed into nightclothes. Her scent lingered in the linens—light and achingly familiar.

He pressed his face into her pillow, breathing in

deeply, grief rising like a tide. Silent tears soaked the fabric.

Later, a dream jolted him awake—Megan slipping from his arms as the train pulled away. He sat up, heart pounding, then lay back, blinking at the dark.

Before dawn, the clatter of Ma stoking the stove stirred him. He exhaled, rubbing a hand over his weary face.

Morning had come.

The first day without Megan.

***

Megan tried to focus on her studies, but her thoughts always returned to Luke. She imagined his voice, the strength of his warm embrace.

Though schoolwork grew easier, the nights remained achingly lonely.

Sometimes she dreamed of him—fleeting glimpses that left her hollow with longing. His letters became her lifeline. She read them again and again, fingers tracing the words like a prayer.

***

At the ranch, life moved on. The first month passed in a blur of labor—gathering harvest, stacking hay, curing meat for winter.

The pantry and cellar brimmed with produce and jars of preserves. The work kept hands busy, but not hearts.

Luke felt Megan's absence like a missing piece of his soul.

***

By late October, it was time for the fall roundup.

For two long days, Luke rode the range with family

and neighbors, driving steers and bulls to market.

Crisp air filled his lungs. The rhythm of hooves and lowing cattle echoed across the open land.

Evenings were spent around campfires—coffee in tin cups, stories and laughter under stars. It stirred memories of his childhood and his tribe—a feeling of belonging.

One night, after the others had turned in, Luke and Grandpa O'Malley sat by the crackling fire.

"How's Megan doing?" Grandpa asked, sipping his coffee.

"She says classes are hard, but she's doing well," Luke said, his eyes focused on the dancing flames.

"And you?" Grandpa read Luke's distant gaze.

"I'm surviving." He paused, eyes shimmering. "She's the reason I came back. And now she's gone. I thought the waiting was over."

Grandpa rested a steady hand on his shoulder. "This is a season of growth. You're learning what she really means to you."

"I already knew," Luke whispered. "Why didn't I just wait a year and spare us both the heartache?"

Grandpa chuckled. "Lad, you'll always be waiting on a woman. But you came back when it mattered. She needed you. You needed her. Fifty miles isn't far. I used to ride to Laramie in a day when I was sheriff. Why not go visit?"

Luke looked up, a flicker of hope in his eyes. "I could ride out Saturday, be back Sunday."

"Better yet—take the train. My treat. Call it an early Christmas gift," Grandpa said with a wink.

Luke grinned. "Thanks, Grandpa."

That night, tucked in his bedroll beneath a blanket of

stars, Luke drifted to sleep with a smile.

*Megan, I'm coming. Just you wait—I'm going to surprise you!*

***

Megan looked toward the weekend with quiet desperation. Days of nonstop studying had left her mind foggy, her body drained. She still had errands to run—supplies to buy, letters to mail, and hopefully one waiting from Luke at the post office. Crawling into bed Friday night, she clutched that hope to her chest. It wasn't just homesickness—she ached for Luke with every breath.

***

In Cheyenne, Luke stepped onto the train platform Saturday morning, dressed in a tailored gray suit and matching overcoat. With his hair tied back and felt hat shading his grin, he waved goodbye to Pa.

*Today is going to be a great day.*

***

"Megan, are you ready?" Tabitha called, giving herself a final once-over in the dormitory mirror.

"Just grabbing my cloak." Megan slipped into her dark blue velvet wrap, the white fur hood framing her face like a soft halo. Her locket gleamed at her throat, and the rich hue of her dress made her green eyes shine. Tucking letters into her purse, she pulled on her mittens and followed Tabitha downstairs.

Outside, the carriage waited, its wheels rimmed with frost. The horses' breath puffed clouds into the cold morning air.

"Hurry, ladies—we're freezing!" Richard called, swinging the carriage door open with a grin.

Tabitha climbed in beside Clint. Megan settled across from them next to Gwen and Richard. The carriage rocked gently as the door shut behind them. Eileen and Tyler had stayed behind to finish a project but planned to meet for lunch.

With a snap of the reins, the horses trotted forward, hooves clopping over the cobbled circle in front of the University.

***

Steam hissed as Luke stepped off the train, the clatter of unloading passengers echoing around him. He scanned the platform, then crossed to a ticket booth under the overhang.

"Hansom cab will get you to the University," the clerk said, nodding to a line of drivers.

"Thank you." Luke made his way to the carriages, agreed on a fare, and climbed inside.

Through the small window, Laramie unfolded—clean streets, tidy storefronts, a quiet charming town.

***

Megan stepped from the carriage onto the boardwalk. Her friends split off—Tabitha and Clint to the milliner's, Gwen and Richard to the cobbler's—promising to meet later for lunch at the café.

Alone, Megan walked slowly, lost in thought. She pulled her cloak tighter, fur brushing her cheeks as the cold nipped at her.

Meanwhile, Luke watched from the cab, eyes scanning the street—then caught a flash of blue. His heart leapt—the hair, the graceful sway of her stride—Megan!

"Driver, stop!" he called, rapping the roof.

Luke leapt out, tossing the driver a coin. "Keep the change!" he called, already running.

"Megan! Megan!"

She turned, startled—then her eyes saw him. "Luke!" she cried. "Oh, Luke!"

She flew into his arms, tears gathering. He lifted her and spun her once before setting her down.

"I had to come," he breathed, "I couldn't stay away."

She laughed through her tears, cupped his face, and kissed him right there in the street. Passersby paused— some smiling, some frowning—but Megan saw no one but Luke.

"I missed you," she whispered.

"I missed you more than I can say." His voice caught.

They held each other tightly, trying to make up for lost time.

"Can we go somewhere?" Luke asked, glancing around.

"I was heading to the post office, then meeting the others for lunch. You could join us."

"No need for the post office," he said, smiling. "You can give me your letter in person. I brought mine too— started writing it, then figured I'd deliver it myself."

"Special delivery," she teased, linking arms with him.

"Not as special as you," he said, gently patting her hand.

At the café, they found a quiet table in the back and shared coffee and a warm Danish. The scent of cinnamon and roasted beans wrapped around them as they sat close, fingers intertwined.

"How is everyone?" Megan asked. "How was the

roundup?"

"All's well. It went smoothly. Still, I missed you the whole time. I kept thinking how nice it'd be to sit by the fire under the stars with you. I want that one day—just us, the crickets, and the night sky."

"Me too," she murmured. "Roundups are my favorite—riding out, bringing cattle home. How are the grandparents?"

"Good. Grandpa O'Malley's the one who told me to come. Even paid my way—said it was an early Christmas gift."

Her eyes sparkled as she leaned in and kissed his cheek. "That's so sweet. I'll write and thank him. He must've known how much I miss you."

"He knew how much I missed *you*," Luke said softly, then leaned back to study her. "How's school—really?"

Megan sighed, glancing around the bustling café. "It's hard. I can't focus. I keep drifting off... thinking about you."

"I know the feeling," he said, grinning. "Good thing chores don't take much concentration."

She smiled and kissed his cheek again, her heart full.

"Megan!" Tabitha's voice rang out.

Megan turned to see Tabitha and Clint just inside, both wide-eyed. Clint looked momentarily stunned. Megan flushed crimson. Luke, beside her, looked entirely amused.

"Tabitha!" Megan rose quickly, startled. Luke stood beside her, a steady hand at her back.

"Megan, who's this?" Tabitha asked, voice syrupy as she clung to Clint's arm.

"This is Luke," Megan said. "Luke, this is my friend,

Tabitha."

"Pleased to meet you," Luke said, offering his hand. "Megan's told me what a wonderful friend you've been."

"Nice to meet you too," Tabitha replied, then added, "Funny—Megan's never mentioned *you*."

Megan winced. "Clint, you remember Luke?"

"How could I forget?" Clint said, sizing Luke up before shaking his hand. Expecting a crushing grip, he was surprised by steady strength and control. His shoulders eased.

"Clint," Luke nodded kindly.

"You've met before?" Tabitha asked, blinking.

"Yes," Clint answered smoothly. "I visited Megan once while traveling. Met Luke then."

"Megan, you never told me your beau was—" Tabitha began, but Clint shot her a warning glance.

"What brings you here?" Clint asked.

"I missed Megan," Luke said simply, sliding his arm around her waist. "Thought I'd surprise her."

Tabitha leaned into Clint, whispering, "Why didn't you tell me about him?"

"I don't see why it matters," Clint muttered, though he smiled.

"It matters to *me*," Tabitha said quietly.

Luke, catching the quiet exchange, offered, "Would you like to join us? We've just started."

"We'd be delighted," Tabitha quickly replied.

"Only if you're sure," Clint said, not wanting to intrude.

"Yes—sit," Megan said, her smile genuine.

"It'll give me a chance to get to know Megan's friends," Luke added, smiling.

"Then I'd love some coffee," Clint replied, removing his coat and helping Tabitha with hers.

They took their seats, the men sitting across from each other.

"They'll have coffee and the same pastries we ordered," Luke told the waitress.

As she walked away, Luke leaned in. "So, what made you both want to become teachers?"

The waitress was back, pouring fresh coffee and setting warm pastries before them, before anyone could reply.

Tabitha added sugar and tapped her spoon against the rim of her cup. "My parents thought teaching was a respectable profession for a woman. So, here I am."

"Very nice," Luke said, watching her with polite interest. He turned to Clint. "And you?"

"I come from a line of newspapermen—*The Sun Tribune*," Clint said, taking a bite of Danish.

"I know it. I read it often," Luke replied, sipping from his cup.

"Well, I didn't want to follow the family path. Journalism has its place, but I'd rather shape minds than headlines. I want to teach at a university—guide future authors, inventors, thinkers. Shape the future."

Luke nodded with quiet respect. "That sounds noble."

"Clint's very smart," Tabitha added proudly. "He could do anything." Then, with a curious tilt of her head, "And you, Luke? What do *you* want to be?"

"I want to be a good husband and father," Luke said without hesitation. "I've had strong examples—both my Indian and adopted fathers. They taught me to lead with love, strength, and wisdom. I want to be a man my children admire, a partner who cherishes his wife." His gaze lingered on Megan.

"I want that too—someday," Clint said, nodding. "A family of my own."

Tabitha leaned forward, a hint of a smirk. "That's lovely, but I meant... profession."

Megan blinked at the shift in tone, surprised. Luke didn't flinch.

"I'll likely keep ranching—it's how I was raised. Or live as my ancestors did, as a hunter and warrior. My people didn't need professions in the white man's sense—we lived in harmony with the land. I've also been trained in the ancient ways of healing." He turned to Megan. "But above all, my greatest role will be caring for my wife and children."

He took Megan's hand, her eyes shimmered.

"That's noble," Clint said quietly. In that moment, he understood—Megan had chosen a man of rare honor.

Tabitha shrugged, nibbling her pastry, clearly unmoved.

Luke turned back to Clint. "Do you know why Megan wants to teach?"

"She's never said," Clint admitted.

Luke's voice gentled. "She wants to teach Indian children on a reservation—to keep them from being sent to distant boarding schools where everything is stripped away. I was lucky—I only had to spend two years there before I graduated. What she's doing is brave. It matters." He looked at Megan, his expression full of pride. "She could've stayed home and married. But she came here."

Tabitha's eyes filled. She reached for her handkerchief. "I didn't know. I'm sorry. No child should ever..."

"We're all proud of her," Clint said. "She's devoted. The reservation's lucky to have her."

Just then, Gwen and Richard entered, scanning the café.

"Hi, everyone!" Gwen called, eyes settling on Luke.

Megan stood. "Gwen, Richard—this is Luke, my beau."

Luke rose and shook their hands. Both looked surprised, then smiled warmly.

"Pull up some chairs," he offered. "Now that I've met most of Megan's friends, we can finally order lunch."

"Not *all* of them," Megan said, waving toward the door. "Eileen! Tyler! Come join us!"

As they approached, she added, "Luke, these are my dear friends Eileen and Tyler."

Luke shook their hands with ease. "What a wonderful group," Luke said. "Let's pull the tables together."

Soon, tables were joined, lunch was ordered, and the earlier tension melted into conversation and laughter. Over steaming soup and fresh bread, the gathering found its rhythm.

When the plates were cleared, Luke stood and offered his hand around the table. "It was a pleasure. But I'd like to steal Megan away."

Knowing smiles followed them as she slipped her arm through his and stepped outside.

From the window, the others watched the couple walk away—side by side, into the golden autumn sunlight.

# Chapter 10

## Fall Semester

"So, what should we do?" Luke asked, as they stepped from the cafe. "We've got the whole day."

Megan smiled. "I want to show you the University—so you'll know the places I write about."

"You sure you won't be embarrassed?" he teased, though something earnest flickered beneath.

"I'm not," she said gently, a flush rising.

"Then why haven't you told your friends about me? Especially that I'm Indian."

"I don't need to explain your heritage," she replied, voice low but firm. "It doesn't matter what they think. I don't see you as just Shoshone. I see all of you—the man I love. That's all anyone needs to know."

His expression softened. "Alright. I'll go wherever you want. I'm just glad to be with you."

He offered his arm, and she slipped hers through.

They wandered the University grounds. The tall gray building gleamed under the sun. Inside, their footsteps echoed through cold halls. They peeked into a grand auditorium with vaulted ceilings and polished benches, passed a busy dining hall, and classrooms filled with chalkboards, maps, and murmurs.

The library captivated Luke. Rows of worn books filled the air with ink and parchment. Megan pointed out rare volumes in a reverent hush.

Upstairs, they passed labs and dorms. At her door, Megan hesitated before opening it. The room looked barren—until he saw the small blue glass bird on the sill.

"The *Bluebird of Happiness*," she said. "It reminds me of you. Now we have a matching pair."

Downstairs, they explored the basement—one side earthy with test plants, the other glittering with ore and minerals. Luke admired how every corner had purpose.

"Thank you for showing me your world," he said as they stepped outside. "It's a wonderful school. Too bad they don't admit Indians—or I'd consider enrolling," he added with a playful smile.

"Maybe one day they will," Megan said, hope lighting her eyes.

"Not for a long time," he murmured, watching the wary looks cast their way.

They sat on a bench beneath a tree, its fiery leaves spinning to the ground like falling embers.

"Luke," Megan said dreamily, "you know what I'd love to do?"

"What's that?" he asked, matching her playful tone.

"Go riding. Could we rent horses? Take an afternoon ride?"

"That sounds perfect," he said, then paused, eyeing her dress. "But you'll want to change. That's too fine for trail dust."

Megan laughed and rose, taking his hand. "I'll be quick. Let's pack a picnic too—I want every minute I can get with you."

Back in her room, she changed into a brown wool skirt and jacket—practical, but still pretty.

They rented two copper-colored mares, sleek and strong. After packing food into saddlebags, Megan mounted and followed Luke out of the livery yard. A stableman pointed them toward the eastern mountains she often admired from her dorm window.

An hour's ride brought them to the foothills, where the world grew quiet and wild. The peaks rose like a painted tapestry—crimson and gold streaked with evergreens. The air was crisp and clean, smelling of dry leaves and sun-warmed earth.

They stopped on a hillside and spread out a blanket. Below, the valley stretched wide—amber fields, cattle grazing, the town a shimmer in the distance. They unpacked their lunch as a bee drifted past and settled on a wildflower. Above them, aspen leaves shimmered like golden coins.

"It's so peaceful," Megan said, taking a bite, eyes fixed on the horizon.

Luke leaned back on the blanket, an apple in hand. "I could live in a place like this. It feels like home."

Megan smiled, savoring the hush between them. "It does."

She rolled onto her side, propped on her elbow, facing him.

Luke turned to meet her gaze. "All I think about is making a home with you. Building a ranch and raising kids. That's my dream."

Sunlight brushed her cheek, setting her eyes aglow, her ebony hair spilling in glossy waves.

"You really are the most beautiful woman I've ever seen."

"Oh, Luke," she whispered, blushing. "You say the

sweetest things. I want all of that too. And I believe we'll have it, one day."

She reached up, fingers gently tracing his smooth jaw. "Why don't you have to shave?"

"It's just how we're made. Do you mind?" he asked, eyes closing at her touch.

"No. I like it."

She cupped his cheek and kissed him—slow, lingering. A low sound escaped him, a breath of longing. He slipped a hand behind her head and drew her in, this kiss deeper.

They pulled apart breathless, hearts racing.

"You're going to drive me wild," he said, lying back to gaze at the sky.

"Sorry," she teased, not meaning it. She nestled beside him, fingers laced through his. "I just want to savor every moment with you."

"Megan, you shock me." Luke turned to her, eyes dancing. Her hair fanned around her, her curves soft beneath her dress. "What happened to the shy girl I knew a month ago?"

"She's growing up. I'll be twenty soon," she said, teasing. "Does it bother you that I kissed you first?"

"Not one bit. I love it. I like a woman who knows what she wants." His smile hinted at a deeper desire.

"Well then," she laughed, "just wait until we're married."

The words made her pulse flutter. She longed for the day they could love without restraint.

"I can't wait," he said softly. "To hold you as my wife—that's my dream."

He kissed her again, with deep tenderness. He drew

back, as a single tear slipped into her hair.

"What's wrong?" he asked, brushing it away.

"Nothing. Everything's perfect. I just don't want it to end. This has been the best day."

Luke studied her, his gaze full of love. "I'm so glad I came. It's the happiest I've been in a long time. And we still have tomorrow. I don't leave until evening—we can ride again."

"I can't. I've got too much studying. If I don't start tonight, I'll fall behind." She hesitated. "Will you come to church with me, then help me study?"

"I'd love to. Sounds like another perfect day—with my Megan."

Their ride back passed too quickly. The sun dipped behind the hills, the air turned cool. At the university steps, Luke kissed her one last time. He climbed into a waiting carriage and rode toward the city lights to secure a room for the night.

The next day passed in a quiet blur. Church was held in the university's grand auditorium, morning light streaming through tall windows. Megan and Luke sat shoulder to shoulder, sharing a hymnal. His thumb brushed hers during the sermon and they held hands through the prayers.

Afterward, they strolled to the café, boots crunching over windblown leaves. Inside, they talked and laughed over bowls of potato soup and soft biscuits.

That afternoon, they slipped into the library's hush. Megan laid out her notes and tried to concentrate, but her eyes kept drifting to Luke, reading beside her, brow furrowed, lips curled in a smile whenever he caught her looking.

As twilight fell, they emerged into the crisp air. Luke's carriage waited.

"One more month," Luke said, forcing cheer into his voice. "Thanksgiving, then Christmas. We can do this."

"We can," Megan murmured. "Tell Grandpa, thank you. Travel safe, Luke. I love you."

She clung to him, arms wrapped tight around his neck.

"I love you so much," he whispered. He kissed her deeply, then stepped away before he lost the will to go. As the carriage pulled away, he leaned out, waving until she faded from view. He sat back, eyes closed, holding on to the warmth of her last embrace.

Megan watched until the carriage disappeared. Then she turned, slipped quietly inside, and climbed the stairs. Passing Tabitha without a word, she lay down fully dressed, curled to one side. She pressed her face into the pillow and wept.

She was already missing him more than she could bear.

***

The next month passed in a blur of textbooks, notes, and longing. Megan counted the days until she could go home for Thanksgiving break. At last, the morning came. She stood in the university's front lobby, watching from the arched window for the carriage to arrive.

"I'll bet you're excited to get home," Clint said, stepping beside her.

She turned, smiling.

He thought she looked regal, untouchable—like a Snow Queen. A vision of winter elegance in her sapphire cloak, ebony hair and emerald eyes framed by the tall windows and gray stone walls.

"Yes, very," she said. "Are you?"

"A little. Holidays can be stressful. The paper never sleeps." He pulled his coat tighter, feeling a chill—the outside world blurred in white and shadow. How could he explain that seeing her every day—so close, yet out of reach—was its own kind of ache?

"Won't you miss Tabitha?" Megan asked, glancing around. It was rare to see him without her.

"I'm sorry for how she treated you and Luke," he said. "I never got the chance to apologize."

Megan's voice softened. "I don't understand why she acted that way. We've been friends for so long...and then to be so cruel. I guess she doesn't like him."

"I don't think it's about Luke," Clint said gently. "I think...she's jealous. Things come easily to you—your beauty, your kindness, the way people love you. I think it's hard for Tabitha to accept."

Megan blinked. "You really think that? That's crazy. She has everything—she's smart, beautiful. She has you."

Clint gave a quiet, bitter laugh. "She doesn't hate you. But jealousy's poison. I've tried to make her feel like she's enough…" He hesitated. "Honestly...I'm still jealous of Luke. I've tried to move on, but no one will ever be like you."

His voice dropped. "Have a good holiday."

Before she could answer, he turned and walked away, the truth finally spoken.

Megan stood frozen. His words echoed in her mind. Then the carriage pulled up, breaking the spell. She crossed the icy stones, her cloak catching the wind. After handing over her bags, she waited her turn, then climbed aboard. At the top step, she paused, glancing back at the towering stone façade before closing the door behind her.

Upstairs, Clint stood at the window, watching her go.

"Goodbye, my queen," he whispered. "I'll miss you." Then he turned and went to pack.

***

Megan stepped off the train into Cheyenne's crisp air. Before she could take a full breath, Luke was there— grinning, arms wide.

"Megan! You're home!"

He lifted her off her feet, spinning her with joy before pulling her into a tight embrace.

She clung to him, burying her face in his coat. Around them swirled noise and motion, but they stood still, wrapped in each other.

"Oh, Luke. It's been too long," she whispered, breath catching. Tears spilled as she breathed in his familiar scent.

"Let's get you home. Everyone's waiting." He slid an arm around her and took her bags.

***

Megan savored every moment of break—home and the steady warmth of Luke beside her. She spent hours in the kitchen with her mother preparing the holiday feast while catching up on classes and ranch news.

On Thanksgiving Day, the family bundled into the wagon and drove to Grandma and Grandpa Hartford's. The house swelled with voices and laughter—uncles, aunts, and cousins filling every room. Later, Bart and Bea's family joined, adding to the joyful chaos.

137

One quiet evening, after the boys were asleep, Megan curled up with Luke on the sofa near the stone hearth. A thick quilt draped over them, a book open across their laps. Pa strummed his guitar while Ma crocheted, the soft rhythm of her hook and the crackle of fire filling the warm silence.

Outside, winter pressed close. But inside was peace. Megan couldn't imagine anything better—except sharing this in her own home someday.

Eventually, Ma and Pa headed to bed. Luke would sleep on the sofa again, Megan in her old room. She knew she should turn in, but stayed nestled at his side, content.

Luke read aloud, his voice low and steady, one arm around her, fingers brushing her cheek. Lulled by warmth and firelight, Megan drifted to sleep with a smile.

Much later, she woke to glowing embers. Luke had fallen asleep, head tipped back, breathing slow and deep. She gently slipped from beneath his arm, eased his legs onto the sofa, and tucked a pillow beneath his head. He sighed and shifted but didn't wake.

Megan brushed his hair back and kissed his cheek before wrapping the quilt around him. She stirred the fire, added a log, and watched sparks leap back to life. With one last look at his peaceful face, she padded softly down the hall to bed.

****

The days passed too quickly. Soon Megan was back on the train, the prairie cold, flat, and endless beneath a slate-gray sky. The land felt as empty as the ache in her chest, each mile pulling her farther from Luke.

She leaned into the glass, her breath fogging the pane

as the rhythmic clatter filled the silence. The warmth of home already felt like a dream. One more long month—but Christmas promised two full weeks where her heart belonged.

***

December on the ranch was bitter cold, though not as harsh as winters past. Luke was grateful—for the barn's shelter, the stacked firewood, and the full pantry. As he worked, memories of lean seasons stirred—days of cold and hunger with his tribe. He thought of his father and those still on the reservation, quietly praying they had enough to endure.

Back at school, Megan poured herself into her studies, finishing final exams just a day before heading home. Though her grades would come after break, she felt confident. Before boarding the train, she bought a few small gifts and tucked them at the bottom of her trunk.

***

Megan stepped into the cottage, bag in hand, Luke close behind with another.

"Ma, I'm home!" she called, joy warming her voice.

Cassie rushed in, gathering her in a tight embrace.

"Megan, finally!" she said, voice thick. She kissed her cheek and held on. Winter had dragged without Megan. Cassie loved her boys, but nothing compared to having her daughter home—a woman to talk to, to share the little things with.

"Oh Ma, it smells heavenly in here," Megan said, slipping off her gloves and hood.

"Vegetable beef stew simmering and rolls just about ready. You made it just in time," Cassie said, smiling

139

through her tears. "Oh, I've missed you."

Luke set the bag down. "I'll grab your trunk."

"Thank you, Luke," Megan said, smiling warmly.

"My pleasure," he replied, stepping back into the swirling snow.

Cassie helped her out of her cloak. "How was the trip?"

"Lovely. The sleigh ride home was perfect—just me, Luke, thick blankets, and jingling harness bells." Her smile lingered.

Cassie stirred the stew. "I can't wait to catch you up. I saved the best stories for when you got here. You must be starving."

"I'm always hungry for your cooking, Ma," Megan said, heart swelling.

She carried her bags into her room to begin unpacking.

Luke returned a moment later, setting her trunk beneath the window. "That's everything. Want help?"

"No, I've got it," she said, elbowing him playfully as he leaned in to peek.

"No peeking!" she added, shielding the gifts.

He laughed. "If you say so." Leaning in, he kissed her cheek and stole another glance.

Megan laughed, heart full—she was home.

***

One evening after supper, the family gathered to decorate the Christmas tree. Pa and Luke had brought home a perfect evergreen, its scent filling the house. The boys strung popcorn and cranberry garlands while Megan and Cassie baked gingerbread men. They hung homemade ornaments, candy canes, and cookies, crowned it with a silver star, and tucked colorful gifts beneath the branches. White candles nestled in the boughs, waiting to glow.

The hearth was trimmed with pine boughs, red bows and holly berries. Below, hung hand-stitched stockings. Pa had even hung mistletoe—stealing a kiss from Ma whenever he could.

On Christmas Eve, they loaded in the wagon and rode to Grandma and Grandpa Hartford's for their traditional supper and devotional.

The house bustled with family—Clancy and Joy's children, Beth and John's, Grandma and Grandpa O'Malley. After supper, everyone gathered by the fire, the children's eyes dancing. Grandpa Hartford settled into his chair to read the Christmas story.

Luke gently squeezed Megan's hand.

"Are you thinking about your family?" she whispered.

"Yes," he said, voice thick. "I miss them...but this is where I want to be." He kissed her cheek softly.

***

On Christmas morning, Johnathan burst into Megan's room.

"Megan! Wake up—it's Christmas!"

She groaned, pulling the covers over her head. "It's four-thirty. Go back to bed!"

"Pa said if I woke everyone, we could open presents. Please?" He tapped her shoulder. "Please! Please!"

She sighed, smiling despite herself. "Alright, give me a minute."

Throwing off the covers, she gasped at the cold, then dressed quickly in a warm skirt and vest. Braiding her hair, she wrapped a shawl around her shoulders and stepped into the kitchen, where warmth and the scent of coffee greeted her.

"Merry Christmas, Megan!" came the chorus.

"Merry Christmas!" she answered, smiling at the candlelit tree, casting a magical glow over the room.

Luke met her with a hug. She smiled up at him, heart fluttering.

"Everyone's awake now!" Johnathan called through Ma and Pa's door.

They emerged moments later, met with warm mugs and cheerful chatter.

"Merry Christmas!" Pa boomed.

"Merry Christmas, Ma and Pa!" came the joyful reply.

"We already did the chores," Johnathan added proudly.

"Well, isn't that a fine surprise," Ed said, beaming.

"Can we open presents now?" Johnathan begged Ma.

"I suppose that's up to Pa," she teased.

Ed lifted his coffee with a twinkle in his eye. "Are you sure you're ready?"

"I'm sure!" Johnathan bounced.

Cassie pulled her shawl tighter. "We could wait until after breakfast…"

"No!" came the unanimous shout.

Laughing, she relented. "Alright, let's open them. We'll eat after."

Luke was already at the tree, retrieving a small gift nestled among the branches. The room quieted as Ma and Pa settled into their chairs, coffee in hand. Megan sat between her brothers—Johnathan on the floor, eyes locked on the pile of presents.

"I want Megan to open this one first," Luke said, handing her a blue-wrapped box, eyes shining.

She raised an eyebrow, heart pounding. "What is it?"

Inside, she found a small wooden box. Her breath caught as she opened the lid—a ring rested in blue velvet.

"Luke…" she whispered, eyes meeting his.

He was already kneeling.

"Megan, you're my dream come true. I promise to love and honor you for the rest of my life. Will you marry me?" His voice trembled.

The room stilled. Ma and Pa exchanged stunned glances.

Tears filled Megan's eyes. "Yes," she whispered, throwing her arms around him. "Oh, yes!"

Luke's face lit up as he kissed her cheek and gently brushed away her tears.

"I love you, Megan—more than I can say. You're my best friend, and I want to spend forever with you."

"That's all I've ever wanted," she breathed, their lips meeting in a tender kiss.

"Yay!" Johnathan cheered, making everyone laugh.

Luke slipped the ring onto her finger as the family erupted in celebration, offering hugs and congratulations.

The last gifts were opened, stockings emptied, but the day's greatest surprise lingered in the air.

Later, in the kitchen, Megan and Cassie prepared breakfast, the scent of baking muffins filling the room. Megan returned to the front room, and Luke pulled her close on the sofa, his arm draped around her shoulders.

Megan gazed at the gold ring on her finger, the garnet glinting in the morning light.

"I can't believe it—we're engaged," she whispered, resting her head on Luke's shoulder. "I'm so happy."

Luke smiled. "I've been thinking about this since October. I couldn't wait until you graduated. And what better day, than Christmas—the day dreams come true?"

"It's perfect," she said, admiring the teardrop stone.

He took her hand, brushing a thumb over the ring. "It looks beautiful on you."

Her smile deepened. "I love it because you picked it." She squeezed his hand, heart full. "But I love you more."

"I love you too," he whispered.

She tilted her head back, lips meeting his in a sweet, lingering kiss.

From the kitchen, Ma called, "Come on, lovebirds—time to eat!"

Laughing, they rose together.

Luke paused, admiring his new pocket watch, reading the engraving: *To my One and Only, With Love, Megan.*

"I'm glad you like it," she whispered, squeezing his hand as they joined Ma.

The kitchen was filled with the scent of bacon, fried eggs, and cornbread muffins.

"Breakfast is ready!" Ma called, slipping off her apron.

Johnathan leapt up, abandoning his toys, while David closed his book and Kurt set aside his whittling. One by one, they gathered at the table.

Outside, soft snow drifted down, blanketing the world in a bed of white. Inside, the house overflowed with love and the joyful spirit of Christmas.

# Chapter 11

## New Year's Eve 1889

News of Luke and Megan's engagement swept through town like wildfire. Friends and family came in a steady stream with warm congratulations.

A few days before New Year's Eve, Bart and Bea Clark arrived, cheeks pink from the cold.

"We couldn't be happier for you," Mr. Clark said, shaking Luke's hand before drawing Megan into a gentle embrace. "Best news we've had all year."

"That's why we want to help you celebrate," Bea added. "We know you're going to the ball and wondered if we might outfit you both. Just an old suit of Andrew's and a gown I wore once. If you don't mind hand-me-downs, it would mean the world to us."

Luke swallowed hard at the mention of Andrew. "I'm not sure we can accept something so generous."

"We were just going to wear our Sunday best," Megan said softly, eyes glistening from their thoughtfulness.

"They're only clothes," Mr. Clark said, taking her hand. "But it would bring us joy to see them worn again."

Megan glanced at Luke. He nodded.

"Then we'd be honored," she said, stepping into their arms.

"Truly," Luke added, clasping Bart's hand. "Thank you both."

***

On New Year's Eve, Megan prepared with care. After a warm, scented bath, Cassie curled her thick dark hair into glossy ringlets, sweeping them up at the sides with gold combs.

"I guess I should put the dress on," she said, rising from the chair.

Cassie tightened the corset and helped her into petticoats before lifting the dress out of the box. Megan's breath caught.

Champagne silk tulle shimmered in the lamplight, adorned with gold lace and beadwork. The low bodice and lace-trimmed cap sleeves framed the sweep of her shoulders; the skirt fell in intricate patterns, pearl buttons trailing down the back to a modest bustle and train. Matching gloves lay folded beside it.

"Oh Ma…it's so grand," Megan whispered, pressing the gown to her chest.

"It's exquisite," Cassie said. "Bea has remarkable taste. I wouldn't be surprised if that silk came from Paris."

Megan's nerves fluttered. "What if I spoil it? It must've cost a fortune."

"She wouldn't have offered it if she didn't trust you," Cassie said gently. "Now let's get you dressed. Luke's not going to believe his eyes."

In the washroom, Luke buttoned Andrew's black suit over a cream shirt, gold vest, and neat cravat. He slipped his pocket watch into place, combed his hair until it gleamed, and tied it back with a silk ribbon. Tonight, he felt like a city gentleman.

Once ready, he waited with Ed and the boys until the

bedroom door opened. Heads turned.

"Megan," Luke breathed, taking her hand and spinning her slowly. "You look gorgeous."

"You look very dignified yourself," she said, blushing.

"Wow!" Johnathan said. "You look like a fairy princess."

Ed's eyes misted. "Just like your ma when we married." He kissed Cassie's cheek. "She's the spitting image of you."

"It was generous of Bea to lend the dress," Cassie said. "That silk is divine—and even more so on her."

Kurt nudged Luke. "Looks like you're getting married tonight."

"I wish," Luke said with a grin. They had promised to wait until Megan graduated, but tonight made the wait feel impossibly long.

"There won't be another girl as pretty at the dance," David added quietly, wishing he'd asked someone to go.

"Thanks, everyone. You sure know how to make a girl feel special," Megan said, sliding on her gloves.

"It's time to take the princess to the ball," Luke replied, helping her into her cloak. After hugs and goodbyes, he escorted her to the sleigh.

The night was crisp and clear, stars scattered across a vast winter sky. Moonlight cast a silver sheen over the snow as Luke tucked blankets around them. The runners whispered over packed snow, sleigh bells jingling in time with the horse's gait.

"I can't believe this is real," Megan murmured, resting her head on his shoulder. "This has got to be the best night of my life."

"Only one better," Luke said softly. "The day I marry you."

"I agree," she whispered, lifting her face to meet his lips.

Town lights soon shimmered ahead, the streets alive with music, carriages, and celebration. Luke stopped before the Music Hall, helping her down and keeping her gown clear of the snow. Two white columns framed the tall doors, a grand wreath with garlands and red velvet bows adorned the entrance.

At the top of the steps, Megan paused. She hadn't been to a New Year's Eve Ball since Andrew. Luke squeezed her hand. "It's going to be fun. Don't worry."

Inside, they left their winter layers with the attendant. The lobby glowed with red-velvet chairs, paneled walls, crimson carpet, and a golden chandelier suspended from the vaulted ceiling. Music swelled as laughter echoed, and guests streamed in from the street.

The ballroom doors opened to a dazzling sight—couples sweeping across a polished floor beneath sparkling chandeliers, an orchestra playing in the corner, a towering Christmas tree at the center. Gold wallpaper, velvet drapes, and garlands crowned every archway.

"It's like a palace," Luke murmured.

"Like a fairy tale castle—and we are the king and queen," Megan said, wrapping her arm through his.

"You are my queen, always." He rested his hand over hers, tender and protective, where it lay on his arm.

"And you are my king," she whispered, eyes gleaming.

Jeremy and Penny appeared in the crowd. "Don't you two look sharp," Jeremy said, shaking Luke's hand.

Penny's eyes lit on Megan's gown. "That's stunning."

"Thank you. You look lovely," Megan replied, noting the peach gown and blossoms woven through her friend's hair.

The orchestra struck a slow polka. "May I have this dance?" Luke asked.

She placed her hand in his, and he led her onto the floor. Skirts swirled, music lifting around them. They had danced before, but tonight felt different—vivid, magical. Her eyes shone as he guided her, his heart full at the sight of her joy.

When the song ended, they clapped with the others, cheeks flushed with excitement.

A fast Viennese waltz struck up, and Luke grinned—thankful Megan had taught him the steps. The lively tempo came easily; he spun her in tight circles, dipping her before sweeping her back up. The room swirled with color, skirts fluttering like petals around black-suited men.

The final note faded to applause. Laughing and breathless, they drifted toward the refreshment tables.

In the far corner, a white-draped table stood beneath a swan ice sculpture, a crystal punch bowl glowing at its base. Platters of cookies and pastries lined one end; at the other, a basket brimmed with festive paper tubes—crimson and gold, cream and silver—tied at both ends.

Luke picked up a crimson one. "What are these?"

"They're party favors. Christmas crackers. Hold the other end...pull!"

The tube snapped, spilling out candies, a gold paper crown, and a faux pink-stone ring. Laughing, Luke slid it onto her finger. "Perfect—now you've a ring on each hand."

"It's all I've ever wanted," she teased, holding it to the light.

He handed her a tiny scroll. She unrolled it, then passed it to him. Luke read aloud, "'The sweet crimson rose with its beautiful hue is not half so deep as my passion for you...whilst my heart lives, you will still be its queen.'" He met her eyes. "That's exactly how I feel."

Her cheeks warmed. "Oh, Luke…"

He tucked the note into his vest. "My queen…"

Megan reached for a silver-and-cream cracker. "Your turn."

This time, candies and a glossy red marble tumbled out. Luke scooped them up, along with another scroll. He grinned. "'The love of your life is right in front of your eyes.' But I already knew that." He kissed her cheek.

"Luke! Someone might see."

"I don't care. You're my fiancée."

She laughed, then read the slip herself. "It's perfect! You have to keep it—it's good luck."

"I don't need luck," he said, patting her hand. "I already have you."

Megan kissed his cheek in return.

"Now who's making a scene?" Luke teased. "You'll get us kicked out."

Megan giggled. "Let's get some punch and sit."

Jeremy and Penny reached the refreshment table as Luke and Megan turned away, flushed and glowing.

"You must've gotten something good," Jeremy said with a wink, having seen their kiss.

"Megan got a pretty ring," Luke replied as she held

out her hand, the oversized bauble catching the light.

"Oh, I love it! I hope I get one too," Penny laughed.

"Go open yours, then come sit by us," Luke said, nodding toward a table near the dance floor.

"We'll be right there," Jeremy replied, and he and Penny each plucked a cracker from the basket.

Luke and Megan settled beside a velvet-draped pillar. Music drifted through the hall, mingling with laughter and clinking glass. Megan sipped punch and nibbled a cookie, careful to keep her gloves clean.

Moments later, Jeremy and Penny joined them, plates in hand. Jeremy now sported a crumpled silver crown, absurd atop his blond hair.

"Nice party hat," Luke teased.

"No, I came with this—it's formal attire," Jeremy said with mock dignity, making Penny giggle.

"I got one too," Megan said, lifting her gold crown.

Penny opened her palm to reveal a tiny bee pin, two candies, and a whistle.

"Oh, how sweet," Megan said, fastening the pin to Penny's ruffled peach bodice.

"How do I look?" Penny asked, beaming.

"Like a flower even the bees can't resist," Jeremy replied, kissing her cheek.

Luke and Megan shared a look of quiet joy. Being surrounded by love felt like standing in sunlight.

After their treats, the four returned to the floor for a lively foxtrot—slow, slow, quick-quick. Luke's hand rested firmly at Megan's back, their steps effortless, her skirts swirling like wind-blown petals. They ended breathless and smiling.

A poised woman with silver curls touched Megan's

shoulder. "You two dance beautifully. Did you study somewhere?"

"No," Megan said politely.

Luke leaned in, smiling. "No lessons—we just love dancing."

"Well…" The woman eyed him closer, then smirked. "I didn't think they taught ballroom on a reservation."

Luke's smile faded, jaw tightening. "You'd be surprised what I learned there. Manners, for one—something you clearly missed." He took Megan's hand and walked away.

Once out of earshot, he exhaled. "Why do they always have to say something?"

"I don't know. But she did say we were good dancers," Megan offered, squeezing his hand.

"It burns me—like I'm not supposed to be educated or refined."

Megan touched his cheek. "You are. You've shown me dances most people don't even know. They have deep meaning and take skill."

His expression softened as she guided him to sit at a table, his hand still cradling hers.

"I could show you one now," he teased, rising.

"You could," she laughed, pulling him back to sit, "but save it for another day."

His eyes glinted. "Only if you promise to dance *my* dances when we visit my tribe."

"I suppose," she said, picturing herself awkwardly stomping around a bonfire.

"Good. I can see it now—you in a white buckskin dress, dancing on our wedding day." His eyes softened at the memory of his dream.

"I doubt I'll look beautiful in buckskin," she teased. "Don't I look beautiful now?"

"Are you kidding? You're the most beautiful woman here. But yes—you'll be beautiful then too." He gazed at her, almost seeing it.

Her smile faded. "Wait—you said *on our wedding day*. Aren't we getting married here?"

"I told you about my dream. You wore a beaded dress with a fringe and belt. I'm sure it was at my tribe's village," he said earnestly.

"I want to get married here—with Ma, Pa, and everyone. Don't you?"

"Well, yes. But I want my father to marry us. He's a holy man. He can wed us on the reservation, with my people." Luke's brow furrowed at her hesitation.

"What about Reverend Gather? You're still a church member. Can't he do it here?" Megan asked, keeping her voice even.

"Hey! Why'd you leave so fast?" Jeremy called as he and Penny approached, a bit breathless.

"Just needed a break," Megan said quickly.

"It's nearly midnight—we wanted to ring in the New Year together," Penny added.

"Us too," Megan said, brightening. "Come sit with us."

"You sure? Looked like you were in the middle of something," Penny said gently.

"We were just talking wedding plans," Megan replied with a smile.

Luke forced a cheerful tone. "Sit—we'll wait together."

"I remember those days—so many decisions," Penny

said.

"We haven't planned much," Megan admitted, taking Luke's hand. He brushed his thumb over her glove, smiling softly.

"So what's been decided?" Jeremy asked.

"Nothing," Luke laughed.

"There's time—you're waiting until Megan graduates, right?" Jeremy said.

"That's right," Megan answered, hope threading her words.

"All I care about is marrying Megan. Where or how doesn't matter—only that it's soon," Luke said, eyes steady on hers.

"That's what counts," Penny said warmly.

"You had it easy," Megan said, gaze drifting. "You're from here—same faith, same pastor. No choice about who or where." She recalled their wedding at the little church—simple and beautiful.

"That's true—but so are you," Penny said, squeezing Megan's hand.

"Not exactly," Megan added after a pause. "Luke's family lives on the Wind River Reservation. His father's a Shoshone holy man, and Luke wants him to perform the ceremony. I thought we'd do it in Cheyenne, so our families could be here—and have it performed by the proper authority."

"What? You don't think my father has proper authority?" Luke asked, voice tightening.

"Sure, in a way. Can't you see? It's not the same as an ordained minister," she said gently.

"No. You don't understand—he *is* authorized. Tam Apo—God, Our Father—*gave* my father the gift to be a holy man. He has every right to marry us."

"Hey, it's almost midnight," Penny said quickly, reading the tension. "Let's dance."

"Come on. Enjoy the night. It's almost a new year," Jeremy said, leading Penny toward the floor.

Luke checked his pocket watch. Five minutes to go. The inscription caught his eye—*To my One and Only, with love, Megan.* He looked up.

"Megan?" His voice softened as he rose, hand outstretched.

She met his gaze, eyes shimmering, lips pressed tight. Still, she placed her hand in his.

"I want to dance the last dance with the most beautiful woman here. My one and only. My queen." His voice was soft, coaxing.

The orchestra began a waltz. Luke bowed; Megan curtsied. It was impossible to stay upset when he looked at her like that—so tender, so proud. His hand at her waist was warm and steady. A thrill passed through her. They glided across the polished floor, her golden gown catching the chandelier's glow.

They circled the Christmas tree, candlelight flickering over silver tinsel and glass ornaments. Megan's cheeks flushed, her heart rising with the music.

Luke couldn't look away. She was radiant, her eyes shining up at him.

"I'm sorry," he murmured.

Her eyes glistened. "You don't need to be. I love you. As long as I'm in your arms, nothing else matters."

The music slowed. "One minute to the New Year!" someone called.

The room quieted to soft murmurs.

"I never meant to argue," Luke said, leaning in. "If marrying you, means marrying here, then here it will be. I love you." He pulled her into his arms, not caring who saw.

"I love you too." A tear slipped down her cheek. Then—a thought. "What if we had two weddings? One here, and one with your family?" Her voice was hopeful, tentative.

"Ten, nine, eight..."

"If that's what you want," Luke said thickly, "then it's what I want too."

"Five, four, three..." They held each other's gaze.

"Two, one—Happy New Year!" the crowd roared.

Megan closed her eyes as Luke kissed her—tender at first, then deepening until the world faded to that single, heart-racing moment.

Cheers swelled, horns blared, and confetti drifted down.

"Happy New Year, my love," she whispered.

Luke laughed, sweeping her into his arms and spinning her once before setting her down. "Happy New Year, Megan," he murmured, still holding her close.

***

They rode home through the moonlit cold, the sleigh's runners whispering over snow, the horses' breath curling in the air. Beneath the wool blanket, Megan's gloved hand rested in Luke's as her thoughts drifted over the evening.

She broke the quiet. "Earlier, when you said 'Tam Apo—God, Our Father—*gave* your father the gift to be a holy man,' what did you mean?"

"'Tam Apo' is the Shoshone name for God," Luke

said. "We pray to Him for healing, guidance, blessings—just like we do in church. My people had no Bible, but they followed thirty commandments passed down for generations. So when I taught from Scripture, much of it was already familiar—just by other names."

"I didn't know that," Megan murmured. "All my life I've heard people call Indians pagans, as if they worship many gods."

"That's not true for my people," Luke said gently. "The Shoshone have always worshiped only Tam Apo, the Creator, the Great Spirit. Our ceremonies give thanks, seek guidance, or bring healing. When I taught about Jesus Christ and the Holy Spirit, some believed. Others feared embracing Christianity meant losing our ways. I try to show them we can follow Christ and still honor our customs."

"You've been a missionary in your own way," she said softly. "I see now where your spiritual strength comes from. Your father and grandfather must've shaped you deeply."

"I learned from Ma and Pa, and them too," Luke said. "The tribal prayers and ceremonies only deepened my faith. I just wish I could lead my father to Christ. Maybe one day."

Megan's voice warmed. "I'm sorry I doubted his authority. I understand now why it matters—to be married by him."

Luke smiled. "Now we'll have both—a Christian wedding and a Shoshone one. Double the blessings."

Her eyes brightened suddenly. "Happy birthday, Luke!"

"I'd forgotten." He laughed and thought, *Twenty-*

*four...and finally with the woman I love.*

"Not anymore," she said with certainty. "I'll never let you forget again." She leaned against him. "I love you. Thank you—for being you. My best friend. The love of my life."

Luke's heart swelled. He drew her closer, kissing her hair. "And you," he murmured, breathing in her lavender scent, "are the best birthday gift I'll ever receive."

# *Chapter 12*

## *January 1890*

The new semester loomed, but Megan wasn't ready to leave.

Luke drove her to the depot, holding her tight on the platform, his breath misting in the cold morning air.

"I'll visit for your birthday—three and a half weeks away, and I'll miss you every second until then." He kissed her softly, swallowing the lump in his throat.

"I love you, Luke. I can't wait to be with you—forever." With effort, she stepped away, valise in hand. One lingering look, then she boarded. Tears fell as she waved from the frosted window until the train carried her out of sight.

***

Ranch life without Megan felt hollow. Luke moved through chores with forced cheer, wearing a smile he didn't feel.

One afternoon, while the boys were at school, he rode out with his pa. The biting wind rattled bare branches as they crossed the snowy fields.

"Son, are you happy here?" Ed asked, tugging his coat tighter.

Luke shifted in the saddle. "Why do you ask?"

"You act happy enough, but I know that look. Restless. Maybe now that Megan's gone, you're itching for your own adventure."

He turned Major into the windbreak of a hill, scanning the horizon for stray cattle.

Luke sighed. "I guess I am. Megan's out there growing and learning, while I'm stuck in the same old routine. I love the ranch, but I want a home and land of my own."

Ed nodded. "I remember that feeling when I met Cassie. Got anywhere in mind?"

"We're thinking Laramie. It's quiet, close to the mountains."

Ed stroked his frost-tipped mustache. "Beautiful, but winters are harsher there. Megan will need to be near a town if she's teaching."

"I've thought about that," Luke admitted.

"We'd love to have you close, but we understand, you're forging your own path."

Luke's eyes lit. "When I visited Megan last fall, we rode into the Laramie mountains. It felt right. Peaceful."

Ed smiled. "Your grandpa O'Malley lived there most of his life. Talk to him. He'll know where the best land is."

"I will. Just talking about it gives me hope."

Ed pointed across the field to a dark shape on the hillside. "Let's check that out."

They kicked their horses into a trot. A cow was stuck in a tall drift to her shoulders. Luke lassoed her, tugging until she lurched free. They herded her back to safety before turning home.

"Pa," Luke said as they rode, "could you spare me for a while? I'd like to visit my father before the spring roundup."

"We'd get by," Ed replied. "I know he'd love to

see you—you said he was angry with you for leaving. Perhaps you two could sort things out before the wedding. Any decisions where that'll be?"

"Megan suggested two ceremonies—one here with the minister and one with my father on the reservation. I think he'd be honored."

Ed's eyes warmed. "That *would* mean a lot to him. We'd love to be there for both."

"Really?" Luke's voice caught. "Thank you, Pa."

"We know it's hard balancing both worlds. Your tribe is part of you. We support you."

They slowed as they reached the main road.

"It doesn't feel wrong to have both, but is it?"

"Not at all," Ed said with an understanding smile. "You'd be honoring both families and beliefs—God knows your heart."

A weight eased from Luke's shoulders. "I'm lucky, I've been blessed with two sets of parents. You and Ma mean everything to me." He quickly wiped a tear away.

"Anything for my son." His throat tightened. "We're proud of the man you've become. Whether you live here or not, you'll always be part of us."

***

Megan's first week back at school was bleak—inside and out. Gray skies pressed low, the wind sharp as a blade as she crossed campus. The university's stone halls felt colder still. The thrill of learning had faded, replaced by heavy books, sleepless nights, and a gnawing homesickness. She longed for Luke, for the life they'd begun.

Tabitha's mood only deepened the gloom. Since Clint had ended their courtship after Christmas, she sulked in their quarters, her bitterness evident.

161

One afternoon, Megan sought refuge in a far corner of the library, sunlight spilling shadows over her notes. She was finishing an essay when the chair beside her scraped back. She glanced up—and froze.

Clint.

He reclined back with ease, ankles crossed, arms folded as if he had nowhere else to be.

"So, how's life?" His voice was light, but his expression carried weight.

"It's good." She answered quickly. Since his breakup with Tabitha, he'd all but vanished from their circle. "And you?" she asked.

He hesitated, his gaze drifting to the book-strewn table.

Megan studied his expression. Shadows deepened the hollows beneath his cheekbones, dulling his tousled golden hair, his eyes so deep blue they seemed to hold a storm.

She waited.

Finally, he exhaled. "I couldn't pretend anymore. Tabitha never stopped comparing herself to you—but it only reminded me she *wasn't* you. I told myself she'd change. She didn't. So I ended it. I wanted what you and Luke have. That kind of love."

He paused, choosing his words.

"I won't lie—part of me still hoped. But when I saw you two together, really saw how happy you are... I knew. Tabitha blamed you for everything. I hope she hasn't taken it out on you."

"That explains a lot," Megan said. She remembered Tabitha's forced smile when she'd seen the engagement ring. "I figured it hurt, but she never said much."

"It did hurt," Clint admitted. "Seeing you with a ring—killed my last bit of hope. I'm trying to be happy for you, but I'd pictured a whole life for us. Teaching, a home, children...but that future's gone." He met her eyes, voice raw. "I wish you'd chosen me."

Megan's heart ached for him. "I'm sorry, Clint. You're a good man. Someday, you'll find someone just as right for you. Don't give up—you'll know her when she comes along." She touched his arm lightly.

He searched her face, emotion glinting in his eyes. A year ago, they'd been sweethearts. So much had changed.

"Thank you," he said. "I didn't mean to unload on you. I just feel like I've ruined everything."

"You haven't. Tabitha's hurting, but she'll move on. She even apologized to me for the café incident. And you—you did the right thing. Staying with someone out of obligation would've hurt you both more."

A rueful smile tugged at his lips. "I hope so." Then, more lightly, "You don't have a sister, do you?"

Megan laughed. "No. But maybe look past the pretty faces. Find someone whose soul speaks to yours—that's where love lasts."

"That's what I want. Someone who makes me better."

She smiled, bittersweet. "You'll find her," she said softly. "Or maybe she'll find you—when you least expect it."

Clint rose and squeezed her hand. "You made the right choice, Megan. You could've had an easy life with me, but you chose something better. I envy Luke. I hope he gives you the world."

"He already has," she murmured.

Clint gave a wistful smile and walked away, still astonished at how she'd slipped through his fingers.

***

Luke was coming Saturday to celebrate Megan's birthday—though it wasn't until Monday, the 28th.

Megan stood on the platform as light snow drifted down. She shifted from foot to foot, trembling with anticipation beneath her cloak. It felt like forever since she'd seen him.

In his last letter, Luke said he'd be returning to the reservation after their visit—just two days together. Megan was happy but worry gnawed at her. What was life like there? What if something happened? What if he never came back?

On the train, Luke leaned toward the frosted window, scanning the crowd. His heart sank. She wasn't there. Was she late?

Brakes shrieked. The train shuddered to a stop. He grabbed his bag, tugged on his coat, and stepped out into the swirling snow.

"Luke! Luke!"

Her voice cut through the crowd. His heart leapt. Megan rushed toward him, cloak billowing. He met her in bounding strides, swept her up, and pressed his face to her neck.

"Oh, Megan. I've missed you." He kissed her, slow and aching, breathing in her lavender laced scent.

She clung to him, feeling as if she were falling and flying all at once. "This is the best birthday gift I could ask for."

He tucked her under his arm, shielding her from the wind. "I'm here, and plan to savor every second."

She laughed, light as air. "Where do you want to eat?"

He led her toward the carriages. "Somewhere quieter than the café?" Luke asked, waving to a driver.

"There's the Mountain Rose Inn. Good food—not crowded. And rooms, if you want to stay."

"Perfect. Driver—Mountain Rose Inn, please."

Inside the carriage, Luke pulled her close and kissed her deeply. He parted only a fraction, his breath brushing warmth across her lips.

"I can't get enough of you," he murmured. "Like dry earth drinking spring rain." His fingers gently stroked her cheek, marveling at its softness.

She smiled. "Lucky for you, I brought plenty of rain." She kissed him again, slow and full of feeling.

The carriage jolted to a stop.

"Well, that was fast," Luke said with a laugh.

They stepped inside, the air smelling of pine and home cooking. A fire crackled in the hearth, casting a warm glow across the cozy dining room. The inn had the charm of a rustic chalet—dark beams overhead, framed mountain landscapes, old skis and snowshoes adorning the walls. A few couples lingered at intimate tables, speaking in hushed tones.

They chose a corner table. A waitress brought menus and steaming coffee, promising to return shortly.

"I'll have the country fried steak, mashed potatoes, and gravy," Luke said. "And a side of biscuits."

"Same—minus the biscuits. I'll just steal his," Megan teased.

The waitress soon returned with a basket of hot biscuits, butter, and honey.

"This place is nice," Luke said, taking a buttery bite and sighed. "And the biscuits are even better."

"They always are," Megan said, spreading butter on hers.

"So, how's school?" Luke asked, eyes steady on hers.

"Hardest semester yet," she sighed. "I just want it to be over. Especially now…" She squeezed his hand. "All I want is to be your wife."

His gaze softened. "That's all I think about. Being home's harder than ever. Everything reminds me of you."

"Same here," she whispered. "I still want to teach—but my heart's not in this anymore. Not like before. I just want it to be over."

Luke looked down, thoughtful. "What if we married a few weeks after graduation? Then had the tribal wedding on the reservation—stay for a month or two for our honeymoon. Traditionally, newlyweds live in their own teepee, alone in the mountains."

She leaned in, intrigued.

"After that," he continued, "we could visit my tribe again. See if you'd want to teach there in the fall. What do you think?"

Megan met Luke's deep brown eyes. The thought of living in a teepee might once have seemed foreign, but with him—it felt like a dream.

"I think it sounds wonderful. Just the two of us while the world goes on without us. I can't think of a single reason not to."

Her eyes sparkled. He gave her hand a soft squeeze.

"Perfect." Luke sat straighter, his voice alight with excitement. "I'll take care of everything—even your dress. My aunt will help." He beamed. "And good news—Ma and Pa want to come to both weddings. Isn't that something?"

Relief flooded her. "I can't believe it." Knowing her parents would be there eased the weight of entering Luke's world—its unfamiliar customs and language. At least she wouldn't be the only outsider.

"I knew you'd be happy."

The waitress returned with steaming plates. The scent of crisped beef, savory gravy, and mashed potatoes filled the air.

"Mmm," Luke murmured, already digging in.

They ate slowly, pausing between bites to share ideas about the wedding and their life ahead.

"Did you mention Laramie to Pa?" she asked, dabbing her mouth.

"I did. Then I talked to Grandpa O'Malley—he used to work here as a deputy. Said it was wild back then but quiet now. He remembered the area we liked. Thought it'd make a good homestead. Maybe we could ride out today, see what's available."

"I'd love that."

With lunch finished, Luke left his bag upstairs and joined Megan for a carriage ride to the university. She slipped inside to change into riding clothes while he waited, then headed to the livery and rented horses for the day.

The snow stopped and sunlight broke through the clouds, turning the landscape into shimmering crystals. They rode toward the foothills, weaving through drifts and snow-laden pines, the mountains rising like giants in the distance.

They stopped at their favorite spot. The valley below

lay hushed and white, a dark stream winding through it. They dismounted and led their horses beneath the evergreens, birdsong breaking the stillness.

Luke took it all in. "This would be a beautiful place to build. House facing the valley, trees for shelter. Only five miles from town."

"I love it already," Megan said, arms circling his waist. "We could plant feed crops, raise horses and cattle...Everything we need is here."

He drew her close, resting his chin on her head. "Home is wherever you are. But if this is the place, I'm in."

She smiled up at him. "It's perfect—just like you."

He kissed her softly. "I could say the same."

They spent the afternoon dreaming aloud, sketching their future. That evening, back at the Mountain Rose Inn, their dreams continued through supper.

The carriage waited at the university, while they shared a long, tender kiss before parting.

***

Sunday slipped through their fingers like sand. The morning passed in church—familiar hymns, a comforting sermon—but their hearts remained restless.

Back at the Mountain Rose, Megan's birthday lunch brought warm smiles, roast chicken, baked potatoes, and laughter, though beneath it all lingered a quiet sadness.

After the meal, Luke surprised her with a small stack of gifts, each one carefully chosen by him and his family. Megan unwrapped them slowly, her heart aching with every token of love.

That afternoon, they wandered hand in hand through town, footsteps soft along the snowy boardwalk. Later, they tucked themselves into a quiet corner of the university library, their conversations light, avoiding what loomed ahead.

As the sun dipped low, they stood on the university steps. Megan's hands trembled as she hugged him, holding on as long as possible. With misty eyes and a brave smile, she whispered goodbye.

She watched the carriage disappear toward the station, tears slipping silently down her face. The ache in her chest settled heavy. Two months—it might as well be forever. Worse, he'd be deep in the Wind River Mountains, far from any post. The thought of no letters unsettled her more than she expected.

***

At the station, Luke checked quickly—Wildfire had been safely loaded into the stock car, just as Pa had arranged.

The train would carry him to Rawlins. From there, three or four hard days of riding remained. Though eager to return, parting from Megan weighed heavy. The constant goodbyes were carving lines into his spirit. He only hoped the days would pass swiftly—and that he'd be back by spring roundup.

Beyond Rawlins, winter struck hard. Snow drifted deep; wind cut like a blade. With no teepee or shelter, the bitter nights left him half-frozen, questioning the wisdom of this journey.

But Wildfire remained his comfort—a loyal companion in the frozen silence.

At night, when sleep finally came, he'd dream of Megan—her smile, her voice, the way her eyes lit when she spoke of their future.

Each passing day, his fatigue grew. More than once, he'd let Wildfire wander off course before he'd realized, his mind in a haze. His limbs ached, his face windburned—but he pressed on.

He passed Fort Washakie without stopping, the outpost quiet beneath a snowy sky. One more day, he told himself. Just one more.

And then—he saw it. Smoke curling against the pale horizon, rising from a ring of teepees in Warm Valley. Relief washed over him—amidst exhaustion, joy, and the first true warmth he'd felt in days.

# Chapter 13

# Winter Camp

Snow blanketed the forest clearing where smoke lazily curled from teepees. As Luke approached the tribe's winter camp, familiar sights and sounds wrapped around him like a memory. Children's laughter mingled with the low hum of voices and the rhythm of women at work, filling the air with quiet harmony.

A dog barked sharply. On a rocky outcropping, a young warrior straightened, spotting the lone rider. Luke lifted a hand.

"Aho!" he called in greeting.

Recognition lit the young man's face. "Standing Elk has come!" he shouted, racing down the slope.

A ripple of welcome swept through the village. Fur-wrapped figures offered smiles and embraces. Someone took Wildfire to feed and water, letting Luke make his way to his father's teepee. The flap opened.

Agwai stepped out, broad-shouldered, long black braids silvered at the temples, dark eyes crinkling with joy.

"Father!" Luke rushed forward, embracing him.

Agwai held him close. "Standing Elk, my son. I knew we'd meet again. I saw it in a vision."

Luke's throat tightened. "I've missed you."

"Come—warm yourself," he said, placing a hand on his shoulder.

"Thank you, Father."

Luke followed him into the spacious teepee, where warmth and familiarity wrapped around him. Cedar smoke and sage perfumed the air, animal pelts softened the ground, and above, Agwai's medicine bag and shield hung from the poles. Clay pots and woven baskets lined the walls. Home.

Prairie Rose slipped in behind them. "You bad boy," she teased, wrapping him in a hug. "Leaving me to care for your father all this time!" A tear slipped down her round cheek.

Luke kissed her head, emotion rising. "I missed you too, Aunt Rose."

Prairie Rose was the closest thing Luke had to his Indian mother. After Bluebird's death, she took Agwai in, later welcoming Luke with the same open heart, loving them both as her own. Short and stout, she carried herself with quiet authority—this lodge was her domain. If she said, "Go to sleep," they obeyed. With saintly patience, she cooked and cared tirelessly for Luke, Agwai, her husband Grey Wolf, and their two sons—all under one teepee.

Two Crows and Spotted Calf burst in, laughing. Now sixteen and seventeen, they were taller but just as wild as Luke remembered.

"Hey!" Luke chuckled as they tackled him with rough hugs.

He hadn't seen them in over a year—they'd been at boarding school when he left. Though their hair was short now, they wore fur and buckskins once more. Both boys, sharp and fluent in English, still idolized Luke.

"Alright, alright—I missed you too," he said, tousling their hair.

Aunt Rose gently scolded them, "Let him be. Sit."

Obediently they settled, plopping down near the fire.

Luke set down his gear, removed his outerwear, and sank onto a buffalo pelt, the fire's warmth seeping into his bones.

Kneeling by the soup, Aunt Rose added more wild turnips and onions to the buffalo paunch suspended with a tripod. She dropped in a few hot stones to boil it, stirring with a bone ladle.

The savory aroma made Luke's stomach rumble. He grinned, catching Aunt Rose's pleased look.

The flap opened and Grey Wolf entered.

"Standing Elk, you honor us. You've been missed."

Luke rose, clasping his uncle's arm.

"Thank you, Uncle. I've missed you all."

Grey Wolf settled beside Agwai. "Brother, your vision is fulfilled. Your son has returned." He asked Luke, "How long will you stay?"

"Two moons. I promised to help with the spring roundup."

Agwai and Grey Wolf exchanged a glance.

"Father, I bring good news." Luke beamed. "I'm engaged—to the woman from my vision. The one with green eyes."

Agwai straightened.

"Her name is Megan. You met her years ago. She's Cassie and Ed's daughter."

"You found the girl with green eyes?" Grey Wolf asked, taking strips of dried buffalo and passing them around.

"I did. She grew up with me on the ranch. She's

beautiful—long black hair, eyes like emeralds. And she carries Indian blood."

Luke bit into the strip of dried meat, savoring the smoky richness.

Agwai looked thoughtful. "Of what tribe?" he asked.

Luke hesitated. This was the moment he'd feared.

"Her mother's family was massacred in Missouri Territory. No one knows which tribe was responsible. But her mother survived—left carrying a child."

Agwai fell silent, then he decided.

"Tam Apo knows and that is enough. He has shown me—she will come here." His brow creased. "But why is she not with you?"

"She's finishing school to become a teacher. I want to bring her here in the spring—if you'll marry us."

Agwai's face softened. "I will. I believe she is meant for you. In my visions, I saw strong seed from her. She will bless you—and our people."

He lifted the sacred pipe, lit it, and raised it to the four directions, chanting a prayer of thanksgiving, then passed it to Luke.

Luke took a turn, then passed the pipe to Grey Wolf.

"Thank you, Father," Luke said, his heart brimming. His father had embraced his path—and the woman he loved.

That night, Luke lay on a buffalo hide, staring through the smoke hole at the star-filled sky. With his body warm, belly full, and heart overflowing, he thought of Megan and drifted into peaceful sleep.

*****

Megan tried to study, but after six weeks without a word from Luke, sorrow weighed on her. Even the weather seemed to mourn, gray skies draping the world in gloom.

One warm afternoon in mid-March, she rode to the foothills, chasing open skies and clean air to ease the ache in her chest.

On a familiar ridge, she closed her eyes and whispered a prayer—for strength, and for the safety of the man she loved.

***

Luke released his arrow in one fluid motion, the shaft piercing the white hide of the mountain goat. It bolted, staggered, then collapsed. He scrambled across the slope, sure-footed on hardened earth. Kneeling beside the fallen animal, he murmured a prayer of thanks before swiftly ending its life.

Working quickly, he gutted the goat, saving the organs and entrails in a leather pouch. When finished, he slung the carcass over his shoulders and began the long trek to camp.

In the valley, spring stirred, but here, snow still clung to shadowed crevices. Though sunny, the mountain wind was biting. Luke welcomed the labor—the burn in his legs, the weight on his back. It grounded him. Still, his thoughts drifted to Megan. He planned to leave in a day or two. He couldn't wait to see her again. Time here had been rich—but his heart was pulling him home—to Megan.

A sudden scream shattered the stillness.

Luke froze.

On a ledge above, a mountain lion crouched—eyes locked, muscles coiled.

There was no escape. The scent of blood had drawn

it. Slowly, Luke lowered the goat and dropped the organ bag. Heart pounding, Luke slowly backed away and drew his knife.

The cat screamed again—a piercing, primal cry—then leapt.

It slammed into him, knocking him flat. Luke fought with all his strength, fending off claws and fangs. He raised his left arm—searing pain shot through him as the cougar's jaws tore flesh and muscle. Luke screamed, bone near breaking under the pressure. Adrenaline surged.

With a desperate cry, he drove his blade into the cat's ribs.

It shrieked, then fell still, blood spilling over both of them. Luke mustered all his strength to roll it off.

"I'm sorry, brother," Luke whispered, breath ragged. Pain roared in his arm. Blood soaked his tunic. His vision swam.

*I can't pass out. Please, God, help me!*

He spotted the bag. Teeth clenched, he yanked the blade free and worked to cut a length of intestine. Looping it around his upper arm, he tightened it using his teeth until the bleeding slowed. The wounds were deep—muscle and bone exposed. Nausea surged. He focused on breathing.

*Stay sharp.*

He needed wooly lamb's ear for clotting. He found the soft leaves and pressed them to the gashes, then tore fleece from the goat and bound his arm tight.

*I have to make it back—for Megan.*

Staggering upright, he stumbled downhill, legs trembling. The valley wavered ahead as the world tilted. Disoriented, he glanced up, but the sun was gone.

"Which way, Lord?" he muttered.

He braced against a tree, breath ragged. Panic clawed at him—until, through the haze, a great bull elk emerged from the trees. Towering antlers. Calm, knowing eyes.

His Spirit Elk.

Its dark eyes met his, then turned—waiting.

Luke followed.

Step by agonizing step, he pushed forward, leaning on trunks. The elk guided him—slow and patient—until trees thinned, and camp came into view.

The elk vanished.

"Help me!" Luke rasped.

A young warrior spotted him, eyes going wide. He rushed to Luke's side, slinging Luke's good arm around his shoulders and shouting for help.

Agwai came running. Together, they carried Luke inside, lowering him to a buffalo hide.

"Luke—what happened?" he asked, eyes fearful.

Luke fought to stay conscious. "Killed the goat… then a cougar attacked. Killed it too." He winced. "My arm...it's bad, Father."

"You did well." Agwai unwrapped and inspected the wound. He turned to the warrior. "Send men to follow his trail—find the animals." Then, to Aunt Rose: "Bring fresh water."

Luke closed his eyes, trusting his father's care. He couldn't feel his arm anymore. Was that a bad sign?

For over an hour, Agwai worked—cleansing, salving, and stitching torn flesh. When he finally loosened the tourniquet, they waited. Slowly, blood returned to Luke's fingers. Sharp pain seared like fire through his arm. He groaned.

His father wrapped the wound with cattail poultice and Usnea moss to fight infection.

By nightfall, fever took hold. Luke tossed in sweat-soaked robes, then shivered with chills. Nothing eased the pain.

Agwai brewed bitter healing teas, and Luke drank them, drifting in and out of fitful sleep. Nightmares came. In one, the cougar lunged again—he thrashed, crying out. All night, Aunt Rose cooled his brow with wet cloths. Agwai smudged the lodge with sage, murmuring prayers as chants echoed outside.

At dawn, the fever broke.

Luke dreamed of Megan—riding beside him on her white horse, laughter bright in her green eyes. He whispered her name in his sleep.

Aunt Rose stroked his hair, singing soft lullabies. He stirred, sipped more tea, and sank into deep, healing rest.

*Please, God...let me return to her*, he prayed.

His breath eased and peace settled. The worst had passed.

*** 

Megan jolted awake Sunday morning, heart pounding. In her dream, Luke had called her name, and she'd reached for him, desperate—only to watch him fade into shadows.

She sat up in the dark dorm room, tears spilled as dread took hold. Something was wrong. She felt it in her bones.

Clutching the blanket, she bowed her head and prayed, pouring her soul into every word.

*Dear Father in Heaven, please keep Luke safe. Watch over him. Bring him back to me.*

A quiet peace settled around her, though the dread lingered.

All day, she repeated that prayer with every breath. She fasted, offering her hunger as a plea—that wherever Luke was, help would find him.

*** 

Luke woke that evening, aching and weak. The fever had broken. With help, he sat up and sipped bone broth made from the mountain goat. The warmth soothed his throat, though his head still pounded.

Over the next days, strength returned. The dizziness faded. Though his arm throbbed, the swelling eased, and the heat was gone. He whispered heartfelt thanks—to God, Tam Apo—for sparing his life and saving his arm.

Agwai spoke solemnly: an evil spirit had tried to take him. Prayer and healing had driven it away. He warned Luke to return quickly to his path. Luke told him of the Spirit Elk that had guided him to camp. Both saw it as a divine sign—his life was spared for a greater purpose.

Two weeks later, he was strong enough to travel.

His father and Aunt Rose promised to prepare for Megan's arrival and the wedding. His horse was packed with food and supplies for the journey back to Rawlins.

He embraced his father and aunt, thanking them for their care. His cousins and uncle wished him a safe journey.

Aunt Rose pressed something into his hand—a necklace strung with four cougar teeth. He fastened it around his neck, deeply moved.

"This will protect you," she said, kissing his cheek. "Be safe, Luke."

"Go in strength, son," Agwai said, pulling him close.

"Tam Apo will guide you. We await your return—with your bride."

* * *

Warm spring weather made travel easy. As Luke neared the valley, winter's grip had loosened—purple flowers carpeted the forest floor, green grass swept the plains, and trees unfurled tender leaves while snowmelt rushed down the mountains in silver streams.

In Rawlins, he spent the night in a modest hotel. At sunrise, he bathed, dressed in his best, and checked his reflection one last time. The train wouldn't wait—and he didn't intend to miss it.

* * *

Two weeks had passed since Megan's haunting dream. She'd written home about her fears and her family promised to fast and pray for Luke's safety.

Saturday morning brought warm sun and the clean scent of rain. After mailing her letters, Megan walked back toward the university. Everything looked bright and beautiful, flowers blooming and children playing. She waved, trading smiles with women hanging laundry in their yards. Her light green skirt and jacket mirrored the cheer in her heart. It was a day that lifted the soul.

As she neared the university, she became lost in thought, barely glancing up at the passing rigs—until a rider caught her eye. Long black hair. Familiar horse—Wildfire!

*Luke!*

Her breath caught.

"Luke! Luke, wait!" she called, running.

He turned. The moment he saw her, he swung down

180

and met her at a run, catching her in his arms.

"Megan," he breathed, burying his face in her hair. He kissed her cheeks, her lips, over and over. Tears streamed down his face.

She trembled in his arms, overcome with relief and joy. Her own tears fell as she clung to him.

"I was so scared," she sobbed. "I thought—"

"I'm here," he whispered.

Her knees buckled and he caught her. He lifted her onto Wildfire and mounted behind her, wrapping an arm around her waist. They trotted out of town, eager to be alone.

She leaned back against him. They were heading toward their mountainside.

Outside of town, Luke slowed. His arm remained around her; her hand resting over his.

She had so many questions, but none found voice. She simply soaked him in, his warmth, his strength.

When they arrived, Luke helped her down and pulled her close, her arms circling his neck. She pressed her cheek against his and wept again.

"I was so afraid," she whispered. "I thought I'd lost you. I don't want to be apart anymore. It hurts too much."

"I know," he said, voice thick. "This time nearly broke me. I don't want to just dream of you—I want to wake up beside you every morning. I love you. So much it aches."

He kissed her neck, her jaw, her lips—again and again, until she was breathless.

"Oh, Luke…" she murmured, trembling. "Why did you stay away so long?"

He hesitated.

"I never meant to," Luke said quietly. "I came as soon as I was strong enough."

He hadn't planned to tell her—not yet—but the weight of it pressed too heavily.

Megan pulled back, searching his face.

"I knew something happened," she whispered. "I dreamed you were being swallowed by darkness. I fasted and prayed. I was terrified—I felt like I was losing you." Her voice cracked as tears spilled down her cheeks.

Luke wiped them away. "I'm well now."

"Tell me what happened?" she pleaded.

He led her to a flat rock, where she could sit. Kneeling before her, he slipped off his jacket and rolled back his sleeve.

Megan gasped.

Fresh scars striped his forearm, edged with fading bruises. Her fingers trembled as they grazed the damaged skin.

"Luke…?" she whispered. Tears welled at the thought of the pain he'd endured.

"I was hunting," he said. "I'd just taken down a mountain goat when a cougar came after me."

Her eyes widened in horror.

"I had my knife when he pounced. He went for my throat—I blocked him with my arm. That's how I got these." He glanced down. "I managed to kill him, but I was bleeding bad. I made it back to camp led by my Spirit animal. Without him, I wouldn't have made it."

Megan gripped his hands, trembling. He rubbed his thumbs over hers.

"My father sewed me up. I fought fever and infection for days, but his prayers and medicine saved me."

She collapsed against him, sobbing. He held her, his hand gently stroking her back.

"You could've died," she cried. "After everything...I couldn't bear it. I couldn't survive losing you."

"No more talk like that." His voice was low. "We have to believe—God is in control. We have a purpose. My father had a vision of you."

She lifted her tear-streaked face. "A vision?"

He nodded, brushing her cheek. "He saw you. Helping me. Helping our people. He saw our children."

Her tears turned to joy. "He saw our children?" she whispered.

He smiled, eyes glowing. "Now I see them too. I see *you*—my wife, the mother of our family."

She kissed him tenderly—full of love and devotion.

He held her close. "You're everything to me," he murmured. "My eternal mate."

"And you are mine." She buried her face in his neck, breathing him in. She pressed a kiss to his skin, and he shivered, a soft moan escaping.

He drew back, breath unsteady, a wry smile tugging at his lips. "Maybe...we should stop for now."

He took her hand, and they walked among the trees. "This is where I see us raising our family." He could see it all—strong walls, a warm hearth, children's laughter.

"That sounds wonderful," Megan said, resting her head on his shoulder as he wrapped his arm around her.

They walked for hours, dreaming aloud, hearts full. Luke built a small fire and warmed food his aunt had packed—smoked meat, flatbread, and dried berries. Megan sat on his bedroll, face to the sun, content to listen to his voice.

The day passed like a dream, riding beneath open skies, kissing under trees, and making quiet promises. Megan wished time would stretch forever. But, in a month, they'd never have to say goodbye again.

* * *

Sunday afternoon, he boarded the train back to Cheyenne, heart already reaching ahead to graduation day—when he would take her home and never let her go.

# *Chapter 14*

# *Graduation*

The family breathed easier when Luke returned. Megan's letter had sparked real worry—and thankfully, their prayers were answered. Luke was alive and whole.

Life on the ranch welcomed him back as if he'd never left. He still missed Megan, but being closer to her—and surrounded by family—brought comfort.

A week later, spring roundup began. For five days, Luke lost himself in the work—riding the plains, herding cattle, branding calves, and castrating bulls. His body knew the rhythm, and his spirit thrived in it. Evenings were his favorite: campfire meals, quiet talk beneath the stars, stories and songs shared in flickering light.

On the final night, Luke sat at the fire, stirring the embers, his mind drifting to Megan—likely in a library, surrounded by sharp-minded students. Tabitha's question echoed: *What do you want to be?*

"You look a hundred miles away," Grandpa O'Malley said, lowering himself beside him.

Luke smiled faintly. "No, just fifty."

"Laramie, then?" Grandpa's gaze lifted to the crescent moon.

"Yeah. I keep thinking about Megan—how smart and driven she is—and wondering why she'd want a man like me. I barely finished high school. She's about to graduate college."

"Don't think like that," Grandpa said. "You've got gifts most men never learn—knowledge and heart those college boys would envy."

Luke stared into the fire. "I've never seen myself that way."

"You know ranching inside and out. You train horses, mend wounds, track game, read the sky, and survive with nothing but your wits. That's earned wisdom. If I had to follow someone on a dangerous trail, I'd choose you—no hesitation."

Luke let the words soak in.

"I'm just not sure what I'm meant for. I know how to provide, protect, and hunt. But in the white man's world, I need to earn money, build a home, and support Megan. I don't want her carrying that alone."

"You already give her what matters most. But if it's a trade you want, give it time. God speaks to those who listen. And remember—Megan chose *you*. You give her what no degree ever could."

Luke swallowed. "It's hard not to compare myself to those university men. They've got plans and titles. I've got...not much."

"That's where you're wrong. You're a quick study. If you wanted, you could go to college—be anything. Even a doctor."

Luke blinked. "A doctor? They'd never let an Indian in."

"They have. Charles Eastman, Dakota Sioux—Boston University graduate. Became a doctor. If he can, so can you."

Luke's eyes widened. "I didn't know that was possible."

"The world's changing. Slowly, but it is. You've got as much right as anyone to chase your dreams. Just find what stirs your heart and follow it."

Grandpa stood, brushing off his pants. "Look at Grandpa Hartford—loved ranching, got hurt, and found another passion—leatherwork. Made a good life. Me and your pa wore the badge because we loved protecting people. It's not where you start, it's what calls to your soul." His eyes warmed with memory. "When I met your grandma, I didn't need to prove myself anymore. She saw me—and gave me peace. That's what you have with Megan. Don't forget it."

He squeezed Luke's shoulder. "Night, son."

"Good night, Grandpa."

Luke sat watching the flames burn low, his heart lighter. He had something men searched a lifetime to find—Megan. His purpose, his match, his future. A smile tugged at his lips as he leaned back, warmed by the fire, imagining the life ahead.

***

"Megan's going to be so surprised." Cassie set the two-layer chocolate cake on the counter, its white frosting swirled to perfection. She stepped back, satisfied.

"We'd better head out if we want to catch the train," Ed said, kissing her cheek. He swiped a finger through the leftover frosting. "Mmm—tastes even better than it looks."

Luke entered, dressed in his best suit. "The team's hitched and ready."

"I'm ready," Cassie said, untying her apron and pulling on her shawl.

Outside, David climbed into the wagon. He'd drive them to the station, then return with Megan in tow. The family could hardly wait to welcome her home for good.

***

Megan snapped her trunk shut, tucking the last item into her valise. She adjusted her graduation cap in the mirror. Beneath her black robe, she wore her favorite purple dress; silver honor cords draped neatly over her shoulders. The locket from Luke rested just above her heart. Pride warmed her, though a quiet ache lingered—she'd miss the friendships, study sessions, and shared dreams.

Tabitha closed her trunk. "You ready?"

"I was ready months ago," Megan said with a grin.

Tabitha linked arms. "I'll miss this place about as much as a toothache." They laughed, their steps echoing down the hall. Since Clint had stopped courting either of them, their friendship had healed.

At the second-floor landing, Megan paused at the window. In the valley below, green crops stretched in tidy rows, prairie grasses rippled in the breeze, and snow-capped mountains rose beyond. Spring had always been her favorite season—this one especially. She was about to be married.

"I'll miss you," she said, hugging Tabitha. "These two years were long, but I'm glad we shared them."

"I'll miss you too. I'm sorry for how I acted before. I've learned a lot—mostly about myself."

"You'll do great wherever life takes you," Megan said as they continued downstairs.

"Thanks for not giving up on me. And I hope you and Luke are ridiculously happy. You'd better write me all about it. And don't skip the juicy parts."

"I promise," Megan laughed. "We'll be at the reservation for a while, but I'll write when I can."

They entered the assembly room, taking seats in the front row as guests filled in. Megan scanned the crowd for her family but saw only faculty filing in.

Fifty-two students were graduating—some in teaching, others in agriculture. Megan sat between familiar classmates; behind her, Clint and Tyler leaned forward.

"Can you believe we made it?" Clint asked, gold cords draped over his gown.

"I'm just glad it's almost over," Megan said. "I'm ready for the next chapter."

"At least you know what that is," Tyler said. "If I can't find work back home, maybe I'll follow Eileen to California." He glanced over; Eileen waved, and he blushed.

"I think God will guide you where you're meant to teach," Megan said.

"Or *love* will," Clint teased. Tyler's flushed cheeks now matched his hair.

Megan looked again—and there they were. Her father's tall frame beside Luke, who gave her a proud smile. She waved and he nodded. She couldn't see her mother, but she knew she was there.

The orchestra began. When the music faded, the university president welcomed the crowd with a brief, dignified address. Professors were introduced, the Student Body President spoke with warmth, and Clint's eloquent remarks drew warm applause.

At last, the moment arrived.

Music swelled as the graduates rose. Megan's pulse

quickened.

"Megan Marie Havoc, *Cum Laude*, Associate's Degree in Education."

Her knees wobbled as she stepped onto the stage. She found them in the crowd—Luke and her parents, beaming. Smiling, she accepted her diploma and crossed the stage.

When the final name was called, the president raised his hand.

"Ladies and gentlemen, I present to you the graduating class of 1890!"

Applause erupted. The graduates bowed and curtsied.

Megan's heart soared. *I did it! I'm finally a teacher!*

In the lobby, students searched eagerly for their families. Megan spotted hers—her parents and Luke—and rushed into their arms.

"Thank you for coming," she said, hugging them tightly.

"We're so proud of you," Cassie whispered, kissing her cheek.

"You've earned this." Ed said, embracing her.

Luke gathered her close. "I missed you so much."

"I missed you too," she breathed, clinging to him, knowing this time she wouldn't have to let go.

He kissed her knuckles. "You were radiant. I'm proud of you."

Her friends arrived with hugs and congratulations. Megan introduced her parents to Tabitha, Gwen, and Richard, then to Tyler, Eileen, and Clint. Laughing and chatting, they drifted toward the dining hall, disbelief in their voices—their school days were over.

Brown and gold streamers twisted above the door-way; a white banner proclaimed *Congratulations Graduates!* The high-ceilinged hall gleamed. A refreshment table stretched the length of one wall, laden with silver trays of cookies and pastries, a crystal punch bowl sparkling at the end.

"Oh, how lovely!" Megan murmured.

"Megan, when's the wedding again?" Eileen asked, piling cookies onto her plate.

"Friday, May second, at Clearwater Pond—just like my parents," Megan said standing beside Luke in line.

"That sounds so romantic! I'd love to come," Eileen said brightly.

"I hope you can. I want all my friends there—but I understand if you can't."

They found seats and Megan waved her parents over. The hall buzzed with laughter and the scent of sugar and spice.

"That's only two weeks away," Eileen said, sitting beside Tyler. "How will you be ready?"

"My ma's been helping. We're keeping it simple. After the wedding, we'll visit Luke's family on the reservation."

"Are you still planning to teach there?" Gwen asked, leaning in.

"I am. I'll apply and see what happens. I'd like to meet the tribe and learn the language too."

"I'll help you learn," Luke said warmly.

"I'm going to California," Eileen announced. "My application was accepted. I could stop for your wedding on the way."

"That'd be wonderful," Megan said, smiling.

Tyler turned to Eileen. "I'll really miss you. I hate the thought of saying goodbye," then thinking, added, "Maybe I'll come to the wedding too, then take a little trip to California. The way you talked about the ocean—it sounds like something I need to see."

Eileen's cheeks flushed. "You should! Everyone should see the ocean at least once." She gave a hopeful laugh. "Traveling together would be so fun."

Across the table, Gwen sent Megan a knowing glance. Megan grinned. Something was definitely blooming between Tyler and Eileen.

Richard, quiet until now, caught the exchange, a flicker of longing in his eyes. "I'll miss you all too, but I'll be glad to get back to the farm. I've missed working with my hands."

"I know the feeling," Gwen said. "Can't wait to get back to the ranch. Maybe I'll ride out to your place—see what all the fuss is about in Casper."

"You should. We're right on the North Platte River. Town's grown since the railroad came through. You could stay with us—we've got plenty of room."

"What about the end of May?" Gwen asked. "The weather should be perfect."

"Perfect. I'll check with Ma—she'll be thrilled. Never brought a girl home before."

"Write with the date and I'll be there." Gwen's eyes sparkled.

"You bet I will." Richard's smile lit up the room.

At the far end, Clint sat down, surveying the happy faces. "You all look so cheerful. Is it just because school's over?"

"Something like that," Megan said with a laugh.

"I'm not going home," Tabitha put in. "I'm off to Boston—to visit friends." She looked at Clint.

"That sounds nice," he said, running a hand through his blond hair.

"What about you?" Luke asked.

"I'm heading home for the summer to work at my father's paper. Then back to college."

Luke raised a brow. "Where?"

"Harvard," Clint said quietly.

The table went still.

"Clint! You never said a word!" Megan exclaimed.

"I didn't want to jinx it. Got the letter a few days ago," he said modestly.

"That's one of the best schools in the country," Gwen said, impressed.

Everyone offered congratulations.

Luke reached across the table to shake his hand. "That's incredible. You earned it. Your folks must be proud."

"I haven't told them yet. They don't really understand why I want to be a professor. But I'll tell them when I'm home."

"They'll come around," Luke said. "Who wouldn't be proud of that?"

Clint smiled faintly. "Thanks. I just hope I can graduate with honors again—maybe teach there one day. That's the dream." He glanced at Megan and Luke. "Speaking of dreams—congrats, you two. The wedding's soon, right?"

"Yes, in two weeks," Megan said, meeting the eyes of her friends. "You're all invited. It'll be small, but we'd love to have you."

"It'd mean a lot," Luke added, giving her hand a gentle squeeze.

"I'm in." Gwen raised her punch glass.

"Me too," Richard said, glancing at Gwen. "Maybe we'll travel together?"

"I'd like that," Gwen replied, grinning.

"I'll be in Boston—but best wishes," Tabitha said, not wanting to be left out.

"Eileen and I will be there," Tyler said. Eileen's cheeks flushed again.

"I'll try," Clint added.

"Thank you," Megan said softly.

Pa stepped up beside her. "Time to head out, Megan. The train's coming."

"I'm ready," Megan said, setting aside her punch. She followed Luke and her parents upstairs, gathering her last things while they carried her bags down.

Megan and Tabitha embraced.

"I'll write—and you'd better too. I want every wedding detail," Tabitha said, eyes shimmering.

"And I want to hear all about Boston," Megan replied, voice catching.

"You take care." Tabitha kissed her cheek and slipped away.

Outside, Megan hugged each friend in turn, lingering with every embrace. Tears stung as she climbed into the carriage. *Goodbye, University of Wyoming*, she thought, turning for one last look at the grand stone building.

She settled beside Luke. His arm slid around her shoulders, and she smiled—full of joy, love, and possibility.

***

When the train finally pulled into Cheyenne, Megan let out a deep, contented breath. She was home. She lingered at the top of the train steps, taking it all in. Then she spotted David.

He looked older—broad-shouldered, confident—but his grin was the same. He ran to her, wrapping her in a bear hug.

"Megan! Congratulations! I'm so proud of you!"

"Thanks, David. Next year it's your turn." She gave him a squeeze. "I missed you all so much."

Arm in arm, they walked toward the wagon. Luke and Ed loaded her trunk, and soon they were rolling through town toward home.

Cheyenne gave way to open prairie—spring grasses swaying, wildflowers bright along the fence lines, birds darting across the road.

Megan closed her eyes and breathed deeply—smiling as the wind brushed her cheek.

Luke watched her. "You look...happy."

"I am."

He sighed in relief. "I'm so glad school's done. I don't ever want to say goodbye to you again."

"Me either." Her smile deepened.

"Everyone was talking about their dreams earlier. Know what mine is?" He kissed her hand. "Being married to you."

"That's mine too," she whispered.

They turned down the lane, and Megan spotted a cluster of wagons near the house.

"What's all this?"

He shrugged, fighting a grin.

The wagon stopped. Luke helped her down—then

the front door burst open.

"Surprise! Congratulations!"

Family and friends spilled out—grandparents, aunts, uncles, cousins, the Clarks with their three daughters. Tears blurred her vision as children ran to hug her.

Johnathan beamed up at her. "I missed you, Megan."

"I missed you too, little brother." She kissed his forehead.

Her grandparents embraced her in turn.

"We're so proud," Grandma O'Malley said.

"I love you both," Megan whispered, blinking back tears.

The Hartfords followed, then Mr. and Mrs. Clark.

"We're so proud of you, Megan. And Andrew would've been too," Mr. Clark said softly.

"You've been missed," added Mrs. Clark. "We hope we'll be seeing a lot more of you."

"I'll be here through the wedding," Megan said, "then heading to the reservation for the summer. If I'm hired—maybe longer."

"Oh? You plan to teach there after you're married?" Mrs. Clark asked gently.

"Yes. If it keeps the children from being sent away, then yes. I just hope the tribe will accept me."

She glanced toward the porch where Luke carried her trunk inside, her expression softening.

"They'll be lucky to have you," Mrs. Clark said. "You're smart, kind, and full of heart. They'll see that."

"And if they're anything like Luke," Mr. Clark said with a wink, "you've nothing to worry about."

"Thank you," Megan replied, touched. "You both helped me through the hardest days. I think Andrew would've wanted me to find happiness again—and now I have."

Luke came from the porch, and she slipped an arm around his waist. He smiled down at her, radiant.

"We can see how happy you are," Mr. Clark said. "And we're happy for you—both of you."

Luke's arm tightened around her. "Ready to head inside?"

"In a minute—I still have more hellos to say."

The Clarks stepped aside, and Luke squeezed her arm before disappearing indoors.

Aunt Beth and Uncle John came forward, followed by Aunt Joy and Uncle Clancy, all warm hugs and bright smiles.

"You've done something incredible," Aunt Beth said.

"It was hard," Megan admitted. "The hardest thing I've ever done. But I made amazing friends—and learned more than I imagined."

"Not just from books," Uncle John said with a knowing smile. "Melissa wrote that you'd changed. Now we see it."

"I miss her," Megan said softly. "She sounds so happy. Maybe there'll be a baby one day."

"I'd spoil that child rotten," Aunt Beth said, clasping her hands.

"Not so fast," Uncle John laughed.

Jeremy and Penny exchanged glances then stepped forward, grinning. "We're making it official," Jeremy said. "Our folks will be grandparents by Christmas."

Megan gasped, hugging Penny. "Congratulations! That's great news."

"We're over the moon," Aunt Joy said. Then, with a

twinkle: "Maybe your parents won't be far behind us."

Megan laughed, blushing. "One step at a time."

"Do you know where you'll live?" Penny asked.

"A few ideas," Megan said. "If I get the teaching job, we'll stay on the reservation for a while. Eventually—maybe Laramie."

"You'll have to let us visit," Penny said.

Ma poked her head out. "Megan! Time for cake."

"Coming!" Megan called, grinning. "That's my cue."

Inside, the kitchen brimmed with laughter. A cheer rose—three rounds of "Hip, hip, hooray!"—until her cheeks flushed and her eyes misted.

"Thank you," she said. "You sure know how to make a girl feel loved."

Later, after the last guest left, Megan sank onto the couch, tired but glowing. Luke wrapped an arm around her, and she leaned into him.

"That was such a nice surprise," she said with a pleased smile.

"Ma planned everything," he said, smiling.

"We just wanted you to know how proud we are," Ma said, settling into her chair with a sigh.

"I couldn't ask for a better family." Megan pulled five envelopes from her pocket. "Cards from the Clarks, both sets of grandparents, Aunt Beth and Uncle John— and from Aunt Joy and Uncle Clancy too."

"Did you open them yet?" Ma asked, leaning forward.

"Not yet." Megan tore one open. A card of pink and purple roses slid into her hand. "From the Clarks." A ten-dollar bill fluttered into her lap. She read aloud, voice catching: "'Dearest Megan, you are one of the sweetest young women we know. We are so proud of your accomplishments and hope you realize how special you are to us. Love, The Clarks.'"

"That's so generous," Ma murmured, eyes misty.

"They're wonderful people," Luke said, rubbing Megan's shoulder.

At his gentle urging, she opened the rest. Each envelope held a crisp bill and a note of love. By the end, she had fifty dollars in her lap and a stack of words she would treasure forever.

Ma handed her one last envelope. "This one's from us."

Pa stepped beside her as she opened it. The card showed a dark-haired girl on a white horse.

"She reminds me of you," Ma said softly, brushing away a tear.

Inside was twenty dollars and a handwritten note.

*To Our Dearest Megan,*

*We love you more than words can say and are so proud of all you've done. You are beautiful inside and out. Your strength, kindness, and talents continue to amaze us. The world is in your hands, and we know you'll use your gifts well. You've always been a blessing and a miracle to us.*

*Love, Ma and Pa*

Megan hugged them both tightly. "You're the best parents a girl could have. Thank you for believing in me. I love you so much."

***

That night, Megan lay in her own bed, the stillness of

home settling around her. For two years she had endured loneliness, doubt, and the ache of missing Luke and her family—nights of relentless study, quiet tears, and unshakable determination. Now, it was over.

And yet...was she ready? The future loomed—full of unknowns, and immense responsibility.

She closed her eyes and whispered a prayer—to be the teacher God intended her to be. Peace replaced fear.

A quiet smile touched her lips as sleep found her. She had reached the end of a long, hard road—and stood at the threshold of a brand new one.

# Chapter 15

## Wedding Preparations

Megan awoke with a renewed sense of purpose. Today marked a new chapter. At the dressing table, she brushed and braided her hair, slipped into her comfortable everyday dress, and stepped from her room, lighthearted and free.

"Good morning!" she called.

Cassie bent over the stove and struck a match to light the fire. She looked up with a smile. "Sleep well?"

"Like a baby. I forgot how comfortable my bed is." Megan kissed her mother's cheek and tied on her apron.

"We're so happy to have you back," Cassie said, gently lowering the cast iron plate over the growing flames.

Megan pumped water into the kettle and set it on the stove. "I'm happy to be home. I missed making breakfast."

Cassie pulled out the coffee tin and added grounds to the kettle. "Any plans today?"

"Anything you need—wedding or chores, I'm all yours." Megan opened the kitchen window, letting in the morning breeze.

"First, your dress fitting," Cassie said, taking down coffee mugs. "Then maybe you and Luke can speak with Reverend Gather. The rest can wait."

"Perfect. We'll go after breakfast."

When Cassie reached for the egg basket, Megan took

it from her. "I've got this—it's my chore again."

The screen snapped shut behind her.

Outside, crisp air brushed her face, dew glinted in the grass, and sunlight laced the trees. Megan swung the basket and smiled at the familiar sounds—rooster crowing, hens clucking.

"Morning, Big Boy," she said, opening the gate. The rooster strutted up, black feathers shimmering.

The hens bustled about, flapping and clucking in their eagerness.

"Good morning, girls!"

Megan greeted each, one by one as they scurried close. "Good morning, Cookie, Clucky, Sunny, Nugget… hello, Red, Ginger. Good morning, Henny, Penny." Off to the side, ill-tempered Sweety skulked, white feathers slightly ruffled. "Hey, girl."

A copper hen darted up, pecking at the yellow flowers on Megan's dress.

"Nutmeg, quit it." Megan gently nudged her back and reached into the feed bin. She scattered grain across the yard, sending the hens into a frenzy.

Sunny found a fat bug and took off running, the rest in hot pursuit. "Run, Sunny!" Megan laughed, heading to the nesting boxes. She lifted the hatch and found the broody hen.

"There you are, Pecky."

The hen glared.

"Now don't start." Megan reached in.

Pecky spun and jabbed her hand.

"Ouch! Come on, now." Using the basket as a shield, she collected twelve warm eggs.

Across the yard, Luke leaned on the corral rail, grinning as she left the coop.

"Don't let 'em get the best of you," he called. "They're just chickens—show 'em who's boss."

"I'd like to see you try," she said, holding up her reddened hand. "Pecky got me good."

Luke swung over the fence and crossed the yard, mock fury in his step. "Want me to roast her for dinner?"

"Nah," Megan laughed, tugging on his sleeve. "She didn't mean it. She's just a chicken."

Luke spun and pulled her into his arms. "Then let me kiss it better."

He leaned in and kissed her, warm and lingering.

"I feel better already," she murmured, melting into his arms, wishing the moment could last forever.

"I do too," Luke said with a grin. "Good morning, Sunshine." He kissed her forehead, took the egg basket, and laced his fingers through her uninjured hand. In the golden light, she glowed—and he couldn't look away.

"Good morning, sweetheart." The words slipped out, making her heart flutter. They'd never used endearments before, but it felt good.

"Did you dream last night?" he asked as they crossed the yard.

"No, but I slept great. Why—did you?" She caught the grin tugging at his mouth.

"I did. Want to hear it?"

"Always."

He sat on the porch steps and patted the space beside him. She nestled in, their shoulders touching.

"We were riding across a wide prairie," he began. "Your hair was flying, you were smiling—free. A herd of wild horses thundered past, every color you can imagine. We herded them home, to a house at the foot of the mountains. Then three little girls ran out to meet us—all giggles and smiles. You scooped up the littlest; I lifted the older two to see the horses. It felt real—it was so vivid. It's the best dream I've ever had."

Megan leaned closer, heart full. "Do you think it could come true—like some of your others?"

"I don't know. But I hope so." His heart swelled at the thought.

"Me too. I can't imagine anything better," she said, already dreaming of the life he'd painted in her mind.

The screen door creaked.

"Mind if I take those eggs?" Cassie smiled at them.

They laughed.

"Sorry, Ma," Luke said, handing her the basket. "We were just soaking up the morning."

"You deserve to," Cassie replied, heading inside.

Luke slipped his arm around Megan. "Oh, yes we do." He kissed her forehead, and she tilted her face up, smiling.

***

Megan tightened the cinch and swung into the saddle. It felt wonderful to ride Snowfire again—the reins in her hands, the sun warm on her back, the scent of spring in the air. She and Luke rode side by side, hooves kicking up soft clouds of dust.

In town, she reined in at the C & H Dress Shop and waved as Luke rode on to his errands. The bell jingled as she stepped inside. Pastel gowns filled the front, each with a coordinating hat. Her heart skipped—she'd chosen her gown's pattern months ago, and now she'd finally see it.

"Good morning!" Ashley called, emerging from the back, looking more than her seventeen years, in the dusty blue gown and elegantly styled auburn hair.

"Ashley! So good to see you again." Megan hugged her. "We didn't get to talk yesterday." With school out, Ashley was able to help out in the family shop.

"Congratulations again on graduating—and your wedding!" Ashley beamed.

"Thanks! Next year it's your turn. Any plans after school?" Megan asked, curious if David and Ashley's friendship might grow closer this year.

"I'll stay here and help my parents in the shop. I'm no adventurer like you," Ashley laughed.

"You never know. The right man might sweep you off your feet—have an adventure of your own."

Ashley's cheeks pinked. "I'll bet you're dying to see your dress. Wait here."

Megan drifted toward a case of glittering combs, imagining which might suit the gown. Ashley returned, dress draped over her arm.

"Well? What do you think?"

"Oh my goodness…" Megan gasped. "It's even more beautiful than I imagined."

"You'll be stunning. Want to try it on?"

In the small, mirrored room, Megan slipped into a corset and petticoats before Ashley eased the gown over her head and fastened the satin buttons down the back.

Megan turned—and gasped. Her dark hair, olive skin, and green eyes glowed against the ivory French lace. The heart-shaped bodice hugged her curves, satin beneath sheer lace; off-shoulder sleeves buttoned delicately at the wrists. Layers of tulle shaped the skirt, the train flowing in soft waves as Ashley fanned it out, revealing the full beauty of the floral lace.

Megan turned before the mirror, hardly recognizing herself. The gown was more elegant than she'd imagined.

"You look stunning," Ashley breathed.

"It's perfect," Megan said, eyes shining. The fit was flawless—like it had been made for her.

"No alterations needed. Just one last thing—we need a veil."

By the hour's end, they'd chosen a medium-length veil with a silver comb. Megan had it boxed with the dress and promised to collect it with the buggy the next day.

Outside, Luke waited on a bench beneath a cottonwood.

"Did it all work out?" he asked, standing.

"Yes! It's beautiful. I can't wait for you to see it." Megan beamed.

"I can see it *now*," Luke said, starting for the door.

"No—you *can't*. It's bad luck for the groom to see the dress before the wedding." She tugged his arm.

He raised a brow. "Strange. I've seen all your other dresses."

"It's tradition. Besides, don't you want to be surprised?"

"I think I'll be surprised enough just seeing you show up," he teased, slipping his arm around her shoulders.

Megan laughed. "Don't worry—I'll be there. I'm looking forward to it as much as you."

***

After speaking with Reverend Gather, they rode

206

home, talking of their trip to the reservation—and their honeymoon.

"What would you say to camping?" Luke asked. "Ride out to our fishing hole, pitch a tent, spend a few quiet days before heading on."

She smiled. "Sounds fun. Let's do it."

***

The next two weeks passed in a flurry of preparations—flowers, baking, quilt-stitching, and hand-delivered invitations.

Days before the wedding, Megan visited Penny in the little one-room cabin she shared with Jeremy. The space was warm and tidy, its meager furnishings brightened by sunlight spilling across the red-checked tablecloth, and lace curtains that stirred in the breeze.

"I'll miss you," Penny said, pouring tea. "I wish you were staying. It'd be nice to have someone to talk to."

"I'll miss you too. I wish I could come back for Christmas, but winter travel's hard. Still, I'll be thinking of you—especially when the baby comes." Megan stirred cream into her tea.

Penny's hand rested on her belly. "It's amazing...But I'm scared. I think about how big it'll get—and how it's supposed to come out." Her voice trembled.

"You'll be fine. Ma had me alone—no doctor—and she got through it. You'll be strong too." Megan squeezed her hand.

"I just wish you were closer. Our mothers forget what it's like the first time."

"I wish I was too. With Melissa far away, you've been my closest friend," Megan said softly.

"All my friends are gone, living their lives. I guess

I hoped you'd stay for good. You just got back...and now you're leaving again." Penny brushed away a tear. "Sorry. I cry at everything these days."

"It's alright. I've missed you too. We dreamed of this—married life. But it's harder than I thought." Megan blinked back her own tears. "I've never been away for a whole year. I don't know how I'll manage."

Penny gave her a reassuring squeeze. "It'll be hard, but you've got Luke. You'll make a home wherever you are. I just hope you come back someday so we can be neighbors."

Megan smiled through tears. "Luke dreamed we had a herd of horses, a home in the mountains...and three little girls."

"That sounds perfect," Penny said wistfully, standing to get more cookies. "Didn't you once say your favorite spot in Laramie was near the mountains?"

"Yes. Maybe one day it'll come true. You and Jeremy could homestead nearby—no need to share space with his parents."

"We've talked about it," Penny admitted. "His heart's in ranching, and I'd love a place that's truly ours. His family's wonderful, but it does get crowded."

Megan nodded. "Luke doesn't want to stay on the reservation forever—just long enough for me to teach. Then we'll find a place of our own, like in his dream."

"In two days you'll be his wife," Penny said softly. "It's been a year since he came back for you. You must be excited."

"I am," Megan admitted, cheeks flushing. "But I'm also nervous. I don't know much about...well...intimacy."

"You're not alone," Penny said gently. "It's natural

to feel unsure. But Luke's kind. He loves you. Trust will carry you through. This part of marriage is a gift—meant to draw you closer." Her hand drifted to her belly. "Look what it brings—a whole new life. It's a miracle."

Megan smiled shyly. "Thank you. I've had so many questions but didn't know who to ask."

"I was nervous too," Penny said. "But when you love someone deeply, giving yourself feels right. Natural. You'll understand."

Megan's smile grew. "I think I already do. Thank you, Penny. You're a wonderful friend."

She thought of the quiet moments she and Luke had shared, the longing she'd felt now made sense.

***

The night before the wedding, Luke and Megan walked along the stream behind the house. The last light faded into a star-pricked sky; crickets sang, and the breeze carried the scent of damp earth. Nestled under his arm, Megan wrapped her own around his waist.

When they were far from the house, Luke stopped. "By this time tomorrow, we'll be married."

"It's hard to believe." Megan looked up at him, her heart fluttering. "We've waited so long—and now it's finally here."

She gazed at his shadowed face, lit faintly by moonlight. She reached up and traced his cheek, her fingers brushing the curve of his neck. She loved everything about him—his strength, his kind eyes, the way his touch calmed her soul.

Her fingers sent a thrill through him. "You are my dream come true," he whispered. "I've never known happiness like this. It took half my life to find you, but

I'd wait all over again if I had to."

He pulled her close and kissed her, slow and deep, the kind that left them breathless. *One more night*, he thought. *Just one—and I'll never have to say goodbye again.*

"Oh, Luke, I love you so much," Megan whispered. "I can't wait to be with you." She wasn't sure if he understood—but soon, he would.

He held her gaze, hearing more than her words. "Neither can I," he said softly, aching for the moment they'd become one in every way.

***

That night, Luke lay in the barn, staring at the rafters, mind full of Megan—her soft eyes, her touch, the way she fit in his arms.

In her room, Megan tossed restlessly, her thoughts a tangle of wedding plans and Luke's kisses, his strong arms around her.

Across the house, Cassie lay awake beside Ed.

"You awake?" she whispered.

"Yeah," Ed murmured, pulling her close.

"I keep thinking how fast everything's changing. Megan and Luke were just kids going off to school. Now they're getting married." She rested her head on his shoulder.

"They've grown into fine people," Ed said, kissing her forehead. "We've been blessed."

"We sure have." Cassie smiled. "Tomorrow's going to be such a beautiful day. Those two have been so patient and worked so hard."

"Not like us," Ed said with a chuckle.

Cassie laughed. "We could barely wait a minute."

"I was no good until you were mine." He kissed her softly.

She rested a hand over his heart. "And I've loved every minute."

Ed smiled. "I'm looking forward to the trip—feels like a honeymoon—just us in the woods. No chores or kids."

"We never really had one," she mused. "It *does* sound romantic."

"I'll make sure it's unforgettable."

"I can't wait," she whispered, kissing him before turning over. "Goodnight, my love."

He curled behind her, pulling her close. "Goodnight, my queen."

# Chapter 16

## Wedding Day

Friday morning dawned bright and purposeful, excitement humming through the house. Outside, chores were finished in record time. Inside, the breakfast table overflowed with lively chatter, festivity filling the air.

Luke rode out with Pa and Grandpa O'Malley to set up the honeymoon camp, then headed into town with Grandpa to dress. Meanwhile, Megan prepared for the most important moment of her life. The wedding was at ten—there was still much to do.

"I'm ready for you, Ma," she called from her dressing table, fashioning the final curl.

"I'm coming," Cassie replied, brushing flour from her hands and untying her apron.

Cassie pinned the ringlets into place, letting some tumble down Megan's back. "Beautiful. Ready for the gown?"

"Yes—just enough time to dress and arrive a few minutes early." Megan stood.

Cassie helped her into the petticoat, then lifted the ivory French lace gown over her head. Megan slid her arms into the fitted sleeves as Cassie worked down the long row of satin buttons, smoothing the skirt and fluffing the train.

"Well? What do you think?" Megan asked, smiling.

"You look beautiful," Cassie said, dabbing at her tears. "It's the most stunning dress I've ever seen."

"Mr. and Mrs. Clark only charged half what it's worth—said it was their gift."

"Not surprising," Cassie smiled. "They've always been generous. Did I ever tell you Bart and Bea's father gave Ed his wedding suit?"

"No! That's so kind."

Cassie reached for the veil, setting the silver comb at the crown of Megan's head. Lace fell in a soft shimmer over her bare shoulders. "Luke won't be able to speak when he sees you."

"Thank you, Ma. I feel beautiful."

"You know what's missing?" Cassie hurried out and returned with a slender box. "Grandma Hartford gave me these on my wedding day. Now they're yours."

Inside lay a silver necklace with a pearl drop and matching earrings. Cassie fastened them with care.

"They're perfect," Megan whispered.

"Especially on you." Cassie's eyes glistened.

"Thanks, Ma. For everything. I couldn't have done this without you." Megan hugged her tightly. "I love you."

"I love you too. You've always been my little miracle." Cassie drew a steadying breath. "You ready?"

"I have everything except 'something blue,'" Megan said, glancing around.

Ed stepped inside and called, "Cassie, Megan—it's almost time. Ready yet?"

"Almost," Cassie said, peeking out the bedroom door. "We're missing 'something blue.'"

Ed rubbed his mustache thoughtfully. "Be ready

when I get back." He strode out, sharp in his Sunday suit and hat.

Cassie glanced at Megan. "Do you have the ring?"

"Right here." Megan handed it over.

Cassie slipped the band into her purse. "Good. I'll load the rest of the food."

Already dressed in her light blue Sunday gown, she pinned on her blue hat over her neat chignon. Satisfied, she gathered the bread basket and headed to the surrey.

Ed rounded the house. "Ready?"

"She's inside." Cassie noticed the flowers in his hand. "What's that?"

"Will these do?" He held up two bluebells.

"Oh, Ed...perfect." She took one, admiring its hue.

"One's for you." He tucked it into her hair and kissed her. "You look lovely, Mrs. Havoc."

She touched his cheek. "And you look dashing, Mr. Havoc. Now go get our bride."

Inside, Megan stepped from her room into warm morning light.

Ed stopped, breath catching. "Oh, my stars...Megan, you look beautiful." His voice trembled.

"Thanks, Pa." She glanced down at the gown. "Didn't the Dress Shop do a wonderful job?"

"They did. But you make it shine." He squeezed her hand.

She smiled. "We should go—it's getting late."

"Oh! I nearly forgot." He held out a wildflower. "Here's your 'something blue.'"

Megan's eyes softened. "Perfect."

He tucked it behind her ear, his voice husky. "I'm proud of you, Megan. You've grown into an incredible young woman—I love you." He kissed her gently on the cheek.

She wrapped her arms around him. "I love you too, Pa. You're the best father a girl could hope for."

Ed inconspicuously wiped at his eye. "Let's get you to that wedding before Luke starts pacing." Megan took his arm, lifting her train with her free hand, and stepped outside.

Cassie wiped a tear away as they crossed the yard to the surrey. "You both look wonderful," she said thickly.

Ed helped Megan into the back, Cassie into the front. Glancing over his shoulder, he grinned.

"Alright then—time to take the princess to meet her prince."

A flutter rose in Megan's chest as the wheels turned. This was it—the moment her life would change forever.

***

Luke adjusted his light blue tie with the silver pin once more. *Why does it never sit straight when it matters most?*

His dark hair gleamed, tied neatly with a black ribbon. He slipped into the tailored black jacket over a crisp white shirt and the blue-and-silver paisley vest the Clarks had gifted him after the New Year's Ball—a gift he'd never appreciated more.

Stepping from the guest room at the O'Malley home, he gave a wry grin. "This is as good as it's going to get."

"Oh, Luke, you look so handsome," Kathy said, stepping over to straighten his tie. "Megan's a lucky girl. I'd say you're the handsomest man in Cheyenne—if your grandfather hadn't already claimed the title."

"I'll take it as a compliment," Luke said, winking.

"Don't listen to her," Patrick called from the mirror. "I *was* handsome once, but those days are behind me. If Kathy's eyesight were better, she might've run off with a fellow like you."

"Oh hush," Kathy laughed, smoothing Luke's tie before kissing Patrick's cheek. "My eyes work just fine, thank you."

"And beautiful eyes they are," Patrick said, returning the kiss.

Luke looked away, grinning. "Alright, lovebirds— let's get moving so I'm not late to my own wedding."

Kathy reached for her blue felt hat and shawl. "I'm ready."

"Let's not keep the bride waiting," Patrick said, ushering them out.

Luke followed with a tray of Grandma's baked goods. After loading the wagon, he climbed into the back.

"Did you remember the ring?" Kathy asked as Patrick helped her into the front seat.

Luke patted his vest. "Right here." He checked his pocket watch—9:15—and felt a flicker of nerves.

By the time they reached Clearwater Pond, guests were already gathering. They parked down the road and walked beneath tall trees to the meadow, where the pond shimmered like glass, mirroring cattails, wildflowers, and a brilliant blue sky.

Reverend Gather approached with a warm smile. "Welcome, Luke. I imagine you're excited—and what a glorious day for it."

"Thank you, Reverend. I don't think a man's ever been happier."

Patrick shook the reverend's hand. "A proud day

indeed."

After a few pleasantries, the reverend moved off to greet others. Kathy and Patrick mingled with relatives while Luke joined a small group of Megan's friends near the water's edge.

"Thanks for coming," he said, shaking hands.

"We wouldn't have missed it," Richard replied, standing tall beside Gwen in their Sunday best.

"I can't wait to see Megan," Gwen said, scanning the crowd.

"She'll be here soon," Luke replied, hoping his voice didn't betray his nerves.

"This place is incredible," Tyler said, taking in the landscape. "No wonder you chose it."

Luke nodded. "It's always been special to us."

Eileen smiled. "I can't wait to see her dress. She's already so lovely."

"She is," Luke said, grinning until his cheeks ached.

Clint stepped forward, extending his hand. "I'm really happy for you. No hard feelings?"

"None at all," he said sincerely.

He glanced at the group. "Truly—thank you for being here. It means the world to both of us."

Luke wove through the gathering, greeting friends and family, but his stomach tightened with each passing minute. Still no Megan.

He checked his pocket watch—ten minutes to go. His hand trembled.

"Luke, I think it's time," Reverend Gather said gently, motioning toward the clearing's edge. His kind smile held quiet assurance. "She'll be here any moment."

The reverend's voice rose over the meadow. "Brothers

and sisters, please take your places. The bride will arrive shortly."

He stepped to the front, the glistening pond behind him, Bible in hand, the day's sacred vows waiting.

Just inside the trees, the surrey arrived. Ed helped Cassie down, then turned to assist Megan, careful of her gown as she stepped to the ground.

Two little girls in pink dresses darted forward—Annabelle and Elizabeth, Aunt Beth's youngest.

"We're ready to carry your train!" Annabelle announced, blonde braids bouncing.

"Mama said to give you these," Elizabeth added, offering a fragrant bouquet of blue and lavender hyacinths with creamy white roses.

"Oh, they're beautiful," Megan breathed, holding them up for her mother to admire.

"They're perfect," Cassie said, eyes misty. She hugged her daughter. "Ready, sweetheart?"

"I've been ready a long time." Megan scanned for Luke, not seeing him but feeling his presence.

Cassie bent toward the girls. "Hold the train above the ground until Megan reaches the front—then join your folks."

"Yes, Aunt Cassie," they chimed, ribbons woven through their hair.

Megan clutched the bouquet and looped her arm through her father's. Ed's proud smile steadied her.

"She's ready," Cassie whispered to the pastor.

Mr. Clark's violin began the wedding march, the soft, lilting notes drifting through the spring air. Heads turned as Megan stepped into view, her father at her side, the little girls following with careful hands.

Luke craned his neck, heart pounding. He drew a breath, straightened. *This is it. Today, my dream becomes real.*

Then he saw her.

She emerged like a vision—lace framing her dark hair, ivory gown gliding over her curves before sweeping into a full skirt. Awe swept through him.

Their eyes met. Megan's emerald gaze shimmered with unshed tears.

Her heart swelled. Luke stood ahead, strong and steady, just as he'd been when he rescued her here a year ago. Her love for him filled every part of her.

At the aisle's end, Ed kissed her cheek and placed her hand in Luke's.

Luke took her hands, blinking back tears. Around them, the world faded. Only her.

"Dearly beloved," Reverend Gather began softly, "we are gathered to witness the union of these two in holy matrimony…"

Megan barely heard him—only felt Luke's touch, his smile, his loving gaze.

"Do you, Luke Standing Elk Havoc, take Megan Marie Havoc to be your lawfully wedded wife…?"

"I do," Luke said, rich with emotion, eyes never leaving hers.

Tears slid down her cheeks.

"And do you, Megan Marie Havoc, take Luke Standing Elk Havoc to be your lawfully wedded husband…?"

"I do," she whispered, trembling with joy.

"You may now exchange the rings."

Luke reached into his vest pocket, took her left hand,

and met her gaze.

"Megan Marie Havoc, I give you this ring as a symbol of my love and my choice to share life's journey with you. I pledge to love, honor, and cherish you—today, tomorrow, and forever."

He slid the gold band with its red stone onto her finger and gave her hand a gentle squeeze.

Megan passed the bouquet to her mother and took the second ring. Holding Luke's hand, she looked into his eyes—immense love emanating.

"Luke Standing Elk Havoc, I give you this ring as a symbol of my love and my choice to walk through life with you. I pledge to love, honor, and cherish you—today, tomorrow, and forever."

She slid the ring onto his copper-toned finger and clasped his hands, smiling through tears.

Reverend Gather lifted his hands. "By the power vested in me, I pronounce you husband and wife. You may kiss your bride."

Luke didn't hesitate. His kiss was soft at first, sealing their vows, then deepened—full of the dreams they had carried to this moment. The crowd erupted in cheers as he lifted her into his arms.

Setting her down, he murmured, voice husky, "I love you, Mrs. Havoc."

"I love you, sweetheart," she whispered, her heart thundering.

Their parents stepped forward, arms wide.

"Congratulations!" came the joyful chorus.

Cassie's tears shone. "We love you both so much."

Ed embraced Luke, then squeezed Cassie's hand. "Reminds me of our wedding—best day of my life."

"Mine too," Luke said with a grin, kissing Megan's cheek.

"I can't believe it," Megan breathed, joyful tears falling. "I'm Mrs. Luke Standing Elk Havoc."

Both sets of grandparents followed with hugs and blessings. David, Kurt, and Johnathan weren't far behind.

"I'm so happy for you," David said, then grinned. "By the way...can I have your room now, Megan?"

"Once we head to the reservation, it's all yours," she said.

"Woohoo!" he cheered—until Cassie teased, "Or maybe I'll turn it into a sewing room."

David groaned. Ed chuckled, pulling him close. "We'll talk later."

Kurt hugged Megan. "You look beautiful...for a sister." He gave Luke a playful pat. "And you clean up well too."

"Thanks, Kurt," Megan laughed. Beside her, Luke grinned.

"I think you're the prettiest sister I've ever had," Johnathan added, earning more chuckles.

"That's because I'm your *only* sister," she teased, kissing his cheek. "Thank you, Johnathan. I love you."

The family drifted off to greet others as more guests stepped forward.

"Congratulations, Megan. It was a beautiful ceremony," Samantha said, drawing her into a warm hug. Her husband, Stephan, followed with a firm handshake and kind smile.

Emotion caught in Megan's throat—it had been so long since she'd seen them. Memories of Andrew's passing flickered through her, but she steadied herself.

"I want you to meet my husband, Luke. This is Samantha, my friend from the telephone company, and her husband, Stephan Butler. His family owns Butler's Butchery."

"Ah, yes—best cuts in town," Luke said, shaking hands. "Pleasure to meet you both."

"Likewise," Stephan replied in a soft German accent. "A joy to meet the man who makes Megan so happy. What a perfect day."

Megan's eyes fell to Samantha's rounded belly. "You're expecting! When's the baby due?"

"End of May," Samantha laughed. "I can hardly move, breathe, or sleep—feel like a pregnant cow!"

With her golden hair catching the sun and eyes alight, she looked radiant.

"You're beautiful," Stephan said gently, kissing her cheek. "Like an angel—soon to be the mother of my child." Samantha blushed, glowing under his affection.

"I'm so happy for you both," Megan said as they walked away—still so in love.

"Good people," Luke murmured.

"The kind who leave a mark on your heart," Megan replied, wiping a tear. "I'll tell you more later."

Relatives, neighbors, and old friends came next, offering warm wishes before heading into town for the reception. At last, her college friends arrived, all smiles and laughter.

"I'm so glad you all came," Megan said, eyes glistening. "I didn't think we'd all be together again. Please come to the reception—dinner, dancing...will you?"

"Of course!" Gwen replied, glancing at Richard. "Our train doesn't leave until this afternoon."

"No better way to spend the day," Richard said smiling.

Tyler turned to Eileen. "What do you think?"

"Yes!" she exclaimed brightly.

Clint stepped forward. "I'd be honored to come too. Congratulations." He kissed her cheek and whispered, "He's the luckiest man I know."

Megan's gaze found Luke's, her hand giving a reassuring squeeze.

After warm farewells, Luke gathered her train and helped her into the buggy, adorned with a sign reading *Just Married*. As the wheels rolled toward town, friends cheered behind them.

Megan nestled close as his arm slipped around her.

"I can't believe it," she whispered. "We're married."

"And I couldn't be happier," Luke said, kissing her softly. "Now that I have you, I'll never let go."

He kissed her again—longer, sweeter—a promise of more to come. The buggy bounced, nearly veering off the road, and they burst into laughter.

# Chapter 17

## *Reception*

In town, they stopped before the grand Masonic Temple where the reception awaited. Luke stepped down and helped Megan from the buggy, his hand warm around hers. Beneath the arched sandstone entrance, he stole a kiss.

"Do we really have to go inside?" he teased. "Can't we just run off and be alone?"

"Patience, my love," Megan smiled, wrapping her arms around his waist. "Soon you'll have me all to yourself."

"I'm counting the moments."

Inside, morning light streamed through stained glass, spilling pools of color across ornate beams and gold-stenciled walls. A crystal chandelier glimmered above a black-and-white marble floor.

"This place is incredible," Luke murmured.

"Just wait until you see the reception hall." Megan led him through the double doors.

Applause and whistles greeted them. Another vaulted ceiling soared overhead, gold-trimmed carvings gleaming in the light of a second chandelier. Red-and-gold drapes framed tall windows, and white columns stood like sentinels around the room. Round tables in white linen held spring bouquets; side tables overflowed with roasts, breads, fruit, pies, and sparkling drinks.

At the head table, Ma waved them over. Ed, in a black suit with a deep blue vest, rose and tapped his glass. The room hushed.

"Friends and family," he began warmly, "thank you for being here on this glorious day. We're grateful for your love as Megan and Luke begin their life together. A toast."

Turning to Luke, his voice thickened.

"When you came to us as a boy, we fell in love instantly. We thought your time would be brief, but months became years, and you became our son. The day we adopted you brought joy beyond words. Letting you go when your father returned was one of the hardest things we ever did. We missed you every day. And Megan…" He met his daughter's teary gaze. "She missed you most."

"We prayed you'd come back. And you did—a miracle that healed us. You didn't just return to visit; you came back for Megan. Your bond began the day she was born—protector, playmate, best friend. Even after years apart, it never broke. What you have is rare—a love that defies time and distance."

Ed turned to Megan.

"Megan, from the moment you arrived, your kind heart shone bright. Through loss and trials, you never stopped giving. You worked hard, sacrificed much, and when Luke returned, your joy returned too. You complete each other—you dream, support, and lift one another."

He lifted his glass. "May your days be full of purpose, your hearts at peace, and your love ever grow. To Luke and Megan!"

"Cheers!" rang out as glasses clinked.

Megan wiped a tear. "Thank you, Pa."

Luke drew her close. "I love you."

"I love you, too."

"Kiss, kiss, kiss!" guests chanted, tapping forks to glass.

Blushing, Megan laughed as Luke kissed her slowly, sweetly. Cheers erupted again. Surrounded by love, it felt like a dream.

Cassie leaned toward Ed. "That was beautiful. You said exactly what I felt." She wiped a tear.

"I just spoke from the heart," he said, kissing her gently.

Reverend Gather rose to offer a blessing, his voice warm and reverent. When it ended, guests lined up at the buffet. Cassie brought a plate for Luke, Grandma O'Malley for Megan, so they could remain at the head table. Amid cheerful chatter, they visited with loved ones, savoring every moment.

It was time to cut the wedding cake.

At the center stood a round table crowned with a three-tiered white cake, pink roses spilling down its sides. Megan took the knife; Luke's hand closed gently over hers. Together, they cut a slice from the top tier.

Luke lifted a piece to her lips. She smiled, savoring it, then broke off a bit for him. He closed his mouth slowly over her fingers, making her giggle as laughter and applause rippled through the room.

As they wiped their hands, soft music drifted from the stage. The orchestra played a gentle prelude while helpers cleared tables for dancing. Megan and Luke mingled, glowing with happiness.

Ashley hurried over to embrace Megan.

"The dress looks divine on you—and the jewelry, perfect."

Ashley wore the rosy-pink dress from the shop, a matching felt hat perched over her light red curls, the rest swept into elegant ringlets.

"Thank you," Megan said warmly. "It was Ma's—she wore it on her wedding day."

Luke leaned in, admiring. "I didn't know that. And this little bluebell—lovely." He brushed back a strand to reveal the bloom.

Clint stepped up, tipping his head to Luke and Megan.

"Thanks for inviting me," he said, his gaze shifting to the striking strawberry-blonde beside him. "Pardon me—I didn't mean to interrupt."

"You weren't," Ashley said sweetly. "I was admiring Megan in the dress we made for her."

Clint turned, surprised. "You helped sew her gown?"

"Not all of it," she said modestly. "My family owns the dress shop—I've been sewing since I was nine." She lowered her eyes with practiced grace.

"Well, I'm impressed," Clint said, watching her. "You clearly have a gift."

Megan exchanged a knowing glance with Luke. "Clint, this is Ashley Clark, a dear family friend. Ashley, meet Clint Miller—my college friend."

Clint took Ashley's hand, kissing the back, his gaze locked on her bright blue eyes. "Enchanté, mademoiselle. Tu as de beaux yeux."

Ashley's heart fluttered. Breathless, she asked, "What does that mean?"

"It's French. 'Nice to meet you, miss. You have beautiful eyes.'"

A flush colored her cheeks. Clint's smile deepened as his heart thudded.

"Thank you," she whispered, lowering her lashes to hide her blush.

Megan stepped in, sensing the spark. "Clint, I didn't know you spoke French."

"My father's French Canadian," he said, still watching Ashley. "He taught me some."

Megan glanced at Luke. "I had no idea."

Clint smiled faintly. "There's a lot you don't know about me. Did I mention my mother's a redhead?"

Ashley looked up, caught off guard by his steady blue eyes. Who was this man?

"No, you never mentioned," Megan said, watching Clint and Ashley. *David might have some competition,* she thought.

"My parents are both redheads," Ashley said, nodding to her mother, who was helping with the chairs.

"She's lovely. I see where you get your beauty," Clint said sincerely.

Ashley flushed. "She was a spinster school teacher until she met my father at twenty-one. Love at first sight."

"He had good taste—and she was wise to wait."

Ashley hesitated. "He first came here hoping to win Cassie's heart—Megan's mother—but found she was taken. He was crushed. But meeting my mother changed everything."

Clint's gaze softened. "I believe it."

"I should let you mingle," Ashley said, stepping back. "Congratulations, Megan, Luke."

Clint caught her hand. "Would you honor me with a dance? After the newlyweds?"

Her heart stuttered. "I'd like that."

"Good." He smiled and slowly let go.

Ashley lingered, shyly answering Clint's questions about her family and schooling.

Ed's voice rose. "Ladies and gentlemen, the newlyweds' first dance."

Guests parted as Luke and Megan took the floor. Megan lifted her lace train; Luke bowed, then pulled her close to waltz.

They moved in perfect harmony. Megan's heart swelled—Luke was hers, her husband. She smiled through tears, her love too big for words.

Luke never looked away, memorizing every breath and step. She was his partner now—his forever—and joy surged through him.

Ashley watched, misty-eyed. Megan's gown flowed like water; Luke tall and confident led tenderly. It was the most romantic sight she'd ever seen. Someday, she prayed, she'd find a love like that.

Clint watched Ashley—her poise, quiet strength, and intelligent eyes captivated him. She glanced up, flustered, then looked away.

Ashley's pulse quickened. Clint's presence was impossible to ignore. Their sleeves brushed; a thrill passed between them. She was moments from dancing with him—the thought thrilled and terrified her.

As the music ended, Luke dipped Megan and kissed her deeply. Cheers erupted.

Ed smiled. "May I have this dance?" Megan grinned and took his hand. Luke offered his arm to Cassie. The next dance began.

Couples joined the floor. Clint offered his hand;

Ashley placed hers in his. They moved to the dance floor, eyes locking.

Tall and slender, she fit perfectly in his arms. Graceful, she followed his lead. He memorized her cheekbones, porcelain skin, long neck, and bright blue eyes.

Ashley floated, lost in the moment. Clint's warm touch and intense gaze made butterflies flutter in her stomach.

Across the room, David watched with envy. He'd missed his chance—Ashley had gone to greet Megan, and now Clint was dancing with her. *Must he always be the center of everything?*

Nearby, Eileen and Tyler swayed and chatted about their upcoming trip, while Gwen and Richard murmured over the beauty of the ceremony.

The song ended, and couples drifted to the edges of the floor, laughter and conversation weaving through the air.

Ed stepped onto the stage. "Friends and family, we'd like to share something special—a song called *Be My Wife.*"

Megan's brows lifted as Luke joined Pa on stage, and took the guitar, while Mrs. Clark took the piano and Mr. Clark the violin.

"Megan, this is for you," Luke said, adjusting the strap.

Cassie slipped an arm around Megan, eyes misting.

Luke strummed a soft chord, glanced to the others, and nodded.

The music began, and his rich tenor rose into the air like a prayer.

*(Verse 1)*

*"After all these years, I found you standing here,*
*By that sunlit pond, a moment crystal clear.*
*When I first saw you on that summer's day,*
*There was no turning back—I had found my way.*
*Our hearts pulled close, through joy and pain,*
*Like broken pieces joined, never to part again.*

*(Chorus)*
*To have and to hold, forever and ever,*
*These sweet moments we share together.*
*I will love you all of my life—*
*If you will only be my wife.*

*(Verse 2)*
*I rescued you, and you rescued me.*
*You fell at my feet, looked up tenderly.*
*Right then I knew—it was meant to be. Can't you see?*
*I wanted you, and you wanted me,*
*Not for a day, but eternally.*

*(Chorus)*
*To have and to hold, forever and ever,*
*These happy days we spend together.*
*I will love you all of my life—*
*If you will only be my wife.*

*(Verse 3)*
*You never need to feel sad or lonely again,*
*I'll stand beside you through sun, wind, and rain.*
*I'll build you a home, together we'll roam,*
*And in our hearts, we'll never be alone.*
*A life well lived, with laughter and grace—*
*A joyful journey, no one can replace.*

*(Chorus)*

*To have and to hold, forever and ever,*
*These tender months we grow together.*
*I will love you all of my life—*
*If you will only be my wife.*

*(Verse 4)*
*You are the one my soul longed to see,*
*The dream I dreamed so endlessly.*
*Could it be true after all this time?*
*Are you still free to forever be mine?*
*Our souls entwined, for all eternity.*

*(Chorus)*
*To have and to hold, forever and ever,*
*These golden years we build together.*
*I will love you all of my life—*
*If you will only be my wife.*

*(Verse 5)*
*So let me stand at your side each day.*
*We'll walk the Sacred Path till we're old and gray.*
*I'll keep you safe in my embrace,*
*Shield you with love, and gentle grace.*
*And together we'll fly when the angels call.*

*(Chorus)*
*To have and to hold, forever and ever,*
*This beautiful life we share together.*
*I will love you all of my life—*
*Because today, you became my wife.*

*(Final Verse)*
*God gave you to me—to honor and to cherish,*
*Bound as one, until our bodies perish.*
*And when the time comes, we'll rise above,*

Luke let the final note linger, soft and full of promise, as Megan's tears slipped down her cheeks.

"I love you, Megan. You're my dream come true."

Handing the guitar to Pa, he stepped off the stage and into her arms. She'd heard the melody countless times, but these words were new—written just for her. Smiling through tears, she cupped his face.

"I love you, Luke. Forever."

"I'll love you always," he murmured, kissing and holding her close.

Cassie watched through joyful tears, slipping her hand into Ed's. He kissed her forehead.

"You'll always be the love of my life. Thank you for marrying me, Cass."

"And you'll always be my one and only," she whispered back.

Guests clapped and dabbed their eyes. Ashley wiped a tear, thinking of Andrew—how Megan had long felt like a sister—and wishing for a love like hers.

"I hope I can have that someday," she whispered to Clint.

"You will," he said, meeting her gaze.

Her heart fluttered at the quiet promise in his eyes.

The celebration stretched on with dancing, laughter, and joyful reunions, but as the afternoon waned, Luke leaned close.

"Let's slip away. The buggy's out front. Let's make a run for it."

Megan laughed. "Let me say goodbye to Ma and Pa first."

They found Cassie and Ed by the refreshment table.

"Ma, Pa, we're heading out. Thank you for everything—it was beautiful," Megan said, hugging them.

"You're welcome, sweetheart. Be safe. Enjoy your time together," Cassie replied.

"We love you," Ed added with an embrace.

Luke tugged Megan toward the door.

"Goodbye!" Ed called.

"They're getting away!" someone shouted.

"Throw the bouquet!" another voice cried.

Cassie appeared with the flowers. Megan turned to the giggling line of women—Ashley, Eileen, Gwen—and tossed the bouquet high. It spun once and landed neatly in Eileen's hands. Cheers rose. Tyler clapped the loudest; she blushed, glancing back at him.

Megan and Luke dashed to their buggy as guests tossed wheat and called goodbyes. They kissed, laughing, as the buggy rolled on, cheers fading behind them.

Ashley waved until they disappeared down the road. Clint stepped beside her.

"I was wondering…" he said softly. "Would you mind writing to me while I'm at school? I'd like to get to know you better."

Ashley's heart skipped. "I'd like that very much."

Clint smiled—and her heart soared at the promise reflected in his eyes.

# Chapter 18

# Camping Honeymoon

The buggy rattled through town, tin cans clanking merrily behind. Once free of well-wishers, Luke slowed the horse and pulled Megan close, stealing kisses whenever he could.

She laughed, breathless, as the buggy swerved. "Luke! We won't make it home in one piece!"

With a sheepish grin, he steadied the reins.

They pulled into the yard and Luke helped Megan down, careful with her train.

"You go change," he said, helping her up the steps. "I'll pack the food."

"Sounds perfect," she said, smiling.

Luke headed to the barn while Megan sat at her vanity, gazing at her radiant reflection. *You're a married woman now...*Her heart fluttered at the thought.

She removed her mother's jewelry, then pressed the little bluebell between the pages of a book. With her veil and hairpins set aside, dark curls tumbled free. She unfastened the buttons at her wrists—then paused. She couldn't reach the ones down her back.

Cracking the bedroom door, she called, "Umm...I need some help."

Luke, in brown trousers and shirt, froze at the sight of her. "I'll be right there." His hands shook, nearly dropping the bread.

Luke entered quietly. The hinges creaked, and Megan jumped. She stood bathed in light, lace clinging to her figure, hair cascading over bare shoulders.

"Just the buttons," she said, motioning behind her.

He swept her hair aside, fingertips brushing her skin. She gasped, shivering. Unable to resist, he leaned in and kissed her neck. She tilted her head back, and he trailed a path of kisses to her ear, making her giggle.

"The buttons," she teased.

"Oh, right," he chuckled.

One by one, he unfastened them, lace giving way to silk and corset.

"There you go."

"Thank you, dear. I've got it now." Blushing, she clutched the dress against herself.

"You sure?"

"I'm sure. Go finish packing." She nudged him out, his chuckle fading down the hall.

Alone, she hung her gown and corset, then dressed in her red frock, sturdy shoes, and stockings. She tied back her hair with a matching ribbon, grabbed her valise, and stepped outside.

Luke waited by the buggy, Wildfire hitched and Snowfire tied behind.

"Let's go, Mrs. Havoc. Our honeymoon awaits."

"I'm ready, Mr. Havoc."

Megan nestled against Luke's shoulder as they followed the narrow trail toward their secluded hideaway.

"Tell me more about that couple we met today—the Butlers?"

"I worked with Samantha at the telephone company," Megan said, eyes on the open plains. "One afternoon, we stopped by the butcher shop to visit Stephan, and we all went for ice cream. From then on, it was the four of us—me, Samantha, Stephan, and Andrew. A week later, we went to a play. On the way home, we were ambushed."

Luke's jaw tightened. "You told me about that night."

She nodded, eyes distant. "Two men blocked the alley. Behind us was Shane—with a gun, out for revenge on Andrew. Stephan charged the thugs, took a beating while Samantha ran for help. That's when Andrew was shot." Tears slid down her cheeks.

Luke drew her close, kissing her hair. "No wonder seeing them again hit so hard."

"If not for them, we might all have died. Stephan, battered and broken, still thought he hadn't done enough. He and Samantha stayed with me until Ma and Pa arrived. I haven't seen them in a while, but I'll always feel close to them."

Luke's voice thickened. "I owe them everything. And Andrew...I don't know what I'd do if anything happened to you. I love you more than I can say."

She turned to him, eyes luminous. He stopped the buggy.

"I love you too," she whispered. "You've always had a place in my heart. Now you're my whole world."

"My darling, Megan." He cupped her face. "Everything I am—is yours."

He kissed her, slow and deep, until they were breathless, foreheads touching—

The sky cracked with a thunderous boom that shook the ground. Both jerked back to see a wall of dark, churning clouds rolling in fast across the prairie.

Megan gasped. "We'd better hurry."

He snapped the reins. Wind howled, dust swirling into a ghostly trail. Daylight dimmed to near-black. Luke veered off the road, driving hard over rough prairie toward their campsite. Lightning forked behind them; thunder rolled like cannon fire. Rain struck in sheets, stinging their faces. Trees ahead bent and groaned in the gale.

At camp, Luke reined in. "I'll get the horses. You take shelter!"

He helped Megan down. She threw her shawl over her head and ran for the white tent, its canvas snapping in the wind.

Luke freed Wildfire and Snowfire. "Go home!" The horses bolted into the storm.

He grabbed their bags, tossing them inside, then vanished into the downpour for the food crate. Megan hauled the bags deeper in, gripping the center pole as the tent lifted and shuddered.

Luke stumbled back in, soaked, and tied the flaps tight. Lightning flashed; thunder cracked overhead, shaking the ground. Hail hammered the canvas.

"Will the horses be alright?" she cried over the noise.

"They'll find their way. Are you okay?"

Another deafening crack. She shrieked and threw herself into his arms, trembling, face pressed against his soaked shirt.

"I'm scared."

"I've got you," he murmured, bracing the pole with one arm and holding her with the other. "Nothing will happen to you. We'll get through this—together."

The storm moved on as swiftly as it came, thunder fading to a distant rumble. Rain softened to a steady patter, the wind died to a breeze.

"Is it over?" she asked in the silvery light.

"Sounds like it." He peeked outside. "The front's passed, but we're in for more rain. We're not going anywhere tonight."

He turned to see her shivering, clothes plastered to her skin.

"Luke, what are we going to do? We're drenched, can't start a fire, horses are gone—our honeymoon is ruined."

He pulled her in, grinning crookedly. "It's not ruined—it's an adventure. We just started the 'cozy inside the tent' part a little early."

She blinked—then burst into deep, shaking laughter that melted the tension. Luke laughed too, holding her close.

When she caught her breath, she smiled up at him. "You're the best. I love you."

"I love you too." He kissed her forehead. "If we had a teepee, I'd build a fire. But since we don't…" His gaze drifted to the bedding at the back of the tent—a thick mattress, warm blankets, and soft pillows. "Only one way to warm up—gotta get out of these wet clothes first."

Her own clothes clung heavy and cold. She sighed. "Turn around."

He obeyed, grinning to himself. She opened her bag, pulled out a nightgown, and peeled off her soaked dress and underthings. Shivering, she slipped into the gown and dove under the blankets. "Okay. Your turn."

Luke had tried to avert his eyes, but a fleeting silhouette in the dim light caught his gaze. Smiling, he shed his boots and wet clothes, changed into his nightshirt, and joined her.

Sliding under the covers, he stayed on his side. "Any warmer?"

"Not yet," she murmured, teeth chattering.

"Come here." He curved his body around hers, arm slipping around her waist. Gradually, heat seeped into their chilled skin.

"Thank you," she whispered, her body softening. Her hand found his over her stomach, fingertips brushing the faint scars on his forearm.

Luke closed his eyes, savoring her touch. "I promised to stand beside you through sun, wind, and rain—remember? Like the song says."

She smiled. "Yes. And what a beautiful song. This day's been perfect...except the storm."

"It's still perfect," he murmured. "Any day with you is perfect." He breathed in her scent—fresh rain and wildflowers.

She gave a soft laugh. "You're so sweet. How did I get so lucky?"

"I think we both did," he whispered. "Two half-frozen newlyweds, a dry bed, and nothing but time while the rain comes down." He kissed her ear.

Her breath caught, warmth running deeper than skin. "Mmm-hmm."

Encouraged, he traced kisses along her neck, brushing his nose against her skin.

Megan's pulse quickened. She wanted nothing more than to be close to him—to share everything. Remembering her talk with Penny, she hesitated only a moment, then turned to face him.

Luke lifted his head. In the soft light, her eyes shimmered. She closed them, and he kissed her gently—lips, cheeks, forehead—each touch melting more of the cold. She turned fully into his arms, and he drew her close until nothing separated them.

In the hush of the rain, they became one—body, heart, and soul.

***

Later, warm and wrapped in each other's arms, they lay listening to the steady rain on canvas.

"What time do you think it is?" Megan traced lazy circles on his chest.

"Five or six, maybe," Luke murmured, stroking her arm. "Why?"

"I'm hungry."

He kissed her forehead. "Me too. But I'm not craving food…"

She laughed. "Silly man. Maybe I should see what I can rustle up for supper."

"No, let me." He sat up, careful not to disturb the blankets. "I packed the food—no need for both of us to freeze."

She hesitated. "You're sure?"

"Positive." He tugged on his nightshirt, crossed the dim tent, and rummaged through the food box. With no fire, options were slim. He returned with a tin plate and slid back under the covers.

"Brr! Your feet are like ice!" she squeaked.

"You'll warm me," he teased. "Here, take a bite." Something brushed her cheek instead, making her giggle as she guided his hand.

"Mmm…strawberry. So sweet."

"Your turn," she said, fumbling and poking his nose.

He caught her wrist, guiding the berry to his mouth, nibbling both fruit and fingers.

Amid laughter, they fed each other until the berries were gone.

"Got anything else in that box of wonders?" she asked, licking her fingers.

"If I had a fire, I'd spoil you," he said with mock regret. "Ah—biscuits from breakfast. Butter and jam."

He assembled them, passing one to her. She ate eagerly. "Perfect. Simple but delicious."

Luke handed her the milk jug. She drank, then smiled. "Best supper ever. Maybe my other senses are sharper without the light."

He chuckled, voice low. "Everything smells, tastes, and feels better in the dark."

He drew her close, kissing along her neck and jaw. She dissolved into giggles, their laughter blending with the rain's gentle patter.

***

The next morning, sunlight brightened the tent to a soft glow. Luke smiled at the sight of Megan asleep beside him. Her lashes fluttered, and he chuckled.

"Good morning, Sunshine," he said.

She peered up. "What's funny?"

"You—my beautiful, *messy* wife," he grinned, holding back laughter.

"Messy?"

"You're covered in flour, jam, and strawberry juice," he said, laughing.

Megan sat up, touching her cheeks—then, upon seeing him, burst out laughing. "You're one to talk! You've got strawberry on your nose, flour on your chin, and biscuit on your chest."

He laughed harder. "You think that's funny? I'm tossing you in the creek to scrub you clean!"

Still laughing, he stood, hoisting her over his shoulder with a playful growl.

"No!" she squealed, kicking as he carried her through the flap, bright sun greeting them.

He patted her backside with his free hand, grinning. "Behave. You need a bath, and there's no use fighting it."

"Noooo!" she squealed again.

"Ahem," a deep voice sounded.

Luke froze mid-step. Megan, hanging upside-down, pushed hair from her face to see who'd spoken.

"Pa!" she gasped.

Luke spun. "Pa!" he echoed, hastily setting her down as they fumbled with their clothes and dignity.

Ed cleared his throat. "Saw the horses by the house—thought something was wrong. I see you're...fine. No need to speak of this again." Leaving their horses behind, he mounted Major and rode off, a laugh trailing behind.

They collapsed into helpless laughter.

"Oh—his face," Megan wheezed.

Luke doubled over. "He thinks we've lost our minds!"

"We have," she gasped, leaning against him.

Gradually they calmed, though the sight of each other set them off again. He brushed off a dusting of flour from her cheek. "Come on, let's get you cleaned up."

They bathed in the cold creek, built a fire, and cooked breakfast barefoot in their nightclothes while their wet clothes dried. Later, dressed and dry, they rode through the rain-washed countryside—prairie grasses waving, wildflowers bright, the air rich with earth and sunlight.

"I never guessed a camping honeymoon could be this fun," Megan said as they rode side by side.

Luke took her hand. "A memory no one else could duplicate. Like I said: Every day's a good day with you."

That evening, Luke caught brook trout, and Megan fried them with potatoes, a gentle breeze carrying the scent of sizzling fish through the trees.

"That was delicious," Luke said, watching Megan dry the last dish and place it in the camp box.

"Wait here." Luke fetched her brush and motioned for her to sit. He knelt behind her, dusk deepening as the creek murmured and fire crackled.

Megan sighed as he brushed long strokes down her back, each one sending a pleasant shiver. He braided her hair and brought the plaits over her shoulders.

"There," he said softly. "All done."

Megan traced the soft plaits. "I love you."

Luke leaned in, hands resting on her shoulders. "Ne en tevitsi tsaa suankanna, tsanavuinde gwehe," he murmured, kissing her cheek.

She turned slightly. "That's beautiful. What does it mean?"

"I love you, beautiful wife."

Megan cupped his cheeks, kissed him slow and sweet. "I love you, too." Rising with a playful grin, she said, "Your turn."

"Yes, ma'am." Luke sat on the log, hair falling halfway down his back, dark as rich earth.

Kneeling behind him, Megan brushed his hair smooth, threading her fingers through its soft silky strands.

Luke closed his eyes. "You're good at this. Feels like you've done it a thousand times."

"I've had a little practice," she teased. "Bun or French braid?"

"Simple braid's fine."

Her fingers skimmed his neck as she braided. He shivered.

"Mmm, nice," he murmured.

She leaned forward, arms circling him, lips brushing the side of his neck. "So are you."

"Come here, my beautiful wife."

He drew her close and kissed her deeply—then swept her into his arms and carried her into the tent.

***

"Tsao tupuninna dehimbe—good morning, sweetheart," Luke murmured, voice low and warm.

Megan stretched—then draped an arm across his chest. "Mmm...good morning, my love."

"Yes, it is." He rolled toward her, kissing her slowly.

"Did you sleep well?" she asked, fingers threading through his hair.

"As long as I wake up beside you." His lips trailed her cheek, nibbling her ear as his hand slid along her back.

She melted into him with a quiet hum.

***

It was late morning before they emerged from their tent. Soon, Megan had sizzling meat and fresh biscuits making their stomachs growl in anticipation.

"My appetite's been wild out here," Megan laughed as she served breakfast. "If we stayed too long, I'd probably get fat."

Luke grinned, taking his plate. "You could, and I'd

love every bit of you."

She arched a brow. "Even if I end up big as a pregnant cow?"

"Even then," he said, laughter fading to tenderness. "Knowing you were carrying our child... Megan, that's the most beautiful thing. A woman growing life—it's sacred. It's your gift."

Her heart swelled. "How do I say, 'I love you' in Shoshone?"

"Ne en tevitsi tsaa suankanna," he said gently.

"Ne...en...tevitsi…" She faltered, watching his face.

"Tsaa suankanna," he repeated.

"Ne en tevitsi tsaa suankanna, Luke," she said proudly.

Emotion caught in his chest. "You're amazing. My dream come true." He brushed her cheek and kissed her, slow and lingering.

***

The day unfolded like a dream—wandering the creek, skipping stones, fishing, and riding through the prairie bathed in spring's golden light.

But too soon, Pa arrived with the wagon to help pack up the tent and take them home.

# Chapter 19

## *The Reservation*

Luke and Megan arrived home with Pa just as the sun dipped behind the hills, the scent of supper drifting from the house. Before the wagon stopped, the boys bounded down the steps.

"They're back!" Johnathan cried, skidding to a halt. "Did you have fun?"

Luke fought a grin. "Yes," he said simply.

David smirked. "Johnathan...they were on their *honeymoon*," he drawled, hoping the boy would catch on.

"What did you do?" Johnathan asked, trotting after him.

Luke glanced at Megan, who hid a giggle behind her basket. "We fished. Rode horses," he said, struggling to keep a straight face.

"I wish I could've come. I love camping."

"Maybe next time, buddy," Luke said, ruffling his hair.

"I'll take you when it warms up," David promised, flashing Luke a knowing look.

"I want to go too!" Kurt called, puffing as he staggered up the steps with a box.

***

Megan stepped into her room and stopped short. "Oh...what a beautiful bed!"

In place of her old one stood an elegant frame with a carved headboard, draped in a new quilt of warm colors.

"Where'd this come from?" she asked, tracing the polished wood.

Cassie appeared, smiling. "It's our wedding gift. The quilt was made by the Quilting Circle."

Megan hugged her, misty-eyed. "Thank you, Ma. It's beautiful."

Luke entered, halting mid-step. "What's all this?"

"Ma and Pa's gift," Megan said, taking his hand. "And the quilt's from the Quilting Circle."

Luke smiled. "It's wonderful. But we leave in a week."

Ed leaned in the doorway. "It'll be here when you come back. And someday, in your own home."

Megan hugged him. "We love it."

Luke pressed a hand to the mattress. "Thank you both. Feels great."

Megan bounced lightly. "I can't wait to sleep on it."

Cassie pointed to a corner where brightly wrapped packages waited. "You've still got wedding gifts to open."

Megan's eyes lit. "Oh, how nice!"

"After supper," Ed said with a wink. "And while we eat, you can tell us about your trip."

As her parents disappeared into the kitchen, Luke leaned close. "I hope Pa didn't tell Ma what he saw."

"If he did, she's not letting on," Megan whispered, sharing a sheepish smile.

***

After supper, they opened gifts and penned thank-you notes.

248

"We'll have almost everything we need to start a home," Megan said, picturing a snug cabin, sunlight spilling through windows as she cooked, kept the hearth, and raised children beside Luke.

***

That night, snuggled in their new bed, they whispered into the dark.

"Are you excited to meet my tribe?" Luke asked, caressing her arm.

"I am," Megan murmured, "but I'm nervous. What if they don't like me?"

"What's not to like?" He kissed her forehead. "They'll love you. You'll love them. It's part of who you are now."

She searched his eyes. "I'll miss everyone here. Won't you?"

"I will. But it's beautiful there. I can't wait to show you."

Her heart eased at the sound of his voice. "If you're with me, I'll be happy."

"Exactly." He lifted her chin and kissed her gently.

***

By Monday morning, they were packed for the long journey. Instead of her finest traveling dress, Megan wore riding clothes and a wide-brimmed hat—ready for the rugged road beyond Rawlins.

On the wooden platform, excitement mingled with the ache of parting. Megan hugged Grandma and Grandpa Hartford, tears brimming. "We love you so much. Thank you—for everything." A quiet fear stirred: would she ever see them again?

"You take care of each other, you hear?" Grandma Hartford said, pulling Luke into a hug and giving his cheek a playful pinch.

"We will," he replied thickly. "We love you."

Grandpa O'Malley clasped Ed's hand. "Don't worry—the ranch is in good hands."

"Thank you," Ed said, relief in his voice.

"I'll keep the boys in line," Grandma O'Malley told Cassie with a wink. "Enjoy yourselves."

"This means more than you know," Cassie replied. "It'll be the honeymoon we never had."

The boys came next.

"We'll try to be back for your graduation, David," Megan said through tears.

"You'd better. Maybe for Thanksgiving or Christmas," he said, voice cracking.

"We'll try—weather permitting," Megan replied.

Johnathan blinked fast. "I'll be almost grown up by the time you're back. You might not recognize me."

Luke hugged him. "No matter how big you get, you'll always be my little brother."

Megan pulled him close. "I love you, Johnathan."

Kurt tried to be brave. "Please come back soon."

"We'll try," Megan whispered, kissing his cheek.

Grandma O'Malley embraced them both. "Write when you can. Be safe. We love you."

"We love you too," they echoed.

Grandpa O'Malley stepped forward. "Don't make me come after you. If money's tight, I'll wire the fare for Christmas. Just promise you'll be back."

Megan hugged him tight. "Thank you, Grandpa. We'll do our best. Take care of everyone. We love you."

His voice softened, eyes shining. "We'll be praying for you."

The conductor's call rang out: "All aboard!"

"We love you! Take care!" Megan and Luke called, waving as they boarded.

Seated by the window, Megan watched her family fade from view, tears slipping down her cheeks. "What if we don't see them again? A year's so long...anything could happen."

Luke drew her close. "We can't live in fear of what-ifs. God's watching over them—and us."

Across the aisle, Cassie dabbed at her eyes. "She's right though...what if something happens to the boys?"

"They'll be fine," Ed said, squeezing her hand. "Grandma and Grandpa will take good care of them."

Cassie managed a watery smile. "I know. I just worry."

"You deserve this trip," Ed said, kissing her temple.

Her nerves fluttered with anticipation. "It might be fun."

"It will," he grinned. "By afternoon we'll be in Rawlins—then nothing but woods and sky. You'll love it."

The day passed in easy talk and laughter, the plains unrolling beyond the glass. Lunch in the dining car broke the journey, and by midafternoon they reached Rawlins. After unloading trunks, they gathered the horses, rented a wagon, and set out north.

Nearly ten miles out, Ed called over the wagon wheels, "We'll need to make camp soon. I want tents up before dark."

Luke pointed to a rise ahead. "Perfect spot—fresh

water, trees for shelter."

He glanced back at Megan, riding beside Cassie. With their braided black hair beneath cowboy hats, they looked strikingly alike—two graceful silhouettes against the Wyoming sky.

"Isn't it breathtaking?" Megan asked softly.

Cassie turned, taking in the sweep of valley and mountains. "It's like a painting."

Below, tall grasses rippled toward streams lined with poplars, fields freshly tilled. To the west, the Wind River peaks gleamed with snow; to the east, red cliffs burned under the setting sun.

"Ma…" Megan hesitated, eyes flicking toward Luke. "I'm nervous."

"It'll be all right, sweetheart. Luke will be with you."

"That's not it." Megan lowered her gaze. "What if I don't like living in a teepee? What if I don't fit in with the tribe? At college, I knew I'd be home for holidays. But this...it feels so far away. I don't know if I'm strong enough."

Cassie slowed. "You're stronger than you think. Remember the verse— 'A man shall leave his father and mother and cleave unto his wife'? This is how it's meant to be. Building a life with your husband is a good and holy thing."

She hesitated. "It might've been easier for me—I had no choice. My family was gone. All I had left were Aunt Mabel, Uncle George, and Ed. But I learned that when you walk life's road together—especially through hard times—you grow stronger, closer."

Cassie's gaze shifted to Luke. "Learning about his people, becoming part of their world—it will bind you in ways you can't yet see. You'll see through his eyes, and he'll see through yours."

Megan's eyes misted as she watched Luke riding ahead, dark hair lifting in the breeze, his fringed buckskin tunic and quiver marking him as a man at home in both worlds. A smile tugged at her lips. "You're right. He looks so proud leading us to his homeland. I want to share that pride—not burden him with worry."

Cassie reached over, squeezing her hand. "Be honest with him. He'll understand. It wasn't easy for him either—coming home, going against his father's wishes, waiting while you finished school. That kind of patience... that's love. Show him the same."

Megan nodded, voice tight. "I will. I love him so much. I want to understand every part of him—and help his people too. I'll try to be brave."

Cassie's heart swelled. "That's my girl. You're a Havoc—and more importantly, a daughter of God. With Him, you can do anything."

"I love you, Ma," Megan whispered, a tear slipping free. "I'll make you proud."

***

That evening, after pitching the tents, they built a fire and cooked supper. The night was clear, stars scattered like jewels, a silver crescent moon rising over the dark mountains. A stream whispered nearby, crickets trilled, and treetops stirred in the cool breeze. Wrapped in blankets, they sat close against weathered logs. Ed strummed his guitar, their voices harmonizing to familiar tunes.

When the hour grew late, Luke stood and stretched. "We'd better turn in. Goodnight, Ma. Goodnight, Pa." He helped Megan to her feet.

Cassie smiled at their glowing faces. "Love you both."

"Love you too," they called, disappearing toward their tent.

Ed tossed a log onto the fire, sparks swirling into the night. Then he drew Cassie into his arms. "What about you, Mrs. Havoc? Ready for bed?"

"Almost," she murmured, breathing in the clean pine air.

From the tent came muffled laughter. Ed chuckled. "Those two. I told you what I walked in on when I brought their horses back. We were never that wild—*were we?*"

Cassie's eyes twinkled. "You don't remember? You tried to dunk me in the watering trough right after our wedding. And later, when I was bathing in the stream—you waited until I dressed and dunked me anyway."

He grinned. "Hmm. Maybe I did forget. But something about being out here with you makes me feel young—and frisky."

His lips brushed hers, then trailed down her neck.

"Ed…" she whispered, fingers threading through his hair. "Maybe it is time to turn in." This trip had been a good idea—maybe the best yet.

***

The next four days were long and sometimes demanding as they wound through rugged passes and broad valleys toward the Wind River Reservation. Each night they camped beneath sheltering trees, but the deeper they rode into the wilderness, the heavier the shadows, the keener the silence.

By noon on the fourth day, they reached Fort

Washakie—a cluster of weathered buildings alive with soldiers, its sturdy fence a stern reminder of order on the wild frontier.

Two armed guards stood at the main gate dressed in crisp blue uniforms.

"Ho there! State your purpose!" one called.

Ed halted the wagon. Luke rode forward and dismounted. "I'm Luka Standing Elk Havoc of the Eastern Shoshone, returning to join my family. I have documentation."

He handed over a folded letter—proof of citizenship and the right to come and go freely. "This is my wife and her parents. She's a teacher, hoping to apply for a position."

The guard frowned. "This is highly irregular." He returned the papers but kept his rifle steady.

Ed spoke evenly. "We're only staying a day or two, just to help our daughter get settled."

"If she's hired, we'll stay through the school year," Luke added. "Otherwise, we'll move on."

"You'll need to report to the main office," the guard said. "Bring your wife. My commanding officer will want to speak with her."

Luke helped Megan down from Snowfire, tied the reins, and followed the guard. Ed climbed down as the second soldier began searching their supplies.

"Only camping gear and clothing," Ed said, his arm slipping around Cassie. His voice was calm, though his eyes were wary—he knew Army suspicion all too well.

The soldier unearthed a hunting rifle. Ed explained its purpose; after a pause, the man set it aside and continued the search.

Inside the fort, Megan stayed close to Luke, uneasy under the watch of armed men along the perimeter. Others paused mid-task to follow them with their eyes as they crossed the yard to a central building.

When Luke and Megan returned, the officer escorted them to the wagon. The search had ended, and a guard reported nothing suspicious found.

Ed met Luke's eyes. "Well? What did they say?"

"They'll let you and Ma stay a few days," Luke said, mounting his horse, jaw tight. "You'll have to check out when you leave."

"And the job?" Cassie asked, glancing at Megan.

Megan's face lit. "I got it!"

Cassie embraced her. "That's wonderful!"

"I'll come back in the fall to finalize everything," Megan said, breathless with joy. "I can't believe it—I'm going to be a teacher!"

***

With Ed following in the wagon, they passed through the checkpoint and returned to the open road.

They crossed the wide prairie until Luke pointed to faint smoke curls on the horizon. "Our teepee fires." From a ridge, the village appeared—a wide green valley cradled by forested mountains, the Wind River glinting along its western edge. South of camp, bareback riders watched over a herd of grazing horses.

Cassie's breath caught. "It's beautiful." Cottonwoods and poplars dotted the riverbank; hundreds of teepees filled the open ground, their people in a mix of buckskin and cotton. "I didn't realize there would be so many…"

"In spring and summer, subtribes gather here to trade," Luke said. "In winter, we split into smaller groups to hunt."

"Should we announce ourselves?" Ed asked, eyeing the camp warily.

Luke nodded. "They likely already know we're coming. But, wait here."

Ed set his rifle beside him, scanning the trees, sensing unseen eyes watching them.

Luke rode down the slope, following worn tracks through the brush. Two braves galloped out to meet him, exchanged a few words, then wheeled back toward camp. He waved the others forward.

Cassie and Megan moved ahead of the wagon to escape the dust, their horses picking carefully down the slope. Ed followed close, riding the brakes to hold the wagon back.

In the village, word spread in ripples—some slipped into their lodges, others gathered to watch.

Luke dismounted and embraced one of the men. By the time Ed, Cassie, and Megan arrived, a crowd had formed.

Megan forced a smile, nerves dancing in her chest. Women approached, murmuring as they touched her red dress and Snowfire's white coat.

A sudden thunder of hooves—young braves charged up, shouting and brandishing feathered spears. Cassie gasped, blanching. Snowfire skittered beneath Megan, who fought to steady her. Luke raised a hand, calling out in Shoshone.

"Luke! What's happening?" Megan cried.

"I'm explaining—wait, someone's gone for my father. He'll settle this."

He lifted Megan from the saddle, holding her close

as he spoke sharply to an especially angry brave.

Ed jumped from the wagon and pushed through the crowd to Cassie. "Luke will clear it up," he told her, voice tight. She trembled, clinging to him.

The crowd parted, and silence fell as a man stepped forward, feathers swaying in his hair, his calm stride radiating authority.

"Apa!" Luke called.

"Standing Elk!" Agwai smiled.

They embraced, warm and firm.

Luke turned to Megan. "Ne gwehe, Megan. My wife. Megan—my Apa, Agwai."

Megan's stomach tightened as the middle-aged man studied her, then gently took her arms. "She is the one," he said in slow English. "The girl with green eyes. Welcome, daughter." He drew her into a warm embrace. "Tsanavuinde."

She knew the word—beautiful.

"Aho, apa nakanden," she said softly. "Hello, father-in-law." Tears welled as acceptance and warmth surrounded her.

Luke introduced Ed and Cassie. "They came for the wedding."

Ed extended a hand. "Good to see you again. Thank you for welcoming us."

Agwai replied with pride, "We are honored that you came for the ceremony. Come—we will celebrate."

As the group moved deeper into camp, Ed glanced back at the wagon.

"Don't worry, Pa," Luke said. A broad-shouldered man embraced him, then led the animals away. "My uncle, Grey Wolf, will care for them."

Luke slipped an arm around Megan's waist as they followed his father toward the village center. Ed and Cassie walked behind, meeting curious stares with polite smiles. Children darted close, giggling as they brushed the strangers before squealing away.

"They think it's brave to touch a white man," Luke chuckled.

Cassie glanced at Ed, unease in her eyes.

He squeezed her shoulder. "We'll be fine."

A petite, round-faced woman hurried up, embracing Luke before turning to embrace Megan with an excited stream of Shoshone.

"This is my aunt, Prairie Rose," Luke said. "She says you're very pretty."

Megan smiled. "Tell her she's beautiful."

Rose's eyes softened at the translation. "She says you are kind," Luke added.

Megan's heart quickened as they reached a large tee-pee, its flap drawn back. Inside, afternoon light glowed through the hide walls, and a small fire danced at the center. Agwai motioned them closer.

"Please, sit," he said, lowering himself onto a pelt. "Your journey was good?"

"Yes," Ed replied. "It's beautiful here."

"I am glad. God—Tam Apa—looks on you with favor," Agwai said solemnly.

"Father," Luke said in English, "can you perform the wedding tomorrow? The Army doesn't want them here long."

Agwai nodded. "Tomorrow, yes."

"Thank you," Ed said.

Cassie turned to Rose. "What can we do to help?"

Rose's smile deepened after Luke's translation. "Rose says everything will be ready by morning. You are guests."

Cassie's eyes shone. "Thank you," she said to Rose.

***

That evening, after pitching their canvas tents, they returned to sit near Luke's family by the roaring bonfire, watching dancers circle the flames, dressed in vibrant regalia. Fringes swayed to the beat of the drums, voices rose in chant, and laughter mingled with the scent of shared food.

As weariness set in, Ed, Cassie, Luke, and Megan offered their thanks before quietly slipping away.

***

"I was so scared today," Cassie whispered in Ed's arms. "I thought I'd overcome that fear. But when those braves came at us—shouting, shaking their spears—it felt like that night again—when they killed my family." Tears spilled, raw and unrestrained.

"Oh, Cass…" Ed stroked her hair. "If I'd known how hard this would be, I wouldn't have offered to come. I was scared too. If anything had happened to you or Megan…" His voice caught. "I'll be glad when this is over. Luke's father welcomed us, but not everyone wants us here."

"I'm glad we came—for Megan and Luke. But I don't want to stay a moment longer than we must."

"As soon as the ceremony's done, we'll leave," he promised, kissing her hair.

Cassie nestled closer. "No wonder Megan was nervous. Living here…it'll be even harder than I thought."

260

"She's strong," Ed murmured. "She'll adjust. And they'll see what we do—Megan's loving, generous, and brave. In time, they'll accept her."

***

"I feel awful," Luke whispered in the dark, arms wrapped around Megan. "I saw Ma's terrified face today...remembered what she's lived through. Then Pa's first wife and child—all that loss. I shouldn't have brought them. I thought only of my father's joy, not how the tribe might react. I've made this harder for everyone."

Megan rested her head on his shoulder. "I was nervous too. When those braves charged, I nearly screamed. I can't imagine how Ma felt. But this isn't your fault. You can't control others—you've done your best."

He held her tighter, sighing. "It'll be better tomorrow."

She smiled faintly as he kissed her forehead. The long journey was behind them. Luke was home—with Megan.

# Chapter 20

# Shoshone Wedding

*oday's the day,* Luke thought, heart brimming as he woke Megan with soft kisses.

"Good morning, husband," she murmured, birds trilling as soft light filtered through the canvas walls.

"Good morning, beautiful," he whispered, brushing her cheek.

Megan nestled closer, returning his kisses with sleepy affection, certain she would never tire of waking beside him.

The sky bloomed pink and orange over the rugged peaks as the family finished a simple breakfast by the campfire. Megan and Cassie had just finished the dishes when six Shoshone women, including Aunt Rose, reached for their hands and gently led them away, laughing and chattering in animated Shoshone.

"Luke, what's going on?" Megan called over her shoulder.

"Go on," he grinned. "You'll see soon enough."

"What do you think they'll do?" Megan whispered to her mother, nerves fluttering.

"No idea," Cassie admitted, wide-eyed. The women carried baskets, blankets, and clay vessels, their beaded deerskin dresses glinting in the morning sun.

They followed a winding trail to the river, water spreading wide between gentle banks. Rose pointed to her chest, then to Megan's buttons, speaking softly but firmly.

"Ma...does she want me to undress?" Megan asked, brow furrowed.

Cassie glanced around the secluded clearing. "I think so."

Blushing, Megan offered a tentative smile. The other women stripped to their breechcloths, waded into the cold water and released their braids, laughter echoing across the river.

Cassie chuckled, unbuttoning her blouse. "After all that trail dust...I could use a bath."

Soon, Megan and Cassie stood barefoot in their underclothes. Rose took their hands, guiding them into the river. There was no shame—only sisterhood. Megan felt it in her bones: each woman, young or old, copper-skinned or pale, reflected divine beauty.

A tall, graceful woman introduced herself as Red Fox, Luke's would-have-been bride, gently lathering Megan's hair with fragrant soap. The icy water and rich scent refreshed her completely. Red Fox introduced the others—Little Deer, Wind Song, and shy sisters Lonnie and Bonnie—each kind and attentive.

Cassie sniffed the soap. "Aloe? Mint? Juniper?" she asked. Rose nodded and repeated the words slowly in both languages. Cassie made a mental note to ask Luke for the ingredients later.

When their hair was washed, the women stepped from the river, wrapping themselves in bright wool blankets. Sunlight warmed them as they sat on river stones, combing in fragrant oil before braiding their hair into twin plaits.

Rose and Red Fox came to Megan's side, gently brushing and braiding her hair while murmuring softly. She closed her eyes, savoring their hands and catching words like bride, beautiful, mother. Her heart swelled.

When her hair was done, the women helped her to her feet. "Come," they said, motioning to follow. Wrapped in blankets, Megan and Cassie carried their clothes back to the waking village. Children spilled from teepees, rubbing their eyes and staring. Some waved shyly, calling "hello" in tentative English.

The women guided them into a large teepee, closing the flap behind them. The wedding preparations had begun.

Inside the teepee, a small blaze crackled in the center, its flickering glow dancing across slanted walls. Fur pelts lay across the floor, offering places to sit. The Shoshone women dressed quickly in their buckskin garments. Cassie reached for her clothes, but when Megan did the same, Rose gently raised a hand.

Silently, Rose set aside Megan's dress and shoes, then unwrapped a carefully folded bundle near the fire. Inside was a stunning creamy-white deerskin dress. The women leaned in, gasping and murmuring admiration.

Rose helped Megan slip it over her head. The leather was warm and buttery soft, with a subtle earthy scent. Wide sleeves reached her elbows, their long fringes trailing to her wrists. The straight skirt, falling just below her knees, was trimmed with fringe along the side seams and hem, the strands swaying to brush her ankles. A straight neckline, modestly revealing her collarbones, was edged in intricate blue-and-white beadwork that flowed down the sleeves and traced the hem.

"Oh, Megan," Cassie breathed. "It's beautiful."

Megan ran her fingers over the smooth leather, the beadwork making her green eyes shine. "Oh, Rose...tsanavuinde—beautiful," she whispered. Rose bowed humbly.

Red Fox lifted Megan's braids and placed them neatly across her chest, then brought a wide beaded belt. At its center, a circle divided into red, black, white, and yellow quadrants glimmered—a symbol she recognized from Luke's belongings. Carefully, Red Fox tied it around Megan's waist.

Tears welled in Megan's eyes. "Thank you...tsanavuinde," she whispered, squeezing Rose and Red Fox's hands. They smiled, nodding gently.

Little Deer stepped forward with a beaded choker—white with a single red square. Megan knelt as she tied it delicately around her throat. Next came Wind Song, holding white bone earrings strung with red beads, which Megan placed in her ears, voice thick with emotion.

"Thank you," she said softly.

Lonnie, the elder shy sister, knelt with white moccasins whose beadwork matched Megan's dress. She slipped them onto Megan's bare feet, lacing them to her knees. Soft, warm, perfectly molded, they completed the ensemble. Megan lifted her hem, marveling at the care and love woven into every piece.

"Thank you," Megan said, slowly turning so the women could admire her wedding attire. "I feel so beautiful."

Last came Bonnie, Lonnie's sister, carrying a length of soft white rabbit fur. With care, she wrapped it around Megan's braids, fastening it with sinew and two beaded discs—white background quartered by blue lines.

Megan traced the fur and beads. *There's meaning here,* she thought. "They're so soft...and beautiful," she murmured.

Cassie embraced her, eyes brimming. "Oh, Megan, you look stunning." She glanced at the women who had given such treasures—each crafted with care. Her voice trembled. "Thank you for making this day so special."

Red Fox translated. Smiling, the women bowed their heads and slipped silently from the teepee, leaving Megan, Cassie, and Rose in a hush that felt sacred.

Megan whispered, "What now?"

Cassie shook her head.

Rose gestured for them to sit, then lit a shallow dish of sweetgrass. Fragrant smoke curled upward as she chanted, sweeping it toward Megan with a feather fan.

Megan bowed her head, clasping her hands in prayer—for strength, happiness, and a long life with Luke. Beside her, Cassie prayed in gratitude and hope for Megan and Luke's new life together.

A tap at the flap broke the stillness. Rose answered, nodded, and motioned for Cassie and Megan to rise.

"It must be time," Cassie whispered.

Megan hugged her tightly. "Here goes."

They stepped into the morning sun and began walking through the village, past clusters of teepees and watchful eyes, toward the central clearing where the bonfire had burned the night before. A slow, reverent drumbeat began.

In the sacred circle stood Luke, cream buckskin tunic and leggings beaded and fringed, dark-blue breechcloth at his waist, black hair braided and wrapped in white fur.

Around his neck hung a white beaded choker and his necklace of four cougar teeth, his copper skin glowing.

Luke's breath caught at the sight of Megan, a smile spreading across his face. She looked luminous; her dark braids, wrapped in soft white fur, framed her like a crown. The beaded belt cinched at her waist bore the symbols of his people—now hers too. The white buckskin dress draped over her like liquid moonlight, the fringe whispering as it swayed. This was the dream he'd carried so long, and now it was coming true.

Megan walked toward him, regal and radiant, the women who'd dressed her watching with pride.

Suddenly, a man burst through the crowd, shouting and shaking his fist. Megan froze. Cassie and Rose moved to shield her as Luke and Ed sprinted forward. Luke seized the man's arm, his voice sharp in Shoshone. Chief Washakie stepped forward, sacred pipe in hand, his calm authority still that of a warrior.

The man glared once more, then shoved his way out. Murmurs followed him as he disappeared into the crowd.

Luke turned to Megan, taking her hands. "He's gone. Don't let him take this moment from us."

Megan blinked back tears and nodded. "I'm okay," she whispered. Luke squeezed her hands, offering a steady smile.

Ed reached Cassie, drawing her into his arms. "You alright?"

She nodded faintly, still pale. "I think so."

Scanning the crowd, Ed caught guarded glances among the solemn faces. Doubt flickered—perhaps not all welcomed this union.

Chief Washakie stepped forward. "Continue. He will

not return." Addressing the people in Shoshone, he eased the tension. Silently, a few slipped away, following the man.

Luke rejoined the circle beside his father.

Ed gave Cassie a quiet smile. "It's alright. The Chief made sure of it."

She nodded, and he moved to stand with Luke and Agwai.

Megan joined hands with her mother and Rose, and together they stepped into the sacred circle.

Luke stood between Agwai and Ed, with Chief Washakie flanked by his sub-chiefs like sentinels. Megan bowed in silent thanks. His headdress dipped in return, his eyes warm. She recalled his words from the night before: *This girl with green eyes who rides the sacred white horse will bring us good fortune.*

At Chief Washakie's signal, the people sat in a wide ring. Ed settled beside Cassie and Rose.

Agwai, radiant in ceremonial regalia, held a sacred hoop in the same four colors as Megan's belt. Passing it to an attendant, he lifted the sacred pipe toward the four directions—east, south, west, north—praying for Tam Apa's blessing.

Then, taking Megan's left hand and Luke's right, he joined them, beginning the wedding rites in Shoshone. Megan caught the word *gwe'etunu*—marriage—and her heart swelled. Luke's deep brown eyes held love and reverence. Surrounded by his people, embraced by their traditions, she felt something stir within her—a connection to her Indian heritage she'd never known. For the first time, that part of her identity awakened, bringing with it a profound sense of belonging.

Luke's gaze lingered on her—she was luminous. His bride. The girl who once felt so far away now stood here, uniting their worlds. Emotion surged—love, reverence, gratitude. Tears burned behind his eyes. This wasn't just a wedding. It was an answer—*his* answer—to every hope, every whispered prayer, every dream.

Megan felt the world narrow to the beat of her heart when she met his eyes. Luke stood tall and still, radiating love and tenderness that made her breath catch, as if she was something sacred. She had never felt so seen, so cherished.

She was no longer just Megan Marie Havoc. She was becoming whole—bound to this man, this tribe, this life. Looking at Luke, she knew she'd never again question where she belonged.

Agwai turned them to each direction of the sacred circle, Megan's hand firm in Luke's. The wind stirred around them as the weight of the moment pressed against her like a rushing river.

They faced east.

"The East," Agwai said reverently, "is yellow. Spring. The dawn of life. It brings fire and light. It is birth. New beginnings."

Megan closed her eyes, letting the meaning sink in. She pictured sunrise spilling over the prairie—the beginning of all things, like this moment, their union.

They faced south.

"The South is red—summer and youth. It is Earth, the giver of food and medicine, where we grow strong."

Megan thought of their own youth, of growing, struggling, and healing—together.

Turning west.

"The West is black—autumn, adulthood, parenthood. It is water, fluid and life-giving."

Her breath caught at the thought of children, someday. Luke's thumb grazed hers, steadying her.

Finally, facing north.

The North is white—winter, the season of reflection and rest. It is air, the breath of life and the mystery beyond."

She imagined silver hair, old age— still beside Luke, stepping together into what lay beyond.

Agwai turned to the tribe, speaking first in Shoshone, his voice rich and melodic, then in English, binding two worlds in a sacred knot. He lifted his hands skyward.

"God, Our Father, bless these two as they make their oaths. Let harmony grow between their worlds. Bind them in body, mind, and spirit. Cherish one another, love unconditionally, accept fully, and forgive always."

He laid his hands over theirs. "Megan and Luka Standing Elk, do you promise to remain faithful to one another all your lives?"

Tears blurred Megan's vision. "I do," she whispered.

"I do," Luke said, voice steady and reverent.

"Then Tam Apa—God, Our Father—gives you to one another. By the joining of hands, I proclaim you husband and wife, bound in this life and the next."

Agwai raised his arms in thanks. A cheer rose— whoops, drumming, joyous cries.

Luke drew her close, kissing her deep and tender. Megan melted into him, her hand finding his cheek.

"I love you, Luka Standing Elk."

"I love you, Megan Marie Havoc," he said, low and fierce.

She bowed to Agwai. "Thank you, Father."

He nodded, solemn and proud.

Rose stepped forward, draping a deep-blue, beaded blanket over their shoulders. Its warmth was nothing to the weight of its meaning—two lives bound as one.

The drums resumed, low as the heartbeat of the earth. A woman's voice rose in song, a haunting chant drifting through camp like wind in pines, stirring something ancient and sacred within Megan.

Side by side beneath the blanket, Megan and Luke walked slowly from the ceremony into the life ahead.

Cries of joy rose from the watching tribe—hands reached to touch the blanket in blessing, others clapped or smiled. Faces blurred before Megan's eyes, but every one bore witness, honoring their union.

Luke's steady presence beside her, his warm hand in hers, grounded her. Through fire and fear, they had found each other. Now, as husband and wife, they walked wrapped in love, family, and the quiet acceptance of a people who had made room for her.

Without warning, Luke swept her into his arms. She laughed, surprised, tucking her head to his shoulder as he carried her toward the shadowed edge of camp. A small crowd followed, pausing where the forest began. A final cheer rang out before they turned back, leaving the couple alone.

Luke carried her to a lone teepee set apart among the trees. He pushed aside the flap and stepped inside, still cradling her close.

"This is our new home," he murmured with a smile. "We stay here until sunrise. It's our honeymoon."

Inside, sunlight filtered through the hide, casting the

space in a golden glow. A small fire circle marked the center. Soft furs piled to form a low bed. Baskets, clay pots and hand-carved bowls lined the walls, each item arranged with care. Megan took in the simple beauty.

Luke laid the wedding blanket at the bed's foot. "The tribe gave us all this," he said. "They share what little they have with open hearts."

Megan's throat tightened. "Most have been so kind... but I understand the ones who haven't. I'm white—an outsider. After all your people have suffered, they have every right to be wary. And still, they welcomed me. That means more than I can say."

"They've been good to me too," Luke said, drawing her close. "My father and Chief Washakie are proud I've returned with you. You've made a strong impression."

"I see why you love it here," she murmured. "This land, your people—are beautiful. There's a quiet strength, a peace...a community I never expected."

"They're your people now too."

He lowered his head. She lifted her face, eyes closing as his lips met hers—warm, tender, sure. The kiss sank into her like rain on thirsty earth. She rose onto her toes, fingers twining behind his neck. Her emerald eyes shimmered beneath dark lashes, her gaze lost in the depth of his.

"*You* are my people, Luke," she whispered, a tear tracing her cheek.

Luke cupped her face, his voice low and reverent. "You're my dream come true." He drew her closer, her softness melting against him. "I waited so long for this. Every lonely day was worth it. With you, I'm whole."

"Oh, Luke..." Her heart swelled, and a joyful sob

escaped. "I'm so glad you came back. After wandering so long, I don't feel lost anymore. I found my home—*you*."

She pulled him into another kiss—deep, tender, and full of promise.

# Chapter 21

## *Agwai*

Ed and Cassie had watched the ceremony with tearful eyes. Once the initial tension faded, they were drawn into the beauty and reverence of the traditions. Though unfamiliar, it felt as sacred as the Christian service they'd attended in Cheyenne. Now, with Megan and Luke vanishing into their secluded lodge, Ed and Cassie were unsure what to do next but unwilling to leave without saying goodbye.

Chief Washakie approached, offering each a firm handshake.

"Congratulations. They will be very happy—I can see that. It is good you have come."

"Thank you," Ed said, glancing toward the path the couple had taken. "We were hoping to say goodbye before we left."

The chief's eyes twinkled. "It is our custom for newlyweds to remain in their lodge until sunrise. You are welcome to stay."

Ed laughed softly, sharing a look with Cassie. "Then we'd be honored."

With a nod, Chief Washakie returned to speak with the sub-chiefs and Luke's father. Ed and Cassie linked hands, heading toward their tent.

Agwai soon approached.

"Chief Washakie says you're staying another day.

Would you like to join me for a ride? I'd like to show you our land."

Ed looked to Cassie. "What do you think?"

Her gaze swept the valley, the river glinting below, mountains glowing in the morning light. "I'd love to."

"Then it's settled," Ed said, sliding an arm around her shoulders.

"Bring your horses to the river," Agwai said with a grin. "We'll ride from there."

***

At the river's edge, Agwai held the reins of his Paint while it drank from the clear, rushing water. Cassie and Ed rode up, their horses' hooves muffled in the soft earth.

"Ready?" Agwai swung bareback onto the striking animal, its hide a bold patchwork of brown and white. Gone was his ceremonial regalia; now he wore a simple buckskin tunic and leggings, a single black-and-white feather in his loose hair. A necklace of bear claws hung at his chest, a sheathed knife at his side.

Ed dismounted to fill two canteens.

Cassie admired the Paint. "That's a fine horse you have."

"A gift from Chief Washakie after a battle—his way of honoring a vision I shared that saved lives. His spirit matches mine," Agwai said, patting the speckled neck. His gaze shifted to the white mare. "But your daughter's horse—that is a rare spirit indeed."

Ed secured the canteens. "We gave her the horse for her sixteenth birthday. They've been inseparable since. An Arabian—fast, fierce, and loyal."

"I can see that," Agwai said as Snowfire pranced, eager to run.

Cassie held the reins steady. "Her name's Snowfire. Spirited and graceful."

"She carries a sacred energy," Agwai mused. "Why that name?"

Cassie glanced at Ed. "It just fit—gentle and calm, yet full of fire, like Megan. They understand each other."

"Then she's Megan's spirit guide," Agwai said, turning his mount north between the ridges.

"Makes sense," Ed said, thinking of all the miles Megan had ridden that mare—through joy and sorrow.

The trio climbed from the valley, the trail steep and shaded by quaking aspens. Ed's chestnut stallion, Major Jr., moved with steady strength, while Snowfire pressed close behind Agwai's horse, eager to lead.

"She's got a mind of her own," Cassie laughed. "She's used to running free with Megan."

Agwai studied Cassie in the saddle. She looked born to it. He wouldn't be surprised if she could race with the same fire as her daughter. He smiled. "She is spirited. When we reach the summit, she can set the pace back."

The camp vanished behind the hills as they climbed. Wildflowers brightened spaces between towering trees. The air was crisp and fresh.

Agwai suddenly pointed to a rocky outcrop. "Look— at the top of that pine."

A bald eagle perched high above, white head gleaming. It launched into the wind, wings wide, shadow sweeping over them before it vanished into the blue with a piercing cry.

"Wow," Cassie whispered.

"It is the most sacred of all birds," Agwai said as they

rode on. "A messenger from Our Father. To see one is a blessing."

Cassie urged Snowfire forward. She glanced at Ed, sharing a quiet smile—both stirred by the land and the people who belonged to it.

At the summit, the grassy path gave way to wind-scoured stone and twisted trees. A chilly gust swept the exposed ridge. Jagged ledges and snow-streaked boulders ringed the peak. From here, the view was endless—mountains layered like waves, some capped in white, others cloaked in green. Far below, the river wound through the valley, their camp reduced to tiny specks. The sun blazed overhead. The sky was deeper blue here—thinner, sharper, more alive.

Agwai gestured toward the valley. "Yuuwaraing Ke'mwahant—Wind River Valley."

Cassie's voice caught. "It's breathtaking."

"What do you call this mountain?" Ed asked.

"In your tongue, this is Wind River Peak. We call it Duku Garer—Mountain Sheep Peak," Agwai said, scanning the slopes for movement.

"Do you often see mountain sheep here?" Ed asked, following Agwai's gaze.

"They're still here, though fewer than before. This is where Luka killed one and was attacked by a cougar—there, on that ledge, just a few moons ago."

A chill traced Cassie's spine.

Ed scanned the outcropping for the signs of blood, wishing he'd brought a rifle.

"You need not fear," Agwai said, sensing their tension. "Cougar is our brother. When the world was young, he helped mankind. We honor that memory and kill only if we must. Even in death, the cougar continues to serve. The pelt is part of Luka's lodge—it will keep him warm, and he wears the teeth for courage—a gift."

They dismounted, tying the horses where grass grew thick. Resting on a flat rock, Agwai spoke softly. "You needn't worry for Megan. I will protect her. Luka will provide."

"Thank you," Ed said, rubbing Cassie's back as she gazed at the endless horizon. "That means more than you know."

"I once left my son in your care. Now I repay the favor. I will treat her as my own, as you treated Luka." Agwai pulled a knife from his belt, shaving a stick to a point.

"It was our pleasure," Cassie said, her voice catching. "Luke—Luka—has been a blessing to us. Especially to Megan." A tear slid down her cheek at the thought of tomorrow's goodbye.

Agwai looked up. "Luka told me Megan is half Indian. That must have been hard—for all of you. I'm sorry...that wicked things happened at the hands of wicked people."

Cassie lowered her gaze, tears spilling freely now. Ed drew her close.

"It wasn't your people," she said thickly. "We know what happened to your wife and daughter. There's good and evil in every nation. We don't blame you."

Agwai nodded. "What happened today—and when you first arrived—must have reopened old wounds. I wish I could have stopped it. But how do we heal, if we cannot forgive? That man lost his family to white man's violence. He carries that hatred still, as many do. We were forced onto this land, and bitterness took root. But anger doesn't heal—it only poisons."

"We're sorry for what's happened to your people," Ed said. "Good and bad exist everywhere. We didn't come to cause trouble—only to support Megan and Luke."

"It was good that you came. You see for yourself that we are not what many believe," Agwai said, his voice calm, without bitterness. "We are not dirty savages, or godless heathens. We believe in the Creator—God, Our Father. We honor the earth and all His creations. Our customs may seem strange to you—as yours do to us. But like your ancestors, we pass down our stories and wisdom to our children."

He paused, then drew his knife lightly across his forearm. Drops of blood fell and darkened the earth.

"You see? We all bleed red. And in time, we return to Mother Earth and feed the worms. That is the circle of life. Our spirits travel on. We live, we die—different paths, but same journey."

He stood, pointing toward the horizon with the sharpened stick. "We once moved freely. The Creator filled the land with every plant and creature so humans could live and care for it. There was more than enough. We followed the seasons and gave the earth time to heal. But now...we are penned in. Too many people. Too little land."

His eyes shadowed with sorrow. "I don't say this to burden you—only so you'll understand. Our people carry anger because they've lost much."

Without another word, he drove the stick into the ground and left it standing.

"We understand," Ed said, his voice thick. "You've

helped us see more clearly than ever. Maybe Megan can help mend what's broken in your people's hearts. She's kind, eager to learn. She wants to teach your children—even as she learns from them." His chest tightened at the thought of leaving her, but deep down he knew—it was the path she was meant to walk.

"If Luka loves her—and I believe he does—then she must be remarkable," Agwai said. "Together, they'll bring goodness to our people and to their family."

"Megan and Luke have already brought healing to us," Cassie replied. "When Luke came, he mended wounds we thought would never close. And Megan... she turned sorrow into something beautiful. You were right—hearts heal through love, not hate. Ed and I are proof."

She took Ed's hand, her eyes glistening—not with pain, but peace. Up here on the mountaintop, beneath the vast sky, everything was clearer.

"Thank you for bringing us here," she said. "For letting us see your world through your eyes."

Ed extended his hand. "We're grateful beyond words."

Agwai clasped it firmly. "And thank you—for returning my son to me." A single tear shone before he turned toward the horses.

Ed helped Cassie to her feet, and together they followed across the rocky ground. Mounting up, they began the quiet ride back to camp.

# *Chapter 22*

## *Saying Goodbye*

Megan stretched, a soft yawn escaping as she stirred from sleep. Beside her, Luke traced the curve of her back with a slow, loving touch.

"Did you sleep well?" he murmured, savoring the warmth of her skin.

"Like a dream," she whispered, brushing her fingers across his cheek. His deep brown eyes were still clouded with sleep. "You?"

"No complaints," he smiled. "Waking up beside you... every day feels like a dream I never want to end." He kissed her palm, lingering there.

A flutter stirred in her chest. "I agree," she whispered, scooting closer.

Still holding her hand, Luke trailed kisses from her wrist to the crook of her elbow. She shivered, eyes drifting shut as his lips wandered over her shoulder, collarbone, and neck before finding her ear.

A breathless laugh escaped her. "Mmm...I hate to say it, but I think Ma and Pa are waiting."

Luke groaned softly, resting on one elbow above her. "I suppose we should be responsible," he said, grinning down at her, hair tousled across the furs. "They say delayed gratification builds character."

"Let's build just enough," she teased, sitting up and clutching the blanket to her chest. She scanned the teepee for her clothes.

Luke lay back, lazily trailing his fingers down her spine, sending another shiver through her.

"Are you sure?" he asked playfully.

"Luke!" she scolded, laughing. "Let's go—so we can come back." She flashed a grin over her shoulder. "Help me find my clothes."

Instead, he folded his hands behind his head, openly admiring her. His copper-toned skin glowed in the soft light, his body relaxed and content.

"No peeking," she warned, raising a brow.

He chuckled. "What haven't I already seen?" The shyness between them was gone, replaced by a quiet freedom.

Megan smirked, and in one swift motion, yanked the blanket off him, leaving him exposed on the buffalo hide. She giggled as he lunged after her, snatching it back.

Victorious, he wrapped the covers around himself. "Much better," he declared, grinning mischievously.

She gasped in mock outrage, cheeks pink with laughter. "Oh, you—!"

Megan reached for the wedding blanket, wrapping it around herself before stepping into her underclothes. As she buttoned up, she caught him watching, his gaze soft and full of love.

"I can't stay mad at you," she said, laughing softly.

She knelt beside him, cupping his face in her hands, and kissed him slowly, deeply.

Luke melted into her touch, her hair falling like silk across his chest. He wrapped his arms around her, pulling her close, his voice a whisper. "I hope not."

***

On the far side of camp, Ed and Cassie packed their tent, lingering with anticipation for their last precious minutes with Luke and Megan.

"How much longer do you think they'll be?" Cassie asked, her heart tugging at the thought of parting.

"Not long, I hope," Ed said, securing the last box in the wagon. "Daylight's wasting, and I'm anxious to see how things are holding up at home."

"I miss the boys," Cassie said with a wistful smile. "I hope they haven't been too much trouble for your ma." She folded her apron, tucking it into a box beneath the tarp.

"Angels, I'm sure," Ed teased.

She laughed, but her gaze drifted toward the silent teepee. Ed stepped behind her, slid his arms around her waist, and murmured, "Truth is, I'm looking forward to some time alone with you. This is our honeymoon too."

She leaned into him, smiling. "I haven't forgotten. And I plan to savor every minute."

***

Agwai approached with Rose and Grey Wolf, carrying a leather satchel of wrapped bundles.

"Rose has prepared food for your journey," Agwai said, offering it to Ed.

"Thank you," Cassie said warmly. She hugged Rose, then paused, having a sudden thought. Removing the silver comb from her hair, she offered it. "I'd like you to have this. You've been so kind—to us, and to Megan. I'm grateful she has you."

Rose's eyes widened. Agwai translated. Smiling, she accepted the comb as if it were a treasure, pressing it to her heart. She spoke softly.

"She thanks you—calls you her White Sister," Agwai said.

Cassie blinked, tears stinging. "I'm honored."

Rose slipped the silver bracelet from her wrist, its band set with turquoise, and held it out.

"Oh no, it's too beautiful," Cassie whispered.

Rose's smile faltered.

Agwai's voice was gentle. "To refuse would offend her."

"I didn't mean to," Cassie said quickly.

"Then take it," he said. "You gave from your heart—let her do the same."

Tears fell as she reached out and Rose placed it in her hands. Cassie drew her into a tight embrace.

"Thank you, my Indian Sister," she whispered. Rose understood, and the two women wept quietly in each other's embrace.

Cassie slipped the bracelet onto her wrist.

"That's beautiful," Ed said, then turned to Agwai. "I have something for you too."

He went to the wagon and returned with a long, white-handled knife in a stamped sheath. Withdrawing it partway, he revealed the stag-antler grip and gleaming blade.

"This served me well for years. A good skinning knife—for your kindness, and for watching over my family."

Agwai accepted it reverently, testing the weight before sliding it into his belt. "It is a fine blade. Thank you." He paused and added, "Wait here."

He disappeared into his teepee and returned with a leather-wrapped hoop. At its center stretched an intricate web threaded with colorful beads, and three eagle feathers hanging below.

"A sacred dreamcatcher," he said, placing it in Ed's hands. "It traps bad dreams until the sun burns them away. Hang it above your bed—it has always brought me good visions."

Ed's throat tightened, thinking of the nights haunted by nightmares.

"This means more than you know," he said, gripping Agwai's hand. "Cass and I both struggle with bad dreams. Thank you, truly."

Cassie brushed the feathers with reverence. "It's beautiful. Thank you."

Just then Megan and Luke appeared, hand in hand.

"Ma, Pa, I'm sorry we kept you waiting," Megan said, cheeks flushed as she hugged her mother.

"It was Megan's fault," Luke teased.

She smirked. "You weren't exactly rushing."

Her gaze caught the dreamcatcher. "What's that?"

"Luke's father gave it to us," Cassie said, lifting it for her to see.

"It's lovely," Megan said, eyes wide. "It might help."

"I hope so," Ed murmured, tucking it safely beneath the wagon tarp.

"Are you ready to go?" Luke asked, glancing at the empty camp.

"Yes," Ed said with a touch of sadness. "Just waiting to say goodbye."

"Do you need anything before we leave?" Cassie asked, maternal instinct rising. "We can leave food or supplies."

"Ma, we're fine," Luke said gently. "We've got

everything we need. Do you have enough for the trip back?"

"We do," Ed answered. "Rose sent food with us. She's been so kind."

Cassie's voice caught. "Then I guess it's time."

She drew Megan into a fierce embrace. "You can come home anytime. Try for Thanksgiving or Christmas. And write—we'll send letters through the fort."

"We will, Ma," Megan said, her voice trembling.

Cassie turned to Luke, gripping his arms. "Take care of my girl. This life is all new to her. Homesickness is no small thing."

"I know," Luke said, pulling Megan close. "I promise—I'll help her through it."

Cassie hugged him, kissing his cheek. "I love you, son."

"Don't worry, Ma. We'll be okay. We'll miss you."

Ed wrapped Megan in a long embrace, kissing her hair. "Oh, my sweet girl. The house won't be the same without you. But this is what you've worked for. Be strong. Do your best and leave the rest in God's hands. We love you so much."

"Goodbye, Pa," Megan whispered. "I love you. Thank you for coming—it meant the world."

"We wouldn't have missed it," Ed said, smiling through tears. He pulled Luke into a bear hug. "Goodbye, son. Take care of each other."

Luke's throat tightened. "We will, Pa. I love you too. Thank you...for everything."

"Write when you can. We'll be praying for you." Ed gave his shoulder one last squeeze before turning away. "Come on, Cass. It's time." He shook hands with Agwai and Grey Wolf.

Cassie gave Megan and Luke one last embrace. "Goodbye, dears. We love you." She turned to Rose. "Thank you for the bracelet—and for watching over my children."

Agwai translated. Rose nodded, smiling. "Goodbye, White Sister," she said in accented English.

"Goodbye, Indian Sister. I hope we meet again," Cassie replied, hugging her. With a final nod to Agwai and Grey Wolf, she climbed into the wagon beside Ed.

With a snap of the reins, the wagon creaked forward.

"Goodbye!" Cassie called, twisting in her seat for one last look.

"Safe travels! God be with you till we meet again!" Luke called, his voice firm despite the tightness in his throat.

"Goodbye, Luke! Goodbye, Megan! We love you!" Cassie's voice faded with the wagon's wheels.

"Goodbye, Ma! Pa!" Megan cried, hand raised until the wagon was gone. Then she buried her face in Luke's chest, trembling as he held her, whispering softly into her hair.

***

Later that morning, Ed and Cassie passed through the fort. That evening they stopped at a quiet clearing off the road.

"I've been thinking," Cassie said, stirring potatoes in a cast-iron skillet. "Do you think Megan will adjust?"

Ed poured water into the kettle. "She's young, and she's got Luke to help her. It'll take time to find her footing, but she's strong. We've seen that."

Cassie handed him a plate, worry clouding her face.

"Some of the people seemed angry. What if they say or do something when she's on her own?"

Ed set his plate aside and took her hand. "Cass, the Lord's watching over them. Our girl's spread her wings—it's time to let her fly. We'll keep them in our prayers."

He bowed his head in a quiet blessing over their meal, and for Luke and Megan's safety.

"Thank you," Cassie whispered. "That helps. But I'll admit—I already miss her. Before, she was only hours away. Now…" Her voice faltered.

"I know." Ed sighed, taking a bite, and thoughtfully chewed. "I miss them too. I was just getting used to having Luke around. I guess it's back to just you and me."

"You know I'm always glad for that," she said, smiling. "After all these years, you're still my best friend."

"And you're mine." He leaned close and kissed her.

As the sun slipped behind the trees, painting the sky in hues of orange and gold, they finished their supper and cleaned up.

Cassie yawned. "Let's turn in soon. I'm exhausted. I didn't sleep much last night."

"Me either," Ed admitted. "It was kind of Agwai to give us that dreamcatcher."

"Do you think it'll work?" she asked softly.

"I'm praying it does," he said. "Those dreams are so vivid—I feel like I'm reliving it all."

Cassie's hand touched his leg. "Oh, Ed…why didn't you tell me?"

"I didn't want to burden you. They came back after Andrew was killed. I thought they'd fade—and mostly they did." He covered her hand with his. "*You* had one last night, didn't you?"

She nodded. "After those men threatened us...it shook me. I still see it when I close my eyes."

Ed pulled her into his arms. "Oh, Cass—this has been so hard on you. That dreamcatcher will help. No more letting fear take root, alright?"

"I'll try," she said, eyes shadowed.

He knelt, lifting her chin. "I'd never let anything happen to you—ever. And Luke will protect Megan. You're safe. She's safe. Believe that."

Tears glistened in her eyes. "I do. You've always cared for me, and I trust Luke to do the same for her."

"That's what a husband does—love, honor, protect, provide. Once we're home with the boys underfoot again, you'll feel better. You'll see."

He held her close as she wept softly against his chest. "Thank you, Ed. I just need a good night's sleep," she murmured, wiping her cheeks and managing a weary smile.

"You do," he said. "I'll fetch a few more logs. Then let's get some rest."

As he glanced back, he thought how precious she was—still trying to be strong under the weight of so much. And silently, he vowed to guard her peace with everything he had.

# Chapter 23

## Honeymoons

The next morning, Luke and Megan rose early, packing only essentials and breaking down their teepee. Luke lashed supplies onto the travois while Rose prepared food for several days. She and Agwai embraced them both, offering blessings and wishes for safe travels.

Mounted on Snowfire, with Wildfire pulling the travois behind, they followed the river into the forest. Warm sunlight filtered through the trees as Megan wrapped her arms around Luke's waist, cheek resting against his back. The gentle rhythm of the ride lulled her in and out of sleep.

The countryside was breathtaking—towering mountains in the distance, grasses rippling in the breeze, wildlife stirring among the trees. Luke led with quiet confidence, already knowing the perfect place to camp. By late afternoon, they reached a small lake framed by forest and mountains, the water glassy beneath the fading sun.

"It's beautiful," Megan said as Luke helped her down.

"It's Bull Lake," he replied, wrapping her in a hug and kissing her head. "Our own private home—for now."

"Just us, far from everything. I love it," she whispered, eyes shining.

Luke kissed her gently. "You're perfect."

She smiled. "Yes, you are, husband."

***

They set up their teepee on the grassy shore. Megan arranged bedding and supplies while Luke went fishing.

"Look—fresh fish for supper!" he called, holding up five gleaming trout strung on a forked willow branch.

"Oh, Luke, perfect!"

Megan proceeded to fry them up in a bit of bacon grease, the savory aroma filling the camp.

"Mmm, smells amazing," Luke said, returning with firewood.

"Wait until you try my biscuits," Megan said, shaping dough and nestling it in the warm ash by the fire.

"I could eat a bear, I'm so hungry," he joked, crouching beside her.

"Let's hope not," she muttered, glancing at the darkening tree line.

He squeezed her shoulder. "We're safe. The fire keeps animals away, and I've got my rifle and bow. If you like, I'll teach you to shoot the rifle."

"Maybe that's not a bad idea." Megan pulled the last fish from the pan. "What I wouldn't give for some milk to make gravy. But this'll have to do."

"This is perfect." Luke plated the trout while Megan added biscuits.

"Shall we say a blessing?" she asked.

"Of course." Luke took her hands, bowing his head in quiet prayer, keenly feeling the responsibility of husband and protector.

"Thank you," Megan whispered, treasuring the sound of his voice.

As they ate, Luke gazed across the still lake. "Plenty of fish, clean water, and deer tracks on the far side. If I leave early, I might bring one down tomorrow."

"What would we do with a whole deer?" Megan asked.

"Use what we need and dry the rest—it'll keep. You'll learn the Shoshone ways soon enough," he said with a knowing smile.

She hesitated. "What will I do while you're gone?"

"Sleep. I'll be back by breakfast."

Her eyes lingered on the darkening wilderness.

"If you'd rather come with me, you can," Luke offered. "Just stay quiet."

Her face lit up. "Yes. If you don't mind."

"Not at all," he said, savoring the joy of sharing the wilderness with her.

*** 

Luke gently shook Megan's shoulder. It felt like she'd only just closed her eyes.

"Is it time?" she murmured.

"Yes, time to go." He dressed quickly, fastening his knife and slinging his bow and quiver across his shoulder.

Blinking away the haze of sleep, Megan pulled on her clothes in the chill. "I'm ready," she whispered, excitement stirring—she had never hunted before.

Hand in hand, they slipped into the dark. The moon sank in the west as dawn stirred in the east. At Luke's signal, Megan nodded, and they crept to the lake's edge, crouching behind rocks. Her legs ached, but she held still, eyes fixed on the willows.

A doe and her fawn stepped into the dim light at the lake's edge. The mother stilled, ears flicking, nose lifted to the breeze, while the spotted young pressed close.

Luke lowered his bow, and Megan touched his arm, understanding his choice without words.

As she shifted, a twig snapped beneath her heel. The doe froze, staring directly at them. Megan barely breathed until, at last, the mother bent to drink and the fawn nestled to nurse. Her heart swelled—she had never been so close to wild deer.

When the deer slipped back into the trees, she thought the hunt finished. But Luke remained still. Then he gave a subtle nod. Down the path stood a buck, framed in the gray light of dawn.

Luke raised his bow. Megan held her breath. The arrow flew with a sharp whisper. The buck bounded, then collapsed. Luke leapt forward, swift as a mountain cat. Megan hurried after him, her knees stiff.

She found him kneeling by the animal, murmuring in Shoshone, cradling its head as its breaths came shallow and quick. With a swift stroke, he ended its suffering.

Megan gasped, tears blurring her eyes. She turned away.

"He's gone now," Luke said softly. "He gave his life, and I thanked him." His voice carried reverence, touched with sorrow.

Megan drew a steadying breath. "I'm okay. What can I do?"

"You sure?"

She nodded. "I grew up on a ranch. Just tell me."

Luke gave a small smile. "Alright."

Together, they worked field-dressing the deer and carrying it back to camp. While he skinned and butchered, Megan fried breakfast—fresh venison with crisp potatoes.

When Luke sat beside her by the fire, he breathed in the warmth and aroma. "I'm impressed," he said with quiet pride. "You did great out there."

"Thank you, sweetheart. It was...intense. I don't know if I'd want to do it again." Megan handed him a plate, then smiled faintly. "But I'm glad I saw the fawn and its mama. I'm glad you let them go."

"I'd never take a doe with a fawn," Luke said. "That little one needs her. Give it a year or two, and it'll be strong enough to survive on its own."

Megan nodded, thoughtful. Watching the whole process had deepened her gratitude for the food before her. "Why did we keep the insides? Back home, we buried them."

"Nothing goes to waste," Luke said. "Every part has a purpose. His sacrifice won't be in vain. I'll show you how to dry the meat, cure the hide, and use the rest for tools and clothing."

She wrinkled her nose. "Even the brains?"

"That's what tans the hide."

Her eyes widened. "Oh...I can't wait to watch."

He chuckled. "I'll teach you. Then you can try it yourself. All the women in our tribe tan hides. I'll even show you how to cut a pattern for moccasins."

"I already have a pair," she said, thinking of her wedding gift.

"Those are beautiful. But these will be your first ones made with your own hands. That makes them special."

Her eyes shone. "I'm excited to learn."

As Megan cleared breakfast, Luke helped himself to another serving. Sunlight filtered through the trees, gilding the clearing as their new life unfolded—bit by bit, stitch by stitch, one lesson at a time.

The rest of the day they sliced venison into strips and hung it above a smoky fire, adjusting the racks so the meat dried without cooking. At sundown they scraped the hide smooth and stretched it taut. By nightfall, bone-tired yet content, they curled together beneath their blankets and drifted into peaceful sleep.

***

"I'll be glad to be back," Cassie said on the third morning, stretching sore muscles. "A hot bath and my own bed sound heavenly. I think I'm too old for sleeping on the ground."

Ed drew her close against the chill. "Hard to believe we'll be home tomorrow night. This honeymoon flew by."

"It's been wonderful," she agreed, "but I miss the boys something fierce."

"Me too. And I'm ready for a break from vacation." He chuckled, rubbing his stiff back. "Camping's hard work."

Cassie smiled. "I look forward to my stove again. Maybe I'll bake a big apple pie. Still, it's been lovely—just us."

Ed's gaze lingered on the dreamcatcher in their tent. "You haven't had nightmares. Looks like it's working."

Her voice softened. "It must be. But this time of year...twenty-one years since my family was killed. I don't think a year's passed without nightmares." Tears filled her eyes, grief rising.

Ed held her, rubbing her back. "Oh, my sweet Cass. You're allowed to grieve."

"I just miss them. And now Megan and Luke are

gone too. I just want us all safe together. You're all that matters to me."

Ed held her closer. "And you're the center of my world. As long as I have you and the children, I have everything."

Her tears now glimmered with joy. "Oh, Ed, I love you. Thank you for asking me to marry you."

"And thank you for saying yes," he said thickly. He lifted her chin and kissed her gently, hoping she felt the depth of his love in his embrace.

***

The days tanning hides and smoking venison passed peacefully. Luke felt content—just him and Megan, alone with the wilderness. He couldn't imagine a better honeymoon.

Megan threw herself into learning moccasin-making. The work was grueling, and at times she missed hot baths and walls that kept wild things out, but her determination grew with each day.

"Want to ride out?" Luke asked after their mid-day meal. "We need herbs and vegetables. I thought we'd explore that ridge—see what's on the other side."

Megan's face lit. "That sounds wonderful."

While Luke saddled the horses, she cleaned the dishes and grabbed a leather bag from the teepee.

"You see that outcropping?" Luke pointed to the cliffs beyond the lake. "That's the Cirque of the Towers."

Jagged gray rock loomed stark and treeless, streaked with snow.

"They look like a giant's fortress," Megan said, marveling.

"We'll skirt to the right," he said, mounting Wildfire.

He waited for Megan to swing onto Snowfire, then gave a nudge, and their horses broke into a gallop across the meadow.

They climbed through aspen and towering evergreens, slowing over loose rock until the trail dipped into a valley.

"There," Luke said. "See that violet-blue patch? Camas."

"They look like the ones near the ranch!" Megan said, spirits lifting.

They dismounted in the flower-strewn meadow. Luke handed her a digging tool, and together they filled the bag with camas and wild onions, tying it shut with leather cords.

"This will make a good stew—if only we had carrots," Megan mused. Cooking here had become a challenge without a pantry.

"Ask and ye shall receive," Luke said with a grin.

She raised a brow. "Carrots? Out here?"

"If you know where to look, there's food everywhere." He took her hand, leading her to a patch of feathery-stemmed white blossoms.

Nearby, the horses grazed contentedly. Megan glanced at them with a smile. "If only we were horses. Life would be so simple."

Luke knelt beside a cluster of delicate white blooms. "Wild carrots—Queen Anne's Lace. See the red dot in the center? That's how you know it's safe. Without it, it could be hemlock—and deadly."

Megan leaned close, fascinated. "That's remarkable."

He tugged a plant free and held up the long, pale root. "Smells like carrot, too."

She laughed softly. "Let's gather some. I'll make stew." Dropping beside him, she pulled at the plants until their bag bulged with roots.

They packed the harvest in Megan's saddlebag and mounted. The descent was slow, horses picking carefully through uneven ground. Below, their teepee glimmered by the lake, nestled in a meadow so green it looked like a painting—peaceful, perfect, wholly theirs.

Then movement caught Megan's eye.

"Luke—do you see that?" Megan's breath caught.

His face hardened. "Oh no." He spurred Wildfire into a gallop.

A black bear clawed at their meat rack, tearing into the venison they'd worked so hard to preserve. Luke nocked an arrow as Wildfire thundered across the grass. The bear rose, growling. He loosed a cry and fired—the arrow struck its chest.

Megan froze. The bear bellowed but didn't fall. Two more arrows hit, yet it wheeled and charged—straight for *her*.

She screamed as the massive form barreled toward her. Snowfire reared and spun in terror. "Luke!" she cried, clutching the reins.

A rifle cracked. The bear stumbled, then collapsed halfway across the meadow. Snowfire reared again, side-stepping in panic. Megan clung to the saddle horn, whispering, "It's alright...we're alright," though her heart thundered.

Luke was suddenly there, grabbing Snowfire's bridle, steadying horse and rider. "Easy now," he murmured. He slid off his horse then helped her down. Her knees wobbled and he pulled her into his arms, steadying her.

"I'd never let anything happen to you," he whispered, voice shaking.

She clung to him, sobbing. "I was so scared."

"I know." He stroked her back. "It's over. You're safe."

"You could've been killed. What if I'd been alone—or asleep?" Her voice broke under the weight of it.

"It was just a hungry bear," he tried, forcing lightness. "You could've taken it down yourself."

But she didn't laugh. "I *hate* it here!" she burst out. "Everything feels scary and strange, and I miss home." The words tumbled, raw and unguarded—things she hadn't even admitted to herself.

Luke's chest tightened. He'd expected hardship but hearing her say she hated it pierced deeper than he imagined.

"I'm sorry," he said quietly. "I know it's hard. Don't let this ruin everything. It's still our honeymoon." He pressed his cheek to her hair.

Her sobs softened. She looked up, eyes glassy. "I don't hate it. I was just scared. When I saw you charge that bear—I thought I'd lose you. I couldn't bear it, Luke. I love you so much."

"I love you too," he murmured, brushing away her tears. "I'll do anything to protect you. Even take you back to Cheyenne, if that's what you want."

She shook her head, tears clinging to her lashes. "No. I want to be here—with you, with your people. I want to teach. I'll be alright." She lifted her chin, steadier now.

"Are you sure?"

Her trembling smile carried quiet strength. "I'm sure."

# Chapter 24

## Living a New Way

The journey home passed peacefully for Ed and Cassie. Even the long train ride seemed to fly by—the gentle sway of the car lulling them into sleep. On the fourth evening they reached Cheyenne, where familiar faces waited eagerly on the platform.

"Welcome home!" Kathy called as Ed and Cassie stepped off.

"Mama!" Johnathan rushed into her arms. "I missed you so much!"

Cassie kissed his tousled hair. "I missed you too, sweetheart. Did you have fun?"

"Yes! But guess what?" he whispered. "Kurt's sweet on a girl! I saw them kiss!"

She chuckled. "Now, no tattling. I'm sure he'll tell me when he's ready."

Kurt hugged her quickly, cheeks flushing. "Did you have a good time, Ma?"

"We did." She kissed his cheek. "Sounds like we've got some catching up to do." She smiled at how fast he was growing.

"Yes, Ma," he mumbled, with a sheepish grin.

Patrick clasped Ed's hand. "Good trip?"

"The best," Ed said. "We'll tell you all about it at home."

"Welcome home, Ma. How was it?" David asked,

giving Cassie a hug.

"Wonderful," she said, handing him her bag as they headed toward the wagon while Ed and Patrick went to retrieve the horses and luggage. "And here?"

"It was fine. Just not the same without you and Pa. We missed you."

"We missed you too," Cassie said with a smile.

She turned to Kathy and embraced her. "Thank you for taking such good care of the boys."

"Oh, it was no trouble. We enjoyed every minute," Kathy said, laughing. "I think it gave Patrick a little taste of what he missed."

Kurt and Johnathan clambered into the wagon bed trying to ignore each other.

"I hope they behaved," Cassie said, giving them a look.

"We did, Ma!" Johnathan said as Kurt nodded.

"Perfect angels," Kathy confirmed, slipping an arm around David's waist. "We're going to miss seeing them every day."

The ride home brimmed with laughter as the boys tumbled over each other's stories. Ed and Cassie listened with quiet joy, fingers intertwined.

"We're definitely home," Ed whispered.

"Yes," she murmured, heart full. "And how good it is."

***

There was nothing sweeter than stepping into the cottage. The mingled scent of woodsmoke, simmering stew, and fresh bread wrapped around them like an embrace. Even the creak of the floorboards and squeak of the screen door felt perfect. Cassie hadn't known how deeply she'd missed it until now.

In the kitchen, a cake gleamed at the center of the table.

"Oh, Kathy—how thoughtful," Cassie said, her eyes misting.

"We wanted your first night back to be special," Kathy smiled. "Just a simple supper."

Cassie hugged her tight. "The house looks beautiful. You truly are an angel. Thank you—it's the loveliest surprise."

That evening, they lingered over the meal, hearts full, before Grandma and Grandpa O'Malley returned to their own home in town.

***

"I sure am going to miss those boys," Kathy said as the buggy rolled along the quiet road.

"Me too," Patrick chuckled. "It was a good stretch, but I'm worn clean out."

Kathy laughed softly. "I am too. But it was worth every bit."

"Yup. Every minute," he agreed, slipping an arm around her shoulders.

***

That evening, Megan and Luke sat by the lake, watching the sun sink behind the mountains as crickets and frogs carried the twilight song. Megan slipped off her shoes, dipping her feet into the cool, glassy water. The chill was a blessing after a long day of tanning hides and smoking meat.

Luke watched her, quietly smiling. She leaned back on her hands, skirt pulled to her knees, sleeves rolled, toes stirring ripples across the mirrored lake. Her loose waves caught in the breeze, moving like spun silk. So peaceful—it made his heart swell with love.

He picked up his flute, leaned against a tree, and began to play.

Megan closed her eyes. The melody was tender, haunting, full of emotion—like a secret spoken only to her. Her heart stirred, hearing the love in every note.

Luke poured everything into the song—her smile, their first kiss, this moment by the lake.

As the last notes faded, Megan turned, breath catching at the sight—his broad chest gleaming bronze, powerful thighs straining beneath soft buckskin, hair spilling like polished obsidian. He looked wild and untamed, like the wilderness itself, yet his gaze was so tender it pulled her in.

"That was beautiful," she whispered. "What's it called?"

"*Megan's Song*," he said, lips curving.

She arched a brow, teasing. "No, really."

"I wrote it for you. I was just waiting for the right moment." His voice was low, gaze steady.

She stepped across the grass and kissed him softly. He savored her lips, then pulled her into his lap. She laughed breathlessly, fingers threading into his hair, and kissed him again—deeper this time. He answered with longing, his hand cradled her cheek, the other at her back.

"Luke...it's beautiful. Thank you," she whispered against his lips.

"It's *your* song. I'll only play it for *you*." His thumb brushed her jaw as he gazed at the fire in her emerald eyes that undid him completely. "It's the song of my heart."

A shiver ran through her at the huskiness in his voice.

"If only I could play you the song of *mine*," she breathed, her eyes dark and deep.

"I think I hear it," he whispered, pulling her close. His lips brushed her skin with quiet passion, their breaths mingling as the last light glowed like the flame of their love.

***

As spring melted into summer, a gentle rhythm settled over their days. Each day Megan walked to the lake for water, the path grew more familiar. Over meals and while stitching moccasins or the soft deerskin dress Luke insisted she have, she practiced Shoshone with him.

They fished and foraged together—Luke teaching her which roots and berries were safe, how to cook them, how to read the land. Afternoons were spent riding through the woods, discovering hidden glades and sunlit trails. Evenings drew them back to the water's edge, feet in the shallows, sharing stories and laughter. At night they lay beneath the stars, watching them appear through the teepee's smoke hole.

"I love it here," Megan whispered one night, her head on Luke's arm watching falling stars.

"I thought you said you hated it," he teased, eyes glinting in the dim glow.

She turned to him. "You know I didn't mean it. I was scared. But now...I feel sure of myself—because of you. You taught me how to live this life. I'm not afraid anymore."

His smile widened. "I knew you'd love it. Just like I knew you loved me."

"Oh, you did, did you?"

"Yup. From the moment you kissed me in Cheyenne," he said smugly.

Megan laughed. "You mean after *you* kissed *me*. And I only did because you saved my virtue. A girl has to show gratitude somehow."

"Ah yes, a maiden must reward her rescuer—with a kiss."

"Well, it seemed polite," she teased, tickling his side.

He chuckled. "You could've cooked me supper, mended my clothes—but no, you chose a kiss." He drew her close, voice tender. "And I'll treasure it forever."

Megan's smile softened. "Hmm...I never repaid you for saving me from that bear." She kissed him deeply, gratitude in her lips.

Luke's eyelids fluttered. "You're welcome, my fair maiden."

"Oh—and when I twisted my ankle?" she whispered, kissing him again.

He grinned. "Seems like you've been saving up thank-yous."

"I don't like owing anyone. I believe in paying in full."

"Well then, what about when you almost got trampled by that horse?"

She kissed him slow and sweet. "You had to reach way back for that one."

"Just collecting what's due. How about when that schoolteacher nearly gave you a licking?"

"That was worth two," she laughed, kissing him twice. Her tone softened. "I loved you so much for that, Luke. You took my punishment without flinching.

You've always been my protector. I don't know if I can ever show you what you mean to me." A tear slipped down her cheek.

"You already have," he said gently. "You married me. That's all I need. Now we'll spend our lives showing how much we mean to each other—building a family, filling our days with joy, making memories worth keeping." His voice dropped. *"To have and to hold, forever and ever. A glorious eternity, we'll spend together. I will love you all of my life. Because—you became my wife."*

She smiled through her tears. *"Ne en tepitsi tsaa suankanna dehimbe—* I love you, sweetheart."

"I love you too, my precious Indian White Dove," he whispered.

He drew her into a kiss—tender, then deep, as if the stars bore witness to the vows they had spoken. Beneath the warm furs, they were wrapped in love, trust, and the passion of an endless summer night.

***

"It's been over two months, and still no letter. Do you think they're alright?" Cassie asked one evening, setting aside her teacup, worry threading her voice.

"Cass, I'm sure they're fine," Ed said gently. "They told us they'd be off on their own awhile, maybe longer than expected. Mail's slow. Just give it time."

"I know... I just miss them," she murmured, eyes drifting to the sunset beyond the trees.

"Me too," Ed said, drawing her close and resting his chin on her hair. Megan had never gone so long without writing. It felt strange—like she lived in another world—and in many ways, she did.

***

"Luke, the other night you called me Indian White Dove. What does that mean?" Megan asked one warm July afternoon as they picked huckleberries on the hillside.

"Did you like it?" He grinned, popping berries into his mouth.

"Yes—it's beautiful. But what does it mean?"

"A dove stands for love and peace—just like what you bring into my life. And you're both Indian and white...so, that makes you my Indian White Dove."

She smiled affectionately. "It's perfect." She straightened, then swayed, nearly spilling her basket.

Luke caught her by the elbows. "You alright?" His brow furrowed at her pale lips.

"I'm fine...just dizzy when I stood," she said, blinking.

"You don't look fine." He'd noticed her napping more lately. "Come on, maybe it's too hot for berry picking." Sliding an arm around her waist, he guided her down the slope back to camp.

"You don't need to fuss," she protested, though unease flickered in her eyes. She'd felt off for days.

At the teepee, Luke rolled up the sides for air. Megan lay on the hides, relieved to rest, while he went fishing. When she awoke, the fire crackled with trout sizzling in the pan. She stepped into the fading light—then the smell hit her. She bolted behind the teepee.

"Don't look!" she cried, arms wrapped around her waist.

He held her hair, rubbing slow circles on her back. "It's alright. I'm here."

Tears streaked her cheeks as she trembled on her

knees.

"Better?" he asked softly.

"A little," she whispered. "I felt fine after my nap—until I smelled the fish."

"Come lay down. I'll bring water." He steadied her inside and pressed a tin cup into her hands. "Here you go, my little Indian White Dove." His heart ached to see her like this.

"Thanks, Luke. You eat—I'll try something later," she murmured.

"I'll be right outside."

She slept until dusk. Luke brushed her forehead when she stirred.

"How do you feel?"

"Better. Hungry, even."

"Start slow. Water first, then a bit of biscuit," he said, offering one from the tin.

As she ate, color returned to her face. That night he held her close beneath the furs, whispering a prayer for her healing as she drifted into sleep.

*** 

The next morning, Megan awoke feeling rested. Luke was already outside chopping wood. She dressed and stepped into the early light.

"Morning, sleepyhead!" he called with a grin. "How're you feeling?"

Before she could answer, a wave of nausea struck. She clapped a hand to her mouth and ran to the bushes.

Luke dropped the hatchet and hurried to her side, steadying her as she shuddered.

"Oh, Megan...you're still sick. Think you ate something bad?" His voice was low with concern.

She wiped her mouth and stood slowly, arms wrapped around her middle. "I don't think so," she murmured, unease stirring. What if it was serious—and they were so far from a doctor?

"I'll make you some broth," he said, masking worry.

Over the next days, Megan forced herself through chores, hiding her constant nausea. She lived on broth and biscuits. Luke saw her pallor linger, her strength fade, and knew he couldn't ignore it.

That evening, as stars pricked the summer sky, he finally spoke his mind.

"Megan, we should go back to the tribe. You're not getting better." He wrapped an arm around her as she leaned into him. "I hoped it would pass, but I'm starting to fear it's something serious."

"Luke, I'll be fine...I'm—*ohaanaai*," she whispered, a tear slipping down her cheek.

Luke froze. "What...what did you say?"

"*Ohaanaai,*" she repeated softly. "Did I say it right?"

"You're...you're pregnant?" The words left him in a stunned rush. Then, wide-eyed, he whispered again, "You're having a baby."

She nodded, tears spilling freely. "Yes. I'm pregnant."

Just days earlier she'd realized her cycle was long delayed. Her mother's words had returned to her—nausea, dizziness, fatigue. She'd waited, but the signs were undeniable.

Relief broke over Luke. She wasn't sick—she was carrying their child. Laughing softly, he pulled her close. "Oh, Megan, that's wonderful."

"I wasn't sure at first...but it's just like Ma described," she said, eyes shining. "Luke...you're going to be a papa."

His heart swelled. "Oh, Megan, my little Indian White Dove...you amaze me." His voice caught as he kissed her, overwhelmed with love.

"I love you," she whispered, arms tightening around him. Joy and uncertainty swirled inside her, even her queasy stomach echoing the mix of emotions.

"When do you think the baby will come?" he asked, already feeling the weight of responsibility. They were far from help—too far.

"Maybe March. Or April. I'm not sure."

"When was your last cycle?" he asked, pondering.

"Right before our wedding. I lost track."

"That's nearly three moons," he said, brow furrowing. "It's mid-July now. The baby could come in February." A chill ran through him. *February*. His mind flicked to his mother—fragile, heavy with child, in the dead of winter.

"Really? That soon?" Megan's brow creased. "But I'll still be teaching."

"No. You won't." Luke's voice was gentle but firm. "We're going back before the snow. You'll have the baby in Cheyenne—with Ma and a doctor." His eyes locked with hers, the firelight reflecting the fierce protectiveness in his gaze.

Megan hesitated. "But what about the children?"

"It's hard enough out here in winter, let alone pregnant. This changes everything," he said, his gaze drifting to her still-flat belly, already imagining it round and full.

"I'll be fine," she murmured. "Women have babies in the wilderness."

"I know. But I won't risk it. You and the baby mean more than anything." He touched her cheek. "You can teach through fall, but not after that. I'm sorry."

Tears welled in Megan's eyes. "I feel like I'm letting them down. All those children…" Her voice cracked.

Luke lifted her chin gently. "Megan, you'll always be a teacher—to our children, to others. One day, you'll be back in a classroom."

She smiled through her tears, wrapping her arms around his neck. "I love you, Luka Standing Elk…so much."

He held her close, feeling the weight of her worry lift. "You're going to be the best mama," he whispered. "I love you, my Indian White Dove."

***

The next month slipped by in a rhythm of hunting, gathering, and preparing for winter. Summer still blazed, though the golden grass and lush reeds by the lake hinted at autumn's approach.

Most evenings, they swam before bed, their days spent checking traps, stitching mittens, and filling baskets with fish and berries. One afternoon, they harvested honeycomb from a beehive, careful with the precious find.

Megan wore her deerskin dress most days—loose, cool, with fringe swaying around her calves. Luke loved seeing her in it, her hair braided, the beaded belt cinched around her waist. Soon, she'd loosen it for the gentle swell of her belly.

Mornings brought nausea, but by midday, she managed. She nibbled on dry biscuits before rising and savored dried rabbit and venison, preferring them to fish. Berries and wild greens became her favorite foods.

"It's time we head back to the tribe," Luke said one

morning, as Megan scrubbed a shirt in the lake.

"Already?" she asked, glancing up with damp sleeves.

"Yes. We need to get back before school starts," he said, gently wringing out the shirt and laying it in the basket.

"If you think it's best…" she said, slowly straightening. Her eyes lingered on the valley. "I'll miss this place."

"Me too," Luke said, smiling at the sight of her, barefoot in the water. "I'll never forget our time here."

"When do you want to leave?"

"Tomorrow morning."

"Then today's our last day of honeymoon," she said thoughtfully. "Let's make it special—a long ride and a big supper. I want this to be the best day ever."

Luke waded in, wrapping his arms around her waist and kissed her cheek.

"Every day is the best day—with you." He kissed her again, warm and lingering. "Besides, our honeymoon's never really over."

Megan giggled, resting her arms over his. "I love you," she whispered, turning to kiss him.

"I love you, too."

***

That afternoon, they rode up the mountain trail to the high ridge overlooking the valley. Below, the lake shimmered like a blue coin, their white teepee a tiny dot beside it. A breeze cooled their flushed cheeks, softening the August heat.

From this height, the world stretched endlessly—rolling hills, deep green valleys, ridgelines fading into the horizon. At last, they began the slow descent. Wildfire and Snowfire picked their way down the rocky path.

"I wonder how Ma, Pa, and the boys are doing," Megan said as the valley opened before them.

"We'll find out soon," Luke replied. "I'm sure there are letters waiting at the fort. We'll write and tell them we're expecting."

"They'll be thrilled," Megan smiled, imagining her parents' joy. "And the boys will love being uncles!"

"They'll also be glad we're coming home for Thanksgiving and Christmas," Luke added, relieved to be near family—and a doctor—when the time came.

"Your father will be sad, though," Megan said softly. "We'll tell him he's going to be a grandpa... then leave before he meets the baby."

"But he'll understand," Luke said quietly.

***

At sunrise the next morning, they ate breakfast and packed in quiet rhythm—folding the teepee, bundling blankets, and loading the travois. When everything was secured, they stood for a long moment, taking in the valley that had cradled them.

"It's strange," Megan said, mounting Snowfire, "how quickly my heart is reaching for what's next. I'm excited to see people again...though I'll miss this place."

"I feel the same," Luke said, swinging up behind her. He nudged Snowfire forward, Wildfire following with the travois. "It's been a beautiful season, but I'm ready to reconnect—with the tribe, with family."

Megan looked back, her gaze sweeping over the still lake and golden hills. "Goodbye, Bull Lake," she whispered. "I hope we see you again."

Luke wrapped an arm around her waist and kissed her cheek. "It'll always be with us—in our hearts, our memories. Even if we never return, I'll never forget it."

"Nor will I," Megan said, smiling through tears. "This is where I learned to live a new way."

314

# Chapter 25

## *Changes*

Luke and Megan finally arrived at the Shoshone village as the sun dipped low. As they entered, two braves rode past and waved a welcome. Megan noticed she no longer drew curious stares, now dressed in soft deerskin, moccasins, and twin braids.

The Wind River Valley had transformed as well; new buildings rose among the familiar teepees, while soldiers patrolled with rifles slung over their shoulders. What had once been lush now lay stark and barren. The river still wound between the towering cottonwoods, but the horizon burned with a hazy orange under the pressing heat.

Luke slid down from Snowfire and helped Megan to the ground, both weary from the long ride but eager to set up their teepee. Just as they finished, Agwai appeared.

"I heard you were back," he said, tightly embracing Luke.

"It's good to see you, Father," Luke said, overjoyed.

Agwai turned to Megan. "How was your journey?"

"Very pleasant, Father," she replied in Shoshone. "We'll never forget it."

He raised his brows, pleased. "Ah, you've been learning. Your students will be proud."

Luke slipped an arm around her. "Father, we have good news. Megan, tell him."

Her eyes sparkled as she announced, "We're having

a baby."

Agwai's grin spread wide. "You have made this old man very happy. Come, eat with us. Your aunt and uncle will want to hear the good news."

As they followed him, a few tribe members welcomed them warmly, while a few stared and others grunted, turning away. Megan tried to ignore the snub, but the subtle sting still hurt.

"How have things been?" Luke asked softly, regarding the changes in the village.

Agwai's face darkened. "A new Indian agent arrived. He's young, impatient, and blind to our ways. He insists we live like white men. Soldiers threaten to tear down teepees if we don't build houses. Some have already surrendered, building homes and taking the government rations," he said, gesturing toward the line of villagers collecting food, clothes, and blankets.

He glanced at Megan, softening his tone. "But tonight, we won't speak of it. Tonight, we celebrate. I am to be a grandfather."

That evening, they shared a meal with Agwai, Aunt Rose, Grey Wolf, and their sons. Luke proudly broke the news.

Rose beamed. "Oh, Megan. Anything you need. I'll be here to help with the baby however I can," she said, giving her hand a squeeze.

Megan glanced at Luke to explain.

"I'm sorry, Aunt Rose. We'll be going back to Cheyenne before the baby's born," Luke said, wrapping a protective arm around Megan.

Agwai looked thoughtfully at Megan. "It saddens us, but we understand."

"It is good to be with your mother when the baby comes," Rose said warmly. "My mother had already gone to the happy hunting ground when I had my boys."

"I'm so sorry," Megan whispered.

"No need," Rose replied. "She watches over us—just as Bluebird watches over Luke, and now you, carrying her grandchild."

Megan smiled, heart eased by the thought of a guardian spirit watching over them.

***

The next day, Megan and Luke rode to Fort Washakie to meet the school's headmaster and collect mail. As they neared the stark white two-story building, Megan's stomach tightened. She entered, knocking on the door marked *Headmaster*.

"Enter!" barked a gruff voice.

Inside, the small office reeked of sweat and paper. The headmaster rose, looking her over with obvious disapproval.

"Hello, Headmaster."

"Mr. Adams," he growled.

"Nice to meet you, Mr. Adams. I'm Mrs. Havoc—the teacher Commander Jenkins hired this spring," she said, offering her hand.

He gave a limp shake. "Mrs. Havoc, about time," he said wrinkling his nose. "Frankly, I didn't think you were coming. School starts in two weeks. It was highly irresponsible of you, waiting this long."

Heat flared up her neck. "I'm sorry, sir. I was away on my honeymoon," she said, trying to keep calm. He gestured to a chair, and she sat.

"That's no concern of mine. Your personal life

doesn't matter here," he snapped.

Megan clasped her shaking hands. "Well…sir…There is something of a personal matter—I'll only be able to teach through the fall. I'm pregnant and will return to Cheyenne before the baby's due. I'm truly sorry."

Mr. Adams scowled. "The Commander should have consulted me." He slammed his ledger closed and stood abruptly. "This is why I oppose hiring married women—or women at all. A woman's place is in the home, cooking and cleaning. Teaching's a man's job. But we're stuck now." He paced, dabbed his forehead, irritation palpable.

"I never intended to let you or the children down. I'll give my best," Megan said. "Over the summer, I began learning Shoshone. I thought it might help—"

"We do not allow children to speak Shoshone!" he barked, finger punctuating his words as his glasses slid down his nose. "You're here to teach English—*English ways*. We aim to train the savage out of them. Understand?" he asked, looming over her, portly belly just inches away. His wretched smell and repulsive words sickened her, insulting the people she loved. He was a pig of a man—inside and out.

Megan clenched her jaw.

"Do—you—understand?" he growled.

Megan masked the fury in her eyes. "I understand, sir," she muttered.

"Good. You'll report here in two weeks. Saturday is move-in day. You've been assigned room 4B in the dormitory next door. Room and board are provided," he said, turning to gaze out the window, dismissing her.

"Pardon me, sir," she said carefully, "but we already have accommodations—"

"That's not negotiable," he snapped, whirling around. "All staff live on school grounds. You're teaching grades one through three. Here's your materials." He jabbed a thick finger at a stack of books.

"And do try to look respectable. You're *not* one of them. Good day, Mrs. Havoc." He sat, pushed his glasses up, and opened a book.

"Good day," Megan said tightly, gathering the books.

Outside, Luke's smile faded at her expression.

"How did it go?" he asked, stepping close. She looked away, fighting angry tears.

"Just fine," she said, bitterly.

He gently took the books as they walked toward the post office. "What happened?"

Her pace quickened on the dusty boardwalk. "He's furious I'm leaving after one term. And he won't let me speak Shoshone to the children. I thought I was here to help—but all they want is to erase who these children are."

Luke drew her to his side. "You *will* help. This is much better than boarding schools. They go home each night, and you'll give them something real—a love of learning. Don't let that man dim your light."

"I'll try," she whispered, blinking back tears.

"That's my Indian White Dove," he said, kissing her cheek.

They reached the small, whitewashed building marked *Post Office* and stepped inside.

"Excuse me," Megan said, "do you have any mail for Mr. and Mrs. Luke Havoc?"

The balding postmaster grinned. "About time! I thought you'd vanished." He reached into the wall of cubbies and pulled out a stack of letters.

"Thank you," Megan said, accepting the bundle—six from Ma, one from each set of grandparents, and one from Penny. She handed him three letters to send, sharing their joyful news.

"All to Cheyenne?" he asked, inspecting them.

"Yes, please." She paid, then stepped into the sunlight beside Luke.

*****

Later, on a blanket outside their teepee, Megan opened the first envelope, smoothing the page. Luke rested with his head in her lap as she began to read.

"*Our dearest Megan and Luke...*" she began but was unable to go on, tears falling.

Luke took the letter and continued:

> "*We made it home safe after four days of travel. It was the honeymoon we never had. Thank you for inviting us—it was beautiful...Home isn't the same without you. Hope you're well and enjoying your honeymoon.*
> *With love, Ma, Pa, and the boys.*"

Megan handed him the next envelope, and together they glimpsed home through words: the garden thriving, hay crops promising, Kurt courting, David learning with Dr. Ward, Johnathan improving his roping skills, and bittersweetly, David no longer seeing Ashley, now courted by Clint.

Megan's voice softened. "They're growing so fast... Poor David, but next year he'll be off to college and loving it. And I'm glad for Ashley and Clint."

Luke took her fingers and kissed them. "I'm glad

we'll be home for Christmas. There won't be too many more with us all together. Ten years from now we'll all be celebrating with our own families."

"Just like us," she added, resting a hand on her growing belly.

Luke raised up and kissed her. "Just like us."

***

The weeks passed swiftly as school approached. Packing their things brought Megan and Luke a pang of sadness; they borrowed a wagon, keeping only what they needed, gifting the rest. Warm hugs and blessings followed them from the tribe.

At the teachers' dormitory, a short, round woman with graying black curls greeted them from the porch. Her black dress, white apron, and starched cap gave her a brisk, capable air.

"Good mornin'! I'm Mrs. Carson—I run the Wind River School Dormitory." Her strong, callused hand clasped theirs warmly. "If you ask Mr. Adams, he'll say he's in charge—but truth be told, I'm the one you'll want when you need something." Her chuckle made her cheeks round and her eyes nearly vanish with mirth.

"Luke Havoc," Luke said cheerfully. "This is my wife, Megan—one of the teachers."

"Of course! Mr. Adams told me you were coming. Room's ready. Bring your things along."

Inside, she pointed out the parlor with its lace-draped windows, the dining room with a polished oval table, and the kitchen at the back. "I cook and my daughter, Missy, cleans," she said, leading them upstairs. The hall stretched long and narrow, four labeled doors on either side. "Yours is 4B at the end. Water closet's at the other end. Keep your room tidy, and Missy will come Saturday for a scrub." She unlocked the door and stepped aside. "I'll let you settle."

"Thank you, Mrs. Carson," Megan said warmly.

Luke set the trunk down with a sigh. "Fall can't come soon enough. That trunk gets heavier every time."

The room was modest but tidy: a rug softened the floor, a small bed stood neatly made with a pale blue blanket, and sunlight streamed through two windows. A pot-bellied stove promised winter warmth; a round table and two chairs made the space almost cozy.

Megan opened the west window, drinking in the warm prairie air, her gaze drawn to the golden horizon. At least she could watch the sunset. But the sight tightened her chest. "I'm sorry, Luke. This isn't how I imagined we'd be living," she said, dabbing her brow with her apron.

He slipped his arms around her. "And how did you imagine it?"

Her eyes softened. "Not shut up in a dormitory. I miss the teepee...the quiet, wide-open valley."

"It's a fine room for newlyweds," he teased gently. "And only for three months."

"But what will you do all day while I'm teaching?"

"Hunt with my father, help in the village. I'll be back every evening for supper with you."

She pouted faintly. "I'll miss working side by side."

He kissed her forehead. "I'll be home every night. Right here."

They spent the next hour making the room their own: cobalt glass *Bluebirds of Happiness* catching the afternoon sun on the sill, embroidered cloth and doilies softening the tables, a family photo on the nightstand. Her deerskin dress was folded away, his bow and rifle rested in the corner. Above the bed they hung his father's dreamcatcher, and at last Megan draped their wedding blanket across the footboard.

When they stepped back, the little room felt touched with home.

"It doesn't look half bad," Megan said, a smile flickering through her wistfulness. "Maybe this won't be so awful."

"I think it looks lovely," Luke said, sliding the trunk beneath the window.

As they stepped out to return the wagon, a woman at the bottom of the stairs struggled with her luggage. She froze at the sight of Luke, arms full, eyes widening.

"May I help you?" Luke asked evenly.

Relief softened her face. "Oh, thank you!" Her brown hair was pinned neatly, cheeks flushed from the heat.

Luke carried her bags upstairs to Room 3B, right beside theirs.

"Looks like we're neighbors," Megan said brightly. "I'm Megan Havoc, and this is my husband, Luke."

"Prudence Wright," she replied, offering Megan a firm handshake before unlocking her door. "This is my second year teaching. You must be the new teacher."

"Yes, grades one through three," Megan said, feeling a flicker of kinship. "What about you?"

"Middle grades—four through six. Two more teachers handle the older students. They'll arrive this afternoon."

Her hazel eyes lingered briefly on Luke before she turned back to Megan. "Have you settled in?"

"Just finished," Megan said. "We'd hoped to stay in the village, but the Headmaster insisted."

Prudence looked again at Luke. "So, you're a tribal member?"

"Yes," Luke answered with a polite smile.

Her gaze shifted to Megan's olive skin and braid. "And you?"

Megan hesitated, then smiled. "No, I'm from Cheyenne. But being married to Luke makes me part of the tribe now, I guess."

Prudence's curiosity sparked. "How did you two meet? That's quite a distance between Cheyenne and Wind River."

Megan laughed lightly. "A long story—for another time. We should return the wagon. Do you have more to bring in?"

"No, this is it. Thank you—it was lovely meeting you." She closed the door gently.

Descending the stairs, Luke glanced at Megan. "She seems kind. Maybe she'll be a friend."

"Maybe," Megan said thoughtfully, climbing into the wagon.

***

That evening, Megan dressed in her olive-green walking dress, buttoning the fitted jacket over her white blouse and fastening a cameo at her throat. Her dark hair was swept into a bun, soft ringlets framing her face, pearl drops glinting at her ears.

Luke, less eager, pulled on a crisp white shirt, brown wool trousers, and a stiff vest and tie. The heat pressed in, his jacket heavy on his shoulders. After smoothing back his hair and polishing his boots, he offered Megan his arm with a warm smile.

"Shall we?"

Megan nodded, slipping her arm through his.

Downstairs, Miss Wright sat in an armchair near the unused fireplace, a book open in her lap.

"Hello again," Megan said.

"Hello," Prudence replied with a smile.

Before more could be said, a short blond man entered with a pale, thin woman at his side.

"John Thompson, and this is my wife, Naomi," he introduced wearily, shaking their hands.

Naomi's fleeting smile barely reached her eyes. Dark circles and the faded blue of her calico made her look as fragile as the dress itself.

"So nice to meet you," Megan said gently. "I'll be teaching the first three grades. This is my husband, Luke."

Luke shook their hands warmly. "Hope the road wasn't too rough."

"Dusty and hot all the way from Utah," John said with a tired grin. "But we're here now. A bath and supper will do us good." He squeezed Naomi's hand, and she looked up at him with quiet gratitude.

"We understand," Megan said kindly. "Four days by wagon after the train was enough. I can't imagine by stagecoach."

Prudence stepped forward. "I'm Miss Wright. Glad to meet you." She broke off as another figure appeared in the doorway.

A tall, dark-haired man in a fine gray suit entered with an easy smile. "Philip Archibald," he said, shaking hands with Luke and Megan.

He nodded to the Thompsons, his grin gentle and knowing. "Those last few days in the stagecoach certainly gave us time to get acquainted," he said, his smooth southern drawl filled the room.

Mr. Thompson nodded slowly.

"You from the South?" Luke asked, tugging at his stiff collar, the ornate parlor already making him uncomfortable. A glance at Naomi told him he wasn't the only one uneasy amid velvet chairs and lace curtains.

"Atlanta, Georgia. Born and raised," Philip replied, brushing back thick, dark hair.

Prudence stepped forward, her green dress shimmering in the light. "Prudence Wright. I teach grades four through six."

Philip took her hand. "A pleasure," Philip said, his gaze lingering on her hazel eyes. "Where are you from, Miss Wright?"

She flushed faintly. "Southeastern Idaho. My family has a farm there."

"I've heard it's beautiful country. Near the Tetons?"

Her eyes lit. "Yes! The sunrise over the three peaks is spectacular."

"I'd love to see them someday—maybe even hike them."

"You should," she said, then added with a polite smile, "I'm sure your wife would love it."

He laughed easily. "No wife."

Her cheeks deepened in color. "It's warm this evening," she murmured.

"Indeed," he said, watching her closely, untouched by the heat.

A young woman in a black dress and apron slipped

in with a tray of lemonade, setting it on the table before vanishing again. Megan guessed she must be Missy, the cook's daughter.

Glasses were passed, and they sipped the cool sweetness with quiet relief.

The grandfather clock struck six. Moments later, Mr. Adams bustled in, gruff as ever, introduced himself, and ushered the newcomers into the dining room.

The table gleamed with fine china, crisp linens, and a bright silk flower centerpiece. At the ring of a bell, Missy hurried in with more food, quickly filling the table and nearby hutch.

Mr. Adams took the head seat, muttered a brusque blessing, and began piling his plate. Megan watched him eat like a man starved. Her own appetite was dulled by morning sickness, but she managed a few bites.

"So, where are y'all from?" Philip asked, glancing at Megan and Luke.

"Cheyenne," Megan said. "Luke's from Wind River."

"How interesting," Philip replied, buttering a roll. "How did you meet?"

Luke squeezed her hand. "I was adopted by a family in Cheyenne. We went to school together, fell in love. The rest is history."

"We married in May," Megan added with a smile.

"Lovely time for a wedding," Miss Wright sighed.

"Not if you want to work for me again," Mr. Adams cut in mid-bite.

All eyes turned as he gestured at Megan with his knife. "This Mrs. Havoc's already expecting and leaving at term's end. Highly inconvenient timing."

Megan flushed, lowering her gaze. Luke drew her

close.

"Megan made me the happiest man alive—twice," he said proudly. "Once by marrying me, now by giving us a child."

"Well said," Philip offered warmly. "Congratulations—I love children."

"Then it's a good thing you're a teacher," Luke teased.

Philip chuckled. "Indeed."

"Congratulations," Mr. Thompson added. "My wife's due in January." He shot Adams a glance. "But it won't affect my work."

Adams rolled his eyes, waving away his empty plate. "Better not. Good grief—is this a maternity ward?"

Stifled laughter circled the table.

"Congratulations to you both," Luke said evenly.

Missy cleared dishes, returning with peach pie. Megan's eyes lit as she took a bite, sighing at its warmth and flaky crust.

"A slice of heaven," Philip declared. "Missy, tell your mama this rivals my mammy's."

"Yes, sir," she murmured, ducking into the kitchen.

"So why leave Georgia to teach here?" Miss Wright asked.

"My pappy believed in education and equality," Philip said. "I was tutored alongside the help's children, learning no mind is lesser. After he passed, I wanted to carry that legacy forward. Every mind has worth, every culture its wisdom. That's why I'm here."

"Wonderful," Mr. Thompson said.

"And you?" Philip asked him.

"Much the same. My wife and I left Utah because we

believe this is where God wants us." He shared a contented look with Naomi.

Philip nodded. "Good people at this table tonight."

"And you, Mrs. Havoc?" Mr. Thompson asked.

Megan smiled. "Teaching was my dream since childhood. I've always felt drawn here. Luke supported me through teachers' college, and once I graduated, we came together. He knows what the boarding schools were like—we want something better. His people are mine too."

Mr. Adams snorted. "Isn't that touching. Now, who wants more pie?" He shoved his plate at Missy for seconds.

"No thanks," Luke said, rising. "If you'll excuse me."

Megan stood as well. "Goodnight. It was a pleasure meeting you all."

Philip and Mr. Thompson rose politely.

"Goodnight," Philip said.

"Goodnight," Miss Wright echoed, her gaze soft with sympathy.

Mr. Thompson helped Naomi up. "We'll turn in, too. Thank you for the meal and the company."

"I believe I'll retire as well," Miss Wright said, setting down her napkin.

Philip rose. "I'm heading that way—may I walk you to your room?"

"Thank you," she replied, taking his arm.

Mr. Adams waved them off with his fork.

In the hallway, Philip glanced at her. "I must confess I'm curious. Why would a lovely, eligible woman choose to teach in such a remote place?"

She blushed. "You'll probably think it's silly."

"Never. Please tell me."

She hesitated, smiling shyly. "It began as a childhood dream. I used to pretend I was an Indian girl—free, close to nature. As I grew, I read everything I could about their culture. Their reverence for the earth, their deep spirituality—it moved me."

He listened as they climbed the stairs, footsteps soft on the wood.

"As the oldest of six, I discovered a love for teaching early on. That passion carried me through college. Seeing this opening, I knew it was meant for me. The Shoshone are remarkable, and their children so eager to learn. I think you'll love it here too."

She finally met his gaze.

"That's not silly," Philip said warmly. "It's admirable. And inspiring."

They stopped at her door. "Miss Wright, I believe it will be a pleasure working with you."

"Thank you," she said softly. "This is my room. Goodnight, Mr. Archibald. It was a pleasure."

She offered her hand. He took it gently and brushed it with his lips. "The pleasure was mine."

Their eyes lingered before she slipped inside, heart fluttering. Pressing a hand to her chest, Prudence breathed deep and smiled. This was going to be an interesting school year.

***

"Luke, are you alright?" Megan asked softly. He'd been silent since they'd left the dining room. She touched his arm. "Talk to me."

He stood rigid, staring out the window like a caged

animal yearning for open space. With a sigh, he loosened his tie, unbuttoned his vest, and opened his collar, as if to ease the tightness in his chest.

"I'm fine. Really." He turned and pulled her into his arms.

"I'm so sorry," she whispered, tears slipping down her cheeks. "The way they spoke about your people...I know most meant well. They do care for the tribe. Well— maybe not Mr. Adams. He's a pig."

That made Luke chuckle, deep and low. He snorted like a pig, and Megan burst out laughing.

Luke's shoulders shook as he laughed harder. "I just pictured that round-bellied man at a trough, shoveling mashed potatoes beside the pigs...pie all over his face. He really is a pig!"

Megan clung to his arm for balance, laughing until her sides ached, then pressed a hand over her mouth, remembering Miss Wright's room shared the wall.

At last they quieted, breathless and smiling. Megan wrapped her arms around him. "I love you, Luke Standing Elk."

He kissed her gently. "And I love you, my Indian White Dove."

# *Chapter 26*

## *School Days*

On Sunday, Luke and Megan slid into a pew among the other teachers and servicemen to worship in the little church. Reverence fell over the congregation as the pastor began his uplifting sermon. They found it comforting—it had been a long time since they'd been in a chapel worshiping with other believers.

Afterward, Mrs. Carson served a hearty Sunday dinner: crispy fried chicken, golden corn, and warm, flaky biscuits. It was scrumptious. Suddenly, Mr. Adams's particular shape made perfect sense.

That afternoon, they rode to Luke's village. Barefoot children waved and called, their laughter brightening the dusty streets between teepees. Megan's heart swelled. Tomorrow she would meet her students—her first day of teaching.

That night, under a light blanket, Megan tossed and turned. Lessons were ready, yet her thoughts would not settle.

"You're still awake?" Luke asked, brushing her arm.

"I can't sleep," she whispered. "I'm nervous... and excited."

"I'm proud of you," he said, voice low and steady, pressing a soft kiss to her cheek. "You're dream is coming true."

"Well, it's only part of my dream," she murmured,

resting a hand on her belly.

"And it's mine too." He laid his hand over hers, fingers entwined. "You were my first dream," he said softly. "And now this little one."

***

"Good morning, children. My name is Mrs. Havoc," Megan said warmly.

"Good morning, Mrs. Havoc," came the reply from those who spoke English.

Twenty-two children gazed up at her, curiosity and nerves mixed in their eyes. All but two had the smooth, copper-toned skin of the Shoshone; the exceptions were the Commander's children, seated in the front row. Megan turned to the blackboard and wrote her name.

"Let's begin by taking roll." She sat and opened the ledger. "Mary Little Feather…"

"Present," a girl called.

Megan smiled, continuing down the list, checking off each name.

Finally, she reached the last name. "Jacob Crooked Arrow?" No answer.

A hand rose. "Mrs. Havoc," said Sarah Singing Willow. "He's deaf."

The only child who hadn't spoken was a small boy in the front row. Megan knelt beside him, pointing to herself, saying her name, then pointed to him and repeated his. His face lit up, and he nodded. Relief washed over her.

For the rest of the morning, Megan faced the class when speaking. She began by guiding students through the alphabet and numbers. Older children encouraged the younger ones. Patiently, she helped the littlest hold pencils for the first time, hands trembling with effort.

She couldn't help but notice how different they looked from yesterday at the village, now dressed in stiff black uniforms and shiny black shoes—government issued.

After lunch, Megan read aloud from the primary reader, holding the book high for all to see. The children listened with rapt attention, eager to answer her questions. Pride swelled in her chest.

"For tomorrow's assignment," she said as the final bell rang, "I'd like each of you to tell a story."

As they filed out, Johnny Red Moon stopped at her desk. "I don't know what story to tell."

"Ask your mother or father to share one with you tonight," Megan said gently. "Then you can tell it to us tomorrow."

He grinned. "Thanks, Mrs. Havoc!" and hurried after the others.

Megan smiled, but her thoughts lingered on Jacob Crooked Arrow. Her heart ached for him. How could he share a story—certainly not with spoken words.

***

"Cass! Cass! A letter came—from Luke and Megan!" Ed called, pulling into the yard and spotting Cassie in the garden.

Cassie sprang to her feet and hurried to him. "Hurry! Open it!" she urged, grinning.

Ed fumbled with the envelope, then handed it to her. "You read it," he said, leaning close as she unfolded the letter.

*Dear Family,*

*We're sorry it took so long to write. We've been on our honeymoon, tucked away in a secluded place called Bull Lake. The valley is breathtaking—tall mountains and a sparkling lake. It felt like a dream. We explored, fished, hunted, and cooked over a fire. Only once did things get a little frightening.*

Cassie glanced up, brows drawn.

"Go on," Ed urged, eyes twinkling.

*One afternoon, a black bear decided to help itself to our dried venison. Luke raced into camp and killed it—now we have both deer and bear meat.*

Cassie shook her head. "I knew something dangerous would happen."

"But it turned out fine," Ed said, wrapping an arm around her.

*I joined Luke on a deer hunt, then learned how to tan the hide and make a dress and moccasins. Luke's teaching me how to survive off the land. I'm living like a Shoshone and loving it. I'm picking up the language and now wear a buckskin dress, moccasins, and braids. Luke likes to call me his Indian White Dove.*

"I *knew* she'd take to it," Ed said proudly. "It's in her blood."

Cassie beamed. "She sounds so happy."

"And that nickname—it's perfect," Ed murmured, picturing Megan in a buckskin dress and braids.

Cassie read on:

*"We have the most exciting news—we're*

*expecting a BABY! You're going to be grand-parents in February!"*

Cassie gasped and flung her arms around Ed. "Oh Ed—we're going to be grandparents!"

"Our baby is having a baby!" he laughed, holding her close.

They wiped their tears as Cassie finished the letter:

*We're planning to come home for the holidays so I can have the baby in Cheyenne. We can't wait to see everyone for Thanksgiving.*

*Love and miss you all,*

*Megan and Luke.*

"Oh, Cass—home for Thanksgiving *and* Christmas!" Ed's voice cracked as he hugged her, overwhelmed with joy.

"We'll get to hold our grandbaby the day it's born," Cassie whispered, tears streaming.

***

The day dragged for Luke. With no hunting or fishing planned, restlessness gnawed at him. By midday he wandered to the corrals, eager to help the young men with the horses. Training had always come naturally, and the rhythm of it lifted his mood.

By sundown, he left camp dusty but content for the first time in weeks. His ranch days and time among the Shoshone had honed his skill, and both tribesmen and Army men took notice. His knack for lassoing and breaking wild horses quickly earned him a reputation, and with it, a renewed sense of purpose.

He returned to the dormitory just in time to wash up

before supper. Opening the door, he found Megan at their small table, red pencil in hand, papers spread before her.

"Hello, beautiful teacher," he said with a grin.

"Hello, handsome husband." Her smile widened as she took in his dusty buckskins, glowing face, and long hair loose about his shoulders.

Luke crossed the room, crouched beside her chair, and kissed her softly. "How was your first day of school?" he asked, pride in his eyes.

"Wonderful. I already adore them. They're bright and eager—most will be reading in a few months. All but one sweet little boy who's deaf. I'll need another way to reach him, but I know it's going to be a great term."

"I knew it would be," he said, settling across from her.

"And your day?" she asked, noticing the spark in his eyes.

"Slow at first," he admitted, "but then I worked with the horses. Even caught a wild Paint no one else could. Rode him a minute before he threw me." He chuckled. "They asked me back tomorrow. One of the Army men said he's never seen anyone handle horses like I do."

"Oh, Luke, that's wonderful! I'm so glad you've found something that makes you happy."

"I'm more than happy," he said, kissing her hair. "Now, I'd better clean up before supper."

With a towel and clean suit in hand, he disappeared down the hall.

***

The next day at school, Megan announced, "Class, now it's time for our story-sharing."

She started with her own story, telling of the black

bear that once wandered into her and Luke's camp. The children gasped and clapped when she finished.

"Now," Megan asked, scanning the room, "who would like to go next?"

To her surprise, Jacob Crooked Arrow raised his hand. Unsure if he understood, Megan knelt by his desk.

"What is it, Jacob?" she asked gently.

He pointed to himself, then to the front.

Megan hesitated, then nodded. Jacob beamed, walking proudly forward. The room hushed as he began to move his hands in fluid gestures—ones Megan had seen Luke's father and Chief Washakie use.

Wordless yet vivid, his story unfolded, showing himself as a small child, burning with fever. Once he'd been called Little Arrow, but after his sickness he couldn't walk straight and became Crooked Arrow. Though his legs grew strong again, his hearing never returned. He shook his head, pointing to his ears. His English name, Jacob, had been given at boarding school. Now he was Jacob Crooked Arrow. Finished, he smiled, hands resting at his sides.

The class erupted in applause as he returned to his seat, glowing.

"Very good, Jacob Crooked Arrow," Megan said warmly. "Thank you for sharing how you got your name."

Jacob's smile widened—she had understood him.

"Who's next?" she asked, heart full, as eager hands shot up.

The last to stand was Johnny Red Moon.

"My story," he began, "is about a white girl who lived in a town faraway. She rode a beautiful white horse and helped her family raise cows."

Megan froze at the back of the room, breath catching.

Johnny glanced at her, then continued. "She was very beautiful, with black hair and green eyes. One day she met a handsome Shoshone man who had dreamed of her for many winters and traveled many sleeps to find her. They fell in love and wished to marry, but first she had to finish school to be a teacher. He waited for her. When she finished, he brought her to the Shoshone village and married her. That's how she became a white Shoshone—and my teacher."

The class burst into applause, louder than before.

Megan smiled, blinking back tears. "That was a beautiful story, Johnny Red Moon. Who told it to you?"

"My mother," he said. "She heard it from Prairie Rose."

Megan laughed softly, deeply touched. "Well, you told it beautifully. Thank you for sharing."

***

That evening before supper, Megan recounted Jacob Crooked Arrow's story as she and Luke stood together in the quiet of their room.

"Well, that's a surprise," Luke said, wrapping her in his arms. "Sounds like you had quite the day, Mrs. Havoc."

"I'll bet you can't guess what the best story was about," she teased, eyes sparkling.

"I'm sure I can't," he said, with a playful smile. "Please, do tell."

"It's one you might know," she grinned, then, repeated Johnny Red Moon's tale word for word.

When she finished, Luke chuckled, gaze soft. "That's

the best story I've ever heard. I especially liked the part about the beautiful girl falling for the handsome Shoshone man." He kissed her gently.

"I loved that part too," Megan whispered. "But Johnny left out one detail—the white Shoshone woman is having a baby."

"Oh, I'm sure that part will be added once the baby arrives," Luke said, drawing her close. "I wish you'd been my teacher when I was a boy—I would've fallen for you on day one."

"Good thing I wasn't," she laughed, arms circling his neck. "Or I couldn't have married you. I think it worked out just right."

"It worked out perfectly, my Indian White Dove," he murmured. "I love you."

"I love you, Standing Elk," she said, then kissed him tenderly.

***

A few days later, Miss Wright came into the parlor and found Megan by the window, reading and sipping tea.

"Mrs. Havoc, how was class today?" Prudence asked, settling beside her.

Megan looked up, pleased. "Wonderful. And yours?"

"Very nice. I taught most of them last year, so I know them well. All good children."

Megan smiled. "I can't believe how quickly I've come to love my students. I already know I'll miss them when we leave." Megan set her book aside.

Prudence poured herself tea. "Some test my patience, but I always end up loving them."

Megan hesitated. "I was curious the other night why

you chose to teach here. Everyone else shared—except you."

Prudence laughed softly. "I told Mr. Archibald, though I felt silly afterward. My reason isn't as noble as yours. As a girl, I used to play 'Indians' with my siblings. That's where my love began. I studied all I could from books, learning about their culture. But I've learned more in a year from these Shoshone children than I ever did from books," Prudence said, stirring in sugar.

"That's not silly at all," Megan said warmly. "It's beautiful. Honestly, I wasn't entirely forthcoming when we met. I let you believe Luke and I were simply school-mates...but we were much more than that."

Prudence leaned in, sensing something deeper.

"When my mother was young, her family was attacked by Indians," Megan said quietly.

Prudence gasped. "Oh...how terrible."

"She barely escaped. While she hid, they burned the house. Everyone inside was killed. When it was over, she stumbled out—only to be found by an Indian man."

"My goodness," Prudence whispered. "That's heart-breaking."

"He forced himself on her," Megan whispered, staring down at her cup. "That's how I came to be."

Prudence sat in stunned silence. "I've read stories like that but hoped they were exaggerations. Like in any people—some good, some bad."

Megan nodded. "Later, my mother went to live with family in Cheyenne and met my pa and fell in love. They married quickly—to cover the fact she was expecting, and everyone believed I was his."

"He must be a good man," Prudence said, now understanding Megan's resemblance to the Shoshone.

"The best." She continued, "Not long before I was born, an Indian man came with his sick wife and little boy. His wife died in childbirth. He left the boy—*Luka*—with my parents and returned to the reservation to bury his wife and daughter. Luke was just four."

Prudence wiped a tear.

"Years passed with no word. Assuming his father had died, they adopted him. He was with us seven years. We grew up like siblings...until his father came back."

Prudence touched her chest. "And took him away?"

"Yes. We were best friends. It nearly broke me. He had to relearn his people's ways, and I had to learn to live without him. But after my first year of college, he returned. We'd both grown, and the love between us had only deepened. We felt whole again and married as soon as I graduated."

Megan wiped her tears, emotions stirred deeper by pregnancy.

Prudence clasped Megan's hand. "That's the most beautiful love story I've ever heard."

"I feel I can trust you to keep this a secret, Miss Wright," she said softly.

"Yes, of course, and please call me Prudence. Friends don't need to be so formal." Her smile was genuine and understanding.

"Then call me Megan," she said, echoing her smile.

Prudence squeezed her hand. "I promise I'll keep your story safe. But you *should* write it down one day. People need stories like yours—real, full of heart."

Megan gave a quiet smile. "Oh, I doubt anyone would want to read a story about a half-white woman marrying an Indian man."

"I think you're wrong," Prudence said earnestly.

"Maybe someday." Megan gazed out the window, her hand resting over her belly. "If I told you every twist and turn, you'd hardly believe it. But I know God's hand was guiding us—even through the hardest parts. And now, here we are, back on the reservation, teaching school... with a baby on the way." A tear slid down her cheek, but she didn't brush it away.

"You're so very blessed," Prudence whispered. "I only hope for something like that one day. A love that deep—and a family of my own. That's my dream."

"You will," Megan said gently. "When the time is right."

Prudence gave a wistful smile. "Sometimes I wonder if I'm destined to be an old schoolmarm forever."

Megan chuckled. "I don't think so. You're bright, kind, and lovely. The right man will find you—perhaps he already has."

Prudence blushed, unable to hide her smile.

"Oh, so you *do* like him," Megan teased, thinking of the way Mr. Archibald looked at Prudence. "He's handsome—and very kind."

Prudence laughed softly. "It's far too soon to think that way. But...maybe. One day."

"Time will tell," Megan said, her heart full—for her friend, and for the little life stirring within her.

***

As the weeks passed, the teachers and their spouses grew close. Supper became a cherished ritual, marred only by Mr. Adams, whose sharp remarks and brooding silences cast a shadow over the table. He remained distant, while the others found warmth and genuine friend-ship.

Each afternoon, Megan and Prudence met for tea, soon drawing Mrs. Thompson into their circle. At first Naomi sat quietly, her words scarcely above a whisper, but as trust grew, so did her voice. She had been raised the eldest of seven in a devout home, carrying both a homemaker's skill and a burden of self-doubt. Around the little table, she began to share those hidden insecurities, and the others answered with friendship.

Children, however, brought out her truest self. She understood them instinctively, speaking their language of the heart. When she offered to play piano for the school and start a choir, her timidity softened into music. The children adored her, and in their songs, she seemed to find her own.

Their afternoons became more than tea—they were sacred hours of bonding. Childhood stories, secret fears, and quiet hopes passed between them like heirlooms. Though few in number, the women leaned on one another for courage, their friendship growing stitch by stitch as they quilted for expectant mothers in the church. Naomi, carrying her first child, stitched with quiet joy, each thread binding her more deeply to the circle.

***

Three weeks into the term, Mr. Archibald could wait no longer. He asked Prudence for a stroll after supper, and she accepted with a soft smile and a blush that warmed his heart.

The sunset streaked the sky with gold and rose, but Prudence hardly noticed, absorbed in the warmth of Philip's presence. Arm in arm, they walked the dusty boardwalks past the white clapboard buildings, stark against the open prairie. Soldiers passed unnoticed, the couple moving in their own quiet world, only aware of each other.

"How are you liking it here?" she asked.

"Quite pleasant," he replied, his smile gentle.

"I'm surprised," she said, glancing at the dry sage and brittle grass. "It's a far cry from Georgia's green hills."

"There's beauty everywhere if you know where to look," he said softly. "I see it now." His gaze lingered on her, making her look away, flustered.

"You need your eyes examined," she laughed nervously. "I think you're imagining things."

"I don't mind if I am. I'm happy with the view," he said in his smooth Southern drawl.

She blushed. "Do you speak this way to every woman you meet?"

His smile faltered. "Do you think I'm a cad?"

"No! Heavens, no," she said quickly, hands trembling. "I just...I can't believe you'd say those things to me. I know I'm not beautiful."

"May I call you Prudence?" he asked gently.

"Yes," she whispered, savoring the way her name sounded on his lips.

"And you may call me Philip," he said, placing his hand over hers.

The simple touch sent a thrill through her. "Alright... Philip," she murmured.

"Prudence, I've known enough people to recognize something rare," he said, eyes steady. "You're not just beautiful on the surface. Your beauty shines from within—your care for the children, your compassion. I speak only from the heart. If it pains you to hear it, I'm sorry. But it *is* the truth."

A tear slipped down her cheek. "I'm flattered...but I'm not used to this. I don't see myself that way." Her dreams were slowly unfolding.

Philip stopped and took her hands. "Beauty is in the eye of the beholder, and I am beholding you. Your mind, your wit, your spirit—they captivate me. The more I learn, the more I want to know."

"You overwhelm me with your kindness," she whispered, heart pounding.

"They're words meant only for you," he said, lifting her hand to his lips. "And perhaps, in time, you'll believe me."

***

Megan began to notice a quiet transformation in her dear friend. She suspected much of that change had to do with Mr. Archibald. Whenever time and weather allowed, he took Prudence on evening walks. On colder nights, they sat in the parlor, sipping tea and reading poetry by lamplight. Megan and Naomi often exchanged knowing smiles. Though Prudence never spoke the words aloud, it was plain to see—she was falling in love.

***

October arrived in a flurry of activity. Between schoolwork and horse training, the days slipped by. Megan and Luke often marveled at how alike their work had become—he earned the trust of spirited horses, she patiently guided Jacob Crooked Arrow and the other children. Progress came slowly, yet surely, for both.

The season brought more than cooler air—it brought color. The prairie blazed with crimson, amber, and gold, and with autumn came another change: Megan's growing belly made the miracle within her impossible to ignore.

One night, around five months along, she lay quietly in bed when she felt something new—a soft flutter low in her belly.

"Luke," she whispered, "The baby's moving."

His eyes widened, and he laid a gentle hand across the small curve of her stomach. "Is it moving now?"

"Not yet. Just wait."

They lay still. Then, as if on cue, a faint ripple stirred beneath his hand.

"Oh! Did you feel that?" she asked.

"I felt it," he breathed. "Incredible. There's really a baby in there."

She grinned in the dim lamplight. "What did you think was in there?"

He chuckled. "I knew…but it felt unreal. Like a dream. But this makes it real."

"I know," she said, resting her hand over his. "I keep wondering…a boy or a girl? Who will it look like? It's hard to picture—like when we were kids imagining marriage. And now, here we are—and I can't imagine life any other way."

"I used to dream about you…about our wedding. But it didn't feel real until I stood beside you. From that moment on, it's been better than I ever imagined." He wrapped her in his arms, drawing her close.

"It really has been," she whispered, pressing a kiss to his lips. "Better than I ever dreamed."

# Chapter 27

## *Autumn*

Outside, the wind howled, while inside Megan and Luke sat warm before the parlor's crackling hearth. She unfolded a letter from Grandma and Grandpa O'Malley and began to read aloud.

*Dear Luke and Megan,*

*We were overjoyed to hear your news—you're having a baby! What a blessing. We know you'll be wonderful parents.*

*It sounds like you're both finding purpose in your work on the reservation. Megan, teaching suits you perfectly. And Luke, we're not surprised you're training horses again—you've had that gift since boyhood.*

*As you asked, we stopped by the Land Office in Laramie. The property you hoped for has already been claimed. Don't lose heart—there are many beautiful places waiting when you return.*

*All is well in Cheyenne. It's hard to believe six months have passed since you left. Your parents keep us updated and are so proud of you both. Melissa gave birth to a healthy boy last week, and Penny is due any day. Soon your little one will be the third great-grandchild.*

*Though we know you hoped to finish the school*

*year, we're glad you'll be home for the holidays. We miss you dearly and hold you in our prayers.*

*With all our love,*

*Grandma and Grandpa O'Malley.*

Luke exhaled sharply, running a hand through his hair. "The land's gone," he muttered. "I should've claimed it sooner. Gone back months ago. What was I thinking? That was our dream." He rose and began pacing.

Megan caught his hand, steadying him. "Luke, our dream isn't gone—it's just taking a new shape. We'll find another place, just as beautiful. Don't lose hope."

Her voice was calm, though her heart ached for the foothills she had loved.

Luke let out a long breath and sank beside her. His gaze softened. "You're right. We would've missed our honeymoon at the lake... and I wouldn't trade those days for *any* piece of land."

He squeezed her hand, disappointment easing in the warmth of her closeness, reminded that whatever form their dream took, they would build it together.

***

With six weeks left before their departure, Megan already felt the ache of goodbye. She had grown deeply attached to her students—their eager faces, their laughter drifting across the schoolyard. Each morning she welcomed their greetings; each afternoon she took quiet pride in their progress.

One crisp morning Jacob Crooked Arrow shyly offered her a purple wildflower.

"Oh, how lovely. Thank you, Jacob," she said, tucking it behind her ear. His grin followed him back to his seat.

That afternoon, Megan sat with Prudence and Naomi in the parlor, sipping tea while Missy's gingersnaps perfumed the air.

"What a pretty flower," Naomi said.

"From Jacob—the deaf boy," Megan said, touching the petals. "He's such a dear child."

"I've seen how the others watch over him," Prudence said. "In white schools he'd likely be sent away—to an asylum."

Megan frowned. "What do they even teach there?"

"The Oral Method only—speech and lip reading. They've abandoned sign language. It's forbidden. Children caught using it are punished, forced to wear gloves tied together."

Megan's eyes darkened. "That's cruel. Jacob speaks volumes with his hands. To silence him would crush him."

"Congress mandated it," Prudence said. "But children still find ways. Where there's will, there's always a way."

Naomi shook her head. "Why not let them use what helps them learn?"

"Exactly," Megan said. "Jacob is as bright as any child. He only falters when he can't read my lips."

Prudence poured more tea. "He's fortunate to be here, with friends who accept him."

Naomi asked gently, "How do you know so much about deaf schools?"

"A friend in teachers' college once planned to teach the deaf," Prudence said. "When the new policy passed, she gave it up. She thought speech training worked for some but was cruel to others. I used to practice sign with her. I still remember the alphabet."

Megan's face lit. "Would you teach me? It could mean so much for Jacob."

"With pleasure," Prudence said.

Megan smiled, then teased, "Not to pry, but how are things with Mr. Archibald? You two stroll together every evening."

Prudence flushed. "He's a true gentleman. Patient with my doubts. I still don't know why he cares for me."

"I do," Naomi said softly. "You make people feel safe."

"And you're a true friend," Megan added.

"And so are you two." Prudence said, eyes shimmering. "Enough about me. How are *you* both feeling?"

Naomi rested a hand on her belly. "A few more months to go. I'm nervous, but ready. It's already hard to bend down and tie my shoes."

"I feel so much better now that the sickness is gone," Megan said. "The baby moves constantly—like she's stretching every direction."

"So you think it's a girl?" Naomi teased.

"Oh, did I say that? Megan laughed. "I guess I'll be surprised if it's a boy."

"I don't care either way, as long as it's healthy," Naomi said, smiling at the gentle kick beneath her hand.

"Do you have names picked?" Prudence asked.

"Not yet," Megan said. "You, Naomi?"

"We like the Bible names—John or Peter. For a girl, maybe Grace, after my mother, or Rebecca, and call her Becky."

"Oh, I love both," Prudence said. "If I ever have children, I'd choose Ruth. She's my favorite in the Bible."

"She's a beautiful example," Naomi agreed, sipping her tea. "Faithful and selfless—staying with her mother-in-law, Naomi, after losing her husband."

"Naomi," Prudence smiled, "you're named after her, aren't you?"

"Yes, my mother loved the story and named me for her faith. I've tried to live up to it."

"And your name, Prudence?" Megan asked.

"It's one of the four virtues. My mother hoped it would guide me. I think it has."

Prudence checked the small watch pinned to her dress. "We should go. Thank you—it's always lovely to talk with you both."

Megan stood and joined Prudence. "We'll see you at supper," Megan said.

Children's laughter drifted on the wind as they stepped outside.

Walking arm in arm, Megan leaned close. "Prudence, I hope you know how lucky Mr. Archibald is. You're remarkable, and he's not the only one who sees it."

"I think I'm the lucky one," Prudence whispered. "To have found friends like you. I'll miss you terribly when you leave."

***

As promised, Prudence and Megan spent lunch breaks practicing sign language. In turn, Megan taught Jacob Crooked Arrow with growing confidence. Though Mr. Adams disapproved, he didn't stop her from helping Jacob after class or on Saturdays.

Soon, Jacob's hands flew faster than Megan could

follow. More than once, she gently caught his fingers, smiling as she signed, *Slow down, Jacob.*

It was as if a door had opened to a world that had always been waiting for him. Megan ordered a book on American Sign Language, and together they devoured each new phrase. She began signing during lessons, allowing Jacob to follow with ease.

Within a month, he could read from his primer and copy words with neat precision. Megan had no doubt he'd one day read and write as well as any student. Her heart swelled with hope for his future.

***

One crisp afternoon near the end of the term, Mr. Adams stepped into the classroom unannounced.

"Mrs. Havoc, I'd like to test your class and see how you're progressing," he said, thumbs hooked in his vest, fabric straining over his belly.

"Yes, Mr. Adams," Megan replied, her nerves tightening.

He paced the room, peering over his glasses. "Let's have your best speller come forward."

Adam Silver Cloud was the obvious choice, but Jacob's eager eyes met hers. Megan made a bold decision. "Jacob Crooked Arrow, would you like to spell for Mr. Adams?" she asked, signing as she spoke.

Jacob nodded and signed, *Yes.*

"What are you doing?" Mr. Adams grumbled. "You know he can't spell."

But Jacob rose with quiet confidence.

"Mr. Adams, he *can.* Please—give him a chance. I'll translate," Megan said firmly.

Mr. Adams scowled, then smirked. "Fine. Have him

spell *deaf.*"

"Sir, he's in second grade. That word isn't on our list," Megan protested. But before she could show him, Jacob's fingers were already in motion.

He signed: *D...E...A... F.*

"What's he saying?" Mr. Adams barked.

"He spelled *deaf,*" Megan confirmed. Turning to Jacob, she signed and said, "That is correct."

The class erupted in applause.

Mr. Adams, clearly rattled, turned so Jacob couldn't read his lips. "Have him spell *dumb.*"

Megan's stomach clenched. Jacob looked at her, confused. *What did he say?* he signed. Some children giggled.

"That word isn't part of our curriculum," Megan snapped.

"Oh, I'm sure he knows it," Mr. Adams sneered. "Might've been the first word he ever heard—if he *could* hear."

Megan marched to the back, fists tight around the spelling list. "How *dare* you. I won't let you humiliate this child—not in my classroom."

"I'm the Headmaster," Mr. Adams shot back. "You're my employee." He brushed past her. "Children, your classmate cannot spell the word. Who can spell *dumb*?"

Jacob's brow furrowed. Then he lifted his hands and signed: D...U...M...B. A tear welled in his eye.

"That is correct," Megan said quickly. "Jacob, you spelled it *perfectly.*"

The class roared with applause. Jacob blinked back his tear, smiling again.

"Hmph," Mr. Adams grunted. "Take your seat.

Arithmetic—someone older this time."

For the next half hour, he drilled them in sums and history. Megan held her composure until at last, he left with a curt nod.

Megan exhaled. "Students, I'm very proud of you," she said, her smile bright. Relief rippled through the room like sunlight after a storm. "As a reward, we'll have another story day. Think of one to share tomorrow. Class dismissed."

The children rushed out—except Jacob. He lingered, signing, *Mrs. Havoc, thank you for teaching me. You are a good teacher*. Then he wrapped his arms around her.

"Thank you, Jacob," she signed back, voice warm. "I was especially proud of you today. You're a joy to teach."

He smiled, eyes shining.

***

That night, Megan lay in bed, her thoughts heavy, replaying the day's events.

"You're awfully quiet," Luke murmured as he climbed in beside her, drawing the quilt close around them. Despite the glowing fire in the potbellied stove, the autumn chill still crept through the room.

"Mr. Adams came into my classroom today," she whispered, mindful of Prudence in the next room. "He tested the children."

Luke brushed a lock of hair from her face. "How did it go?"

A tear slipped down her cheek, catching the moonlight. Before she could speak, a sob broke free. Luke gathered her close.

"I shouldn't have called on Jacob Crooked Arrow,"

she managed. "He was so eager—and Mr. Adams humiliated him. Made him spell *deaf* and *dumb*. How could anyone be so cruel?"

"Some people just are," Luke said gently, kissing her damp cheek. "You didn't do anything wrong."

"I feel so awful. I never taught him those words—I didn't even know he knew them."

"You've said he's smart. Maybe he taught himself."

"I *am* proud of him," she whispered. "You should've seen Mr. Adams' face when Jacob spelled *deaf.* He didn't expect it. Then he turned away so Jacob couldn't read his lips for the next word. The class laughed. Jacob looked crushed. But when he realized what the word was, he spelled it before anyone else could."

Luke held her tighter. "Then Jacob won. And it won't be the last time. God gave him strength for a reason. He'll face trials, but he has a gift—and you helped him find it."

He kissed her again, voice thick with feeling. "I'm proud of you, my Indian White Dove. You're changing lives. You're doing the Lord's work."

Megan pressed against his chest, tears of joy softening her sorrow. "I'm so lucky to have you."

"And I'm blessed to have you," he murmured, stroking her hair as his heart swelled to overflowing.

***

"Prudence, would you like to ride into the mountains with me?" Philip asked one evening as they sat in the parlor. "The leaves are turning, and they won't last much longer."

"I'd love to," she said smiling.

"Saturday afternoon, then?" He'd been eager to explore the hills for weeks.

"Could we invite Megan and Luke?" she asked hopefully.

"I think that would be wonderful. They'll know the best trails."

"I'll ask Megan tomorrow," Prudence said, already imagining the crisp air and blazing colors.

***

That Saturday, the four rode along the winding Wind River, passing the Shoshone village, where teepees had given way to rows of wooden shanties. Megan's heart sank. Change was settling, like an early frost.

Blanket-clad figures watched as the riders passed, children darting forward with shy waves. Megan lifted her hand in return, her chest swelling. Beside them the river ran slow and silver, cottonwoods whispering overhead as golden leaves spun down across the horses' backs. The damp, earthy scent of water and fading leaves filled their senses with a wistful peace.

"When did they get the blankets?" Megan asked, riding beside Luke.

"A few weeks ago—they're part of the rations," he said, nodding toward the colorfully striped wool.

"But why wear them outside?" Megan asked.

"It's a sense of pride," Luke explained. "My people don't weave wool. Blankets like these must be traded—two horses for one. The Navajo weave beautifully, but Hudson Bay blankets are thicker, better for winter. Wearing one is like putting on your best dress for church."

Prudence leaned closer. "I've seen them in ceremonies. What do they represent?"

"They're sacred," Luke said. "At our wedding,

Megan and I were wrapped in one. They're also given in honor. Every tribe treasures them."

"But isn't it strange," Prudence asked gently, "to accept something from the very people who confined them here?"

Luke's gaze swept over the camp of framed shacks. "Maybe. But at least this was useful. Most wear white man's clothes now and live in framed houses. We don't have a choice. The buffalo are gone. Teepees can't be repaired without hides. Blankets help us endure."

"I always admired their buckskin clothing and tee-pees," Prudence murmured. "It breaks my heart."

"Me too," Luke said softly.

They rode on as the trail climbed into the hills. Birches and aspens flickered gold, scarlet maples blazing between them. The crisp air carried the scent of pine, while feathery clouds drifted across the bright blue sky. Birds flitted and chirped overhead, and a squirrel skittered up a trunk.

"It's beautiful here," Philip said, drawing a long breath. He'd been quiet since passing the village, his thoughts lingering there.

"Autumn is my favorite season," Luke said. "It only lasts a few weeks before the snow starts. This year my people chose to winter in the valley, relying on rations. I pray it's not a mistake."

"I hope not either," Prudence murmured. Supplies had come late last winter.

As the climb steepened, Megan leaned into Snowfire's steady rhythm. Luke slowed Wildfire for Philip and Prudence, whose horses strained on the rocky incline as much as their riders.

At last they reached a broad outcrop. The view swept across the valley below. Luke pointed to a rugged slope beyond the pines. "That's where I was attacked by a cougar. I'd just taken a mountain goat. He leapt from that rock."

Megan and Prudence gasped. Megan had heard the story, but seeing the place made her stomach twist. She could almost picture it—Luke, bleeding and alone.

"How did you escape?" Philip asked, the hair on his neck prickling.

"I dropped the goat, but it was too late. He attacked and bit my arm before I could stop him. I used leaves and the goat's fur to slow the bleeding. I thought I'd die. Then...my Spirit guide came—a bull elk. He led me back to camp. My father's medicine and prayers saved me." Luke touched the strung teeth around his neck. "These remind me."

Megan's eyes filled. She remembered the dream that had haunted her during his absence, and his return with scars.

"Megan was praying for me," Luke added softly. "Fasting too. I believe her faith—and my family's—kept me alive."

She reached for his hand.

"Your Spirit animal?" Prudence asked. "Does everyone have one?"

"My people believe everything has a spirit—plants, animals, even the land. If we listen, they guide us. My elk came first when I decided whether to return here, then again on my vision quest, and that day with the cougar. He's sacred to me."

"That's remarkable," Philip said.

"Anyone may seek a vision," Luke said. "It begins with weeks of prayer. Then you go alone into the mountains to fast, pray, and wait. The Spirit speaks in a vision. It was the most spiritual experience of my life."

He nudged his horse forward. The others followed in silence, each imagining what such a vision might reveal.

Philip glanced once more toward the slope where Luke had faced death and been led home by a Spirit animal.

As they crested a grassy rise, Luke pulled up and pointed to the distant range. "Just a day's ride through there is where Megan and I spent our honeymoon. A quiet valley with a lake—Bull Lake. We camped there three months."

"I miss it," Megan sighed. "The lake was cradled by granite ridges and wooded hills—a fortress of peace. We foraged, fished, and hunted. Luke even shot a bear."

Philip blinked. "A bear? On your honeymoon?"

Megan gave Luke a wry smile. "It's not like we went looking for one."

"We found it raiding our deer meat," Luke said with a chuckle. "I tried to scare it off, but it charged Megan. Two arrows slowed it, but I had to use my rifle. Dropped it with one shot—thankfully."

Prudence gasped. "I would've fainted!"

"I almost did," Megan gave a weak smile. "It was terrifying."

"You were lucky," Philip said. "Luke, maybe your name should be Luck. You're the kind of man I'd want in the Wild West."

Luke grinned. "It's not luck—it's learning. Living with nature is something my people have always known."

"It's a skill you've mastered," Philip said, impressed.

Luke turned back to the trail, Megan close beside him. Prudence and Philip exchanged wide-eyed looks, half expecting a wild beast to leap from the trees.

They rode on until Luke paused at a clearing overlooking rolling forest and stone. He breathed in deep the clean mountain air. Megan's cheeks glowed with the chill, her eyes shining with wonder. Up here, on one of God's majestic peaks, the freedom felt exhilarating; with each step higher, the world's troubles fell away.

"I can't believe we waited this long to see this," Megan whispered, gazing over mountains cradling valleys and silver streams feeding the Wind River below.

"This is incredible," Philip said. Far beneath, the camp looked like scattered dollhouses by golden trees. A hawk's piercing cry drew his eyes skyward.

"That's a red-tailed hawk," Luke said as it effortlessly rode the updrafts.

"To fly like that—how glorious it must be," Prudence murmured.

"Maybe someday, you will," Philip said, watching her peaceful face.

She laughed. "Don't be silly. I've no wings."

"You never know. When we leave this world, I believe we'll soar in spirit—over landscapes more beautiful than this," he said.

"I've never thought of it that way." Prudence pictured herself gliding above treetops, brushing the river with her fingertips.

Philip studied her. "It would only be heaven if you were there with the one you love."

Her smile softened. "Yes. To live forever with true

love—that's heaven." Her chest ached. She longed for what Megan and Luke shared, admiring the Indians' freedom from society's chains.

"There's such a thing as heaven on earth," Philip said, gazing at Prudence.

Megan and Luke exchanged a knowing glance. "Shall we keep going?" Luke asked, urging his horse forward.

A few miles brought them to the crest. They tied the horses and stepped onto a rocky outcrop where wind sharpened, and scraggly pines clung to the slope. Snow-capped peaks stretched north and south, valleys below a quilt of autumn color. The river shimmered like molten silver.

Luke led Megan a short distance away and drew her close. "Now this," he said, kissing her cheek, "this is heaven. I'm on top of the world with the woman I love—who carries our child. What more could I ask?"

Megan leaned into him. "You're right. This is heaven."

Prudence watched them, the wind lifting their dark hair against the wide sky. Luke in fringed buckskin, Megan in leather and suede—they seemed part of the land itself.

Beside her, Philip caught her expression. He reached out, slowly intertwining his fingers with hers. His heart pounded at the feel of her soft skin.

Prudence's breath caught. She had dreamed of this— yet the joy blooming in her chest was greater than she imagined. Closing her eyes, she let the warmth of his hand steady her.

Philip's gaze lingered on the horizon, then returned to her—more beautiful than the view itself—the woman who held his heart. He studied her profile: soulful green eyes, soft brown hair, lips pink from the cold.

Prudence looked up. His warm, brown eyes held hers, full of tenderness. She blinked back tears and smiled.

Moved by the shimmer in her eyes, he leaned in and whispered, "If I had to die right now, I'd die a happy man. I thank God I came here."

"I'm thanking Him too," she whispered, gently tightening her grip on his hand.

# Chapter 28

## Making Plans

By late afternoon, they returned to the Shoshone village. Luke led them to a grassy clearing near the river's edge and dismounted.

Megan, revived by the wind and sky after weeks indoors, slid from her saddle and guided Snowfire to the riverbank. "This was exactly what I needed."

Prudence dismounted, brushing dust from her skirts. "Yes, a much-appreciated break from the fort."

"Thank you, Luke," Philip added, leading his horse to water. "Prudence and I couldn't have managed this terrain without you. You're a natural. People would pay well for your skill—you should consider guiding professionally."

Luke chuckled. "You think folks would pay just to ride through the mountains with me?"

"I do," Philip said, glancing across the river. Beyond the horses, Megan and Prudence laughed, their voices mingling with the river's song. "Wealthy men would pay dearly for a wilderness hunt. You're a tracker, a hunter—you live off the land. That kind of knowledge is rare."

Luke's gaze drifted to the mountains. "I've always felt alive in the high country—riding, hunting, sleeping under the stars. To earn a living that way would be close to paradise."

"You could even guide trips to remote lakes—the one

you and Megan visited on your honeymoon. From what she told us, it sounded like a sportsman's dream. I'd pay for a trip like that—and I know others who would too."

"Maybe not here, but near Laramie," Luke said, warming to the idea. "Megan and I have always dreamed of starting a horse ranch there. I could train horses, and now and then guide fishing or hunting trips."

"I hope you do," Philip said. "Dude ranches are gaining popularity. Wealthy Easterners—and even Europeans—are eager to experience the frontier. You'd draw even more interest being Shoshone. Buffalo Bill's show proved that. Those stories drew me to the West."

Luke grinned. "Thanks, I'll think it over."

"No thanks needed—just let me be your first guest," Philip said with a grin. "Four or five days in the wild— nothing but sky, water, and quiet."

"It's a deal," Luke said, shaking his hand. "You'll be first on my list."

"Then I'll spread the word—you'll have more business than you can handle."

Luke was beginning to truly enjoy Philip's company. An idea stirred. "Would you like to meet the Chief? Chief Washakie would be honored to speak with you," he said, just as Megan and Prudence returned.

"I'd be thrilled," Prudence said, eyes bright.

"It would be a true honor," Philip added, never imagining he'd meet the revered man.

"Wait here," Luke said, striding into the village.

Megan stroked Snowfire's mane. "You'll adore him. He's so charismatic. It's no surprise he was chosen as Chief. He's wise, articulate, and deeply respected."

Moments later, Luke returned. "He'd like us to join

him in the center of camp."

They secured their horses and followed Luke past children playing games between the wooden shanties.

"Miss Wright! Did you come to see where we live?" called a boy from her class, bounding up with bright eyes.

"I came to meet the Chief," she said warmly. "But your village is beautiful."

He beamed. "Thank you, Miss Wright," he said, then rejoined his playmates.

There, in a wide stone-lined circle stood a man with snow-white hair, gleaming beneath an eagle-feather headdress that trailed to his feet. Tall and commanding, his presence seemed magnified by the regal plumes. He wore a red calico tunic beneath a bearskin robe, buckskin leggings, with bear claws and beads draped across his chest.

Prudence and Philip joined Megan and Luke, standing respectfully as Luke stepped forward.

"Chief Washakie, these are the teachers I mentioned—Miss Wright and Mr. Archibald."

Prudence's hands trembled. She'd learned of his bravery and wisdom but never imagined meeting him. "Chief Washakie, I'm honored to meet you," she said, offering her hand.

"The honor is mine," he replied warmly, clasping hers in both of his. "We're fortunate to have you guiding our youth."

Prudence was struck by his kind eyes. "Thank you, sir."

He smiled, patting her hand. "Such a lovely woman— and wise too. Some lucky man will have a fine partner one day." With a wink at Philip, he added, "If only I weren't already married…"

Laughter rippled through the group.

The Chief gripped Philip's hand. "Mr. Archibald, it's a pleasure."

"The pleasure is mine, Chief Washakie. I hold you in the highest regard," Philip said, tipping his hat.

"It is I who respect you," he replied reverently. "You help our children walk in both worlds. We give them their ancestors' ways; you give them the new language and knowledge. Both are sacred."

Philip bowed his head. "Thank you, sir."

The Chief turned to Megan. "My dear Megan, you've bloomed like a desert rose." His eyes flicked to her growing belly. "Agwai proudly speaks of becoming a grandfather. You and Luka Standing Elk must be full of joy."

Megan's voice caught. "We *are* happy, but it'll be hard to leave."

He squeezed her hand. "Child, your presence has left a mark. The children will carry your teaching—especially my great-nephew, Crooked Arrow. You gave him a rare gift."

Megan blinked back tears. "Miss Wright deserves the credit. She taught me sign language so I could teach Jacob."

The Chief nodded. "Words, yes—but more than that, you gave him hope. And that's what our people need most." He leaned forward and kissed her cheek.

Tears streamed down Megan's face. "Thank you, sir."

"I hear you carry a new name—Indian White Dove.

It suits you. Go to your Cheyenne home, build your family, and remember us with love."

"I will," she said, smiling through tears.

Chief Washakie laid a hand on Luke's shoulder. "Luka, thank you for bringing these good people to me—and for sharing your wife with us. Tam Apa will bless you for your sacrifice."

"He already has," Luke said, drawing Megan close. "We have a baby on the way. I have more than I ever dreamed."

The Chief's eyes shone. "You have stayed true to your path, and it has rewarded you. But it is not over. I see a future brighter than you imagine." He bowed slightly. "If you'll excuse me, I must meet with the Indian Agent."

"Thank you for making time for us," Philip said gratefully

"Thank you, Chief Washakie," Prudence added.

He turned to leave. "Luka—Megan, come see me again before you go. I'd like to say goodbye."

"We will," Luke and Megan promised.

***

Later, the four lingered outside the dormitory in the late afternoon light.

"Luke, thank you. Today was unforgettable," Prudence said, shaking his hand.

"The pleasure was ours," Luke replied, clasping Philip's next.

"I meant what I said," Philip continued, more serious now. "You'd be perfect for guided trips—or even a dude ranch. I'd invest. Let's sit down before you leave."

Luke slipped an arm around Megan. "I'll talk it over with Megan and get back to you."

Philip tipped his hat. "Good. We'll see you at supper." He offered his arm to Prudence, who smiled as she linked hers with his.

Inside their cozy room, Megan peeled off her jacket and collapsed onto the bed with a sigh. Luke knelt, untied her shoes, and eased her legs up.

"Thank you," she murmured as he rubbed her feet. "I'm worn out. It's been ages since I rode that far."

"I was afraid it might be too much," he said.

"I'd feel this way even if I weren't pregnant. I've gotten soft, being cooped up so long. A short nap, and I'll be good as new," she assured him, eyes closed.

"Then rest," he said gently, working the stiffness from her feet.

Soon Megan was asleep, a faint snore escaping her lips. Luke smiled, touched by her sweet vulnerability.

It had been a beautiful day, one he would always treasure—but he'd decided this was Megan's last ride until after the baby came.

He slipped into bed beside her, careful not to wake her, and drew the wedding blanket over them. Curling close, he laid a hand on her belly, feeling the flutter of life beneath his palm.

The baby was strong; even the fort doctor had said so. Still, Luke wouldn't take chances. They would return to Cheyenne. He would keep them safe.

With Megan in his arms, he let sleep carry him into quiet peace.

***

The couple strolled arm in arm along the fort's boardwalk, their steps unhurried. Around them, the day wound down—soldiers shuttered the post office, the mercantile dimmed, the smithy locked, and lanterns flickered in the bathhouse and mess hall. Neighbors passed with easy nods.

Their path ended at a weathered split-rail fence, silvered by sun and time. Beyond it, the valley opened wide in sage and tawny grass. The sun slipped to the mountain's edge, and the sky deepened into lavender hush. Prudence rested a hand on the top rail. "It's so beautiful," she sighed contentedly.

Philip broke the silence. "Prudence—I'd like to court you."

Her eyes locked on the horizon, afraid the moment might vanish like the sun behind the mountains. With emotion rising, she managed, "I'd like that very much."

He drew a steady breath. "I've thought of you since the first day I saw you. I waited until it seemed right. Forgive me if I'm too forward, but...could you see us—someday—as husband and wife?"

"I can't think of anything I'd want more than a life with you," she said, turning but still unable to meet his eyes.

Philip gently tipped her chin up, forcing her to meet his heartfelt gaze.

"There's nothing I'd treasure more than forever by your side," he said earnestly.

Then, in the golden hush of sunset, he leaned close, kissing her—softly, reverently—leaving them both breathless.

***

Megan stirred, rolling onto her back with a soft sigh. Luke lay beside her, his smile warm in the faint lamplight.

"Feel better?" he asked.

"Much," she murmured, turning to face him. Dusk had settled over the valley, leaving the room dim and cool.

"I'm glad." He leaned in to kiss her.

She lingered, then asked, "So what's this about guiding hunters and running a dude ranch?"

"It was Philip's idea," Luke said. "He thinks it could be a solid business."

"I know you'd be wonderful at it. But what about your dream—raising horses?" Megan propped herself up on an elbow.

"I could do both. Use the horses we raise for the trips." His voice brightened. "Philip knows wealthy folks and foreigners who'd pay to be guided by a real Indian through the mountains. We'd be doing what we love—together. You could help cook, we'd camp in the woods..."

He got up, excitement building. "We'd teach them about nature, survival—the way we know. Maybe not hunting, but fishing and camping." He turned up the lamp and began to pace. "Picture it—kids riding to a mountain lake, learning to fish. At night, stories, songs, and stargazing. They'd fall in love with it like us."

Breathless, he came to sit beside her. Her heart swelled at the spark in his eyes.

She cupped his cheek. "You really want this, don't you?"

"I do. Don't you?"

She kissed him sweetly. "If it's your dream, I believe in it. And if Philip can send guests, it might actually happen. But it's a big job, Luke. We'd need help. It's like running a hotel in the woods. Promise me you'll think it through."

"It's not just my decision." He drew her into his arms. "This is ours. I won't take a step unless you're beside me. You and the baby—our family—come first. Always."

He rested his cheek atop her head, fingers gently stroking her back.

She chuckled. "Now you've got me excited too. We could work with family. Jeremy loves horses. Penny and I could cook."

She laughed, picturing it. "Crispy fried fish, Dutch oven potatoes, peach cobbler..." She gave him a squeeze. "All this talk's making me hungry. Let's head down for tea and biscuits."

He drew back to look into her eyes. "I love you, Megan. You're an amazing woman—my Indian White Dove." He kissed her softly.

She smiled against his lips. "Mmm. I love you too."

***

In the days that followed, their conversations bloomed with ideas and dreams. They spoke of building a guest lodge—offering families a taste of the Wild West, enriched by Indian tradition and mountain beauty.

"When we get back to Laramie, the first thing we need is a homestead plot," Luke said one night, lying beside Megan. "Maybe Jeremy will want land nearby. We could build side by side—work together."

"I thought we were staying in Cheyenne until after the baby's born," Megan said, snuggling close, the pot-bellied stove glowing warmly in the corner.

"We will," Luke replied, eyes bright. "But we could

stake our claim now, then return in spring to build. We'll stay with Ma and Pa through winter, save what we can, and move once the weather turns. We could build a cabin with Pa and the boys lending a hand."

Megan smiled but remained cautious. "Shouldn't we talk to Jeremy and Penny first? This is happening so fast."

"You're right," Luke admitted. "I'll write him tomorrow. But I'd still like to stop in Laramie—just to see what land is available."

***

"Have you thought it over?" Philip asked a few evenings later as they sat in the warm parlor, sipping tea.

"We have," Luke replied, excitement in his voice. "We'd love to pursue it—but we'd need more than the two of us." He glanced at Megan, crocheting beside Prudence near the fire.

"You'd need a small team," Philip agreed.

"We imagine it as a family adventure," Luke said. "City kids riding horses for the first time, fishing, gathering at a campfire, sleeping in teepees. Just think of their wonder."

Philip's eyes lit. "Brilliant. You could share your Shoshone heritage—archery, beadwork, tanning buckskin. The possibilities are endless." His gaze lingered on Prudence.

Luke gazed out the dark window, vision unfurling: teepees in a circle, a fire pit at the center, horses in a corral, guests exploring the hills. "This dream lives deep in me. Megan and I want families to know what we've been blessed with. But we'll need help. Our cousin and his wife love the outdoors. I've written them, hoping they'll join us."

"I'm glad," Philip said. "Your passion will keep people coming back. I'd be honored to be part of it." He winked. "And if all goes well, I hope Prudence will be by my side when it opens."

Luke's gaze softened on the women. "You've chosen well."

Philip's voice lowered. "Let me help fund it. I believe in this dream—and in you. Just as you know the elk is your Spirit guide, I know in my heart we're meant to bring this dream to life."

Luke nodded, stirred. "I've prayed on it. I know it's right. If you truly want to help, I won't refuse. I'll estimate costs—horses, teepees, a lodge, wages. It won't be cheap, and profit may take years."

"Take all the time you need," Philip said. "Come spring, we'll start building. It can be ready by summer."

"That's what I hope," Luke replied. "But it's a large investment."

"Don't worry about the money," Philip said, setting down his cup. "Consider it a loan. My father left me a generous inheritance, and I'd rather use it to build something lasting. You and Megan have good hearts—you'll touch lives with this dream."

Mr. Thompson entered with his wife on his arm. "Good evening, gentlemen. How's everyone tonight?"

"Very well," Philip said.

"Doing fine," Luke added, then smiled at Naomi. "And how are you, Mrs. Thompson?"

"Good, thank you," she said warmly, resting her hands on her round belly before joining Megan and Prudence by the fire.

"She looks radiant," Philip observed.

"She is," Mr. Thompson agreed. "Even though she's uncomfortable, she never complains. I hear her awake at night, though she tries not to disturb me. I never realized how hard it must be—carrying all that weight."

"I think Mr. Adams might have an inkling," Philip murmured, and they chuckled.

"In truth, she's remarkable," Mr. Thompson said, his gaze softening. "Always kind, always patient. Sometimes I wish she'd scold me more—might make me feel human."

"We men are prone to folly," Luke said with a wry smile. "Megan's only fault is carrying guilt that isn't hers. Years ago, a young man died protecting her honor, and she still blames herself. She also grieves what was done to my people, as if the burden were hers. I remind her it's not."

"There's evil in the world," Philip said. "I saw it in the South. The war ended before I was born, but cruelty lingered—men still trying to dominate others. But there are good men too. My father was one. He helped people, no matter their color or class."

"You're a reflection of him," Mr. Thompson said gently. "I'm sure you miss him. Naomi misses her family too. But I'm grateful she has Megan and Prudence—they comfort her."

"And she comforts them," Luke said. "Megan often says how much she enjoys Naomi's cheerful spirit."

"The children adore her," Philip added. "And her choir is as fine as any I've heard in the South."

"She'll miss it when the baby comes," Mr. Thompson said. "And we'll miss you and Megan when you leave."

"We'll miss you too," Luke said softly.

"You leave in a week or so?" Mr. Thompson asked.

"Yes," Luke replied. "We want to reach Cheyenne before the mountain passes close. It'll be hard for Megan to say goodbye—especially to the children—but we know it's time."

"We plan to stay in close contact," Philip said. "And if our plans go as I hope, we'll see each other often."

Mr. Thompson raised a brow. "Plans? What are you plotting?"

Luke chuckled. "Nothing shady. We're dreaming of a guest ranch near Laramie—families can ride horses, fish, camp under the stars... and learn a little about Shoshone ways."

"Luke and I dreamed it up together," Philip added.

Mr. Thompson's eyes brightened. "That sounds incredible. You couldn't ask for better men to run it." He lifted his teacup. "To success."

They clinked cups with a smile.

"Come visit next summer," Luke said. "We'll give you the tour—and a discount for good friends. Tell your family in Utah. The more, the merrier."

"You bet we will!" Mr. Thompson laughed.

***

A week later, a letter arrived from Cheyenne in Jeremy Holden's neat hand. Megan tore it open, heart racing, and read aloud as Luke listened.

*Dear Luke and Megan,*

*We were thrilled to hear from you. It's been too long. We can't wait to welcome you home.*

*Penny is a month from delivery, busy sewing*

Luke swept Megan into his arms. "Can you believe it? Jeremy *and* Grandpa O'Malley are joining us! Megan, it's happening—we're going to build the finest guest ranch in the West." He kissed her forehead.

Megan gazed up, eyes shining. "It's unbelievable. With Jeremy, Penny, Grandma and Grandpa—it'll feel like home. I can hardly wait."

That night, she drifted asleep resting her head on his shoulder as he held her close. Their future was taking shape, and everything felt exactly right.

***

A frantic knock shattered the silence, jerking them awake. It came again—louder, more urgent.

"Mr. and Mrs. Havoc! Please, wake up—I need your help!" a trembling voice cried from the other side of the door.

# Chapter 29

## Farewell

Luke sat up as the knocking grew urgent. Megan stirred, rubbing her eyes.

"What is it?" she murmured.

"I don't know." He lit the lamp and pulled on his trousers as the knock came again. "I'm coming!"

Mr. Thompson stood pale in the doorway. "Please—come quickly. Naomi needs help. She woke in pain. She's bleeding."

"Go back—we'll be right there," Luke said, turning to Megan. "Get Mrs. Carlson. I'll fetch the doctor."

Megan raced through the hall, nightdress and robe billowing. Prudence's door creaked open.

"What's happening?" she asked, sleepy.

"It's Naomi. Go to her—I'll get Mrs. Carlson," Megan whispered.

Downstairs, she knocked softly. "Please wake up. Naomi needs you."

Moments later, Mrs. Carlson appeared, hair wrapped in a white scarf, eyes alert.

"What is it, child?"

"Naomi's bleeding and in pain. Luke's gone for the doctor," Megan explained.

"I'll be right there."

Megan hurried upstairs. Mr. Thompson held the door and stepped aside, feeling helpless.

Inside, the dim light revealed Naomi in bed, curled in pain, Prudence at her side.

Megan knelt close. "Naomi, what's happening?"

"It hurts...I'm bleeding," Naomi gasped.

"Mrs. Carlson's coming. The doctor too. You'll be alright," Megan whispered.

"Pray...for my baby," Naomi choked, tears falling.

Together, Megan and Prudence bowed their heads in a fervent plea for strength and life.

Naomi whispered, "Thank you."

Mrs. Carlson entered with hot water and towels. "Lordy, child," she said, voice motherly. "Let me see what's what." Carefully, she examined Naomi, then crossed to the basin to wash her blood-soaked hands.

Mr. Thompson whispered, "Is the baby alright?"

"We'll do our best," she said quietly. "It's too early. The afterbirth is separating. She needs surgery. Keep her calm until the doctor arrives."

Pale and shaken, he moved to Naomi's side, gently rubbing her back. "Shh...you'll be fine. Just hold on." He brushed away a tear as her trembling eased and she drew a deep breath.

Luke and the doctor burst in. The doctor murmured instructions, scrubbing at the basin. "Mrs. Carlson, I'll need you. Everyone else—out."

Luke wrapped Megan in an arm. "We've done what we can." She followed, glancing back with a whispered prayer. Prudence trailed behind, sobs escaping.

Philip opened his door. He stepped out just as Prudence flew into his arms. He held her close, then looked to Luke for answers.

Mr. Thompson emerged, dazed. "The doctor...had to

put her to sleep. He's cutting the baby out now," he said hollowly.

Luke placed a reassuring hand on his shoulder. "She's in good hands."

Mr. Thompson covered his mouth, shoulders quaking. Luke guided him back to their room, sat him down, and asked Megan to make tea.

In the hallway, Philip stroked Prudence's back, her quiet weeping piercing him.

"Come," he murmured, leading her into her room where a lamp glowed. He eased her into a chair near the potbellied stove and set a teapot to warm.

Prudence tried to stifle her sobs, but thoughts of Naomi's suffering broke her again.

Philip pulled up a chair, gently stroking her braid. Even tear-streaked, she looked beautiful—her compassion only heightening it.

His steady touch slowly calmed her trembling. She lifted her glassy gaze, so raw and vulnerable, his heart ached.

"I love you," she whispered.

The words struck like lightning. His heart thundered. Tenderly, he brushed away her tears and kissed her, lips speaking what words could not.

Pulling back, his eyes deepened. "I love you, too," he said, low and sure.

More tears spilled as she folded into his arms, her bittersweet sobs soaking his shirt.

***

A soft knock broke the stillness. Mrs. Carlson entered Luke and Megan's room, her face lined with fatigue.

"She's asking for you," she said gently.

Mr. Thompson rose at once. "The baby…?" He couldn't finish.

Her voice caught. "No, dear. But Naomi needs you."

Without a word, he rushed past her. She followed, closing the door softly behind.

A sob broke from Megan as she clung to Luke, her knees giving way.

He caught her and carried her to the bed, laying her down gently. The night's weight—grief, fear, helplessness—had overcome her.

She wept into the pillow while Luke stroked her hair, murmuring reassurances. He knew her tears were for Naomi and John, but also for the fragile life within her, shadowed by uncertainty.

Clutching the blanket, Megan closed her eyes and poured her heart into prayer—for Naomi, for John, and for the child in her womb.

***

Sunday dawned gray and hushed. Megan lay curled beneath the quilts, too weak to rise, even the thought of dressing felt impossible.

Luke stayed near. While she slept, he read softly from the scriptures, pausing to pray—first for John and Naomi, then for Megan and their child.

Later, he slipped downstairs for breakfast. Mrs. Carlson moved quietly through the dining room, setting out warm platters.

"She's resting," she told the others gently. "Weak, but she'll recover in time."

Mr. Adams gave a terse nod, muttered his condolences, and began to eat.

Grief hung in the air like smoke, yet the Headmaster

seemed untouched. Luke pushed his plate away—his appetite gone.

A dull ache throbbed in Luke's chest. John and Naomi were the kindest souls he knew. Why must the purest bear the heaviest burdens? Alone, he wept for them—and feared for himself. He wasn't sure he could survive losing Megan or their child.

Toward midmorning, Megan stirred. Luke sat at the small table, dressed in buckskins.

"Are you going to church?" she asked faintly, eyes shadowed.

He rose and brushed her cheek. "No. I'd rather stay here with you."

She offered a wan smile. "You should go. I'll be alright. I just need rest."

He hesitated, then kissed her forehead. "Only because you ask. Try to eat—I brought biscuits. I'll be back soon."

He changed, tied back his hair, and slipped out, praying she'd find peace in his absence.

When the door clicked shut, Megan turned into the pillow—and broke.

Sobs came in gasping waves, raw and uncontainable. Beneath sorrow lay shame—a terrible, aching relief. Her baby still lived. How could she face Naomi, carrying life when Naomi's arms held only loss?

All Naomi's dreams—her whispered hopes, the tender life she had carried—had vanished. Megan felt unworthy to even mourn.

*Why them, Lord?* Her sobs softened into prayer. *They deserved joy, not this. Oh God, please...wrap them in Your mercy. Help them understand. Help me understand.*

*And please—please don't let me lose my baby too.*

She lay still listening, hands resting gently over her womb.

***

Luke slipped into the chapel just as the opening prayer ended. Scanning the pews, he spotted Mr. Thompson near the front—Naomi's place held by Prudence and Philip.

Quietly, Luke joined them, sitting beside John. The man turned, eyes red-rimmed, offering a faint smile. Luke wondered why John wasn't with Naomi. Then again, he was here while Megan grieved alone.

The reverend stepped forward, delivering a sermon Luke would never forget.

He spoke on Abraham and Sarah—how God had given them Isaac in their old age, then commanded Abraham to offer him as sacrifice. Luke's throat tightened; he knew the story well.

"When Isaac asked his father what they would offer, Abraham answered, 'God will provide.'" The reverend's voice dropped. "Isaac obeyed his father, laying upon the altar in trust and faith. Just as the knife was raised, the angel of the Lord stayed Abraham's hand…"

His gaze swept the room. "Abraham glimpsed what it meant for the Father to surrender His only begotten Son. In that obedience he felt, in part, the weight of divine love—a sliver of the sorrow and the immeasurable grace God bore for us."

Silence fell. "Will we obey, even when it costs us everything? Are we stronger than Abraham—or more beloved than Isaac? Can we yield to what God asks, though it breaks our hearts?"

He read from Romans: "For I am persuaded, that neither death, nor life... shall be able to separate us from the love of God.”

Mr. Thompson bowed his head, tears slipping silently down his cheeks. Prudence dabbed her eyes as Philip gently squeezed her hand.

The final prayer rose, and when the *amen* fell, the congregation filed out in hushed reverence.

Prudence and Philip walked side by side beneath a low, gray sky, Luke and John trailing behind.

John spoke. “The Lord knew I needed that today.”

“We all did,” Luke answered quietly. “How is Naomi?”

“Weak. Sad. But she’ll recover. The doctor gave her something for rest—she lost so much blood. She asked me to thank you all. She worried none of you slept.”

They paused at the dormitory steps.

Prudence touched his arm. “We were glad to help. Naomi’s our dear friend.”

John’s voice thickened. “She needs you and Megan more than ever—maybe visit after supper?”

“Yes, after supper.” She gave him a reassuring smile.

John tipped his hat, climbing the steps with slow, heavy footfalls.

“That poor man,” Philip murmured. “What a burden he carries.”

Prudence turned to Luke. “How’s Megan?”

“She’s worn out—in every way. But perhaps seeing Naomi will help them both.”

***

Megan stirred as Luke stepped inside.

“How was it?” she asked, voice thick with sleep.

“Comforting,” he said, slipping off his overcoat.

"John was there."

She sat up. "He was? How is he?"

Luke watched as she crossed to the stove, adding coal with a soft clink of iron.

"He's grieving but bearing it with grace. He asked if you and Prudence might visit Naomi after supper. He thinks it would help—just knowing her friends are near."

Megan froze, then slowly reached for her dress. "I don't know, Luke. Just looking at me—carrying this baby—it'll only hurt her more. Maybe in a few days."

As she fumbled with her buttons, Luke gently caught her shoulders.

"Megan, she needs you. You'll have to face her sometime. We're leaving soon—you'll want to say goodbye. Don't let this moment slip away."

Her lashes trembled, tears spilling. "I just can't," she whispered, then broke into sobs.

Luke held her close. "My brave Indian White Dove, what if it had been you? Wouldn't you want your friends near? Naomi has no mother to lean on. She needs the comfort only a friend can bring."

Megan sniffed, wiping her eyes, thinking of Naomi—gentle, selfless, always giving. Even in pain, she would've reached out. That was Naomi—Christlike.

"I would want her with me," Megan admitted

Luke lifted her chin. "Just be there. That's all she needs."

He kissed her forehead. She gave a faint, tearful smile.

"Alright," she whispered. "I'll go. I just hope I don't make it harder."

"You won't," he said. "You'll remind her she's not

alone."

***

After supper, Megan and Prudence walked quietly down the dim hallway, hands clasped. Megan knocked at Naomi's door.

John answered. Without a word, he stepped aside and left them.

Naomi lay propped against pillows, bathed in sunset's glow. The warmth lit the room but not her skin. Her lips were pale, eyes shadowed, her long braid spilling over one shoulder. She looked as fragile as the day they first met.

When she lifted her arms, they rushed to her side. No words—only the rustle of skirts, the creak of the floor, and shared weeping.

At last, Naomi spoke, her voice raw. "Thank you for coming. I've tried to be strong for John...but I needed *you*. I needed *this*." She brushed her cheeks with trembling fingers. "Thank you for letting me cry."

"Naomi," Prudence said thickly, "we're here for you—always. You're our sister. When you suffer, we suffer too. And when you rejoice, we'll rejoice with you. You don't have to carry this alone."

Megan lamented, "We're so sorry."

Naomi gripped their hands. "Last night...after the surgery, I asked to see her. She was so tiny, perfectly formed...she looked like she was sleeping. But she wasn't. And in that moment, something inside me shattered. A piece of my soul went with her."

Megan and Prudence held her hands tight as tears streamed down their faces.

"I wanted to die," Naomi's voice broke. "To wake to

a world without her felt unbearable. Until I realized—John still needs me."

"We understand," Prudence whispered, stroking her hand.

"While John was at church—at my urging—I prayed harder than ever. Not for a miracle, but for strength to accept His will. And then...something sacred happened."

Her voice steadied. "A warmth came over me—real, tangible—as if someone wrapped me in a blanket. Then I heard a voice. Not in my mind, but aloud. Deep, resonant, yet full of love. It said: *She came to gain a body... and now waits for you in Heaven. One day, you will raise her.*"

She trembled. "Then came the light. Not sunlight, but something purer, filling the room. Though the fire was cold, I was warm. I felt held—in my Savior's arms."

Her sobs softened, touched with awe. "He told me I'm a worthy woman. That I will have more children. That I will raise a righteous legacy unto Him."

Megan and Prudence wept and smiled through tears, the Spirit a quiet fire within.

"Oh, Naomi," Prudence whispered, "what a sacred gift. You *are* a choice woman. The Lord *will* bless you. He hasn't forsaken you."

Naomi nodded. "When I told John, he said he'd felt something too. At church, the reverend's words struck deep. We believe—though our hearts ache—our little girl is where she belongs. And one day, we'll be with her again."

Megan shook her head in wonder. "Your faith...it's so strong. How do you hold to it through this?"

Naomi's gaze softened. "I could turn away. But what

would that change? It wouldn't bring her back. It would only deepen the pain. I'd rather walk through this valley with my Savior than face it alone. He loves me. And He wants what's best for us."

She squeezed their hands. "It doesn't mean He'll spare me sorrow. But He walks with me through it. If I feel alone, it's only because I've turned away. He never leaves us. Never."

"Oh, that I had your faith," Megan murmured, wrestling with the anger she'd felt toward God for taking Naomi's child. "I don't think I could bear it as you have."

Naomi pressed her hand. "You would, if the time came. We all choose—surrender or resentment. And I believe you'd choose faith. You already follow Him. I see it in your patience and love. I'm so blessed to know you both. Thank you for taking me in from the day I arrived."

No," Prudence whispered, eyes glistening. "We are the blessed ones. You inspire us."

***

On Monday morning, classes were suspended in honor of the Thompsons' loss.

Mourners gathered at the tiny grave, silhouettes etched against a silver sky. Frost jeweled every branch and blade, breath rising in soft clouds. Across the way, Shoshone children stood in rows, hands folded. At Miss Wright's signal, their voices rose—*Amazing Grace* drifting pure and haunting, threading the air with angels' song.

When the final note faded, Prudence quietly stepped beside Philip. Naomi and John sat hand in hand, ringed by friends and congregation. The soft earth yielded, cradling the small wooden box in its final resting place.

The reverend spoke reverently. "We gather to lay to rest little Grace Naomi Thompson, beloved daughter of John and Naomi. The body we return to the earth is but a shell, a spirit called back too soon, awaiting reunion in glory at the Lord's coming."

He read from Psalm 23: *"The Lord is my Shepherd; I shall not want…"*

John and Naomi rose together to scatter soil across their daughter's resting place, faces pale with grief. Megan turned into Luke's arms, muffling her sobs. Prudence clung to Philip's hand. Mrs. Carlson cried out, clutching her trembling daughter, Missy. At the back, Mr. Adams stood apart, arms crossed, head shaking at the disgrace of it all.

The mourners filed back to the dormitory, where Mrs. Carlson had laid out ham, rolls, potatoes, and pies. Friends added their own offering, a quiet testament to sorrow shared.

The reverend closed with a blessing of peace and comfort. Guests ate in silence, voices hushed. In the parlor, Naomi and John received friends by the fire, answering whispered condolences with quiet grace.

*** 

Tuesday marked the last day of school before the long Thanksgiving break. The children, though eager for dismissal at noon, wore somber faces—for it was also Mrs. Havoc's final day.

Standing before the class, Megan smiled gently.

"Before the bell rings, I want you to know how deeply I'll miss you. It's been an honor to teach you. You are bright, good-hearted children. I trust you'll work hard and show your new teacher the same kindness you've shown me."

Jacob Crooked Arrow raised his hand. Megan nodded and he stood to sign, his movements fluid and sure.

Megan translated, steady despite the ache in her throat.

"Mrs. Havoc, thank you for being our teacher—for the time and care you gave us. We made you a gift."

From the back, Johnny Red Moon stepped forward, holding a necklace of brightly strung beads. Megan bowed her head as he draped it around her neck, then hugged her tightly.

She smiled through misted eyes. "Thank you. It's beautiful. I'll treasure it always."

The bell rang. Yet the children lingered, lining up to hug her and whisper tearful goodbyes. Megan wiped her eyes, knowing it might be years before she returned.

Jacob was last, brown eyes shimmering as he signed slowly: *I love you, Mrs. Havoc. I'll miss you.*

Megan knelt, hands trembling as she signed back: *I love you too, Jacob. I'm proud of you. Keep learning. I'll see you again, someday.*

He hugged her once more, then dashed out the door.

Megan slipped on her coat and gathered her things. She took one last look around—so many memories lived here—some challenging, some triumphant. She only hoped she'd left enough light behind. With a wistful glance, she closed the door.

At the Headmaster's office, she knocked.

"Enter," came Mr. Adams' gruff reply.

"I've finished for the day. Thank you again for allowing me to teach here," Megan said, setting a stack of books on his desk and turning to leave.

"Mrs. Havoc," he sneered after her, "against my better judgment, I let you stay. I only hope your replacement has the sense not to marry and bear children. That path brings only misery—as we've seen with the Thompsons. Good luck, I suppose, with your life as a wife and mother."

Megan turned back, chin lifted, a knowing smile curving her lips.

"I don't need luck. I have everything I ever hoped for—a fulfilling role as a teacher, a loving husband, and soon, a child of my own. I chose this life freely, and it brings me joy. It's *you* I pity. Your world is small and bitter, sustained only by food and resentment."

She closed the door firmly behind her. As she walked back to the dormitory, her shoulders straightened. The ache of leaving lingered, but she couldn't help the smile tugging at her lips. She would not miss Mr. Adams—not for a moment.

*** 

"Well, that's the last of it," Luke said, closing the trunk. Their room stood bare—ready for the new teacher.

"I didn't think I would," Megan murmured, folding her apron, "but I'll miss this place."

"It wasn't so bad," Luke said. "We made friends. Found moments of joy."

She smiled faintly. "We should go if we want to be back before the stage."

Luke hauled the trunk downstairs. Megan followed with their bags.

"Mrs. Carlson?" Megan called toward the kitchen. "We'll be back in an hour—we're going to the village to say goodbye to Luke's father."

"Don't forget to say goodbye to me," she called over her shoulder.

"Never," Megan said warmly. "We left our things in the hall so the new teacher can settle in."

"Much appreciated. Mr. Jacques is due soon," Mrs. Carlson said.

They borrowed a rig and descended into the valley. Megan gazed at the quiet landscape—leafless trees along the river, smoke curling from chimneys, a few villagers moving slowly through the cold.

They stopped at a modest wooden home. Luke helped Megan down and approached the door. Rose greeted them with a warm smile, pulling them inside. The room was dim but cozy, warmed by a pot-bellied stove. Fur-lined bedrolls were stacked in one corner, and baskets of food and folded clothes in another. A single window let in a pale shaft of light.

"Welcome," Rose said, embracing Megan. "It's good to see you."

"We wanted to say goodbye before heading back to Cheyenne," Luke said. "Is my father around?"

"He'll be back soon," Rose replied. "But first—I have something for you." She guided Megan to a chair by the stove and placed a cradleboard in her lap.

Megan's breath caught. She traced the smooth wood, the buckskin lacing, the intricate beadwork. Tears filled her eyes. "It's beautiful. Thank you."

Luke embraced his aunt. "Thank you." He stepped to the window. "I hope Father returns soon. The stage won't wait."

As if on cue, Agwai entered, smiling. "Son, come. I

have something for you."

Outside, Luke's uncle stood beside two Paints—a four-year-old colt and a mare, both with brown and tan spots. Luke stared. "Father...these are the ones I broke in the fall."

Agwai nodded. "They're yours. The tribe wishes to give them to you. You trained them well. They will serve you—and breed strong."

Luke stepped forward, wrapping his arms around his father. "Thank you. This means more than I can say. I love you, Father."

"And I love you, my son," Agwai said, voice thick. "We'll miss you both. I'll pray for your safe return—and your child's health. Write to us. Miss Wright can read your words."

Megan embraced her father-in-law, tears spilling freely. "Thank you, Father—for everything. I'll miss you."

A strong voice called, "Luka! Megan!" Chief Washakie approached, shaking Luke's hand and gently taking Megan's. "I couldn't let you leave without saying goodbye. Thank you—for teaching our children."

"Thank you, sir," Megan said, wiping tears.

The chief kissed her cheek. "Blessings on your family. May Tam Apa guide you safely home—and back again."

"Thank you," Luke said, offering a grateful smile.

He turned to his family. "Give our love to the others. We'll miss you all."

"Goodbye, my son," Agwai said, embracing them both. "Kiss the little one for me when she comes. Tell her about us. And come back."

"We will," Megan whispered. "I love you."

"And I love *you*, child." Agwai swiped at a tear.

Rose hugged Megan again, then placed the cradle-board in the wagon, the horses tied behind. Luke helped Megan up and climbed in beside her.

As they pulled away, they waved, hearts heavy. Luke didn't know when they'd return, but he knew the love of family would always be waiting.

***

At the fort's gate, they passed the trading post, where a Shoshone woman sat cross-legged behind handcrafted wares. Her eyes followed the wagon with quiet hope.

Luke eased back on the reins and swung down.

"What are you doing?" Megan asked. "The stagecoach could be here any minute."

"I want to pick up a few Christmas gifts." He selected several items from the blanket and returned.

"These should do nicely," he said.

She smiled, cradling the package. "I hope there's room."

"I'll make room," Luke laughed. "Even if I have to carry them to Cheyenne."

***

Back at the dormitory, Megan joined Naomi for a final, tearful goodbye.

Downstairs, Megan and Luke hugged Mrs. Carlson.

"A little something for the baby," she said, pressing a blanket into Megan's hands.

. "Missy and I will miss you both terribly."

"Thank you—for everything." Megan kissed her cheek.

394

Mrs. Carlson pulled Luke into a firm hug.

"Take good care of her," she said warmly.

"Yes, ma'am."

Just then, the front door opened, and a tall, broad woman stood blocking the entry, two bags at her feet.

"Is this the teachers' dormitory?" she asked boldly.

"It is," Mrs. Carlson replied.

"I'm Miss Jacques—Patricia Jacques. The new teacher."

Megan and Luke froze, luggage in hand.

"Welcome," Mrs. Carlson said, quickly recovering. "Let me show you to your room."

Megan touched her arm gently. "Goodbye, Mrs. Carlson."

"Goodbye, dear," she said, squeezing Megan's hand.

Stepping onto the boardwalk, Megan and Luke's eyes were drawn to movement.

In front of the school, Shoshone children stood with Mr. Archibald, Mr. Thompson, and Miss Wright. A soft, haunting melody rose—a Shoshone farewell song, lifting like a prayer.

They set down their luggage.

Prudence stepped forward, wrapping Megan in a tight embrace. "I'll miss you, dear friend. You'll always be in my prayers—and my heart."

"I'll write," Megan whispered.

Mr. Thompson offered a quiet handshake, gratitude in his eyes.

Mr. Archibald approached with a travel bag in hand. "We'd best be going if we want to make that stage," he said.

"What?" Megan blinked, astonished. "You're coming with us?"

Philip nodded. "Business in Laramie. And I'd like to see you home safely."

Prudence's eyes widened. "You're leaving? For Thanksgiving?"

"I'll be back before school resumes," he promised, squeezing her hand.

Prudence's heart ached. "I'll miss you."

"I'll miss you, too," he said, slipping her arm through his.

Together, they walked to the post office, where the stagecoach waited. Their luggage was promptly loaded. The horses stamped restlessly, their breath rising in clouds.

Luke swung onto Wildfire, glancing back at Snowfire and the Paints tied behind, eager for the journey.

Megan and Prudence embraced one last time. Then, Megan stepped into the coach and Philip closed the door. She leaned out the window, tears streaking her cheeks.

"Goodbye!" voices called, fading into the brisk autumn wind.

The stage lurched forward, wheels crunching over frozen ground, carrying them from friends, family, and the place that had become home.

# Chapter 30

## Going Home

Luke waited for the stagecoach to pull ahead, letting its dust settle before nudging Wildfire forward. A glance back confirmed Snowfire and the two Paints followed smoothly on taut leads. His heartbeat fell into rhythm with their hooves. He meant to match the stage's pace all the way to Rawlins—twelve grueling hours. He only hoped Megan could endure the ride. The horses he trusted; they were strong and surefooted.

Behind him, Fort Washakie blurred into the low, gray sky. Wind whipped the prairie, rattling dry grasses and stealing warmth. Inside the coach, thick curtains shut out the chill, dimming the light. Six passengers sat knee to knee, shoulder to shoulder, bags jammed at their feet. The air soon thickened with wool, dust, and silence.

Wind howled, sliding through the curtain seams and nipped Megan's shoulder pressed to the wall. She shivered, pulling her coat closer, and worried for Luke.

Two hours in, the stage halted at the first way station and three fresh teams were hitched. Luke arrived soon after, his horses lathered and steaming. He cooled them down, checked their legs, then led them into the stable for water.

In the drafty shack, Megan and Philip sat with fellow travelers, filling themselves with ham and bean soup and stale bread. Luke entered quietly, drawing glances.

Megan scooted over and patted the bench beside her.

He sat, red-faced and wind-bitten. A bowl was pressed into his hands, and he hunched over it gratefully.

"Luke, you're freezing," Megan whispered, taking his hand. His skin was red beneath the scarf and gloves.

"I'll be alright," he said, squeezing her fingers, though his own ached as the feeling returned. Riding had kept his core warm, but his hands and feet were numb.

"Maybe you should ride inside. We could pay for another seat."

He shook his head. "No. I'll be fine."

The driver's call rang out. They finished the last bites of supper, bundled up, and climbed aboard. Outside, the fresh team pawed the frozen ground, eager to run.

Luke saddled Snowfire, tying the others behind. As the stage pulled away, he followed closely.

The sun split the clouds, momentarily gilding mountaintops before disappearing. Dusk spread in shades of steel, soon swallowed by night. Inside the coach, a lantern swung from the ceiling, flickering with each jolt. Megan gave thanks for the metal box of coals beneath their feet, warming the blankets over their legs.

The coach, suspended on wide leather straps, rocked and swayed with each jarring blow from the trail. Hooves thundered. A snort or whinny now and then cut through the wind as the team strained to haul the weight of wood, iron, and weary souls uphill. Megan's heart lurched as the wheels tilted sharply on a curve, the coach leaning precariously before settling. Her pulse steadied, but unease lingered.

The ceaseless motion turned her stomach. She breathed the cold air leaking through the curtains to quell the nausea.

Conversation faded away. Philip lowered his hat and dozed. Wedged between him and another man, Megan hunched forward to avoid being pressed on both sides. Shifting brought little relief to her aching back. The promise of a faster journey no longer appealed.

Across from her, a young man pinned between two broad companions caught her eye. He gave a faint, knowing smile. Megan returned it, then lowered her gaze, resting gloved hands over her rounded belly, bowing her head in silent prayer for the miles still ahead.

Outside, Luke narrowed his eyes against the wind, keeping the swaying lantern in sight. Without it, the road would vanish. At this speed, one misstep could leave them stranded.

Doubt crept in. Was this wise? Wouldn't a slower wagon have been safer? But then he pictured Megan, warm inside, and pushed the worry aside. She was safe— that mattered most.

Still, the cold gnawed at his throbbing fingers and toes. Snowfire tossed her head, tiring after ten miles of leading. Luke urged her on gently, scanning the horizon for the next stop.

At last, the stage halted at a lonely shanty. Passengers spilled out to stretch, use the necessary, and sip hot but weak coffee.

Luke arrived stiff as wood, sliding from Snowfire, every joint complaining. He led the horses under the lean-to, watered and rubbed them down, but doubt pressed harder than the saddle. One hundred miles. Twelve hours. Already it felt too much—maybe even for the horses.

Philip appeared, breath fogging the air. "Let me ride a leg," he said. "You need to warm up. I can't stand another minute in that rocking coffin." He chuckled, but concern darkened his eyes.

Luke shook his head, rubbing down a flank. "They're my responsibility. I'll get them there—even if it takes another day."

"Hogwash," Philip replied. "We're partners. Your wife needs you whole. Let me help." He was already swapping the saddle to a Paint.

Luke exhaled. "Fine. Thank you." He handed over his buffalo coat, scarf, and gloves. "Take these. You'll need them."

Philip tugged them on, tightening the scarf. "Get coffee. I'll be fine."

"Yes, sir." Luke gave a weary grin before heading toward the shanty's glow.

Megan met him at the door, brows furrowed. "Are you alright?" she asked, eyeing the wool coat on Luke.

"I'm fine," Luke said, pouring steaming coffee and downing it in two burning gulps.

"Why are you wearing Philip's coat?"

"He insisted I rest. I told him no, but he's stubborn. At least he'll be warm." Luke refilled his cup.

"You needed a break," she said, silently thanking God for Philip's steady heart.

The driver's call rang out. Luke was the last to board, glancing back. Philip sat tall in the saddle, raising a hand in salute.

"Keep the lantern in sight!" Luke called over the wind.

"I will!"

There were three more stops before Rawlins. If they traded off, Philip believed they could make it—and now, Luke dared to hope so too. With the heavy coat and mittens the ride was survivable.

Inside, Luke settled beside Megan. He nodded to the others, but few responded, conversation had long since died. Only four hours since leaving the fort, but it felt like another lifetime. Soon, warmth from coals and shared body heat seeped into his bones, and within minutes his head dropped forward in sleep.

Megan leaned into him, comforted by his closeness. He was utterly spent. Nestling against his shoulder, she closed her eyes and tried to rest.

The coach jolted. "Whoa!" the driver shouted, rousing the dozing. Luke stirred, blinking.

"We're at the next stop," Megan whispered with relief. The baby had kicked her ribs for miles. Finally, a chance to breathe.

Luke climbed down and stretched, cold slapping him awake. He turned, scanning the dark road for Philip.

Philip saw the lanterns ahead and sighed with relief. Drawing the reins, he brought the horses to a staggering halt.

Luke caught the bridle, running a gloved hand down the lead's steaming neck. "How was it?"

"Fine," Philip said, though his tone betrayed him. He dismounted stiffly, understanding at last what Luke had endured.

Luke didn't press. He led the horses to the corral, then gave Philip a light shove toward the shack. "Get coffee. Warm up."

Philip didn't argue, forgetting he still wore Luke's

coat.

When the horses were exchanged and the coach reloaded, the men swapped coats again. Without ceremony, the journey resumed.

His watch showed nine—half the miles remained. Fatigue tugged at Luke despite the brief rest. His mind drifted. Once, he slowed too much and had to urge the horses faster before the lantern vanished. He blinked hard, shaking off the haze.

Inside, Megan faced her own battle. Her back throbbed, hips ached, knees stiffened. She forced her thoughts on Laramie—family, homecoming, and new beginnings. At last, she drifted into sleep, hope resting lightly in her chest.

She woke with a jolt at the next stop. Snow had begun to fall—broad, soft flakes drifting like feathers. The wind had eased, and the night felt gentler. Climbing from the coach, she searched the road anxiously until Luke appeared, dismounting with steady movements. Relief swept through her. She rubbed Snowfire's neck as they settled the horses. Luke nodded his thanks, then went for a hot drink before they moved on.

As passengers reboarded, Luke and Philip exchanged coats and places again. Luke gratefully sank into the seat beside her, every limb aching.

"I heard wolves an hour back," he murmured. "Prayed they wouldn't follow. Looks like they didn't."

The thought chilled her more than the air. She clutched his hand and leaned close. Within minutes, he slept again—and soon she followed, lulled by his warmth and the coach's rhythm.

By the final way station, it was one in the morning.

The passengers reboarded, irritable, sighing and shifting restlessly; one man taking a secret pull from a flask.
Megan, though no drinker, almost envied him. She felt
raw, stripped bare by the road. This last stretch frayed
her spirit, stretching time unbearably thin.

Outside, Luke strained to keep the swaying lantern
ahead in sight. Heavy snow coated his body and buried
the road. Snowflakes flew at him like sparks, dizzying
his head. He wiped his eyes with soaked mittens, the
cold a brief clarity before fatigue blurred it again.

The forest closed in, dark and watchful. He strained
for any sound, half-expecting wolves—or something
worse—to lunge from the gloom. Only the horses' breath
and pounding hooves broke the silence. Again and again
he glanced back, sure something followed. Exhaustion
pressed in like fog. He swayed in the saddle, half-dream-
ing, barely upright.

Inside, Megan battled despair. She imagined casting herself into the white sea beyond the coach. The air
grew stifling, sour with damp wool, sweat, and breath.
The stagecoach rocked and groaned like a storm-tossed
ship, every lurch pounding her spine. Nausea surged; her
vision swam.

Philip noticed her pallor in the dim light. "You
alright?"

"I'll be fine," she whispered. "How much longer?"

He checked his pocket watch. "Three o'clock. We
should be close."

She exhaled shakily, hand to her chest. When the road
finally leveled, the rocking eased, and hope returned.

"We must be in Rawlins," she murmured. She turned
to Philip. "Will you look?"

He lifted the flap. A breath of cold swept in; beyond, lamplight flickered across snow-laden houses. "We're here."

Megan nearly wept with relief. As the coach door opened, she stepped down and faltered. Philip caught her elbow, guiding her to a bench beneath the hotel eaves.

"I'll get our things," he said, hurrying back.

The coachman tossed luggage down as the horses stamped and snorted, steam rising from their manes. Megan rubbed her knees and stood when she saw Luke riding into the lamplight. She met him as he dismounted—blanketed in snow—only the copper-toned skin around his eyes visible. Pulling down his scarf, he offered a weary smile.

"Thank heavens we made it," she said, voice cracking.

"I agree," Luke replied, brushing snow from his coat. "Never again," he vowed. "I'll take the horses to the livery. Get us a room—we'll sleep a few hours before the train leaves."

"What about the trunk?" she asked as it landed beside the other bags.

"I'll help," Philip offered, returning with the rest. "Once she's settled, I'll lend a hand with the horses."

"Thank you," Luke said quietly, then followed the teamster down the street.

Inside the hotel, warmth wrapped around them like a balm. A kind-eyed clerk stepped forward.

"Looking for a room?"

"Yes, please," Philip said, guiding Megan to the counter.

"Mr. and Mrs.…?" the clerk asked, pen poised.

Philip replied quickly, "Oh—no. Not married. Two rooms. One for Mrs. Havoc and her husband—he'll be along shortly—and one single for me. Philip Archibald."

"My apologies," the clerk said, flushing. "I saw the ring and assumed."

"No offense taken," Philip said easily. Megan looked away, cheeks pink.

They carried the trunk and bags upstairs. The clerk lit the stove and promised to send Mr. Havoc up. Megan thanked them, then slowly unbuttoned her coat, peeling off the scarf she hadn't touched in twelve hours.

Catching her reflection, she blinked. Her cheeks were pale, lips drained of color, eyes shadowed with fatigue. Strands of hair escaped her bonnet in tangled wisps. "What a fright," she murmured, untying and setting it aside.

She splashed her face, slipped into her flannel gown, and sank into the mattress's welcoming warmth.

Luke climbed the narrow stairs, each step a trial for his aching limbs. At the door, he turned the key carefully, hoping Megan slept.

Lamplight revealed her beneath the quilt, face serene against the pillow. He kissed her cheek. *Almost home,* he thought. Relief washed over him. The worst was behind them.

His raw wind-chapped skin burned, but he hardly noticed. Every part of him equally hurt. He peeled off his coat, hung it by the stove, undressed, and slid beneath the covers. The soft mattress—and warmth of her—lulled him swiftly to sleep.

A knock thundered at the door. "Sir, it's eight!" the clerk called.

Luke jerked awake, voice hoarse. "We're up—thank you."

He turned and gently shook Megan's shoulder. "Darling, it's time."

She stirred, groaned, then pushed back the quilt with resolve. Her body protested, but she sat up, hand bracing her back. From her bag, she drew her purple travel dress, saved for this final stretch. Though wrinkled, it would ease with wear. The bodice felt snug, the waist tighter than she remembered, but she managed to fasten it above her growing belly.

Quickly, she pinned up her hair, dabbing color to her cheeks and lips. Shadows still lingered beneath her eyes, but the rouge softened them.

"Ready?" Luke asked, already dressed in his brown Sunday suit.

She nodded, tying her bonnet's ribbon under her chin. "I'm ready."

Luke stepped close, eyes warm. "You look lovely," he said, kissing her cheek before helping her into her coat.

***

With Philip's help, the horses and trunk were loaded just in time. As the train lurched toward Laramie, the difference was immediate. Compared to the bone-rattling stagecoach, it felt almost luxurious—warm, spacious, mercifully smooth. The railcar rocked gently, wheels clattering in a steady rhythm.

Even so, fatigue lingered. They took turns walking the aisle, then found the dining car, where hot coffee and loaf cake revived them. Outside, wintry plains blurred past in silver and white. Inside, china clinked softly against the hush of conversation. Megan sat quiet, eyes on the frosted window, her thoughts already home. She only half-listened as Luke and Philip discussed plans for the guest ranch.

They reached Laramie at noon beneath a pale sun. The horses were unloaded, the trunk left under the station master's watch. Philip stayed with the animals while Luke wired Pa in Cheyenne—their next train left at five. They had just enough time to file their homestead claims.

Mounting up, they rode through the unusually empty streets. A hush hung over the town. Megan noticed their favorite bustling restaurant was oddly quiet along with nearly every other business.

They reached the Land Office. A sign read: "Closed."

Their hearts sank. Of course—Thanksgiving. In the rush of travel, they'd lost track of days.

Philip circled in back, seeing life in the attached dwelling. He returned to the front and firmly knocked.

A curtain twitched. A small man scowled through the glass. "Can't you read? Closed."

Philip held steady. "We see that. But we've come a long way. Might you make an exception?"

"It's Thanksgiving," the man huffed.

Megan stepped forward, voice soft. "We're sorry to trouble you, sir. But please—we've come so far."

Her hands rested on her rounded belly, eyes shimmering. The man faltered. With a grumble, the curtain dropped. Moments later, the bolt clicked, and the door opened. His eyes widened when Luke entered—tall, stoic, unmistakably Indian.

"What do *you* want?" he asked gruffly.

"I'm here to file a homestead claim," Luke said

evenly, arm resting around Megan. "My wife and I plan to settle here."

The clerk's expression hardened. "I can't file claims for Indians. Your land's on the reservation—where you belong."

Philip, worn thin after the long night, cut in, voice sharp. "Enough. This man is a U.S. citizen with full rights under the Homestead Act. I'm filing 160 acres, too. Now show us the available plots—we've a train to catch."

The clerk bristled but, seeing resistance was useless, rolled out a map with a muttered curse. "These are left," he said, jabbing at parcels near the wooded slopes to the northeast and west.

Luke's anger burned steady, but he stepped forward, nodding. At last, one step closer to their dream.

"We'll need to ride out and survey the land," Philip said, slipping a five-dollar bill partway from his pocket. "If you'll open again when we return, we'll make it worth your while."

The clerk's eyes flicked to the bill. "Fine. But don't be long. My ma's got turkey in the oven, and I'm not missing it."

They rode toward the edge of town, spirits uplifted. Fresh snow blanketed earth, clinging to trees and rooftops. Megan pointed out the university's stately buildings, looming like castles above the whitewashed countryside.

Five miles on, they reached the tract they'd marked. Even in snowy stillness, the land felt alive. Luke and Megan dismounted and stood hand in hand, gazing over the valley—160 acres of rich pasture, bordered by forest and backed by rising foothills. A silver stream threaded through the trees to water fields below.

"It's perfect," Megan whispered, leaning into Luke's arms.

Philip nodded, already picturing the ranch—a lodge beneath the pines, corrals on the open ground, trails leading into the mountains. He chose the parcel just northwest of theirs, expanding their reach. They prayed Grandpa O'Malley and Jeremy might secure land nearby.

Back at the office, the clerk stood in his coat, glancing at his watch. He grunted but held the door. One by one, they handed over their chosen plots, watched him enter them in the ledger, paid the fee, and saw Philip slide an extra bill across the counter. The clerk pocketed it without a word.

With deeds in hand, they stepped into the crisp afternoon, hearts full.

"You might as well come home with us for Thanksgiving," Megan said. "You can get a room in Cheyenne and meet the family—your future partners, too."

Philip smiled, weary but content. "How could I refuse? A home-cooked supper sounds mighty fine after all we've been through."

Back on the train, contentment settled over them. Megan squeezed Luke's hand as he unfolded their deed, reading the words with quiet reverence.

"It's finally ours," Luke murmured, eyes shining.

Megan rested her head on his shoulder. "Our own homestead." Her voice thickened. Sleep soon claimed her, filled with dreams of the home they'd build.

The screech of brakes jolted her awake. Outside, a small crowd gathered on the platform.

"Look! There's Pa!" she cried, heart leaping.

Luke grabbed their bags and followed her out, Philip close behind. Megan ran to her father, eyes brimming.

"Pa!" she cried, throwing herself into his arms.

"Megan!" Ed caught her, tears streaking his weathered cheeks. *My little girl is home.*

Remembering her condition, he gently set her down, studying her with love. She looked radiant, though travel had left shadows beneath her eyes.

"Pa!" Luke stepped forward, dropping the bags to embrace him. "It's good to see you."

The two men held each other a long moment before parting. Megan turned to Philip.

"Pa, this is Mr. Archibald—the friend we wrote about."

Philip extended a hand. "An honor, Mr. Havoc. Your daughter and son invited me for Thanksgiving. I hope I'm not imposing."

"Not at all," Ed said, shaking firmly. "Let's get your things and be on our way."

He helped Megan into the wagon and tucked the bags at her feet. "Wait here—we'll fetch the trunk and horses." She watched the three tall figures go, their camaraderie already forming.

As they drove through Cheyenne, Megan pointed out buildings with nostalgia and pride, sharing happy memories.

"This is a right nice town," he said, quietly impressed. The city had electric lights, telephones, and paved streets, yet it retained a friendly charm.

As the wagon turned out of town, Megan leaned toward her father. "How's everyone?"

"Doing fine," Ed said warmly. "Your ma's been counting the hours. She stayed behind to have supper hot the moment you walked through the door."

"And the boys?"

Ed chuckled. "Back in school, always into something. I'll let them tell you their tales."

Megan glanced back. Luke and Philip sat on crates, talking land and water rights, while the western sky glowed lavender over the rolling hills.

"It's beautiful country," Philip said, admiring the mix of farmland, prairie, and woods.

"Wait until you see the homestead," Luke replied, heart swelling. He saw it again—walking home beside Megan, lifting her into the air as a little girl, riding back with her after his long absence. The land held pieces of his soul.

Philip fell into quiet awe as Ed turned down the lane. Branches arched into a natural tunnel, leaves carpeting the road. A small house appeared, nestled among the trees, cozy and welcoming. A red barn and outbuildings stood nearby, solid and well-kept.

The front door burst open as the wagon stopped. Cassie ran out, skirts flying, eyes brimming. Ed helped Megan down, and she rushed into her mother's arms.

"Oh, how I've missed you," Cassie whispered, clutching her.

"I missed you too," Megan choked, smiling through tears.

From the barn came shouts. "Megan! Luke!" The boys ran to meet them—David taller, Johnathan leaner, Kurt more solemn. They embraced Megan, jostling Luke with laughter and playful hugs.

Philip was introduced and folded easily into the circle, the Havoc family's warmth wrapping around him like sunlight after storm.

Megan stepped inside; the scent of roast turkey making her mouth water.

With Ed and Philip's help, the trunk was carried in. Luke went to the barn with the boys, already talking about the new Paints.

Megan paused in her old bedroom. The patchwork quilt lay neatly across the bed—just as it had on her wedding day.

"Didn't David move in here?" Megan asked, setting down her bag.

"He did for a while," Cassie said gently. "We packed your things, then set them back again. He's back in with his brothers."

Megan traced the quilt's edge. "Thank you, Ma." Her voice broke, and tears spilled.

Cassie drew her close. "What is it, sweetheart?"

"I just missed you all so much. And the journey... it was harder than I expected." She wiped her eyes. "I'm just glad to be home."

"As am I," Cassie whispered, brushing away a tear. Her gaze dropped to Megan's middle. "And look. You must be—what, six months?"

"Almost seven," Megan said, resting a hand on her belly. "Doctor says late January."

"You're hardly showing."

"That's not how I feel," Megan laughed. "I feel like a bloated cow."

Cassie chuckled. "Oh, I remember that feeling. You must be exhausted. How was the stagecoach ride?"

"Awful," Megan said, shaking her head. "I'd be happy never to ride one again."

"Well then, let's get some food in you and put you to bed. A warm meal and long sleep will do wonders."

Cassie guided Megan into the kitchen and eased her into a chair at the waiting table. A white cloth lay beneath her rose-trimmed china, crystal glasses and gleaming silverware. The hutch overflowed with steaming platters and brimming bowls.

Across the room, Ed and Philip admired the rifle mounted above the hearth, commenting on the fine craftsmanship.

Luke entered with the boys, all crowding the sink, laughing as they jostled for space.

Cassie turned with a smile. "Ed, it's time."

"Yes, ma'am," Ed said with a wink, casting her a fond glance.

Once all seated, Ed bowed his head and spoke the blessing, voice full of thanks—for safe returns, for food, and for the friend among them.

Laughter rose quickly, mingling with the clink of dishes and the hearth's crackle. Megan looked around the table, heart swelling. The long miles, the weariness— gone in the warmth of voices and home-cooked comfort. She was home. Surrounded by love, wrapped in peace.

Luke leaned back, soaking it in—Ma's laughter, his brothers' chatter, Megan's hand steady in his. Their eyes met, and in the quiet passing between them lay the truth: here, in grace and gratitude, they were exactly where they were meant to be.

# Chapter 31

## Planning the Future

Philip was glad he'd come. The Havocs were warm, gracious people, and the Thanksgiving meal had been extraordinary. After thanking Cassie and Ed for their hospitality, he rode with David back into town for the night.

"Thanks for taking me," Philip said glancing at the stars. "I imagine you'd rather be visiting with Megan and Luke."

David shook his head. "I'll have time. It's no trouble."

Philip glanced over, impressed with the young man. "Megan mentioned you'll be graduating this spring. What's next?"

"Medical school," David said, eyes on the moonlit fields. "I've been apprenticing with our town doctor. He says I'm a natural... but I'm not so sure."

"I doubt he'd say that lightly. Do you enjoy the work?"

David's face lit. "I love it. The human body—it's miraculous. The more I learn, the more certain I am only God could have designed it."

Philip nodded. "I believe that too. You've got the mind for medicine—and more importantly, a caring heart."

David smiled, then faltered. "What good is a heart, if

the one you give it to chooses another?"

"Someone you cared about?"

"We were close for years. I thought maybe... but she chose someone else. I was just 'good old David.'"

Philip placed a hand on his shoulder. "Heartbreak's never easy. But the Lord rarely closes one door without opening another. If she wasn't right, someone better suited to your heart is waiting."

David looked skeptical. "You really believe that?"

"I do. I've lived it."

David glanced over. "Really?"

Philip settled back, the wagon rocking steady. "Back South, I courted refined, proper ladies—charming, polished—but I wanted more than manners. I prayed, following a quiet tug west to Wind River Valley, where they needed a teacher. The moment I arrived, I knew I'd found my purpose."

He paused. "And then I met her. A teacher with fire in her spirit and gentleness in her heart. Compassionate, strong, imaginative. I didn't fall for her beauty—though she has it. I fell for her light. She makes me want to be a better man."

David thought for a moment. "You think I'll find that someday?"

"I don't think—I know. She's out there, being shaped by the same hand shaping you. And when the time comes, you'll know."

David nodded slowly. "I try to let it go. School and the practice help. But seeing Megan and Luke so in love... it stirs everything again. I want that."

"You will. Trust God's timing."

The golden lights of the Cheyenne Hotel came into

view. David drew the horses to a stop.

"Thank you, Mr. Archibald. For everything. I'll keep praying—and hoping."

Philip climbed down, suitcase in hand. "Happy Thanksgiving, David."

David smiled. "See you tomorrow."

Philip tipped his hat. "Tomorrow."

***

After a warm bath, Megan finally climbed into bed. Luke joined her moments later with a weary sigh.

"Feels like the longest day of our lives," he murmured, curling an arm around her waist.

"It does," she whispered, eyes closing. "But worth every mile. I'm glad we're home."

"I'm home anywhere you are," he said, kissing her before sleep claimed them.

***

"Can you believe it?" Ed said, pulling Cassie into his arms. "All our children, safe under one roof."

Cassie snuggled close. "Feels like a dream. I just wish it could last."

"We'll treasure every minute," he murmured. "And soon, a new little soul—maybe a tiny Cass or Meg."

"Or a little Eddie or Luke," she teased, kissing his cleft chin.

He chuckled. "Let's hope the baby favors their pa, not their grizzly grandpa."

Cassie smiled. "You're as handsome as ever."

Ed gave her a squeeze. "Sometimes I think life couldn't be sweeter. *'These happy years we spend together...I will love you all my life, because I made you*

416

*my wife.*"'"

Cassie kissed him gently. "'*To have and to hold, forever and ever.*'"

***

The sun was up when Megan and Luke finally emerged to the scent of fresh bread.

"Well, good morning, sleepyheads," Cassie said, kneading dough.

"Good morning, Ma," Megan murmured, rubbing her eyes.

"Morning," Luke yawned, tugging on his suspenders.

Cassie smiled. "Breakfast was hours ago, but there's plenty." She set the dough beneath a towel.

"I'll help," Megan offered, tying on her apron. Soon the kitchen filled with the sizzle of eggs, crisping bacon, and steaming coffee.

"David went to fetch Mr. Archibald," Cassie explained, adding golden pancakes to a platter. "They should be along any minute."

"I hope so," Luke said, piling his plate. "You'd be mad to pass up a meal like this."

As if on cue, the front door opened.

"Good morning, Mrs. Havoc," Philip said, stepping inside.

"Good morning, Mr. Archibald," Cassie replied, flipping a pancake. "Hang up your coat and join Megan and Luke."

"Thank you kindly. I've eaten, but I wouldn't turn down a cup of your coffee." Philip hung his coat.

Cassie poured coffee, handing it to Philip, and joined them at the table.

"Luke," Philip said, stirring cream, "might we visit your cousin after breakfast?"

"Sure. Megan wants to see Penny too—we'll all ride over together." Luke reached for more pancakes.

"She'll be thrilled to see you," Cassie added. "Folks are excited you're back."

"Me too, but I'm glad we left when we did," Megan said softly. "Though I miss the children and our friends."

"But not Mr. Adams, I'm sure," Philip teased.

Megan shook her head. "No, I won't miss him. That man perturbs me."

"I think he's about to get a taste of his own medicine," Luke said with a glint.

"Oh?" Philip asked.

"As we left, his new teacher arrived. A large, loud *woman*."

"I thought a *man* was hired?" Philip frowned.

"So did he," Megan grinned. "Mr. Adams told us a Mr. Pat Jacques was due that day."

"But it turned out to be *Miss* Patricia Jacques," Luke chuckled. "There must've been a mix-up."

"I'd love to see that encounter," Megan said, laughing.

They all joined in, picturing the flustered schoolmaster.

"I'm sure I'll hear all about it," Philip said, sipping his coffee.

Megan's smile dimmed. "I just hope she's kind. I hated leaving the children, not knowing if they'd be alright."

"They'll manage," Luke said, squeezing her hand.

"And you," Cassie added gently, "are exactly where

you need to be.”

Megan looked up at her mother and smiled.

***

That morning, Luke, Megan, and Philip called on Jeremy and Penny. The door burst open, and Penny pulled Megan into a fierce embrace.

“I’m so glad you’re back,” she whispered.

“I’ve missed you too,” Megan said, blinking back tears.

“We brought our friend, Mr. Archibald,” Luke said, drawing Jeremy into a hearty hug.

Philip tipped his hat. “A pleasure. I’ve heard only the finest things.”

Inside their one-room home, Penny set out coffee and oatmeal cookies, and soon the conversation flowed. By the time they left, Jeremy and Penny were committed to the venture. Jeremy and Grandpa O’Malley would ride to Laramie the next week to secure adjoining land—the foundation of their guest ranch in the Wyoming hills.

***

The ride into town passed quickly as the trio spoke of the future.

“I’ll come help once school ends,” Philip said. “Then return in the fall to teach with Prudence.”

Luke grinned. “Shouldn’t you bring her with you this summer?”

Philip cleared his throat, feigning surprise—the matter of his proposal still a secret.

“Oh, you must,” Megan said. “She’d love the mountains.”

Philip nodded. “I’ll have to ask.”

"You should," Megan urged. "I think she'd say yes."

"I'll speak with her," he replied, thinking of something long-lasting.

Luke leaned closer, raising an eyebrow. "You ought to ask more than that."

Megan, pretending not to hear, smiled. She knew Prudence hoped for a proposal.

At the O'Malleys', the scent of beef stew and fresh bread filled the air. Simple furnishings, lovingly kept, gave the home a warm charm.

Patrick, tall and broad with silver hair and kind eyes, shook Philip's hand. "Luke says you're from the South. Planning to stay in Wyoming?"

"I do. The land, the people, the chance to build something lasting...it feels right."

Kathy poured tea. "But will you keep teaching at the reservation?"

"For now," Philip said. "But when I have a family, I'd like to raise them here—with mountains and fresh air."

Patrick squeezed Kathy's hand. "My heart's in the hills too."

Kathy smiled. "We hope you won't mind two old folks tagging along."

Philip shook his head. "Not at all. We'd be honored to have your wisdom and experience. Right, Luke?"

"Absolutely," Luke said. "We'd be blessed to have you."

"And I'll help however I can," Kathy added. "Cooking, cleaning, watching little ones. I miss the sound of children in the house."

Megan squeezed her hand. "We'd love your help—

but only if it brings you joy. These are your golden years, savor them."

Patrick chuckled. "We've done enough savoring. A little adventure keeps us young. If you'll have us, we're in."

Philip extended his hand. "Welcome aboard."

They spent the next hour trading ideas. As they stood to leave, Kathy offered, "Won't you stay for lunch? It's nothing fancy—just soup and fresh bread."

Megan looked to Luke, her stomach rumbling.

"I'd be honored," Philip said.

And so they stayed, sharing laughter and hearty bowls of stew, breaking warm bread as their dream took shape—on the horizon of a shared future.

***

That afternoon, after taking Philip to the depot, Megan joined Cassie by the hearth while Luke and Ed rode out. The room was hushed, save for the fire's crackle and the whisper of crochet hooks.

"Tell me about your teaching," Cassie said, handing her a steaming cup of tea.

Megan smiled softly, recalling schoolchildren's mischief and triumphs. They laughed over humorous stories, her voice faltering when she spoke of Jacob Crooked Arrow.

"And the other teachers?" Cassie asked, her hands busy with a baby blanket.

"Prudence is in love," Megan said smiling. "I think she and Philip will marry soon."

"I like that Philip," Cassie nodded. "Steady. Thoughtful. I'm glad you were surrounded by such good souls. It helps when life gets heavy."

"It does," Megan whispered, her gaze lowered.

Cassie set aside her work and clasped Megan's hand. "What is it, sweetheart?"

Megan swallowed. "Naomi—Mr. Thompson's wife—she lost her baby, Ma…" The words broke on a sob. Cassie drew her into a tender embrace.

"Oh, darling," she murmured, tears slipping down her own cheeks. "That poor woman…"

"It's breaking my heart," Megan said raggedly. "Why did she lose her child? It doesn't seem fair."

Cassie held her until the sobs quieted. "We're not always given answers, only the chance to trust. I believe God's with Naomi and John, comforting them."

"They say they've found peace," Megan whispered. "But sometimes I think—it should've been me."

Cassie drew back, startled. "Why would you say that?"

Megan looked down at her hands folded over her belly. "Because I've been given so much—Luke, this baby, our new home. And Naomi... she's so faithful."

Cassie cupped her cheek. "Don't measure blessings against another's sorrow. We each walk a different road—some smooth, some steep. Yours hasn't been easy. God doesn't bless because we earn it, but because He loves us."

She brushed back a strand of Megan's hair. "When I carried you, I felt ashamed of how you came to be. But then Ed brought love and hope. Over time I saw you not as a burden but as a blessing—a miracle. And you *were*, Megan. You still *are*."

Through tears, Megan whispered, "I love you, Ma."

"I love you more than I can say." Cassie kissed her

brow.

"Thank you...for listening."

"I always will," Cassie said, smoothing her daughter's cheek.

"I think I need rest," Megan said softly.

"Go on," Cassie urged. "But remember—God wants you to feel joy, not guilt for blessings. Only gratitude. And you already have that."

Megan nodded faintly, her smile tired but sincere. She slipped into her room, folded her hands in prayer, and gave thanks—for her safe return, for family, and for comfort on Naomi's behalf. With her tears spent and her mother's love in her heart, she drifted into peaceful sleep.

***

Luke and Ed rode in companionable silence, the only sound the soft clop of hooves and the lowing of cattle. Luke breathed deeply the late autumn air, his travel-worn limbs loosening.

"You look content," Ed said as they crossed the pasture where cattle nosed through dry grasses.

"I am," Luke answered with a faint smile. "And relieved." His voice caught, and he looked away.

"Relieved?" Ed asked. "I thought leaving your people might weigh on you."

"It does. But more than anything, I'm grateful that Megan's home, with Ma and a doctor nearby. That's what's important." Tears burned behind his eyes.

Luke stared at his gloved hands. "Pa…" He hesitated.

Ed slowed his horse. "What is it, son?"

"I don't know what I'd do if I lost Megan. Or the baby." His voice cracked. "Naomi and John just lost their baby—it came too early. Naomi nearly died. Megan's struggling. I'm trying to be strong, but I'm scared, Pa. Deep down, I'm scared."

His horse stopped to graze. Luke bowed his head, heart heavy.

Ed drew beside him, laying a firm hand on his arm. "Luke, fear is part of loving deeply. I know it well."

Luke looked up, surprised. "You do?"

"I do. When Mary died, I blamed God. I buried myself in work and anger. It took years before I could open my heart again. When Cassie came into my life, I healed—but when she reached the same stage of pregnancy as Mary, fear came roaring back. I tried to hide it, but Cassie felt it. Telling her drew us closer."

Luke listened, eyes on his father's rugged face.

"You don't have to carry this alone," Ed said. "Let Megan in—honesty will bind you closer."

"I just love her so much," Luke said, voice raw. "We fought so hard to be together, and now...it feels like everything's finally right. But what if something goes wrong?"

Ed nodded. "It's easy to fear joy when it feels too good. But joy is meant to be cherished. Don't let fear rob you of your earned peace."

Luke exhaled slowly, the weight easing. "You're right. She's my wife, we're starting a family, and we've got land of our own. It's everything I dreamed of."

"Then rejoice in it," Ed said with a smile. "Hard days will come again. But for now, savor the blessings."

Luke nodded. "Thank you, Pa."

Ed's expression softened. "Life's made of moments—bits of joy tucked between the work and worry. The Lord gives tender mercies, but it's up to us to hold them close when the road gets rough."

Luke looked out across the fields, wind lifting his dark hair. A quiet smile returned. "You're right. We've had so many beautiful moments—our weddings, the honeymoon, just being together."

"That's the spirit," Ed said, turning toward home. "Now let's get back before your ma calls supper without us. Another blessing—good food and better company."

Luke chuckled, falling in beside him. "Amen to that."

***

That night, as wind blew outside, Luke curled around Megan beneath the quilts, his chest warm against her back. She sighed, slipping her icy feet against his legs.

"Mercy, your feet are like ice," he gasped, chuckling as he pulled her closer.

"Sorry," she whispered, laughing. "I should've warmed them by the fire."

"I don't mind," he murmured, kissing her hair. "I'll warm them for you."

They lay in hush, fingers laced. After a moment, Megan spoke.

"Luke...I love you more than I ever thought possible. And sometimes that love—" she faltered "—it frightens me. You, riding through the snowstorm, terrified me. If anything happened to you…" Her voice trembled. "You and this baby—you're my whole world."

"I've felt the same," Luke said quietly. "Naomi nearly died losing her daughter. It shook me. I want to protect you from everything. You've brought more peace and joy than I ever believed I'd know. I can't imagine life without you."

She turned, brushing a kiss across his lips, a single

425

tear slipping into her hair.

"I hope you never have to," she whispered. "But if tomorrow were my last day, I'd still be grateful. These months with you have been the happiest of my life. I won't let fear steal the joy from them."

Luke cradled her face. "My little Indian White Dove. I don't want to live in fear. I want to dream of what's ahead."

"Then from now on," she said, steadier, "I'll treat each day as a gift. I don't want to waste the time we have. It's too precious." She paused. "I'm sorry I've been so heavy-hearted."

Luke shook his head. "The dark won't last forever. We'll find our light again. Just let me hold you—until the ache fades and only love remains."

She nestled deeper, his heartbeat steady beneath her cheek. Wrapped in his arms, her fears melted away, and with a contented sigh, she drifted into dreamless sleep.

# Chapter 32

## *Holidays*

Though the house was crowded with seven under one roof, an easy rhythm soon took hold. Winter days were warmed not just by the hearth but by the joys of preparing for Christmas.

One snowy evening, the family gathered near the fire. Ed sat in his worn chair, peering over the newspaper. David was buried in a medical book. Luke strummed a tune, the melody weaving with the crackle of flames and wind's low howl. Johnathan and Kurt battled over a checkerboard, while Megan and Cassie stitched tiny garments in soft yarn for the baby.

Megan paused, eyes on the fire. "I wonder how our friends are faring."

"That reminds me," Ed said, setting aside his paper. "You got a letter today. I forgot with that horse throwing his shoe."

"That's okay, Pa." Megan took the letter, smiling at the familiar handwriting. "It's from Prudence."

She unfolded the letter, and the room hushed in anticipation.

Luke asked, "Anything good?"

Megan's eyes twinkled. "Prudence writes, 'Mr. Adams met Miss Patricia Jacques not long after you left. True to form, he launched into a tirade—but Miss Jacques, tall as he and twice as firm, scolded him until he turned red as a beet. She demanded an apology—and got one. Since then, he's been nothing but cordial. Philip and I suspect he might even be sweet on her.'"

Luke chuckled. "I'll be. Didn't think *anyone* could put Mr. Adams in his place."

David grinned. "Sounds like he met his match."

Laughter rippled through the room.

"Oh!" Megan read on. "She'll be in Laramie this summer—wants to help at the lodge. Philip and Prudence, Jeremy and Penny...it'll be wonderful."

"I'm glad," Ed said, settling back. "Sounds like you'll have plenty of help."

"I hope Naomi and John can visit too," Megan added wistfully.

"If Naomi's well enough, I'm sure they will," Luke said, moving beside her.

Megan smiled, already picturing summer meals and walks among the pines.

"What else?" Luke asked.

"She thinks Philip will propose soon."

Luke laughed. "Good for him. Would be simpler if they came married—less fuss over bunking arrangements."

Megan shot him a playful look as laughter rose again.

Cassie grinned. "You two will have everyone married off by summer."

David looked up, feigning offense. "What about me? Any sweethearts for *me*?"

"Maybe at the New Year's Eve Ball," Megan teased.

David frowned. "Doubtful. But I'll probably see Ashley and Clint. I heard he's visiting for the holidays. Wouldn't be surprised if there's an announcement."

Cassie's smile softened. "We're still going to the Clarks' for New Year's supper. Do you want us to bow out?"

David hesitated, then shook his head. "No. Better not make it more awkward." He snapped his book shut and stood. "I'll fetch more firewood."

Megan gave Luke a look and nodded toward the door.

Luke stood. "I'll help. Goes faster with two."

Outside, the night pressed close—silent and heavy with snow, low clouds veiling the stars. Their boots crunched over hardened drifts as golden light spilled from the kitchen window across the yard.

Luke glanced upward. "Looks like another storm's coming."

David brushed snow from the logs. "Seems so."

Luke hesitated. "I know it'll be hard, seeing her again. But someone's out there for you. Someone worth the wait."

David kept his eyes on the woodpile. "Even Kurt's courting someone. Maybe love isn't for me. Maybe I'm meant to serve—not be loved."

He turned away, but Luke caught the tear on his cheek.

"You know," Luke said softly, "I was once promised to the Chief's niece."

David paused, surprised. "Really? What happened?"

Leaning against the pile, Luke's breath curled in the cold. "It was arranged—me, the Shaman's son, she the Chief's niece. A strong match. She was kind, beautiful. But I didn't love her." He glanced toward the glowing windows. "My heart already belonged to Megan. I returned—uncertain, hoping—and waited nearly a year before we married. It was worth every moment."

David stacked another log into Luke's arms. "I understand. But it hurts—to imagine a future, only to see it vanish. I think a part of me will always love her."

"Maybe you will," Luke said gently. "First loves leave their mark. But hearts heal, and when you least expect it, someone new will appear and it will all make sense."

David exhaled. "I hope you're right."

Luke grinned. "Besides, you're just a pup." He scooped snow and hurled it into David's face.

David sputtered, blinking snow from his lashes. "Just because you never grew up doesn't mean I won't." He fired back, narrowly missing Luke's shoulder.

"Missed me!" Luke laughed, sprinting for the porch—only to take a snowball to the back of the head.

"You won't get far hauling all that wood!" David crowed, launching another snowball.

Luke dropped the logs, dove behind the porch rail, and struck David square in the chest.

The front door creaked. Kurt peeked out. "What's—" A snowball splattered beside his face.

"Snowball fight!" David shouted, launching another.

Kurt retreated laughing. "This means war," he muttered, yanking on his coat and slipping out the back door, he pelted David from behind.

From inside, Johnathan called, "What's going on?"

Cassie, amused, peered through the frosted window. "They're having a snowball fight."

"Wait for me!" Johnathan bundled into coat and mittens and charged out with a cry.

Ed joined Cassie, resting a hand on her shoulder as

they watched. Megan came to the window just in time to see Luke get pelted from all sides.

"Uncle!" Luke surrendered, arms raised.

Breathless and flushed, the brothers tumbled into a snowdrift, laughter spiraling into the crisp air.

"It's good to have you home," David said quietly.

Luke grinned. "It's good to *be* home." He scooped a fresh handful and launched round two.

***

Christmas passed, leaving warm memories in the Havoc home.

Megan cherished the Christmas Eve gathering at Grandma and Grandpa Hartford's: pine wreaths, mincemeat pies, and full hearts. Nestled beside Luke beneath a sparkling tree, she listened to the Nativity story, grateful for every loved one gathered close.

Luke sat in quiet contentment, joy tempered with sorrow, remembering the loss of his mother and sister. Yet he no longer felt caught between two worlds. With Megan and their child on the way, he felt truly home.

That night, Megan lingered in their room, gazing at the walnut cradle her father had refinished. She pictured their baby wrapped in the blanket Cassie had crocheted, beneath Luke's dreamcatcher swaying like a soft prayer.

The next day brought joyful news: Penny had delivered a healthy boy, fair-haired like his father, said to be the image of Grandpa Clancy.

When Luke and Megan visited, Penny beamed from her bed. "Come see. Isn't he just like his pa?"

"He certainly is," Megan said, brushing the baby's cheek.

Luke patted Jeremy's back. "You did good, partner."

Jeremy laughed. "Penny did most of it."

The men slipped away with coffee mugs, leaving the women to marvel at the infant.

"How was it?" Megan asked, cradling the baby.

"Hard. Frightening. Beautiful," Penny whispered, stroking her son's downy hair.

"I'm scared," Megan admitted, marveling at the fragile weight in her arms. "How can something so small bring so much pain—and joy?"

"Because he's perfect," Penny said softly. "I'd go through it all again. I love him more than I ever imagined."

"He's wonderful," Megan murmured, breathing in his newborn scent.

"We've named him Jeremiah," Penny said proudly. "After Jeremy's grandfather. But Jerry suits him for now."

"I love that," Megan said, smiling at the sleepy infant. As if agreeing, he yawned and stretched, curling his fists like tiny seashells.

"Doesn't he do the sweetest things?" Penny asked, wonder shining in her eyes.

"He's amazing," Megan whispered. "I can't wait to hold my own."

"Soon," Penny said, brushing her thumb across Jerry's cheek. "I have a feeling it'll be a girl."

Megan laughed. "You think so?"

"I do. Just imagine—our little ones growing up side by side."

"Cousins and best friends," Megan said dreamily, then sighed. "I wish Melissa lived closer. I hoped she'd come for Christmas, but winter travel is hard."

"Maybe this summer," Penny said. "A reunion at the guest ranch?"

"That would be perfect," Megan agreed.

The baby fussed, and Megan handed him back.

"I think he's hungry," Penny smiled.

Megan hugged her. "We'll visit again soon."

Luke drained his coffee, bidding Jeremy farewell with a glance at Jerry, now nestled against Penny.

"Wasn't he the sweetest baby?" Megan whispered as they rode away.

Luke smiled. "A precious little soul."

"Do you hope it's a boy or a girl?"

"Either is fine. But if it's a girl, I hope she has her mother's eyes."

Megan's gaze lingered tenderly. "And if it's a boy, I hope he's the very image of his father."

***

The family welcomed the new year in the warmth of home, though the two eldest boys were away at the New Year's Eve Ball. David had gone reluctantly with Kurt and his sweetheart, Hannah—curious more than confident. Megan's teasing suggestion that he might meet someone special lingered with him.

At the house, the rest of the family celebrated quietly, with laughter and stories by the fire. They played games, savored confections, and as midnight neared, counted down together before lifting glasses of cider in a joyful toast.

When goodnights were said, Megan and Luke slipped to their room.

"Happy birthday, Luke," she whispered as the hush of the house settled.

He smiled, drawing her close. "Thank you, sweetheart."

"Do you have a wish?" Her arms circled his neck, eyes dancing playfully.

"I do. A full day and night *alone* with my wife. Once the baby comes, quiet moments will be rare."

Her heart swelled. He was right. Soon their days would blur with feedings, diapers, and sweet exhaustion of parenthood.

"I'll see what I can do," she murmured, brushing his lips with hers—a tender promise for the year *and* his birthday.

***

At midday, the family gathered for a simple but heartfelt birthday. The kitchen filled with the scent of chocolate cake, and each offered Luke a thoughtful gift. His favorite was a finely crafted pocketknife from Ed and Cassie—a tool both practical and symbolic, passed from one generation to the next.

Megan handed him a pair of thick, forest-green socks she'd knitted. "The rest is still in the making," she said with a mysterious smile.

That afternoon, preparations began for the New Year's dinner with the Clarks. The men shaved, dressed in dark suits, and knotted their ties. The women curled one another's hair, pinned it high, and slipped into their finest gowns. Though familiar, the evening always stirred a flutter of excitement—like stepping briefly into another world.

In her room, Megan fretted before the mirror. At eight months along, her figure required accommodations. "I look like a circus tent," she sighed, smoothing the empire waist over her rounded belly.

Luke finished buttoning his black suit in the washroom, thinking the whole affair a great to-do for one meal—but tradition held weight.

Back in their room, Megan tied the black ribbon that secured the cameo at her throat. Her crimson gown, trimmed in ivory lace, framed her neckline with elegance. Puffed sleeves brushed ivory gloves, while pinned curls and soft ringlets framed her cheeks. Still, she eyed herself uncertainly.

"I suppose this is as good as it gets," she murmured—just as Luke stepped in.

He froze, breath caught. Her beauty, made radiant by the life she carried, left him undone.

"As good as it gets?" he echoed, wonder in his voice. Crossing the room, he kissed her gloved hands. "You're the most beautiful woman I've ever seen."

Megan's breath caught. The look in his eyes—tender, reverent—was all the reassurance she needed.

"Thank you, Luke," she whispered, a tear glinting in her emerald eye.

He kissed her softly, careful not to disturb gown or hair. Pulling back, he smiled, dreamy and sure.

"You," he said as if seeing her anew, "are truly something to behold."

***

Bart and Bea welcomed the family with warm embraces and lively chatter. Coats vanished into the arms of the staff as guests were ushered into the parlor, where coffee, tea, and quiet hospitality awaited by the hearth.

As David expected, Clint and Ashley sat together on the settee—Clint sharp in a black tuxedo, Ashley radiant in deep blue velvet that shimmered in the firelight. They rose to greet Luke's parents with practiced charm. David lingered by the doorway, until initial pleasantries passed before approaching. He had avoided the couple at the New Year's Eve Ball, but tonight there was no escape.

Squaring his shoulders, he stepped forward—then faltered as a young woman emerged from behind Clint. Brown curls tumbled past her shoulders, green eyes sparkled with rich warmth. Whatever David meant to say vanished.

"David, it's good to see you," Ashley said sweetly, as if they didn't pass each other daily at school. "You remember Clint?"

"Yes," David replied, dryly. "Clint." He offered a hand.

Clint clasped it. "Good to see you again. Ashley tells me you're apprenticing with the town doctor. Admirable work. We need more good physicians, don't we, Ashley?"

Ashley nodded, gaze fixed on Clint. "I always said David was the smartest in class. He'll make a fine doctor."

"Thanks," David murmured, the praise faded as her eyes adored Clint instead.

The young woman extended a gloved hand. "I'm Hazel." Her voice was clear, melodic. In her cream gown trimmed with lace and satin ribbons, she looked almost angelic—porcelain skin, rosy cheeks, lips curved like a bow.

"David," he replied, taking her hand more easily than he felt.

"My apologies," Clint added. "I should've introduced you sooner. Hazel's my sister. She's been traveling with me and will stay with our aunt while she recovers. Hazel hopes to become a nurse—she'll begin college after graduation this spring."

"You're drawn to the healing arts too?" David asked.

"Oh yes," Hazel said, eyes alight. "It's been my calling as long as I can remember."

Before more could be said, Clint and Ashley excused themselves to greet Megan and Luke.

Left together, David and Hazel drifted to a quiet corner, talking over hot chocolate. Conversation flowed—medical texts, training, the best schools in the West. With every shared thought, their connection grew.

Around them, Cassie and Ed spoke with Bart and Bea, Luke and Megan gathered by the hearth with Clint and Ashley. At the piano, the Clark girls led Johnathan and Kurt in song at the piano.

Soon, Bea rose and announced, "Supper is ready."

The party filed into the dining room, glowing with firelight, dressed in pine garlands and red bows. A chandelier bathed the long table in warmth. Gold-rimmed china, crystal goblets, and gleaming silver shimmered beneath red tapers nestled in holly.

Megan's gaze lingered on the empty chair beside hers—Andrew's. The memory of his quiet strength rose bittersweet. She met Mr. Clark's eyes and offered a faint smile.

Bart stood, raising his glass. "Before we begin, I'd like to wish Luke a happy birthday." Cheers rang out. He continued, voice thick with feeling. "Thank you for carrying on this tradition. Bea and I treasure your friendship. Through joy and sorrow, you've stood by us—and we are grateful. To true friendship."

"To friendship!" guests echoed, smiles warm, glasses clinking.

Then Bart lifted a hand. "If I may—Clint has something to share."

Clint rose, clasping Ashley's hand. "I've asked Ashley to be my wife—and she has accepted."

Applause erupted. Clint kissed her hand, beaming with pride.

David sat stunned. Beside him, Hazel leaned close, her whisper brushing his ear. "Isn't it romantic?"

He turned, managing a smile. "Yes. Yes, it is."

Hazel's grin widened in pure sweetness. David's pulse stirred.

"Isn't love wonderful?" she whispered again as the first course arrived.

"I hope to find out one day," David murmured, leaning close, catching the faint scent of rosewater.

Hazel blushed. "Me too."

Platters appeared—prime rib, roasted potatoes, winter salads, and warm rolls. Hazel handed David the basket, their fingers brushing. Just a moment, but enough. Her hazel eyes lifted to his, bright and unguarded. He smiled; she flushed but did not look away.

Around them, conversation flowed—cheerful and familiar. Ed recalled meeting Cassie at the church picnic, then Bart not long after arriving in Cheyenne. Bart chuckled over the barroom brawl that landed him in jail beside Clancy, while Bea smiled, remembering their first supper together—a simple meal that became the start of something more.

They spoke of opening the C & H Men's Clothing Store, where Bart and Bea grew closer, and of Cassie's time as a seamstress. Weekly dinners had faded as families grew, but roundups and holiday suppers kept their bond strong.

Ed remembered the roundup when Clancy saved Grandpa Hartford from the angry bull—the same fall Patrick proposed to Kathy. They agreed it was providence when Joy moved in with the Hartfords and later married Clancy.

There were triumphs—the growing town, thriving businesses—and hardships too, like the bitter winter of '87 that nearly ruined every rancher. Yet through it all, they endured.

Silence followed Andrew's name. His loss lingered, but the stories now brought soft smiles as well as tears. Bart, eyes misted, thanked Megan for keeping his memory alive. Luke squeezed her hand beneath the table as she wiped her eyes, quiet joy in her face when Ed and Cassie spoke of Luke's homecoming.

"So many blessings," Cassie said. "So much to be grateful for."

"And look how our family keeps growing," Ed added with a smile. "Megan's child on the way, Ashley and Clint marrying this spring. A new year, full of promise. Here's to 1891—may it bring rejoicing and more memories to come."

He raised his glass. "To 1891!"

"Hear, hear!" voices echoed.

After dessert—spiced cakes and hot cider—they returned to the parlor. The piano rang with familiar songs, laughter and games filled the room, then quieter conversations as the evening deepened.

David and Hazel were rarely apart. Whether sipping

tea or tucked in quiet corners, their ease with one another grew. They shared dreams and values—a kinship rooted in kindness and compassion.

Hazel admired David's wit, but more than that, his sincere heart. Like him, she felt called to care for others, hoping to nurse before raising a family.

As the hour grew late, Hazel asked, "Would you write to me?"

"I'd love to," David said, finding paper at a rolltop desk. They exchanged addresses, and she tucked his away like a treasure.

"I do hope I'll see you again soon," she said with regret.

"I'm sure you will," he answered gently. "Ashley and Clint will marry in the spring. We'll meet again then." To his surprise, the words no longer stung.

Hazel touched his hand. "I wish tonight didn't have to end."

David hesitated. "When do you leave for your aunt's?"

"Tomorrow morning. The nine-thirty train."

He smiled. "Let me take you to breakfast before you go."

Her face lit. "I'd like that very much."

Leaning in, David kissed her cheek—a swift, earnest gesture. "I'll be here at seven-thirty," he promised, pulling on his coat.

Hazel lingered in the doorway, her smile glowing in the faint light. "I'll be waiting."

* * *

The second part of Luke's birthday gift arrived the next morning—wrapped not in ribbon, but surprise.

Over breakfast, Megan smiled over her teacup. "We'll be spending the day in town—and the night at the Cheyenne Hotel," she said shyly. "I saved from my teaching wages to pay for it."

Luke's eyes lit up, but before he could answer, the younger boys rushed out, satchels swinging.

"David, you'll be late for school," Cassie called as she passed the bedroom door with a basket.

David stepped out, smoothing his hair beneath his hat. "I'm going to see Hazel off first."

Cassie's knowing smile followed him. "Alright, but don't dawdle."

Grinning, David stepped out into the brisk morning.

Luke watched him go, then turned back to Megan. "I think he's nearly as happy as I am."

She laughed, and he kissed her cheek.

"Maybe another wedding's not far off," Luke teased.

"Oh, you," Megan said, swatting his arm. "Let them finish school first." She kissed him lightly. "Now, go pack. Your birthday adventure awaits."

"You don't have to tell me twice." He rose with boyish eagerness, and Megan, rolling up her sleeves, turned to the dishes, her heart full.

***

In town, David stopped the buggy at the coffeehouse and quickly helped Hazel down, steadying her on the slick walkway.

"Thank you," she said, slipping her arm through his. Her green traveling dress and bonnet set off her bright eyes.

They lingered over breakfast, conversation easy, laughter gentle, glances held too long. Too soon the meal ended. David paid and helped her back into the buggy.

At the depot, the train whistle echoed faintly. On the platform, steam curled around them as they stood hand in hand.

"All aboard!" the conductor called.

"Safe travels," David said, voice catching. "Write to me."

"I will." Hazel's gloved fingers tightened, then she stepped close, arms slipping around his neck. Her lips brushed his cheek, feather-light, lingering.

His heart raced, her scent and warmth clinging.

"Goodbye," he whispered.

"Goodbye, David." She mounted the steps, then reappeared at the window, waving with a bright, wistful smile.

He stood watching until the train vanished in the winter haze. Only then did he return to the buggy, the rhythm of hooves barely registering. All he could hear was her laughter, feel the warmth of her cheek—the world seemed softer, lighter, with Hazel in it.

***

Luke's birthday gift was one he would never forget. He and Megan spent the morning strolling hand in hand through Cheyenne—pausing at shop windows, making modest purchases, sharing laughter in the crisp winter air. After lunch at a familiar restaurant, they attended a stirring play, and by evening dined in the hotel's elegant room, where lamplight shimmered off crystal glasses. And afterward, to Megan's quiet surprise, they danced.

She hesitated, uneasy beneath curious eyes, but Luke, grinning like a boy, reminded her it was his birthday. With a sigh and a smile, she gave in.

Dressed in crimson velvet, Megan let him lead her onto the floor. Chandeliers spilled golden light across the parquet as a string quartet played. Ornate paintings looked down, statues stood in silence, and thick draperies and lush carpets softened the grand hall.

As they waltzed, Megan relaxed. Luke's hand at her back, the music's rhythm, the spell of the evening—she felt she had stepped into a dream. For once she was not a teacher or ranch wife, but a princess dancing with the man she loved.

"You're glowing," Luke whispered, eyes smoldering.

"It's warm in here," she teased, a smile on her lips.

"You're beautiful," he said, voice low and certain. "Even if you don't believe it. Everyone else can see."

"I'm just glad you still do," she murmured in his ear.

"I always have," Luke replied. "From the very beginning. I love you, Megan. Always."

He drew her close and kissed her, slow and tender.

"Are you ready to go?" he asked, voice hushed, meaning clear.

"I'm ready," she said softly, her eyes saying more than words.

# Chapter 33

## Baby Havoc

January dragged for Megan, each snowy day blurring into the next. Outside, the world lay beneath a heavy white blanket; inside, time felt suspended. Discomfort and quiet anxiety shadowed even her birthday. Though she wore a cheerful face, fear lingered—what if something went wrong?

To others, she appeared calm, weathering the final month with grace. But in a letter to Prudence, she allowed her honesty to flow freely.

She offered heartfelt congratulations on Prudence's engagement to Philip, wishing she could be there to share every detail. She confessed how much she missed the children, the school, and her dearest friends—especially Prudence and Naomi. Though grateful to be back in Cheyenne, Naomi's grief weighed on her, and she asked gently how her friend was faring.

Then Megan wrote of sleepless nights, of how difficult each breath and step felt. She admitted to irritability, then guilt, ashamed that her complaints sounded ungrateful. Naomi would have endured anything for the chance to hold her child. Tears blurred her words. Resting a hand on her belly, she asked forgiveness for her selfishness before closing the letter with love.

A week later, Prudence's reply arrived. Megan retreated to her room and read it by lamplight, winter pressing against the panes.

> *My dearest Megan,*
>
> *I'm happier than I ever imagined. Philip and I will marry once the school term ends—likely in Laramie. We'll be neighbors!*
>
> *Naomi's doing better. Her health has improved, her smile is returning. She's taken up the choir again, teaches Sunday School, and helps Jacob with his signing. Step by step, she's moving forward.*
>
> *Please don't be ashamed of your feelings. No one expects you to be more than human. Soon this will be behind you, and once that sweet child is in your arms, the discomfort will fade to memory. I keep you in my prayers. God is near. He will not abandon you.*
>
> *With all my love, Prudence*

Megan pressed the letter to her heart, a smile breaking through her tears. Comfort bloomed as she whispered a quiet prayer—for Prudence, for her kind words, and for the new life soon to come.

***

February arrived, bringing final touches to tiny garments lovingly stitched and tucked away, waiting. She thought of Agwai and Rose as she gazed at the cradleboard, imagining her baby resting there one day, hoping someday they might see the child.

Late one night, Megan awoke with a start. A dull ache bloomed in her back, then tightened her abdomen. She held her breath. Another pain came.

A soft smile touched her lips. *It's happening.*

Excitement and nerves mingled as she breathed through the rhythm of contractions. She tried to rise without waking Luke, but another wave forced her back down, trembling as cold seeped through her flannel gown.

Luke stirred, reaching for her hand. "What's wrong?"

"I...I think I'm in labor."

He sat up at once. "Should I get Ma?"

"Not yet. First babies take time."

"Are you cold? Do you want to get back under the covers?"

"No, just help me with my robe and slippers. I need to walk."

Luke wrapped her robe around her and slipped on her shoes. They paced quietly until the chill drove them to the front room fireplace. He stoked the embers, settled her on the sofa, and started tea.

Cassie emerged, instantly alert. "Is it time?" She hurried to Megan's side.

"The pains started about an hour ago," Megan said. "It may be a while, but I couldn't sleep."

A contraction tightened her face; she closed her eyes, breathing slowly.

"You're doing fine," Cassie murmured, rubbing her shoulder. "Just keep breathing. That's it."

Luke returned, handing them tea before sitting at Megan's side, her hand in his.

Day dawned—Ma cooked breakfast while Megan returned to bed, Luke nearby.

Ed entered as Cassie set pancakes on the table. He kissed her cheek. "Should I fetch the doctor?"

"After breakfast," she said. "There's still time."

The boys gathered for the blessing, voices hushed. David lingered near Megan's door until Cassie reassured him the baby wouldn't come while they were away. Reluctantly, they left for school with Ed.

Luke ate quickly before returning to Megan, who now sipped sugared tea but refused food. Sweat glistened on her brow despite the chilly room. Her breath came in shallow bursts between moans, her world narrowed to the waves of labor.

Ed returned with the doctor an hour later.

He entered her room with a warm smile. "So, today's the day."

Megan managed a faint smile before another sharp pain stole her breath.

"Let's give her space," the doctor said, "And I'll see how far along she is."

Luke and Cassie stepped out, closing the door behind them.

Soon the doctor rejoined them at the kitchen table, his expression bright.

"She's coming along well. If all goes as it should, we'll have ourselves a baby by afternoon."

Luke shot up and hurried back to Megan. Cassie poured coffee for the doctor.

"Come warm yourself," she said. "Can I fix you something?"

"Don't mind if I do. Busy morning, no breakfast yet."

Cassie quickly warmed pancakes and eggs, setting a hot meal before him.

In the bedroom, Megan clung to Luke's hand.

"The baby may come this afternoon," she whispered, her voice weary.

The pain was staggering—an axe in her spine, a blade across her belly. Her legs shook; there was no easing it. She barely held on, fighting back tears.

Luke brushed her damp forehead and hummed an old Indian lullaby, one his aunt had sung when he was fevered. Megan's breathing slowed. He burned sage and prayed—for her, the baby, himself.

In the kitchen, Ed joined the doctor.

"You should be a grandfather before supper," the doctor said. "She's strong. She'll do just fine."

"We hope so," Ed replied. "She's still our baby. It's hard to watch her hurting but you've given us some comfort."

"Reassurance eases suffering too," the doctor said with a small smile. "'Mind over matter,' as they say— or: 'If you don't mind, it doesn't matter,'" he chuckled, quoting Twain.

Ed chuckled. "No wonder you're good at what you do."

"And I'd be lost running a ranch," the doctor replied. "We all have our place."

Morning stretched into afternoon. Megan labored on, worn thin. Dr. Hathaway left to check another patient, returning an hour later.

The boys came home to find Megan still laboring. Stricken by her cries, Cassie sent them to their grandparents until it was over.

Megan gave birth to a beautiful baby girl, sometime after supper. Dr. Hathaway guided her through the final moments, Luke and Cassie close beside her.

"Oh, my sweet Indian White Dove—you've done it!" Luke whispered, kissing her damp forehead.

The newborn's cry filled the room. Wrapped snug, she blinked up with stormy-gray eyes as Megan held her for the first time.

"Oh, my darling girl... you're finally here," Megan whispered, tears falling as she kissed her cheek.

At her mother's voice, the baby furrowed her brow and let out a wail.

"She's telling you all about it," Cassie said, laughter breaking through tears.

Luke kissed the child's head, soft with black fuzz. She calmed briefly under his gaze before crying again.

Cassie squeezed Megan's hand. "She's precious... just like her mama."

Megan closed her eyes in a silent prayer—for her child, for strength, for the love around her.

When Megan opened them, Luke was kneeling beside the bed.

"I love you," he said, voice thick with emotion. He kissed her tenderly. What she had endured seemed beyond belief. He'd ached all day, wanting to carry her pain. Now it was over. Joy filled every corner of his heart.

"I love you, too," she whispered. Her arms trembled with fatigue, but she held her baby close, already lost in the deepest love she'd ever known.

Ed slipped into the room once Megan was settled. He shook the doctor's hand before the man stepped outside for air.

"Oh my... a baby girl," Ed murmured, voice rough. He kissed Megan's forehead, eyes glistening. "She's as pretty as her mama."

Megan managed a tired smile. "Thanks, Pa. Want to hold her?"

"Are you sure?" he asked, glancing at Cassie.

"Yes," Cassie said gently, lifting the baby from Megan's arms and passing her to Ed. "We've all had our turn."

Ed cradled the tiny bundle. "What a sweet little thing," he whispered, studying her copper cheeks, downy hair, and delicate lashes. Tiny fists pressed to her face as she slept, content from her first feeding.

Spent, Megan leaned into Luke. Tears slipped quietly down her cheeks as her body surrendered to relief.

After a moment, Ed handed the baby back. "Time for Mama and babe to rest. Congratulations."

"Thanks, Grandpa," Luke said with quiet pride.

Ed chuckled, joined by Cassie. Megan opened her eyes briefly, offering a faint smile before drifting off again.

"We should let them sleep," Cassie murmured.

The baby was laid beside Megan, who curled protectively around her daughter. Luke moved to the far side of the bed, watching in quiet awe as the two most precious people in his world slept in peace at last.

****

An hour later, the boys returned, eager to meet their new niece. A soft knock stirred Megan from sleep. Luke, still at her side, smiled down at her and their daughter.

"Come in," he said softly.

The boys entered, faces lit with wonder as they gathered around the bed. Nestled between Megan and Luke, the small bundle slept peacefully, a round face framed in thick black hair.

"Oh, she's so pretty," Johnathan whispered.

"She's so small." Kurt leaned closer.

"Congratulations," David said, giving Megan a gentle hug. Each brother followed with a kiss to her cheek.

"What's her name?" Johnathan asked.

Luke glanced at Megan. "Mary Bluebird," he said, his voice catching. "For her great-grandmother Black—and my mother."

"Mary Bluebird Havoc," David repeated. "I like it."

"I'm going to call her Bluebird," Johnathan declared, beaming. "She's tiny—just like a little bluebird."

Luke's heart swelled. "My mother would've liked that," he said with pride.

***

Later that evening, after a simple supper, the little family retired for the night.

Luke lay opposite Megan, watching the angelic infant sleeping.

"Does life get any better than this?" he asked, wonder in his voice.

Megan brushed her daughter's silken cheek. "If it does, I can't imagine how. This feels like heaven."

Luke's hand rested on Megan's waist, love lacing his words. "To have you—and now her—it's more than I ever hoped for."

"I feel the same," she whispered. "The moment they placed her in my arms... it was instant love. Miraculous."

His gaze lingered on the baby. "Now I understand why a parent would give their life for a child. I'd do anything for her. I want to give her everything—just as I've tried to give you."
"And it's been more than enough," Megan said. "You've made me feel cherished. I didn't think I could love you more than on our wedding day—but I do."

She smiled at him as the room fell into hush, lit only by lamplight and the breath of new life between them.

***

The next month passed in a blur of cherished moments as kin, neighbors, and friends came to meet Mary Bluebird. Joy filled the house with grandparents, three doting uncles, and adoring parents. Mary rarely lay in her cradle. Megan often joked the only time she held her was to feed her.

Letters arrived from Prudence and Naomi, both overjoyed at the news. Naomi wrote she and John planned to travel to Laramie for Prudence's wedding and linger awhile among friends.

Meanwhile, Luke exchanged letters with Philip as they finalized lodge plans. Supplies would arrive once the ground thawed enough to lay a stone foundation. Construction was set for May: lodge, barn, corral. It would serve as their home until cabins could be built that fall. Luke, Jeremy, and Patrick planned to leave by May first for construction. Philip already had fishing trips booked through July. Megan fretted over the preparations, but Luke reassured her it would be ready.

For Megan, the weeks were full—feeding, burping, changing. She often marveled at her mother's ease in raising four children. The cradleboard proved a blessing; with Mary snug on her back, Megan could work while the baby watched or slept, soothed by gentle motion. Evenings brought laughter as the boys took turns entertaining her, eager for her coos and smiles.

As April waned, Cassie thought often of the parting ahead. Spring had come fully now. The prairie greened under steady sun, calves frolicked, wildflowers bloomed.

One soft afternoon, Megan carried Mary to the porch and joined Cassie to watch the men drive the horses in from pasture. Luke's Paint mare, heavy with foal, trailed after Snowfire, Wildfire, and two newer horses now part of the herd.

Luke rode past the house, lifting a hand in greeting. Megan waved back, heart full. She would miss him dearly once he left in a few days.

"Look, Mary, there's your papa," she said as the baby kicked and wriggled, eyes fixed on the horses.

Luke dismounted, closed the gate, and jogged toward the porch. "How's my little girl this fine afternoon?" he asked, arms outstretched. Mary squealed, lifting her chubby arms. He swung her high, laughing, then kissed her round cheek.

"She's had her nap—ready to play now," Megan said, smiling.

"Then Papa will play," Luke grinned, kissing Megan before carrying the baby toward the corral.

Megan leaned back, content, grateful for the brief rest as she watched them together.

"I'll sure miss that little girl," Cassie murmured, eyes on Mary's kicking feet. Nearly three months had flown, and the baby was now a plump bundle of joy, quick to smile at anyone.

"She'll miss you too," Megan said. "And so will I."

"We'll visit as often as we can," Cassie promised. "She's my only grandbaby. I intend to spoil her every chance I get."

"Come anytime. We'll always look forward to it."

# Chapter 34

## Building the Lodge

Moving day came sooner than they expected. The lodge had risen with astonishing speed and Luke sent word—it was time to settle in. With a mix of eagerness and sorrow, Megan and Cassie packed the last of Megan and Luke's things. As the wagon rolled away, Megan cast one last look at her childhood home, whispering a silent goodbye.

From the Laramie train station, they rode north by wagon—Megan, Cassie, Kurt, and Johnathan—bringing the rest of Luke and Megan's belongings. David regretfully stayed behind in Cheyenne to tend the ranch and continue his medical training.

As Kurt steered into the foothills, Megan's heart quickened. There, nestled beneath the wooded mountains, stood the lodge—grander than she'd ever imagined.

"Is that it?" Johnathan asked, peering around Cassie.

"It must be," Megan breathed. Months apart from Luke now made sense—all his effort had gone into this place.

"It's huge," Kurt muttered as they entered the yard.

The towering A-frame rose between two-story wings, a wide porch stretching across the front. Megan climbed down, taking the sleeping baby from Cassie.

At the sound of wheels, Luke and Ed emerged from

the barn, running to greet them.

"Welcome home!" Luke called, gathering Megan close and kissing Mary's fuzzy head. His heart swelled—it had been weeks since he'd seen them.

Ed drew Cassie into his arms. Though it had only been a week, it felt longer. Cassie took sleeping Mary so Luke and Megan could unload.

"She's grown an inch," Ed murmured, gazing at the baby in Cassie's arms.

"She missed you," Cassie said.

"I missed her—but I missed you more," he whispered, kissing her tenderly.

"I can't wait to show you everything," Luke said, hoisting luggage.

Megan grabbed her bags and followed him up the steps. Luke threw open the heavy door.

"We hired extra hands—got it up fast. Still shelves and cupboards to finish, but it's ready."

The main hall soared, log walls and timber beams giving it a rustic grandeur. A long table stood near the kitchen, wagon-wheel chandeliers overhead. Overstuffed chairs circled a great stone hearth, sunlight spilling through tall windows.

"Won't those windows let in cold?" Megan asked, eyeing the treetop view they afforded.

"Shutters outside—close tight when snow comes."

"Smart," she murmured, picturing a crackling fire during a storm.

"Come see our room." Luke bounded upstairs. "Four bedrooms on each wing, each wing with its own washroom. Philip insisted we build it right. There's even a clawfoot tub. Downstairs—an office and two more bedrooms for guests who can't climb stairs."

Megan followed, speechless. From the balcony she gazed down at the vast room, then into their bedroom—bed, bureau, dressing table, and plenty of space. A window overlooked the woods, letting in the spring breeze.

"It's wonderful," she said.

Luke pulled her close. "And this is only the beginning. Come see the barn."

Outside, the barn loomed twice the size of the one back home.

"Sixteen stalls," Luke said proudly. "Room enough to winter the horses. Corral's even got a chute to saddle up quick for guests. Hay's coming next week; straw's already in the loft."

Megan turned slowly, amazed. The land she'd last seen in November was transformed.

"How'd you manage it all?"

"Every hand we could find. Philip hired a crew. Still work to do, but we'll be ready for guests."

"But first the wedding," Megan said, already tallying the list. "I have meals to plan, beds to make, linens to buy, shelves to fill…"

Luke chuckled, adoring her beautiful face. "I love you," he said, catching her in his arms swinging her around with a laugh. "I've missed you."

"I missed you too," she said, meeting his kiss.

***

By week's end, the lodge stood proudly complete. The great room held leather sofas, carved tables, and the scent of pine, sawdust, and fresh leather. Plaid blankets dressed the guest beds, antlers and gleaming fish adorned log walls, and a framed landscape lent elegance.

Sunlight streamed through tall windows flanking the hearth, crimson drapes deepening the glow, while woven rugs warmed the plank floors. In the kitchen, a cast-iron stove, icebox, pump-fed sink, and well-stocked pantry promised hearty meals. Outside, a bunkhouse awaited the hired hands who would tend horses while Luke, Jeremy, Philip, and Patrick led guests into the wild. Upstairs, the staff filled the east wing—the west wing ready for guests. Every detail was in place, just in time.

The day before Ed, Cassie, and the others were to leave, the family gathered behind the lodge to celebrate. A fire pit ringed with logs became their circle. Dutch oven chicken and potatoes simmered over the flames, filling the twilight with rich aromas.

As night fell, Luke circled the fire in a quiet dance, drumbeats echoing into the trees. Megan held baby Mary close, her heart swelling with pride and gratitude. They sang campfire songs and told stories—some old, some new. Kurt, Johnathan, and David spent their last night in the teepee pitched nearby. Each one held Mary, reluctant to let her go.

That morning, Prudence had arrived by train, bustling with wedding plans. Even Grandma and Grandpa Hartford made the journey, calling it the first Hartford-Havoc-Holden reunion—not one to miss.

It was a night of laughter and reflection. Ed strummed a slow cowboy tune while others gazed into the fire. Prudence and Philip sat wrapped in a blanket, whispering. Penny cradled baby Jerry, snuggled against Jeremy's side. David stared into the flames, thinking of Hazel— grateful for his visit with her after months of letters.

Patrick and Kathy held hands, grateful to experience such joy in their later years. Grandma and Grandpa Hartford quietly remembered the blessings Cassie had brought into their lives. Clancy and Joy watched their eldest son and grandson with quiet pride. Beth and John shared a tender smile, missing Melissa and her family.

Luke tossed another log onto the fire, then sat near Megan's feet. Watching the flames, he thought of his tribe and family—how much they would have loved such a gathering. His father would have been proud. Looking up at Megan, he offered a silent prayer for the land, the people, and the love now surrounding him. She smiled as he squeezed her knee and joined in the singing.

When the song ended, Cassie slipped an arm around Megan and lifted her gaze to the star-swept sky.

"I never imagined, twenty-two years ago, that my life would turn out like this," she murmured. "The world I knew vanished overnight. I thought all was lost... but look at the life God gave me. Your pa, the love of my life. You, Megan—my miracle daughter, more precious than I dreamed. Then Luke when I needed healing most, then three more sweet boys—and now this little angel." Cassie touched the baby's cheek. "You're my legacy. Because of you, my life is blessed beyond measure."

Tears slipped down Megan's cheeks as she leaned into her mother. "Oh, Ma, you've always been my light. I've learned so much from you—your courage, your joy, your faith. Your legacy—*Cassie's legacy* is more than the life you've built—it's who *we* are, because of *you*."

Cassie kissed Megan's cheek. Together, they sat beneath the stars, hearts full, bound by love and gratitude.

***

The next morning, the ranch buzzed with farewells and gratitude as kin packed up and left for the train. With tears falling freely, Ed, Cassie, and the boys embraced Megan, Luke, and the baby one last time with promises to write and return in the fall.

No sooner had the wagons vanished, than the women threw themselves into readying the lodge for guests. Prudence's parents were due that afternoon, along with Philip's mother, and Naomi and John. Laughter and hurried steps echoed through every room.

By mid-afternoon, Philip and Luke set out for the train station while the women finished chores and prepared supper. The lodge gleamed—fresh linens on beds, warm blankets over sofas, books on shelves, candles on the hearth.

"I daresay it looks splendid," Prudence said, admiring their work. "Goodness! It's almost time. I'm so excited to see my parents—it's been nearly a year."

"And I can't wait to see Naomi and John," Megan added. "I imagine you're a little nervous about meeting Mrs. Archibald."

"I am—a bit," Prudence admitted, tucking a stray hair into place.

"She'll adore you—just as we do," Penny said, giving her hand a squeeze.

"Thank you," Prudence said, smoothing her new dress.

Megan glanced out the window. "They're coming!"

With a joyful squeal, Prudence dashed through the doors, skirts flying. Megan and Penny followed, each with a baby in arms as the first wagon arrived.

Luke reined in the team and jumped down. John

helped Naomi from the wagon.

"Naomi!" Prudence cried, embracing her.

Naomi laughed, hugging her tight. "It's so good to see you."

Megan approached with Mary on her hip. "You made it."

Naomi's smile deepened. "And this must be little Mary."

Mary grinned and reached out to touch Naomi's cheek.

"She's a charmer," Megan said fondly, then asked, "How was the trip?"

"Long, but the train was pleasant enough," Naomi admitted.

"And you, John?" Megan offered him a warm hug.

"Couldn't be happier. Ready to rest—and lend a hand." His gaze lifted to the lodge. "This place is remarkable."

"Come inside," Luke said, hefting their cases.

While they entered, Prudence lingered as another surrey rounded the bend. Philip reined in the horses.

"Mama!" Prudence cried, rushing to her mother's arms, laughing through tears.

"Papa!" Prudence hugged her father next. "I'm so glad you came."

"We wouldn't miss it for the world," he said, beaming.

Philip helped his mother down. Petite and elegant in a peach gown with a matching parasol, Mrs. Archibald carried herself with polished grace, her dark hair streaked with silver.

She extended a gloved hand. "Philip told me you

were lovely, but he was far too modest. You're exqui-site."

Prudence blushed. "I'm honored to meet the woman who raised such a fine man."

"And I, my soon-to-be daughter," Mrs. Archibald said, drawing her close.

Prudence laughed softly. "Yes—very soon. I trust you met my parents?"

"We did," Mrs. Archibald said. "Though they grow potatoes and we cotton, we're farmers all the same." She smiled at the thought, though she'd never plucked a boll herself.

One look at Mr. Wright's calloused hands told her he worked his own land. Prudence, too, bore the quiet confidence of one who worked hard. That pleased her. Philip had chosen well.

"Mother," Philip said gently, "let's go inside where it's cooler."

Inside, guests washed up and rested before supper. In the kitchen, Megan, Prudence, Kathy, and Penny laid the final dishes on a table set with care, platters of steaming food ready to welcome them all.

Soon, everyone gathered around the long table, con-versation flowing easily. Patrick and Kathy spoke with Mr. and Mrs. Wright and Mrs. Archibald about their travels, while Naomi and John caught up with Megan and Luke and met Jeremy and Penny.

When the talk quieted, John cleared his throat. "We've been saving some good news to share in per-son." He glanced at Naomi, smiling.

All eyes turned. Naomi, blushing, reached for his hand.

"We're expecting," John said simply. "Due in November."

Cheers and congratulations rang out.

"Oh, Naomi, I'm so happy for you!" Megan said, grasping her hand.

Prudence squeezed Philip's hand beneath the table. "What wonderful news."

The evening passed in cheerful busyness. Guests toured the lodge, admired the views, then gathered around the great hearth, trading stories and laughter until late. Weary and full from supper, they retired with warm embraces and soft goodnights.

Tomorrow was the wedding—eleven o'clock sharp.

Philip lay awake longer than he expected, heart thrumming with anticipation, until sleep brought dreams of the life he and Prudence would soon begin.

Down the hall, Megan and Luke lay side by side, Mary asleep in her crib. A breeze stirred the curtains, while crickets and rustling leaves whispered through the open window.

"Thank you, Luke," Megan whispered. "For building this place. For bringing us all together. Isn't it wonderful news about Naomi and John?"

"It is," he murmured, his voice unconvincing and distant.

She turned her head. "What's wrong?"

He kissed her forehead. "Nothing."

"I don't believe you," she said with concern.

Luke exhaled. "I love it here. But sometimes I miss the quiet—just you and me, like our honeymoon. A place of our own, where I can kiss you whenever I please. A home for us and Mary."

Megan considered this. "I understand. But it's only for the summer. Then we'll have our own place again." She kissed him gently.

"I guess I'll save up my kisses until then," he teased.

"You know, we're alone *now*," she laughed, pulling him close.

He brushed her neck with his lips, and she giggled. "Shh, you'll wake Philip," he teased—just as a soft snore drifted through the wall.

****

Morning dawned in a flurry of excitement. Prudence, with her mother's help, styled her hair and stepped into her gown. Philip dressed carefully, pacing as he practiced his vows.

Downstairs, Mrs. Archibald joined the women in the kitchen, while Luke and the men finished chores and decorated the buggy with tin cans and a painted sign.

By a quarter to eleven, the preacher arrived along with neighbors from church. At the stroke of eleven, the clock chimed, and the phonograph played the wedding march. Prudence entered on her father's arm, radiant as she crossed to where Philip stood. Pink ribbons and candles brightened the mantel, sunlight pouring through tall windows in a golden glow.

Hand in hand, they exchanged vows and rings, sealing them with a kiss as applause filled the room. Megan wiped away a tear.

While guests mingled, Megan and Penny warmed the food. The table was set with platters heaped high, and Mr. Wright and Mrs. Archibald raised toasts to the couple.

Afterward, music filled the lodge. The newlyweds

led the first dance, soon joined by others, laughter swirling with the melodies.

By mid-afternoon, Prudence and Philip changed into traveling clothes. With bags packed, they dashed out the door as guests showered them with wheat and waved farewell.

On the train, tucked away from the bustle, Prudence slipped her arm through Philip's and took his hand.

"I'm so happy, Mr. Archibald," she said, eyes shining.

Philip smiled, squeezing her hand. "Me too, Mrs. Archibald," he murmured, stealing a kiss as the train carried them into their new life.

# *Chapter 35*

# *Standing Elk Lodge*

Philip and Prudence returned from their honey-moon just as the first guests were set to arrive. With bags scarcely unpacked, they dove into preparations, while Patrick rode off to collect the guests from the train station.

Outside, Luke waited in traditional buckskins. His braided hair and claw necklace caught the sun as the surrey rolled up, curiosity brightening the passengers' faces.

"Welcome to Standing Elk Lodge," Luke greeted with a warm smile.

A portly man climbed down first, cigar between his teeth.

"Good to be here, my boy," he boomed, pumping Luke's hand. "I'm Mr. Tuttle. This here's my son, Cody."

A lanky boy of fifteen followed, nervously brushing hair from his eyes.

"Luke Standing Elk," Luke said, steadying his grip on Cody's hand.

"Wow... a real Indian," Cody whispered, wide-eyed.

Luke chuckled. "I sure am."

A tall, thin man in a fine suit and white spats came next, mustache twitching.

"Jeffery Hendricks—call me Jeff."

Philip appeared as the last guests arrived—a trio of his old friends from Georgia—greeting him with backslaps and laughter.

"Fellas," Philip said, "this is Luke Standing Elk—my partner and your guide."

A deep drawl answered. "Howdy! Jim Bishop. Known this rascal near all my life," he said, gripping Philip's shoulder, then shook Luke's hand, followed by soft-spoken Lester Martin, and the overly confident Charlie Brewster.

Luke welcomed each in turn. "Grab your things. Supper's at six—we'll go over plans then."

Their voices followed him inside, light and carefree.

That evening, the long dining table glowed beneath wagon-wheel chandeliers. Plates brimmed with hearty fare, and conversation flowed as freely as coffee.

"My boy Cody's been dreamin' of the West since he was knee-high," Mr. Tuttle said, clapping his son's back. "Cowboys and Indians, dime novels—you name it. And here we are, ready for the real Wild West."

Cody flushed but smiled, pleased despite himself.

Jeffery chimed in, dabbing his mouth. "I'm a lawyer back East. Always meant to see this country before I'm too old to climb a hill."

Jim Bishop let out a laugh. "My wife's visiting her folks, so I figured it was high time I had an adventure."

Charlie smirked. "At least your wife's glad you're gone. Mine'll raise a storm when I get back. Told her I'd earned this trip after years of slavin' for her father. He near exploded when I said I was headin' west for fishin' and fresh air. But worth every glare so far." He grinned, clapping Philip's back. "Thanks for the invite, friend."

Philip lifted his glass. "It's a blessing having you all here. May you make memories worth keeping."

Smiles circled the table before Naomi's voice broke the hush. "And what about you, Mr. Martin?"

Lester's hands folded, eyes low. "It was always my father's dream to see the West. He never made it." His voice faltered. "So I came in his place."

Naomi leaned forward, voice warm with empathy. "I'm so sorry. But I believe he's with you—especially now."

Lester's chin quivered as he managed a trembling smile. "The moment I saw the mountains, I felt it. I knew he was here."

A reverent pause held the room before Charlie lifted his glass. "To memories made, and dreams fulfilled."

"Here, here," came the chorus as glasses clinked and hearts swelled.

***

At first light, the men rose to the hush of a sleepy lodge. The eastern sky glowed faintly, promising a fair day. Bags were packed for the four days ahead. The air was filled with the creak of leather as horses were saddled and provisions strapped to the pack animals.

Each guest was paired with a mount. Those unfamiliar with riding received a quick lesson—mounting, dismounting, guiding with reins. There were fumbles and stiff saddle shifts, but by sunrise, the company was ready.

Philip, Luke, Jeremy, Patrick, and John embraced their wives, then mounted. Luke led, steady as always, while others rode alongside novices, offering quiet guidance. Patrick brought up the rear to keep the group together.

Back at the lodge, the women savored the rare peace. Tea, conversation, and long-postponed projects filled the day while babies played nearby—a blessing after weeks of cleaning and cooking for crowds.

Meanwhile, on the trail, Luke's patience was tested.

Not far in, Cody's horse veered toward lush grass. The boy drifted off trail, clinging helplessly to the saddle horn until Jeremy retrieved the reins and led them back.

"You've got to show him who's boss," Jeremy grinned. "You're named after Buffalo Bill—might as well live up to the legend."

Cody chuckled, sitting taller in the saddle.

Charlie, brimming with confidence, galloped into a meadow—only to forget how to stop. Yanking the reins too hard, the horse reared. Charlie tumbled backward, thankfully landing in soft grass. Bruised pride aside, he laughed as Patrick hauled him up and caught the runaway horse.

Jeff fared no better, his mount brushing him against trees or diving through brush until Philip fetched him back on course.

Things didn't ease up. Mr. Tuttle's horse crowded Lester's, nipping at its flank. Lester's mount jumped aside, but the biting horse caught Lester's calf instead, leaving a red welt. Luke rode back, gently reminding Mr. Tuttle to keep his distance.

Delays piled up. By midday, Luke called a rest, wondering if they'd reach the lake before nightfall. The trail climbed steadily through swaying pines, wildflowers pressing close. By mid-afternoon, saddle sores and stiff backs had men walking beside their mounts. Luke noted their faces—he'd overestimated their stamina.

At last the lakeside camp appeared—the relief was audible. While Luke and his men set up tents and supper, guests stripped boots and dust-caked clothes, plunging into the cold water with yelps and laughter.

As dusk settled, a hearty meal was served to the now-rowdy group. Someone passed a bottle of whiskey as songs and laughter rose beneath a star-strewn sky. Watching from a distance, Luke shook his head with mild frustration. This wasn't the quiet journey he'd envisioned. These men were more suited to parlors and carriages than forests and saddles.

By morning, the quiet camp stirred to the scent of coffee and frying bacon. One by one, men emerged from tents—bleary-eyed, stiff, and dirt-smudged. Luke caught Patrick's eye and stifled a grin. Guests shuffled to the fire, clutching tin mugs of coffee as Jeremy and John returned with firewood.

Breakfast—bacon, eggs, pancakes—gradually eased complaints, bringing smiles and cheerful banter.

"I think I slept on a rock," Mr. Tuttle groaned, rubbing his back.

"Pine boughs and moss make a fine mattress," Luke replied. "Gather some tonight and I'll show you."

"Will do, my good man," Mr. Tuttle said, lighting a cigar as he ambled off.

Luke returned to the fire ring and called everyone to their feet. It was time for the first fishing lesson.

They walked down to the lake, sunlight shimmering on glassy water. Luke showed the old ways first—catching fish with bare hands. Then woven traps and the spear. Finally, baited hooks and choosing the best pools.

Charlie and Jim, already skilled fly fishermen, wandered off down the shore. Luke reminded them firmly to return by midday; he had no intention of searching the woods after dark.

Soon the men spread along the bank. Lester remained quiet while Jeff filled the silence with cheerful chatter. Both returned fishless but in high spirits, Jeremy and Patrick close behind.

Philip and the others returned in time for a hearty meal, appetites sharpened by the mountain air. Charlie and Jim, though, stumbled in much later—laughing too loud, their breath heavy with whiskey and light on fish. By then, only a single sandwich remained. They shrugged it off with rough jokes and backslaps, but the levity rang hollow. Uneasy, Philip tried to take the bottle, murmuring apologies to Luke.

Charlie jerked it back.

"I paid good money for this," he snapped, voice thick with liquor. "It's my vacation. I'll do as I please." He stumbled toward the lake, cursing under his breath.

With bellies full and heat rising, the men reclined under the trees, hats pulled low for a quick nap. Restless, Luke wandered to the water's edge, where Charlie sat hunched on a rock, head in his hands.

"Hey there," Luke said gently.

Charlie looked up, eyes bloodshot. "Hey yourself."

"Mind if I join you?"

Charlie shrugged. "Long as you ain't here to lecture me."

"Wouldn't dream of it." Luke settled on a log, drew his knife, and whittled in silence.

The lake lay calm, mirroring sky and trees. Charlie stared at it a long time before speaking.

"Tell me, Luke—why can't a man be boss of his own life? Feels like someone's always telling me what to do—first my pa, then my wife, now her pa. Never once been asked what I wanted."

Luke let quiet hold the space.

Charlie gave a bitter chuckle. "Truth is, I don't even know anymore. Married young, took a job at her pa's mill soon after. Hot, noisy place. Cotton dust chokes your throat, your lungs—*and* your soul."

Luke raised a brow. "Then why stay?"

Charlie scowled. "Started out wantin' to please her... help her folks. The longer I stayed, the more I hated it. Now... I don't even recognize myself." His voice cracked. Shoulders shaking. "God help me, Luke—I'm sick of my life."

Luke sat quietly listening.

Charlie wiped his face, muttering, "Didn't know it ran this deep. Guess I needed distance to see it. Every day I drag home, only to be scolded. The bottle's the only thing that helps me forget." He dropped the bottle with a sigh. "But I swear I'm not like her pa—he's cruel."

Luke drew a long breath. "Maybe your wife's afraid you'll *become him*."

Charlie fell silent. A duck landed nearby, ripples widening. He watched them fade. "You think a man's choices ripple like that?"

Luke nodded.

"Did you ever dream of doing something else?" Luke asked.

Charlie smiled faintly, eyes distant. "When I was a kid, I wanted to work on trains. Loved the sound, the steam. I'd sneak to the depot just to watch. That whistle meant freedom. The ride out here... felt like a sliver of that dream."

"So what's stopping you?"

Charlie toed the dirt. "Everything. How would we eat? What would my wife say—her parents? I wouldn't know where to begin." He let out a frustrated breath. "It's just not in the cards."

Luke stood, brushing wood shavings from his lap. "Didn't you just say a man ought to live his own life? Maybe take your own advice."

He turned to leave.

"But how?" Charlie called after him.

Luke paused. "Be strong. It's your life. Don't wait until it's too late—like Lester's pa."

Then he walked up the hill, leaving Charlie with the lake, the bottle, and the echo of his own heart.

***

That evening, they gathered around the fire beneath a starlit sky. Luke noticed Charlie hadn't brought his bottle. When Jim asked, Charlie shrugged. "It's gone." The guides exchanged quiet relief.

Jeff surprised them with a harmonica, and at their urging, he played lively tunes. Luke joined with his guitar, music and laughter mingling with the night air until cold and weariness nudged them toward tents.

"Luke, did you find those branches and moss for my bed?" Mr. Tuttle asked, lingering by the fire.

"There's plenty around. Didn't you gather any?"

"I told Cody, but he didn't know what to look for," Mr. Tuttle said. Cody ducked into the tent.

"I'll show you tomorrow—too dark now," Luke said.

"A lot of good that'll do me," Mr. Tuttle muttered, grinding his cigar into the dirt before crawling into his tent.

***

The next morning, Mr. Tuttle grumbled about his back again.

"I'll show you where to find the boughs after breakfast," Luke promised, stirring the skillet over the fire.

Later, the party split: Patrick and Philip led one group north, Luke and Jeremy took the others south. As they walked, Luke pointed out edible plants, occasionally stopping to gather samples. Cody, Mr. Tuttle, and Jeff listened with interest, Jeff looking particularly polished against the rugged backdrop in his new gear.

"Here's the moss, and spruce boughs. See how soft?" Luke chopped a few branches, handing Cody the hatchet. "Keep this hand back."

Cody worked carefully. "Look, Pa! I've got enough for a bed!"

"Well done, son." Mr. Tuttle beamed, picturing a good night's sleep.

"Carry them back later. Let's keep moving," Luke said.

Jeremy brought up the rear, eyes scanning the woods after spotting bear scat earlier.

"Oh—huckleberries!" Luke crouched, popping berries into his mouth.

The others joined, hands and tongue soon purple.

By late afternoon, they returned with stringers of fish and a hat full of huckleberries. Laughter echoed along the trail. Even the horses seemed livelier. Jeff, flushed with sun and pride, carried six gleaming trout on a forked branch.

"You're lucky," Jeremy teased. "I've never been outfished by a city slicker."

"Beginner's luck," Jeff said, beaming.

That night, they feasted on fried fish until they couldn't eat another bite. Conversation drifted long past dusk as the fire burned low and stars gathered overhead.

"Will you show us an Indian dance?" Cody asked shyly.

"I'll do better," Luke said, standing. "I'll teach you." He pulled Cody up and beckoned the others into a circle. Reluctantly, they brushed off their trousers and joined hands in a circle around the fire. Luke chanted, voice rising and falling, feet pounding a steady rhythm.

Clumsy at first—their steps grew steadier, and laughter faded. Firelight flickered in their eyes. They gazed skyward, stars shimmering in the deep blue. A solemn reverence settled over them.

When the dance ended, they stood breathing hard, hearts full of emotion.

"This dance," Luke said, voice low, "asks God, Our Father—Tam Apa—to help us. He is near. Listen and he will guide you."

They sat cross-legged, gazing into the flames.

"We're not here by chance," Luke continued. "You didn't come just to fish or escape your routines. You were led here. You've discovered strength, insight—maybe even who you truly are."

He looked around the circle.

"Jeff—you have the instincts of a hunter. My people would welcome you."

Jeff's face glowed, proudly.

"Lester, your father's spirit walks with you. You honor his memory."

Lester nodded, eyes shining.

"Jim, you're a leader. Your family and frends look to you. Guide them well." Jim smiled sheepishly as Charlie nudged him with a grin.

"Charlie, you're finding your path. Keep walking it."

Charlie offered a soft smile.

"Cody, you're becoming a man. In my tribe, boys your age go on a vision quest—fasting and praying alone. You needn't go far but find a quiet place and listen for guidance. The Lord will answer."

Cody nodded solemnly.

Luke turned to Mr. Tuttle. "Your son is watching. Make sure what he sees is worth imitating."

Mr. Tuttle bowed his head, staring into the fire.

"Our path is filled with trials," Luke continued, sliding a glance at John, then around the circle. "But with courage—and God's help—you'll walk it well. It has been my honor to guide you, show you the mountains, teach you to live off the land, and be at one with God and nature. *This*," he said, sweeping his gaze around the camp, "*is my dream.*"

Solemn silence fell over the circle, hearts full, eyes glistening.

"Thank you, Luke, for sharing your dream," Patrick said finally. "There's something healing here—in the woods, with good men, and in God's presence."

Jim chuckled. "Okay, let's not get too sentimental. Our wives might think we've gone soft."

Chuckles rose, lightening their hearts into quiet joy.

***

The next morning, after a hearty breakfast of huckleberry pancakes, bacon, and strong coffee, they broke camp. The return to the lodge was brisk—warm baths and soft beds quickened their pace. Even the horses seemed eager.

They arrived just in time to wash up before the supper bell. The women welcomed them with open arms and warm kisses. That night's meal was a feast: fried chicken, mashed potatoes with gravy, flaky biscuits, and all the fixings. The men ate heartily, appetites sharpened by fresh air and good company.

From the kitchen doorway, Megan watched, smiling at the color in their cheeks, the easy laughter, and the way even Cody walked taller. They had gone into the wilderness as individuals—but returned as comrades.

And so began the first season of Standing Elk Lodge and Luke's dream.

# Chapter 36

## Luke's Dream

Summer passed in a blur of guests and adventures. The men spent long days guiding in the mountains, returning briefly to tend chores before the next outing. The women kept busy cooking, washing, and managing the lodge. Though stretches apart were hard, they cherished quiet hours together.

Saturdays became sacred—trips to town for supplies or an evening at the Opera House. Sundays were for church, picnics and buggy rides, or simply rocking on the porch.

When John and Naomi left for the reservation before school resumed, their absence left a quiet ache. Megan knew Philip and Prudence would soon follow—they'd promised one more year of teaching before permanently returning to Laramie. The four couples had grown close, and parting was not easy.

***

With guiding season over, work on Megan and Luke's house began. Lodgepole logs, boards, and windows piled up just south of the lodge. From her bedroom window, Megan smiled, trying to imagine their house.

"I can't wait! Today's going to be the best day ever," she said, pulling on her wool skirt and vest. "Ma and Pa will be here soon. They won't believe how big Mary's gotten."

She lifted Mary from her crib. The baby kicked and cooed, chewing her rattle.

"You're so big—nine months old and sitting on your own," Megan said, slipping the nightgown over her downy-soft hair.

Luke leaned in to tickle her belly. "Such a big girl," he said, earning a wide smile.

Megan laughed, struggling with squirming feet. "You two aren't making this any easier," she teased as Mary's stocking slipped off again.

Bundled in the surrey, they set off. The crisp fall morning was bright and clear, the hills ablaze with gold, amber, and crimson. Leaves rustled underfoot, the air rich with earth and pine.

At the train station, the platform hummed with reunion—kisses, hugs, and happy tears.

"I missed you so much!" Cassie said, wrapping an arm around Megan as they rode home together.

"I missed you too," Megan answered.

"And you, my little Bluebird—I missed you most!" Cassie said, lifting Mary onto her lap. "You've grown so much," she whispered, kissing her copper cheek and smoothing her hair beneath her bonnet.

"Better soak up all the baby time you can," Megan teased.

Ed turned from the front seat, taking Mary's chubby hand. "Save a little time for Grandpa, too. I miss my baby bunting."

"I'll leave you some time in the evenings—once you've finished working," Cassie added with a wink, making Ed chuckle.

Luke listened as the family caught up—Johnathan

boasting of roping calves, Ed relieved that the roundup was a success.

At the lodge, Grandma and Grandpa O'Malley welcomed them with hugs.

"Land sakes, how you've grown," Kathy said, kissing each boy's cheek.

"We've missed you something fierce!" Patrick added, pulling them in for bear hugs. Next came Cassie and Ed with warm embraces.

Ed clasped Patrick's arm, noting the hard muscle. "I think you've grown too."

Patrick chuckled. "Fresh air's done me good. I feel stronger than I have in years."

"Well, *Grandpa*," Ed grinned, "let's put that to the test—we've got three houses to build before winter."

Patrick grinned back, more than ready to prove himself.

Jeremy and Penny welcomed them with baby Jerry, who squirmed until Cassie scooped him up.

"And how's my great-nephew?" she said, bouncing him. "Good grief, you're solid as a brick."

"His mama's milk—must be mostly cream," Jeremy teased.

Penny blushed, pride softening her smile.

Once greetings ended, the men—joined by hired hands—headed to the building site. The women stayed at the lodge, cooking and visiting until suppertime.

The men worked steadily, soon shedding coats as the crisp air gave way to sweat. By evening, the foundation was laid and the root cellar dug.

The next day, they walled the cellar and laid the main floor. From the lodge, the women watched with pride, later carrying lunch to the site.

"It's so big!" Megan exclaimed as Luke led her through the framework. "Much bigger than Ma and Pa's house."

"I made sure we'd have plenty of room—with two stories," Luke said, sliding an arm around her. "For all the children we'll raise here."

Megan laughed, her eyes teasing. "How many are we talking—ten?"

"As many as God gives us," Luke said solemnly. "But I'm hoping for at least a dozen."

She elbowed him playfully. "You'll need another wife to help with that."

He swept her into his arms. "No one but you, my Indian White Dove," he murmured before kissing her soundly.

***

The house rose quickly, timber by timber beneath clear autumn skies. Log walls climbed two stories high, the silhouette bold against the trees. Stones were laid for the hearth, the chimney rising above the peaked roof. Rafters were crowned with shingles, window panes framed, solid doors hung.

By Friday, the cookstove and water pump were placed, the bathroom shining with porcelain and brass. Saturday finished the work—furniture arranged, dishes and linen set, rugs spread, pantry stocked.

That evening, the house looked and felt like a true home. After hugs and well-wishes, the family left Luke and Megan alone in their new place.

It was well past dusk when Megan laid Mary in her crib, the baby breathing softly beneath her quilt. She had just turned away when Luke's voice called from the porch.

"Megan! Come quick!"

Alarmed, she hurried outside. "What is it?"

Standing at the railing, he pointed west. "Look."

Low in the sky, a radiant streak glided silently, trailing a shimmering plume across the heavens.

"Oh my," she whispered. "A comet?"

"It must be," Luke murmured. "What else shines like that?"

They stood together, arms entwined.

"It feels like the heavens are rejoicing with us," Megan said in awe.

Luke nodded. "A gift from God. A blessing for our new beginning." He tipped her chin and kissed her gently, sealing an unspoken vow.

When they parted, he searched her face. "I've missed this—just us. No borrowed space. Only you, me, and our home."

Her eyes shone. "It's more than I dreamed. You, Mary... this house... it's more than I ever hoped."

She kissed him again, slow and lingering. With a soft laugh, Luke swept her into his arms.

"Mrs. Havoc," he said, voice husky, "it would be my honor to carry you across the threshold."

He carried her inside, nudging the door closed with his boot, never breaking her gaze. Lamplight glowed on polished floors, the hearth crackled with warmth. Crossing the parlor, he entered their bedroom and shut the door.

His lips found hers again—tender, reverent, deep. In the sacred hush, wrapped in firelight and the scent of pine and linen, they began their first night in their new home—heart to heart, soul to soul.

***

Autumn lingered warm and golden as Jeremy and Penny's home rose west of the lodge. Smaller than Megan and Luke's, it was no less charming. Within weeks they were settled, their laughter mingling with the quiet woods.

Not long after, Patrick and Kathy's modest home took shape on a homestead south of Luke's, finished just before the first snow.

In November, a letter arrived from Naomi and John. Megan read it aloud by lamplight, her voice trembling with joy:

> *Dear Megan and Luke,*
>
> *We are overjoyed to share that we have a beautiful baby boy—Donavan Fredrick. He has his father's eyes, and John insists he's inherited my gentle ways. He's a good baby, growing stronger each day. The delivery was smooth, and we are grateful beyond words for his safe arrival. Though we still ache for little Grace, our hearts are full, with God's mercy and provision.*
>
> *With love,*
>
> *Naomi and John.*

Tears glistened on Megan's cheeks. "Oh, Luke—a baby boy. What blessed news."

***

That Thanksgiving, the lodge rang with warmth and laughter. Philip and Prudence arrived glowing with news of their own—they were expecting a child in late spring.

"We hope to move back soon," Prudence shared as she helped Megan in the kitchen. "If all goes well, we'll have a home ready before the baby comes. Mr. Adams wasn't pleased," she added with a wry smile. "But one look from Miss Jacques shut him right up. Then he offered congratulations—I nearly fainted."

Megan grinned, pulling golden rolls from the oven. "How are things between those two?"

Prudence chuckled. "Better than anyone would guess. He's changing, Megan. Kinder. And smitten with Pat. I used to think she was too blunt, but now... I admire her honesty and strength. She's exactly what he needed."

Leaning closer, she whispered, "You'll never guess what."

"What?"

"He asked her to call him by his first name."

Megan's eyes widened. "He did? What is it?"

"Laverne. She calls him Vern."

"Laverne?" Megan stared. "That's a girl's name."

"It was his grandmother's. He was teased as a boy and never told anyone—until Pat."

Megan shook her head, smiling. "Well, I'll be…"

Cassie entered with a jar of pickles. "You'll be what?"

"Mr. Adams has a schoolmarm crush!" Megan burst into laughter.

"The sour-faced headmaster?" Cassie asked, pouring pickles into a bowl.

"The very one," Prudence replied. "He's met his match."

Cassie laughed softly. "Even a beast can become a prince when the right one comes along."

The three women chuckled, agreeing there might be

hope for anyone—even a schoolmaster.

***

Thanksgiving dinner filled the long table with family, stories, and laughter as snow softened the world outside. Philip and Prudence shared news from the reservation—updates on friends, students, and the quiet strength of family adapting to change. Gratefully, Jacob Crooked Arrow was thriving in his studies and a favorite of Miss Jacques.

At the far end, Ed and Cassie caught up with Patrick and Kathy. David, home briefly from medical school, spoke of long hours studying and Hazel's letters from nursing school. Johnathan and Kurt recounted school adventures—Kurt's junior year, Johnathan's shy confession of a crush. All begged Luke and Megan to come home for Christmas, insisting it wouldn't be the same without them.

***

That night, most had gone to bed, but Megan and Prudence lingered by the fire. Luke and Philip were in the office, leaving the women to savor the quiet.

"I still can't believe I'll be a mother by summer," Prudence said, resting a hand on her stomach. "I'm so happy, even though the nausea's been terrible. The stage ride nearly did me in. Poor Philip was beside himself with worry."

Megan squeezed her hand. "I remember it well. Miserable."

"I hate leaving so soon," Prudence said softly. "It's been so lovely to be back. We think of you as our truest family now."

"I feel the same," Megan said, voice thick with emotion.

Kathy entered, easing into a chair with her crocheting. "You girls don't mind if I join you?"

"Of course not, Grandma," Megan said warmly.

"We were just talking about how connected we feel—like family," Prudence added.

Kathy's gaze softened as she worked the yarn. "I understand that well. After I lost my first husband and sons in the war, I felt so alone. I had Beth and Joy, but they were young."

"That must've been devastating," Prudence said gently.

"It was. Then Ed came back from the war, and for a moment I could breathe. But after losing Mary... I lost him too, in a way. Kansas held too many memories, so he left. When he asked us to come to Cheyenne, I hoped I might find my place. I did—I met Patrick. He was my new beginning. I felt a connection from the moment we met."

Kathy chuckled softly. "I hesitated—telling him to find someone younger. But he wouldn't hear of it. Said I was the one. And now, I'm living the happiest days of my life."

"Oh, Grandma, that's beautiful," Megan said, rising to hug her.

Kathy's eyes misted. "You and your family have brought me such joy. Every child, grandchild, and great-grandchild has filled my life with more than I ever dreamed. One day, you'll understand."

"I think I already do," Megan whispered. "When Luke returned, my heart was whole again. And now, with little Mary, I feel as you do—like life keeps growing richer."

"I love you, dear," Kathy said, taking her hand. "You and Luke were meant for each other. It was part of the Lord's plan."

"I feel it too," Prudence added, eyes glistening. "As if God intertwined our lives."

Megan smiled through her tears. "I feel like you're the sister I never had."

"A kindred spirit," Kathy said knowingly.

Just then, Patrick appeared in the firelight, resting a hand on Kathy's shoulder.

"Am I interrupting?"

"Not at all, dear," she said, covering his hand with hers.

"I was wondering if you were coming to bed. I'm getting lonely," he teased.

"I was just saying goodnight." She set her yarn aside and rose.

Megan hugged her tightly, then kissed Patrick's cheek. "Goodnight, Grandma. Goodnight, Grandpa."

"Sleep well, dears," Kathy said as they disappeared into the quiet.

***

That Saturday, Prudence and Philip returned to the reservation, settling back into teaching's steady rhythm. She still loved working with the Indian children alongside Philip, John, and Miss Jacques, yet the spark had dimmed. Her thoughts often drifted to spring—the promise of a home with Philip on their own land. That hope carried them through the gray days.

***

Winter in Laramie held its own quiet beauty. Megan, busy with the new house and little Mary, found her days full—cooking, cleaning, rocking the baby, keeping the fires warm. Having Luke home more often brought steady joy.

She loved hearing about his work with the horses, especially the new colt born that winter. They visited him often, grateful for the barn's warmth. Luke spent hours felling trees for the barn he hoped to raise in spring, splitting firewood, finishing small projects indoors. The winter proved mild, and on many weekends they rode into the hills. Grandma and Grandpa O'Malley gladly watched Mary and Jerry whenever the young couples went to town or rode beneath the wide Wyoming sky.

Shortly after New Year's, a letter came from Philip. The next season's schedule was full; all the rooms were booked. He asked Luke and Jeremy to arrange for extra help by spring.

As snow gave way to thaw, the plains awakened—grass pushing through softening earth, wildflowers among the pines, buds swelling on oak and poplar. Megan took Mary on long walks behind the house, following the stream. In a sunlit patch of rich soil, she found the perfect place for a garden. With the season shifting, she felt the weight of all that lay ahead: the planting, the lodge opening, and the busy life soon to come.

***

When the school year ended, Prudence and Philip returned to Laramie, welcomed with open arms.

The next week Philip and a crew began construction. With local help, walls rose, and a roof was set within days; the interior followed quickly.

A week before the birth, Prudence and Philip moved in. He stayed close, skipping the season's first trip. When their son arrived—a healthy, brown-haired boy—they named him Patrick Philip Archibald.

"We'd like to name him after you," Philip told Patrick. "You've become like a father to me."

Patrick's voice softened. "I'm honored, but why not after your own father?"

"We did. His name was Philip too."

Patrick nodded, eyes misting. "Thank you. You've made an old man very happy."

*** 

July 1892

Cassie gazed out the train window as the plains stretched golden beneath the summer sky. "You know, Ed," she said softly, "it doesn't seem so long ago I first rode this train to Cheyenne. And yet, so much has changed."

Ed smiled, eyes warm. "Time slips past. I still remember the first time I saw you—walking into church with George and Mabel. You looked so lovely...and a little lost. You've got more color now," he added, brushing a graying strand from her forehead, "but to me, you're as beautiful as that first Sunday."

Cassie leaned against his shoulder. "Do you remember our first trip to the pond?"

"I'll never forget," Ed said. He remembered her tears, her confession, the moment she told him she was pregnant—and how he'd held her close, kissing away her pain.

"I couldn't believe you still wanted me," Cassie murmured. "Pregnant—and with an Indian's child. I thought no man would ever want me."

"My darling Cass," his voice was steady, "I wanted you from the moment I met you. I loved you then. I love you more now." He kissed her brow. "After losing Mary and the baby, I never thought I could love again. But God knew how to mend what was broken. Look at the life we've built."

"You've been everything to me, Ed—my strength, my friend, my love."

"I'll love you forever, Cass," he whispered. They held each other in quiet peace as the train carried them toward Laramie.

Later that afternoon, brakes squealed, and the whistle marked their arrival. Passengers stirred, gathering bags and hats. Ed and Cassie stepped onto the platform, hearts light.

"Do you think the children will be surprised?" Cassie asked, glancing around.

"I'm counting on it," Ed replied, guiding her toward the carriage.

It wasn't like them to travel unannounced, but with David home from college and the boys able to manage the ranch, the timing felt right. When Ed suggested surprising Luke and Megan—Cassie eagerly agreed. They hadn't seen them since New Year's. Now, with the garden ripening and summer in full swing, it felt the perfect moment for both a family visit and an anniversary escape.

The carriage rattled up the dusty lane toward Luke and Megan's homestead. As it stopped before the log house, Cassie leaned forward, eyes bright. "Do you think they're home?"

After paying the driver, they stepped down. He tipped his hat and rattled off toward town.

"We'll soon find out," Ed said, carrying their bags. Cassie knocked. No answer.

"Let's check around back," Ed suggested.

They rounded the corner and found a dark-haired toddler near the garden, hands dusted with earth, while Megan knelt, weeding vegetables.

Mary saw them first. With a squeal, she stumbled up and ran to them, arms wide.

"Mary!" Cassie cried, sweeping her into a tight embrace as Megan turned.

"Ma! Pa!" Megan gasped, joy lighting her face. She rushed to them, laughter and tears mingling as she held them close.

"We wanted to surprise you," Cassie said, eyes shining.

"You nearly gave me a heart attack!" Megan laughed.

"Where's Luke?" Ed asked, glancing toward the trees and flourishing garden.

"At the lodge—he'll be home for supper," Megan said. "He'll be over the moon. We've missed you so much."

Inside, shade and cool drinks refreshed them as conversation flowed. As Megan stood to stretch, Cassie's gaze caught on her daughter's waist—the soft swell beneath her skirt.

Megan grinned. "I was going to write...we're having another baby!" she announced, cradling her belly.

Cassie hugged her. "Oh, that's wonderful! When?"

"End of November," Megan beamed. "They'll be nearly two years apart." She scooped Mary into her arms. "Are you going to have a baby brother or sister?"

"Baby. My baby," Mary declared proudly, wriggling free and crawling into Cassie's lap.

Cassie and Ed laughed, showering her with kisses. "Yes, Mary," Cassie said, "your very own baby brother or sister."

***

July 1897

Another blazing July sun gilded the Wyoming prairie. Five summers had passed since that surprise visit, and life had only deepened in sweetness and purpose.

Megan rode beside Luke across the open range, her dark hair streaming like a banner. Astride Snowflake, daughter of her cherished Snowfire, she tilted her face to the sky, laughter spilling as the wind kissed her skin. It was a day for riding—for remembering how much she loved this land, this life, and the man beside her.

Luke watched her with quiet reverence. The years had only made her more radiant. That first moment in Cheyenne still lived in him, as did the memory of nearly killing to protect her. It only made this peace more precious. She had always drawn him in like the moon pulls at the tide, and across years, silence, and distance, his love had only grown deeper.

She caught his gaze, blew him a kiss, and he laughed aloud, her spirit running through him like sunlight on water.

As the herd trotted through the corral gate, they slowed their mounts. Luke swung down to close the gate while Megan dismounted, tying Snowflake to the post.

"These may be the prettiest horses we've ever raised," she said, slipping her arms around him, resting

491

her head against his chest.

He pressed a kiss into her hair. "They are. But not without your help—and Jeremy, Patrick, Philip... I couldn't have done this alone." He glanced toward the house with a smile. "And thank heaven for the cook and housekeeper at the lodge. I love knowing you're home with the children, where your heart belongs."

"Girls! Come see the new horses!" he called.

From the porch came the patter of small feet and peals of laughter. Mary, now seven, led little Cass by the hand, dark braids bouncing. Four-year-old Kathy followed close behind as they ran through the grass toward the corral.

"Mama! Papa! Pretty horses!" Mary cried.

Megan scooped Cass into her arms. "Look, darling— see the horses?" The toddler squealed, clapping, green eyes alight with joy.

"Horsey! Horsey!" she shrieked, her eyes a mirror of her mother's—and her namesake, Grandma Cassie.

"Kathy, do you want Papa to hold you?" Luke asked, crouching. She twirled a braid around her finger and nodded.

"Oh Papa—they're so pretty!" she exclaimed as he lifted her.

"Me too, Papa?" Mary asked. Though growing tall, Luke didn't hesitate. He swept her up, one daughter in each arm, while they leaned over the fence rail, wide-eyed with wonder.

Megan stood close, her heart blooming. "Luke," she said softly, "I just had the strangest feeling—like I've lived this before. Like a dream."

His expression stilled. "Megan...it *was* a dream. One

I had before we married. I saw this—you, me, the horses, our daughters running to us. This *exact* moment."

Her breath caught. "I remember," she whispered. "You told me long ago. It was beautiful then...and now— it's our life." She touched his arm, warm and sure. "I love you, Luke Standing Elk. Always."

He pressed a tender kiss to her lips. "And I, you—my Indian White Dove. Now, always, and forever."

And so their days unfolded like a dream—woven from sunlight and shadow, hard work and quiet joys, the steady rhythm of seasons passing and children growing. Beneath wide Wyoming skies, with horses grazing and wind whispering through the grass, Luke and Megan built a life both ordinary and extraordinary: rooted in love that endured beyond hardship and time. And in the hush of each evening, as stars kindled overhead, they gave thanks for it all—two souls bound as one, forever home.

The End

# *Acknowledgments*

With deep gratitude, I thank my husband, Bruce Blake, for his steadfast support, and my friends and family for their unwavering love and encouragement. My heartfelt appreciation goes to my dear friend and line editor, Peggy Jefferson, whose wise edits and positive spirit helped bring clarity and grace to every page. A warm thank you as well to Eric G. Reid and his remarkable team at Skinny Brown Dog Media for transforming my words into a work of art—one I will forever treasure. To all of you who helped bring this dream to life, I offer my sincerest thanks.

# *A Note From The Author*

Thank you for spending time with Luke and Megan. I write these stories slowly, with a lot of listening—to history, to place, and to the quiet corners of the heart—and I love sharing the small discoveries along the way. If you'd like to keep walking with me, visit *YBlake.com* for updates, behind-the-scenes notes, and occasional extras. For gentler, more personal letters (early pages, field notes from research trips, and what I'm reading), join my reader list at *yblake.com/newsletter*. It's the best way to hear from me directly, without algorithms or noise.

I'm grateful you're here.

# *About the Author*

Yvette Blake is a historical romance author whose work explores identity, home, and the ties that hold when the world pulls apart. Set against the wide skies of nineteenth-century Wyoming, *Luke's Dream* continues her fascination with cross-cultural love, community, and courage. A longtime researcher of Western history, Blake blends archival detail with a storyteller's heart to craft novels where tenderness and truth share the same page. When she isn't writing, she can be found combing library stacks, mapping scenic byways, and collecting small details that make history feel alive. Enjoy the entire Cassie's Legacy series—*Cassie's Miracle, Cassie's Blessings, Megan's Promise*, and *Luke's Dream*—at *YBlake.com.*

CASSIE'S LEGACY — SERIES LIST

Book 1: *Cassie's Miracle*
EPUB — 9781957506050
Case Laminate — 9781957506333
Cloth™ — 9781957506227
Perfect Bound — 9781957506234

Book 2: *Cassie's Blessings*
EPUB — 9781957506753
Case Laminate — 9781957506746
Cloth™ — 9781957506739
Perfect Bound — 9781957506722

Book 3: *Megan's Promise*
EPUB — 9781965235102
Case Laminate — 9781965235096
Cloth™ — 9781965235089
Perfect Bound — 9781965235072

Book 4: *Luke's Dream*
Hardcover (Case Laminate) — 978-1-965235-94-2
Hardcover (Cloth™) — 978-1-965235-95-9
Perfect Bound (Paperback) — 978-1-965235-96-6
eBook (EPUB/Kindle) — 978-1-965235-97-3

Short Story, YA Friendly: *Cassie's Big Move*
Hardcover (Cloth™) — 9781957506043

www.ingramcontent.com/pod-product-compliance
Lightning Source LLC
Chambersburg PA
CBHW031233310726
48971CB00004B/996